The Nine Week King

RÄCHAL MONIGATTI

DEDICATION

For Jack and Doreen

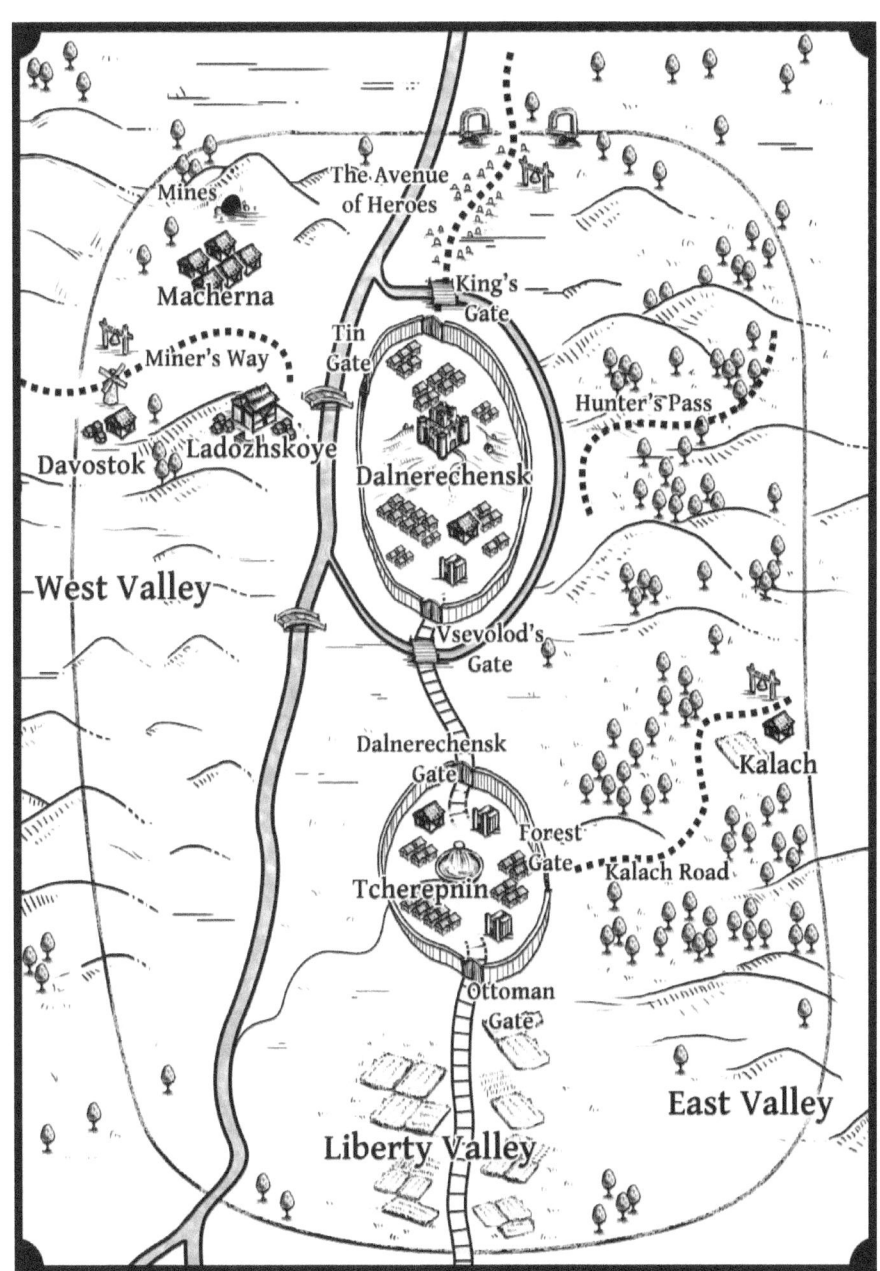

The Descendants of Vsevolod

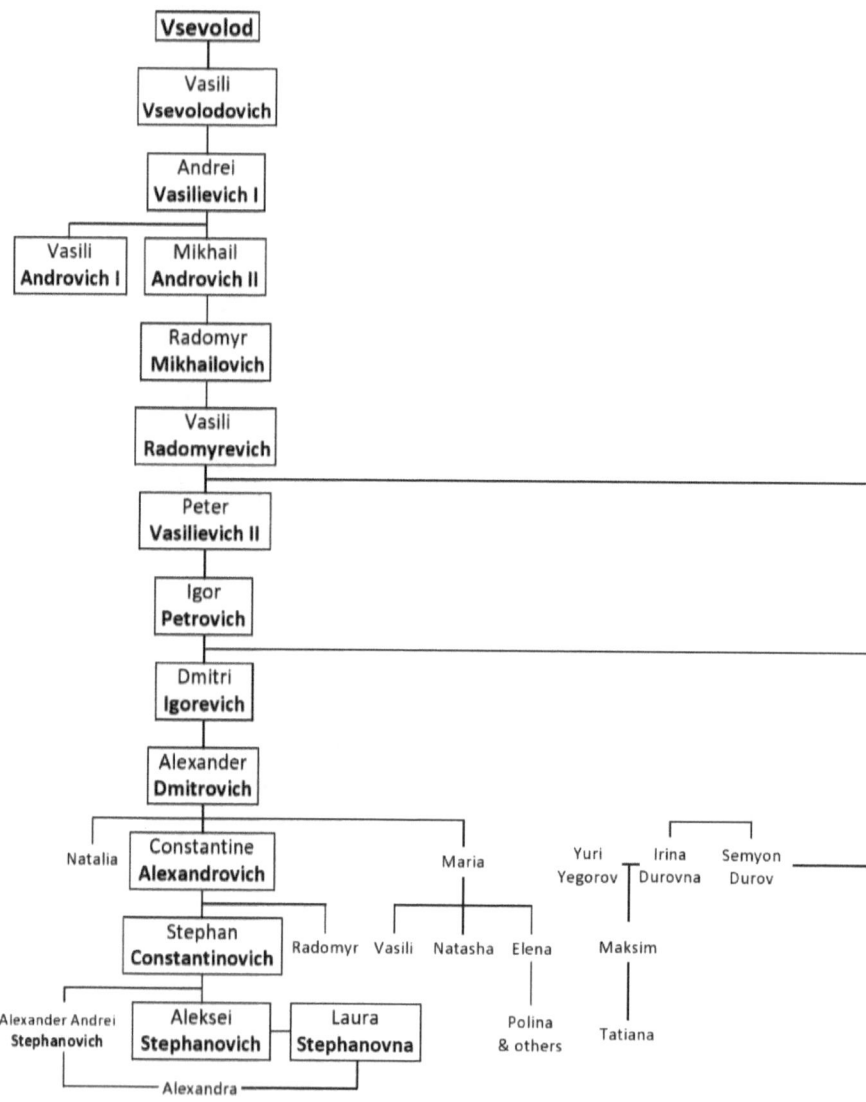

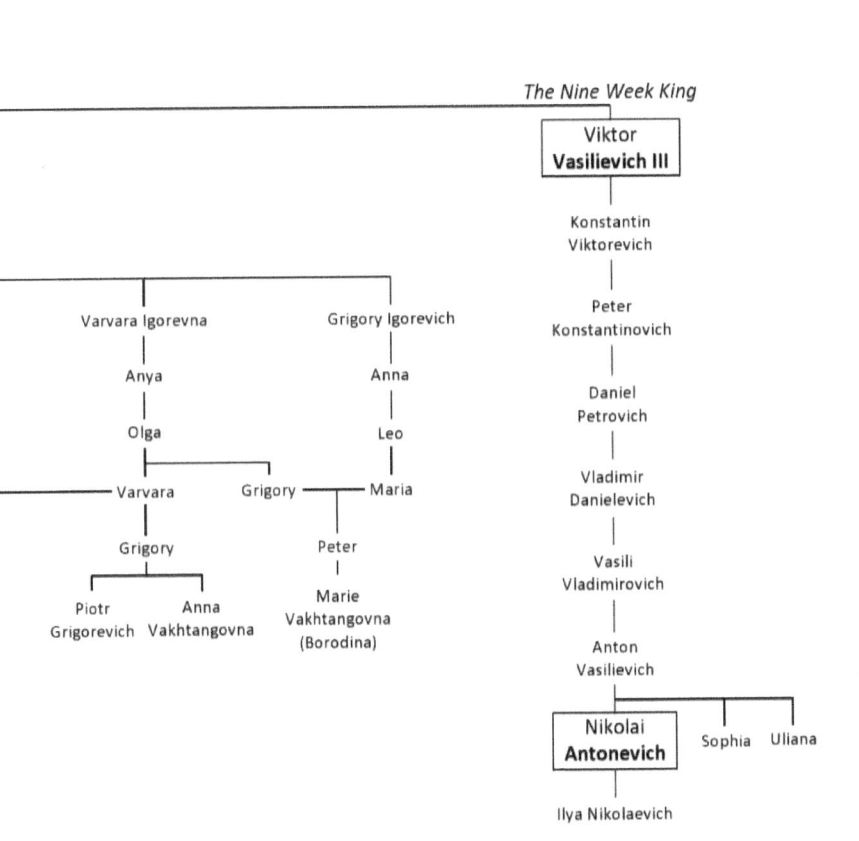

The Nine Week King

Viktor
Vasilievich III

Konstantin
Viktorevich

Varvara Igorevna

Grigory Igorevich

Peter
Konstantinovich

Anya

Anna

Daniel
Petrovich

Olga

Leo

Vladimir
Danielevich

Varvara — Grigory — Maria

Vasili
Vladimirovich

Grigory

Peter

Piotr Anna
Grigorevich Vakhtangovna

Marie
Vakhtangovna
(Borodina)

Anton
Vasilievich

Nikolai
Antonevich Sophia Uliana

Ilya Nikolaevich

PROLOGUE

October 1905

Prinz Sebastian gave the document a cursory glance and signed it, passing it to his adjutant, who handed him another. He signed that too, humming to himself as he thought about the hunting excursion he had planned for the afternoon.

'Any other orders of business?' he asked, handing back the document.

'Baron Fredrik von Schmidt has sought an audience with you, *Ihr Magistät*' the adjutant said, laying the documents on the cherry wood sideboard.

'Who owns the factories in München? What does he want? Send him in.'

The adjutant bowed and crossed the rich expanse of the study and opened one of the white Rococo doors, calling to the man seated in the adjacent room.

Prinz Sebastian watched the young blonde step into the room and bow respectfully. He was immaculately dressed in a fashionable sable jacket, his hair swept back and brushing his collar. He was handsome and youthful, and he moved with grace and poise.

'*Euer Hochwohlgeboren*' he said, beckoning him forward. 'Why have you requested this audience?'

Fredrik straightened and came closer.

'Please forgive my forwardness' he said, keeping his eyes lowered. 'I have come to ask permission to visit your house guest.'

Prinz Sebastian blinked in surprise.

Fredrik bowed his head. 'My uncle, Axel von Schmidt, *Burggraf* of *Schwarzschwanwald*, was informed by our cousin Countess Ivanova of Dalnerechensk that Her Highness Laura Vakhtangova was your house guest. Countess Ivanova said that - that Her Highness was in poor health' he shut his eyes. 'I am, of course, distressed to hear so and wish to ask your

1

permission to visit her.' He stopped talking and waited, holding his breath.

Prinz Sebastian watched him coolly. By all accounts Fredrik von Schmidt was a kind and honest man, and not one person could fault him in courtesy and etiquette. *It must be a desperate love to make him come here uninvited. Prinz* Sebastian wanted to refuse.

'She is in poor health *Euer Hochwohlgeboren*' he said, more brusquely than he had meant to sound. 'I invited her here where the air might do her some good. She has had a severe shock and I do not wish to upset her further.' He shot him a hard look.

'I understand, *Ihr Magistät*' Fredrik said quietly. 'Forgive my rude intrusion.'

He bowed and began to walk backwards from the room.

'Her melancholy has not lifted' *Prinz* Sebastian went on more quietly, forcing Fredrik to stop in his tracks. 'If you can make her smile you will be welcome here. She often sits by the lake.'

Fredrik hesitated then bowed low and walked out of the room, straightening up in the antechamber. The adjutant closed the door and Fredrik strode out of the chateau, marching around the precisely clipped garden to the path that led to the large, ornamental lake.

As he walked he tried to organise his thoughts, to get the words in the right order, wondering what he could say to her. Snippets of gossip had flooded through the lips of European nobility; the accounts of what had happened often contradicting each other. Some whispered of revolution, others whispered of plots to overthrow the monarchy orchestrated by the Tsaritsa and Ilich Rukavishnikov - the man who became Dalnerechensk's Prime Minister. There were rumours of scandal, and the name *Knjaz* Rurik, Russian Ambassador to Dalnerechensk, had been mentioned several times. All anyone knew for sure was that the royal family was dead and a frail Laura Vakhtangova, the sole survivor, had arrived seeking refuge in Varennikov Castle one month later.

Prinz Sebastian had recently attended a masque in Varennikov Castle, the home of Countess Ivanova's parents, and had been shocked at the pale appearance of the young Tsaritsa. The Prince had stayed on after the birthday celebrations for Count Varennikov, his concern growing, and after witnessing a particularly spiteful attack from Marie, at whose wedding the Prince and Fredrik had both met Laura, *Prinz* Sebastian had ordered her trunks to be packed and taken her to the pretty chateau that served as his hunting lodge in the Bavarian Alps.

Fredrik stopped thinking. The landscaped, artificial lake stretched away from the chateau, silver and white with frost. Near the shore was a large fountain of bronze and marble, silent and still. Before him, seated on a wicker chair and facing the lake was Laura. He too was shocked at how pale she looked, how dull and lifelessly still, like some beautiful doll. She must have heard him approaching but did not stir.

2

He coughed quietly, as much to alert her to his presence as to clear the thick nervousness from his throat. She did not stir and he stepped beside her, bowing low.

'*Eure Hoheit*' he said, and when she didn't acknowledge him he straightened, a little embarrassed. 'I am sorry to hear of your illness' he said in French, remembering that was the language they both knew well enough to converse freely. 'I thought I could -' he stopped, the embarrassment rising. 'I thought I might read to you' he said, pulling a slim volume of poetry out of his jacket pocket.

Still she did not answer him. Embarrassed and at a loss with what to do Fredrik sat on a chair beside her and opened the book, beginning to read aloud. The poems were in his native tongue, and so at the end of each he would translate the German into French. He read for an hour before finally folding shut the book when *Prinz* Sebastian approached.

He stood and bowed deeply, miserably, and *Prinz* Sebastian came forward, taking Laura's arm gently.

'Come, I have brought your coat, the afternoon is getting chilly' he said, folding it around her shoulders and helping her to her feet.

Fredrik bowed again.

'I will take my leave *Ihr Magistät*, Your Highness' he said somewhat stiffly. 'I apologise for my rude intrusion and I will not return again. I hope your health returns to you.' He bowed again.

'Read to me tomorrow' she said.

Her voice was faint and small, and her eyes still looked glassy and dull, but she had finally spoken to him, and Fredrik tried not to yell with joy. *Prinz* Sebastian smiled sadly and gently guided her away from the lake.

1

'Vladimir Lenin would not speak so flippantly of revolution if he knew what it really meant' she said softly.

Fredrik looked up from the book he had been reading aloud, realising how gloomy the day had become. The snow was whispering against the large windows of *Prinz* Sebastian's library and the fire in the grate had died down. Laura sat opposite him in a high-backed chair, her face pale and dappled with shadows. A tear, glinting in the firelight, slid down her cheek.

'He would not speak so if he knew of that terrible sound; the voices of hate and anger and violence' she went on, staring unseeingly past him, into her memories. 'The sound of battering rams against the door, the splintering of wood...

'Ilich had whipped them into a frenzy, but he couldn't control them that night, so they rushed to the castle mad for blood, our blood.' She blinked and more tears ran down her cheeks. 'There was a secret tunnel, we escaped, and we ran into the forests of Dalnerechensk.

'Ts - Tsar Constantinovich was - sick - his heart - so we carried him on a stretcher made from my shawl, but - but he died, and we dug his grave with our own hands.' She blinked again, and Fredrik yearned to lean across, to lay his hand on hers gently.

'We were captured, by *Knjaz* Nikita Rurik. He was en route with his army to invade Dalnerechensk. He tied me behind his horse and made me walk all day, and then in the evenings he would try to seduce me. He threatened to torture me...' she stopped talking, her voice fading away.

Fredrik's hands tightened.

'I escaped' she whispered. 'I jumped into the river. Al-Aleksei followed me, but he drowned in the river and - and I never saw him again. He jumped in to save me...

'I went back to Dalnerechensk, because I knew what Nikita would do when he got there, I knew he would kill men, kill women and children. I had the treaties, I could stop him; but I was so afraid they would kill me. I thought they might shoot me on the spot and not listen to me, not know what I could do to save them...' she trailed off again.

'Men would not speak of revolution if they knew what bodies looked like torn apart by cannon balls' she went on. 'How men sounded screaming for their mothers and their God and their legs. And that terrible smell of burnt blood and gun powder -'

'Stop' Fredrik pleaded, looking sickly. 'I am so sorry for the horrors you have endured.'

'I can't forget those sights' she whispered. 'They haunt me. I am haunted by the faces of those I will never see again.'

Fredrik quickly plucked his kerchief from his pocket and pressed it into her hand, wishing he could pull her into his arms. At long last she sighed quietly, wiping her tears.

'I am sorry for making a spectacle of myself' she said, straightening up. 'I am sorry to distress you with these terrible tales; I remember how you were even distressed at Marie's language.'

Fredrik smiled then, remembering the wedding festivities at Varennikov Castle for his cousin Marie. It was where he and the American Princess had overheard the cruel argument between Marie and her little sister Ekaterina whilst walking through the ruined west wing together.

'My distress is diminished in the joy that you have spoken to me, moreso than in the months I have spent here reading to you' he smiled.

There was just a hint of a smile that touched her lips, then it was gone again.

'It is late *Eure Hochwohlgeboren*' she said, rising from her chair and causing Fredrik to rise too.

'May I call on you again tomorrow?' he asked.

'You may. But bring something more entertaining than Lenin.'

He smiled and bowed and she left, slipping along the cold corridors to her rooms in the hunting lodge.

She tip-toed over to the crib in her room and peered in. Her daughter was sleeping fitfully and Laura smiled softly, stroking her finger along the soft skin on the back of Alexandra's hand. Her birth had been the most humiliating and painful experience of her life; without a stitch of undergarments on and her legs propped open for the doctor, the midwife and the servants bringing boiled water and towels to see. The pain had been terrifying, and the little, lamb-like cries of Alexandra had been the strangest and strongest sound she had ever heard; a sound that had reached down into her heart and opened a deep chasm of fear for her daughter.

She leaned down and kissed her gently, then quietly made her way across to the bedroom, beginning to strip for bed. She pulled back the cold covers and slipped between them, shutting her eyes, trying desperately to stop her thoughts from turning to Olaf.

She could not bring herself to tell anyone that her daughter was Olaf's child; Olaf, who had protected her as they escaped from Nikita's army, who had made love to her, who had been executed for a spy by Ilich's government. She could tell no one that her daughter was not Aleksei's child; she did not want her to grow up with the stigma of being a bastard.

By Dalnerechensk law no illegitimate children could come to the throne. Aleksei had inherited a throne that had not been intended for him, by right it should have gone to his older brother Alexander Andrei. But he had gone mad and secretly abdicated, disappearing from public view. Dalnerechensk believed their mad prince was dead. They didn't know the truth Laura had discovered, that Alexander Andrei was the stable groom Olaf - that the true heir was the father of her child.

The complicated legality and the scandal couldn't make her forget that she had loved him, and that his execution meant he had been hung from a tree in the forest until the bones had fallen from the rope. That thought made the blackness swirl around her; brought the pain back fresh and raw.

What could she have told Dalnerechensk? That their mad prince was the father of the heir to the throne? It was madness that caused the revolution in the first place. Could she have told them they had executed not a traitor but their own Tsar? How would the people have turned on Ilich and the government? Alexander Andrei had been loved by his subjects. She could do nothing, and so she had let a lie protect her daughter.

She sniffed loudly, buffing her puffy face with her knuckles, burdened by the weight of secrets.

2

'Good morning Your Highness' Fredrik smiled, bowing and handing over a large present. 'I have brought you something more entertaining than Lenin.'

She laid the box on the table of the small parlour and lifted the lid, staring at the strange shoes with a metal blade along the bottom.

'What are these?' she asked, holding them up.

'*Schlittshuhen*' Fredrik said. 'Ice shoes. Come, let me show you how to use them.'

He offered her his elbow and led her down the path to the ornamental lake. Fredrik tested the thickness of the ice on its surface then stepped onto it, steadying her as she joined him. Together they made their way to the fountain where Fredrik stopped and placed the box he was carrying on the ice.

She sat on the marble edge of the fountain and he knelt before her, carefully removing her shoes and lacing on the skates, then sat beside her to lace on his own. She eyed him, astonished at the ease with which he balanced on the thin metal strips and gingerly got to her feet, holding tightly to the fountain for support.

Fredrik offered her his hands and she tottered unsteadily, clumping along the ice as she tried to walk. He stopped her and patiently explained how to glide, coming to stand beside her, one arm carefully around her waist as they slowly circled the fountain.

The rush of the wind brought up the colour in their cheeks and their eyes sparkled with moisture. Laura found herself enjoying the moment, and for the first time in a year a real smile touched her lips. She looked up at Fredrik, watching the way strands of his golden hair blew across his forehead and cheeks.

She stopped, looking away, glancing carefully at the path to the chateau, then the wide lanes that bordered the ornamental lake.

'What is it?' Fredrik asked, glancing around them too.

She hesitated, not knowing how to tell him of the terrible years of Lady Ramkinson's school, of how disobedient girls were beaten with a riding crop, of how even now she was terrified of being caught doing something wrong. She felt somewhere deep down that it was wrong to be enjoying herself with this handsome man, that it somehow dishonoured the memories of Olaf and Aleksei.

She turned away, gliding back to the fountain where she sat and began to tug undone the skates. Fredrik knelt before her and helped her put her shoes back on, sitting quickly to pull his own on.

'Thank you *Eure Hochwohlgeboren*, I enjoyed this much better than Lenin' she said quietly, standing up and forcing Fredrik to do the same. 'Perhaps more than I should have' she added quietly.

'Your Highness' he said gently. 'It is no terrible thing to be happy again.'

'It is a terrible thing to dishonour a good man' she said.

'Perhaps you do not understand what goodness is' Fredrik said, then cursed himself for his words, watching that terrible, hard look settle in her features.

'Good day *Eure Hochwohlgeboren*' she said coldly and stamped away from him.

Fredrik followed her helplessly back to the chateau, quickening his pace when a flurry of snow tumbled out of the clouds. Laura had already disappeared when he reached the terrace so he stepped in, heading for *Prinz* Sebastian's study.

'Ah, *Eure Hochwohlgeboren*. I have read an intriguing treatise, I would like to hear your opinion on it' he said, handing over a piece of paper.

Fredrik had come to take his leave, anguished that Laura did not return his feelings and had resolved to depart the chateau immediately. But he bowed and took the document, running his eyes over it. *Prinz* Sebastian began discussing it earnestly, but Fredrik was distracted and confused, and tried to follow the conversation as it wandered from Socialism to city infrastructure to native plants.

'*Ihr Magistät*' he said finally. 'I thank you for the generous hospitality that you have shown me but feel I cannot intrude here any longer.'

'If you must' *Prinz* Sebastian said, glancing at his window. 'But the weather has worsened, you cannot leave tonight. A room will be aired for you; you will leave in the morning.'

'As you command *Ihr Magistät*' he said and bowed low.

Some small part of him wondered if the Prince had deliberately wasted his time to force him to stay but he dared not ask him. For some time he had been aware that *Prinz* Sebastian's feelings for Laura ran deeper than a paternal desire for her well-being, and he wondered now, as he had many times, if *Prinz* Sebastian was waiting for Laura to come out of mourning to ask her to marry him. *If so, he wouldn't concoct reasons for a rival to stay...*

He shut his eyes, desperately pained. The Prince was kind and respected, wealthy and aristocratic. He would make an excellent husband for the Empress of Dalnerechensk.

'*Arbendessen* will be served soon' *Prinz* Sebastian continued in his usual straightforward way, checking his pocket watch. '*Prinzessin* Alexandra does fuss if her routine is upset.'

Fredrik could do nothing but bow and follow *Prinz* Sebastian to the dining room.

3

'Alexandra stop it! Stop crying!' Laura shouted at the wailing thing in the crib, grabbing her hair and sobbing. '*Please stop crying!*'

The door to her small sitting room was pushed open with a knock and Fredrik stood there, a robe hastily thrown over his borrowed nightshirt.

'I've fed her, I've bathed her, I've cleaned her and I don't know why she won't stop crying!' she wept, shaking.

'Allow me Your Highness' Fredrik said softly. 'I will soothe Princess Alexandra, try to get some sleep.'

'But -'

'Please' he interrupted. 'You are in need of rest. I will care for her with all your tenderness.'

He bowed, picked up the screaming child and cradled her gently as he slipped out of the room. Laura hesitated, wanting to run after him and grab her daughter back, feeling hot with shame when she wished he would never bring her back; wanting to fall asleep for a hundred years. *I'll just rest until I'm calm again* she told herself, wiping away her tears and perching exhausted on the edge of the chair.

She awoke with a start some time later, aware of the hours that had gone. An icy fear gripped her when she realised she could no longer hear

Alexandra crying. A quick check told her the crib was empty and she lurched to her feet, pushing open her sitting room door. The corridor beyond was cold and empty. The rooms hastily made up for Fredrik last night were also empty and she rushed on, stopping when she saw the warm firelight spilling onto the landing from *Prinz* Sebastian's library.

She took a brief second to compose herself then stepped into the doorway, peering in. Fredrik was asleep in a chair by the fire, Alexandra asleep on his chest, her little face turned into his neck. Laura stepped closer, a tender feeling rising in her, resting her head against the door frame as she gazed at them.

But the feeling was bringing a memory with it, a memory of late nights standing outside Aleksei's study, watching him pour through document after document, trying to find some way to alleviate Dalnerechensk's economic depression. She had loved him as she stood in dark doorways watching him; she had seen a man so few had ever seen.

Gently she stepped in and closed the door, crossing over to the chair. She stroked Alexandra's head tenderly then trailed her fingers down her small back, stopping when she was so close to Fredrik's fingers she could feel the heat of them. His eyes opened.

'Your Highness' he said, blinking himself awake. 'Forgive me for what I said this afternoon -'

She stopped him gently.

'Aleksei was a good man' she said. 'But good men can do terrible things. Before I came to Marie's wedding, *Knjaz* Nikita Rurik had been sent as an ambassador to Dalnerechensk. He was handsome and sophisticated, and I was told I must pander to his every whim. So much depended on his good will. It was easy to be charming and agreeable - and I was so very young, and lonely' she sighed sadly.

'Tatiana spread vile poison about me, that I was unfaithful, that I was Nikita's mistress. None of it was true, but it made my husband despise me, it made him sick. An ulcer wracked him with pain and he spurned me for his mistress. Nikita was only toying with me; he was so unkind the day he left Dalnerechensk' she shut her eyes tightly.

'And I came to Marie's wedding, hurt and - and foolish' she sighed. 'I wanted to hurt Aleksei for what he had done to me. I am sorry I encouraged your attentions when I should not have' she stopped.

'*Knjaz* Rurik was cruel to toy with your heart' he said quietly. 'And you were cruel to toy with mine. But I forgive you.'

She gently gathered Alexandra to her, letting her small head rest in the curve of her neck as it had done to Fredrik's. She folded her arms around her, cradling her carefully.

'Thank you *Eure Hochwohlgeboren*' she said quietly. 'You have been a great comfort to me these last weeks. Goodnight.' She stepped out.

'Goodnight' he called after her.

4

Laura rose and kissed her daughter, lifting her out of the crib to feed her, wincing slightly. When Alexandra was full she burped her gently then dressed her in a pretty lace garment, tying a matching bonnet on her head. Alexandra burbled happily to herself while Laura stood, pulling on a corset she laced not without some difficulty and stood before her wardrobe.

Gently she reached out and touched the sleeve of the black dress she had worn for many months, stroking the material sadly. She had decided it was time to come out of mourning, yet her other dresses suddenly seemed too bright, too garish; even if they were Marie's dull castoffs.

Finally she selected a grey silk and pulled it on, pinning her hair back simply. She stood in front of the mirror, surprised at how wan she seemed, like some wisp of smoke. She hesitated before the door, wondering if she should change into the black dress again, then picked up her daughter and carried her down to *Prinz* Sebastian's study before she could change her mind.

He made a sound of delight when he saw her, rising smiling from his seat to kiss her hand.

'It is good to see you out of mourning Your Highness' he said, crooking a finger at Alexandra and cooing.

Quickly he instructed his adjutant to bring a chair for her and offered her some tea. Laura sat and thanked him, accepting a cup and sipping carefully so as not to spill any on Alexandra.

'I have grown very fond of you in the time you have spent here' *Prinz* Sebastian said.

'And I of you' she said, setting the teacup on its saucer and rocking Alexandra gently. 'Your Majesty, will you do me the great honour of being Alexandra's godfather?'

He smiled, but it was sad at the edges. 'Of course' he accepted. 'Nothing would make me prouder.'

'I am glad. You have been so kind to me, and it eases my heart to know that should anything ever happen, my daughter will be safe and protected.' She kissed his hand gently.

He held her hand for a moment longer than he should have, then let her go, shuffling the papers on his desk.

'You will excuse me, Your Highness, I have much that requires my attention this morning. Please eat without me, Baron von Schmidt will be glad of your company.'

She stood and bowed, taking Alexandra with her as she made her way to the small dining room. Fredrik was seated inside, wearing the rumpled clothes he had worn yesterday. He stood and bowed to her when she stepped in, smiling as she seated herself beside him.

'You look radiant this morning' he said.

'Do you say that to all the girls with dark bags under their eyes and tired skin?' she asked, arching an eyebrow, lightly mocking him.

'It was rather short-sighted of His Majesty not to provide you with a handmaiden or at least a nursemaid to help you.'

'He did offer. I turned them both away.' She lowered her eyes.

'Whatever for?' he asked, laying down his fork in shock.

She was quiet for a moment then said: 'The girls I went to school with were raised by nurses, and they talked about their mothers in such cold and distant ways. I didn't want Alexandra to feel about me like that, she's all I have left of -' she stopped and bit her lip. 'But to tell you the truth, one more sleepless night with her screaming and I'll gladly sell her to the gypsies.'

Fredrik laughed and reached across to collect a dish of quince, his fingers passing so close to her hand she could feel the heat of them again. Quickly she moved away, glancing at the door.

'Do I make you uncomfortable Your Highness?' he asked quietly. 'You sometimes seem - ill at ease.'

'Forgive me' she said, but did not offer any explanation.

Before an awkward silence could fall Fredrik busied himself with pouring tea for Laura, placing a few morsels on her plate while she rocked her gurgling daughter.

'Would you permit me to introduce you to my aunt who is currently visiting us?' Fredrik asked when she had finished eating, aware of how little it had been. 'Allow me to extend a warm invitation to you on behalf of my uncle. We would be honoured to have you stay in München with us.'

'That is very kind' she said quietly. 'I would be glad to meet new friends'

'Excellent' he smiled. 'I will return to München today to make arrangements. My brothers will be thrilled to see you again.'

'And I them' she said honestly. 'If you will excuse me I shall write a letter to my father.'

'Of course' he said, rising as she rose and bowing.

Laura left, taking her daughter up to her rooms, wondering why she could not feel happier at meeting old friends again.

5

It was nearly a week before Laura left *Prinz* Sebastian's chateau, with the German Prince reluctant to say goodbye.

'I shall miss you, Your Highness' he had said, gruff with tears.

'And I you' she had answered, her lip quivering. 'I cannot thank you enough for the great kindness you have shown me.'

'You must promise to write frequently' he had pressed and Laura had agreed, kissing his hands then waving goodbye as the handsome carriage set off on its long way to the outskirts of Munich.

'Here is my uncle's home, *Schwarzschwanwald*, Black Swan Forest' Fredrik said after many silent hours as they turned into a stately driveway lined with skeletal trees. 'It was designed by Karl Friedrich Schinkel himself.'

The driveway was divided into two by a narrow, artificial lake, a frozen rectangle a hundred metres long and five metres wide. Two pretty bridges arched over the lake, cutting it into precise thirds. At the top end of the lake sat a fountain, adorned with nymphs holding water jugs that dripped ice stalactites onto the frozen surface. Behind it rose the white façade of the classical home, three stories high with a porch supported by fluted columns.

They stopped in front of the steps and a cold driver jumped down, placing a step before the carriage door. The door to the house flew open and two boys tumbled out, racing down the marble stairs to greet them. Fredrik opened the carriage door and jumped down. They both threw their arms around him, hugging tightly, babbling away excitedly in German.

'Remember yourselves' Fredrik chided, but he was smiling, and reached up to steady Laura as she stepped down from the carriage.

Kurt and Gustav bowed low to her, reigning in their enthusiasm when they saw that she had a child. Burgrave Axel von Schmidt stepped out of the house and bowed low, smiling.

'Welcome, Your Highness' he said, coming forward to kiss her hand. 'It is a pleasure to see you again.'

'Thank you for your kind invitation' she answered, allowing herself to be led up the stairs under Axel's guidance.

'I have prepared rooms for you that overlook the gardens' he said, leading her into the foyer. 'You must be tired from your long journey. Heidi and Gertrude will be your hand and nurse maids -'

'I require no handmaiden' Laura interrupted.

Axel stopped, surprised, his arm still gesturing at the two women that stood in the rich, wood-panelled foyer. 'Your Highness -' he stuttered.

'I require only a nursemaid, not a handmaiden' she continued firmly.

'I could not, in good consciousness Your Highness, leave you without someone to attend to you in your rooms' Axel continued, bewildered.

Laura looked carefully at the expressions of surprise, shock and worry on their faces and shut her eyes, masking her unhappiness.

'Do they speak Russian?' she asked faintly.

'No Your Highness'

'French? *English?*' she tried, despairing.

'Only German, Your Highness' Gustav explained.

'We shall find you a German tutor' Fredrik smiled.

'Allow me' Gustav and Kurt cried at the same time.

'How could I refuse such enthusiastic tutors?'

The boys grinned and excitedly led her through the house, showing her the antechambers and the magnificent galleries and ballroom. Laura watched them carefully as they walked. It had been almost eighteen months since she had seen them last. The youngest brother, Kurt, still had his boyish blonde locks, some still ringlets, but he tied them back with a black ribbon at the nape of his neck. He was now thirteen and had grown four inches, becoming lanky and a little ungainly, as sudden growth spurts often made young men.

Gustav, now seventeen, had lost his sulky pout and had become surer of himself. He too had grown a few inches, and was now the tallest and darkest brother, his brown locks cropped and tousled romantically on his forehead. He wore a coat of slightly rough material, but it was cut fine and fitted him well.

Alexandra, tired and fussy from the long journey from the Alps, began to grizzle and wiggle in Laura's arms.

'I have prepared a nursery for *Prinzessin* Alexandra' Axel said, beckoning them up the elegantly carved, curved staircase in the foyer. 'Please forgive me if it is inadequate, I did not expect to be making a nursery in this home so soon.'

He pushed open one of the doors and Laura caught her breath. The room was mostly barren, but the large windows were draped with brocaded curtains and a beautifully carved crib stood in the centre of the room, in front of the fire. It was too far back to be in danger from wayward embers, but a fire screen protected it as well. A hoop of lace arched over the crib and the delicate material waterfalled over the sides.

'Oh, it's beautiful' she whispered.

Forgetting herself she moved to step forward, then sharply checked herself, stepping back and clutching Alexandra tighter.

'Your Highness?' Axel asked, concerned.

'The Dalnerechenskers have a superstition about nurseries' she said by way of explaining herself.

'But surely you do not -' Fredrik started then stopped, unnerved by the look on her face.

She flinched.

'No I do not' she said quietly, finally. 'But it is a tradition that is important to my people, so I will honour it.'

But doing so would mean letting go of her daughter she realised. No one else had cared for her since she had been cleaned and placed in Laura's arms after her birth. *She needs rest, and it will only be a little while* she consoled herself, giving the fussing baby to the older of the two servants that had followed them upstairs. She bobbed a curtsey then crossed the threshold of the nursery and laid Alexander in the crib, beginning to rock it gently.

'Allow me to show you to your rooms' Fredrik said, noting how reluctant Laura was to leave. 'Do not worry, Gertrude has been a midwife and a nurse for many years, *Prinzessin* Alexandra is in safe hands.'

Laura allowed herself to be led a short way down the corridor. The rooms Axel had furnished for her were modest in size but lavish in decor. The parlour was bright and the wood panelling glowed in the sunlight. The dressing room had an area tiled in Italian marble on which stood an iron claw-foot bathtub. A richly carved folding screen divided the bathroom in half and a large armoire and a vanity stood on the carpeted side of the room. Her travelling trunks were already in the dressing room and the younger maid, Heidi, began hanging up her dresses.

'I hope you will be comfortable' Fredrik said, opening the door to show her the beautiful bedroom.

'It looks blissful' she said. 'If you will excuse me, I am tired from our journey. I will rest until this evening.'

He bowed and excused himself, closing the door behind him. Laura sighed and shrugged off her travelling cloak, stepping into her dressing room. Heidi turned and curtseyed to her, asking something in German as she took the cloak from her. Laura looked at her blankly so Heidi crossed to the armoire and pulled it open, gesturing to the recently hung dresses.

'Yes, very nice' she murmured, embarrassed at the language barrier.

Heidi pointed to Laura's dresses and mimed eating something out of a cupped hand, saying *arbendessen* then gestured to the dresses hanging in the closet. Laura realised she wanted her to choose a dress to wear for dinner that night.

'Dark red' she said without thinking, then reached out and touched the one she meant.

Heidi smiled and pulled it out, shaking out the creases in it and hanging it over the dividing screen. Laura went back to the bedroom and lay down on the bed, rubbing her eyes tiredly. She hadn't realised she had drifted off until she woke a few hours later with the polite knock on her door.

'*Eure Hoheit, Seine Hochgeboren kompt*' Heidi said, pushing open the bedroom door and carrying in the red dress.

'What?' Laura asked, still half asleep, then her brain began processing what she had heard. *Hochgeboren* – High Born – she had said. That meant Axel and not Fredrik, who was titled *Hochwohlgeboren* – High Well Born.

Laura rubbed her face to rouse herself then rose, stretching. She felt hands clasp the back of her dress and jerked away, rounding in horror on Heidi.

'No!' she cried, stopping the bewildered girl, who reached out again, saying something Laura couldn't understand. 'No!' she shouted, pulling away.

The door to her rooms hurriedly opened and Axel looked in, alarmed.

'What is wrong?' he demanded, eyeing the maid who had fallen into a submissive posture, shaken and upset. Quickly she spoke to Axel, who then turned surprised to Laura. 'Your Highness, she is only helping you undress –'

'No' Laura snapped, shaken. 'She may turn out my clothes for me and clean the room and whatever else maids do in your house but she is never to help me dress or undress. Never. Tell her.'

Axel started to protest then stopped and turned to the shaking maid, dismissing her with a gentle word. Heidi dipped a curtsey and hurriedly left. Laura turned away, trying to calm herself down, feeling stupid and hot with shame.

'The evening meal is ready Your Highness; would you care to join us?' Axel asked finally.

'I will join you shortly' she managed, and Axel bowed and closed the door behind him.

Laura, wiping her cheeks, went quickly into the dressing room, splashing her face in the basin of water that sat on the vanity. She pinned her hair up carefully then dressed in the dark red dress, smoothing the bodice down against her. It did not quite fit her properly, she found it near impossible to cinch the corset tight on her own, but she had lost weight since she had last worn the dress.

She felt ugly, eyeing herself unhappily, then turned away from her reflection and joined Axel in the corridor, slipping her hand into his offered elbow.

He led her to a lavish dining room, brocaded in blue and burgundy, and over to the table where Kurt, Gustav, Fredrik and a man and a woman whom she did not recognise stood. The company at the table bowed deeply when they stepped into the room, and Axel led Laura to the head of the table, seating her himself.

'Your Highness, may I present my sister Countess Marbeckel, and her husband, Count Marbeckel' Axel said, repeating the introductions in German. The man and the woman bowed to her again and Laura dipped her head forward politely.

She gestured for them to sit and bowls of soup were placed before them. Axel seated himself on her right and provided translations for her as conversation flitted up and down the table. She was for the most part ignored by the Marbeckels until the Countess asked Laura a direct question. Her husband muttered something that was not as inaudible as it should have been and Laura noticed how Fredrik's face tightened.

'My sister could not help noticing that you wear no jewels' Axel said. 'She asks why it is that you do not?'

Laura eyed the gems dripping from Countess' throat, noticing how her fingers delicately rested on the diamond encrusted cuff she wore on her other hand, surreptitiously drawing the eye to them. She then guessed what her husband had said that made Fredrik react so; she still wore one piece of jewellery: her wedding ring.

'I have none' she answered. 'They were all taken in the revolution.'

There were gasps when Axel translated that comment. Count Marbeckel made another comment and his wife laughed.

'Kurt, Gustav; would you please begin your lessons with me tomorrow? I can see I am desperately in need of them' Laura said, twisting her mouth into something that might have been a smile, but it did not reach her eyes.

6

'Good morning Your Highness' Gustav said, bowing low when she stepped out of her bedroom dressed in dark green. 'It is a fine day, not too cold, I thought perhaps you might like a walk in my uncle's woods, I know you were fond of them in Dalnerechensk.'

Laura shut her eyes, wounded at his suggestion, then took the hat and muff that Heidi held out. She opened her mouth to say something to her, but stopped when she realised she couldn't apologise to a servant, and she wouldn't understand her anyway. That didn't stop her from wanting to, but she closed her mouth and followed Gustav with an unquiet heart as he led her out to the garden.

Kurt was waiting impatiently on a stone bench and stood and bowed when they appeared. Eager to get started he pointed at the house and said *Haus*, enunciating clearly for Laura.

'We thought perhaps to tell you the names of objects -'

'*Garten*' Kurt interrupted excitedly, gesturing to the area they stood in.

'- so that you might get used to the pronunciation before we start some simple sentences.'

'*Wald!*' Kurt added, pointing to the trees beyond the high garden wall.

Laura took a deep breath, turning the names over in her head before she hesitantly said *Haus, Garten, Wald* and pointed at each one. The boys applauded as if she had said something profound and she felt ridiculous yet pleased all the same.

They began a small tour of the garden, and Kurt excitedly called out the names of anything that caught his eye, even his own shadow. Laura did her best to keep up with the pace of the lesson, distracted, but glad of Kurt's enthusiasm, as it stopped her from thinking too much, stopped her thoughts sliding to Olaf.

'Enough' Gustav said, curtailing Kurt's enthusiasm, and they walked in silence for a while through an avenue of yew trees, clipped into strange shapes, arriving at a gate in the garden wall.

Gustav opened it and ushered Laura and his brother through, surprised at the hesitation he saw in her. But she did not stop, walking into the white dusted trees of the forest. Deep in the woods, set aside in a small clearing, stood a small copse of pine trees, planted in neat rows. A set of wagon tracks led to and away from them, disappearing into the forest near where they stood. As they approached the little copse they could see one tree was missing, cut close to the ground, and pine needles and footprints littered the ground.

'Thieves?' Laura asked.

'More likely Wilhelm' Gustav explained, picking up a sprig of needles. 'I do so enjoy the scent of cut logs in the fireplace.' He lifted the sprig under his nose and shut his eyes, breathing deep. He stopped at the sound from Laura. 'Your Highness?' he asked, surprised at her tears.

She picked up her skirts and ran, from the memory of Olaf teaching her the plants in the Hunting Forest of Dalnerechensk, shutting his eyes in simple pleasure as he had breathed in the scents of the trees. She ran from her guilt and anger and hurt. Olaf was gone and it was her fault.

She raced into the house and upstairs to her room, flinging herself down on the carpet to sob miserably. There was a quiet tap on the open door then it was pushed closed behind them, and Laura found herself in gentle arms, a hint of delicate perfume wafting over her.

'I miss him so much!' she cried in French, knowing that Heidi couldn't understand her but didn't care. 'It was my fault, and I never got to say I was sorry for it, never got to see him again!'

Heidi soothed her, rocking her gently, smoothing down her hair with her hand. Laura gulped and sobbed, incoherent with grief, a mess of hiccupping slobbery tears. It took almost an hour but at long last she got herself under control and sat back, her mouth dropping open when she saw it wasn't her servant at all. Instead before her sat a pretty blonde dressed in a fine silk coat.

'Who are you?' she gasped, going red with embarrassment.

'I am Countess Emilie von Schmidt, Your Highness' she said in French, with only a trace of an accent. 'My husband is Count Karl von Schmidt. I am delighted to meet you, Your Highness' Emilie went on. 'I'm sure we will be close friends.'

Laura's blush deepened when she realised this woman had understood all she had said, and scanned roughly through her wept words, trying to see if she had blurted out anything incriminating. Emilie got to her feet, dusting off her coat and curtseyed to her.

'Forgive me for my outburst' Laura started, getting to her feet too, but Emilie waved it away.

'There is nothing to forgive' she smiled. 'If it pleases you, I would like to introduce my son to you, and it would be such an honour to meet your daughter!'

'Give me a few moments, I will join you shortly' she managed.

Emilie curtseyed and let herself out of the room, closing the door behind her. Laura crossed to her dressing room, wincing as she caught sight of her messy face in the mirror. She sat at her dressing table and put her face in her hands, sighing.

The red hot shame hadn't faded yet, and for a moment Laura fervently wished she was back in the Alps, hiding from the world. She had learnt to hide anger, fear and jealousy as a student in Lady Ramkinson's ghastly school, but never had she learnt to hide the searing misery of grief. She had forgotten what it meant to have eyes on her, judging her; forgotten how difficult it could be to be a queen.

She was not ready to be thrust into the public eye again. She thought about locking herself away in her room but sighed, knowing she couldn't. She could make Emilie wait for hours until she was fully composed, but there were such things as grace and courtesy. She couldn't send Heidi with a note, the girl didn't understand her, and by the time one of the brothers had come to translate she may as well have left her rooms herself.

Besides, her breasts were sore, Alexandra would need feeding again soon.

She wiped away the crusting mess on her cheeks then stood and washed her face properly in the basin of water. She patted it dry then pulled out her hair and repinned it tidily. She took off her green coat and hung it in her wardrobe, smoothing down the bodice of the charcoal dress and eyeing herself critically.

Finally she turned away, and still warm from the afterglow of shame she pulled open the door to the corridor.

Kurt and Gustav were waiting worriedly outside her door, and bowed when she stepped out.

'Your Highness,' Kurt started worriedly, but stopped when she took his hands and kissed his cheek, and then Gustav's.
'I hear your eldest brother and Countess von Schmidt have arrived' she said. 'I will bring my daughter to meet them. Please escort me to the nursery.'

Gustav offered her his elbow and she took it, Kurt scampering on ahead. Another crib had appeared in the room and another nursemaid was chatting amicably to Gertrude as she folded sheets and blankets, placing them in the crib. They both stopped and curtseyed to Laura and Kurt instructed Gertrude to pick up the burbling baby, bringing her back to Laura.

Laura kissed Alexandra's forehead, gathering her into her arms. She excused herself from the company of the von Schmidt brothers and stepped into the small room beside the nursery. Axel had placed a nursing chair in this room where Laura could feed her daughter in comfort, and the small sideboard table held a collection of cloth diapers, towels and face cloths to see to Alexandra's feeding and toiletry.

Laura sat, and after a careful look at the door she unbuttoned her dress and unhooked the flap on her nursing corset, exposing her breast. Alexandra nuzzled at her then began to drink, and Laura reached into the sideboard, pulling out a towel she placed over her shoulder, ready to pat the wind out of her daughter.

When Alexandra was full she burped her, righted her clothing, cleaned up the milky vomit from the back of the nursing chair and carried her down to the foyer where Axel, Karl, Fredrik and Emilie stood. On Emilie's hip sat a baby, more alert and less floppy than Alexandra. They saw her and bowed as she arrived.
'Your Highness, it is a pleasure to see you again' Karl said, coming forward to kiss her hand. 'Allow me to introduce my wife Emilie and my son Helmut.'
'A pleasure' she said, forcing down the heat of the remembered shame. 'This is my daughter *Prinzessin* Alexandra Alexeevna Vakhtangovna.'

It was not her proper title, but she couldn't say it out loud, she could barely think it, as it was the same title that – she stopped, knowing if she even thought his name now she would start crying all over again. As one the brothers, Axel and Emilie all bowed deeply to the baby, Karl and Emilie coming forward to take the tiny hand and kiss the back of it.
'She is beautiful' Emilie smiled.
'Come, you must be exhausted from your journey. Let us retire to the drawing room for some refreshment' Axel said, leading the way from the foyer.

7

Laura rose early, unable to stay in bed. She was still debating whether she should move the crib into her room, anxious about Alexandra, but felt a guilty relief that she didn't have to see to her when she cried at night, or change dirtied diapers anymore. Despite not having to see to her, she had woken twice when she heard Alexandra cry, and had made it down the corridor twice before the crying had stopped again. She had pushed open the nursery door the first time, seeing Gertrude rocking the crib gently, singing softly in German. The second time she had stopped in the dark corridor, listening hard in the silence, before forcing herself to turn around and head back to bed. But sleep had not come again.

She dressed in a purple so dark it was nearly black and headed to the nursery, her full breasts squashed painfully in the nursing corset. Emilie's maid Claudette greeted her quietly, as she spoke both German and French, and quickly brought Alexandra to her. Laura slipped into the room next door and freed her tender breast from the constraint, wincing as Alexandra began to feed.

In the silence that folded around them, Laura stroked Alexandra's cheek with the back of her fingers, wondering if she should sing to her. No one had taught her any Russian nursery rhymes, and she couldn't remember all the words to the songs her mother had used to sing. So she stayed silent, rocking Alexandra gently after she had finished, until she drifted off to sleep again.

She smiled gently and rose, righting her clothing and taking her back to the nursery where she gave her back to Claudette. It was still early, too early to make her way to breakfast, so she decided to explore some of Axel's home, padding down to a gallery in a little used wing of the house. It was filled with portraits, some small and intimate, others grand and imperial; their subjects staring down from steeds or chaise lounges. The corridor was still dark so Laura crossed to the drawn curtains at the window and pulled them open, surprising Fredrik who was walking across the internal courtyard. He bowed to her and she dipped a small curtsey, knowing he would soon join her. She turned away and walked slowly along the gallery, gazing at each face, opening each curtain she came to, stopping in front of a particularly attractive dark beauty.

The door at the far end opened and Fredrik stepped through, smiling, remembering the pleasant afternoon they had spent walking through the West Wing of Varennikov Castle.

'I'm afraid that you will find no ghosts here Your Highness' he smiled, bowing, before coming to join her.

Her cheeks coloured. 'I spent so much time in the West Wing when I returned there Ekaterina was afraid I would turn into the Grey Ghost' she said, then she dropped her eyes. 'She was so very worried for me.'

'Why did you spend so much time there?' he asked quietly.

She sighed. 'I felt like a ghost' she shrugged. 'It seemed right.'

She turned away from the look on his face, taking hold of the curtain to pull it open.

'Allow me' Fredrik said quickly, and his fingers brushed hers gently as he took hold of the material, flinging it open.

Laura wasn't sure if the touch was accidental or not, and the warmth of his fingers had stirred something strange in her. She quickly checked that they were still alone, folding her hands together before her, turning to eye the comely woman in the painting again.

'Who are these exotic beauties that your uncle populates his house with?' she asked, changing the subject.

'Countess Mariana von Schmidt' Fredrik smiled sadly, joining her again. 'She was my mother.'

'She is beautiful' Laura said, knowing where Gustav got his romantic dark looks from. 'I am terribly sorry.'

'This is my grandfather' Fredrik said, swallowing down the lump and gesturing to the painting beside the countess. '*Fürst* Otto von Schmidt, a non-royal prince and cousin to *Prinz* Sebastian's father. Otto had sixteen children; my father the second eldest and *Onkel* Axel the youngest. My grandmother loved children' he smiled. 'When my parents died she took my brothers and me in, to grow up together with her youngest. She had many daughters, but only three sons. I used to think she had so many children because she wanted more boys. This is grandmother' he smiled, gesturing to another portrait.

Slowly he led her to other portraits, explaining how each relative fitted into the many branches of the family tree, finally showing her Ulrich Schmidt, the smithy who had turned his attention to more delicate metalwork, producing such exquisite pieces that he had even come to the attention of Sigismund, Holy Roman Emperor and King of Germany, who conferred Letters Patent on Ulrich, admitting him into the *Niederer Adel* – the Lower Nobility. His descendants, through further Letters, alliances and marriages, now found themselves speckled throughout the *Niederer Adel* and the *Uradel* – Ancient Nobility. Fredrik's family was now employers of jewellers, rather than the craftsmen themselves.

'The Dalnerechenskers love children and large families' she said quietly. 'It was only my father and I at our wedding. What a great disappointment I must have been.'

'You could never disappoint anyone Your Highness' Fredrik soothed.

She looked away, turning to eye a portrait of a chubby toddler, one of Fredrik's many cousins, nieces and great-nieces.

'Tell me about this Dalnerechensk superstition of nurseries' he said, changing the subject.

'It is four hundred years old' she said, still eying the toddler. 'Vsevolod is highly revered in Dalnerechensk. He was their first Tsar, and he defended Dalnerechensk against the might of Russia and Ivan the Terrible. His wife, Natasha, built the nursery in the castle, down to the last detail, pouring her heart into it. But she never had any children. The Dalnerechenskers say she went to her grave miserable and cursing that any tsaritsa who set foot in her nursery before the birth of her first child would remain childless. Since then no tsaritsa has ever set foot inside before the birth of their first. Some refused to *ever* set foot inside, especially if their first was not a son.

'All Vsevolod's descendants come from the single son he had with his second wife. *He* had twenty seven children, not all of whom were legitimate. There are many laws in Dalnerechensk about marriage and inheritance and mistresses and so on. And many punishments' she added quietly, looking away.

'Your Highness' he said, stopping her.

Quickly she looked around, stepping away from his touch.

'Excuse me *Euer Hochwohlgeboren*, I think it is time for my German lessons with Gustav and Kurt.'

Fredrik could do nothing but bow helplessly and watch her leave.

8

The knock on the door startled Laura out of her reverie and she realised, somewhat embarrassed, that she had been staring too long at the groundskeeper Wilhelm as he raked the snow from the garden paths. Behind her Heidi answered the door, dropping a curtsey to Emilie.

'I hope I am not interrupting?' she smiled.

'No' Laura smiled too.

'Would you accompany me on a shopping excursion Your Highness?' she asked, excited. 'Axel has promised a feast for his birthday, he has invited half of the gentry of München, and I simply have no dress that would do.'

'I couldn't leave Alexandra -'

'She is in safe hands Your Highness, Claudette and Gertrude are very experienced, they will see that she comes to no harm. Besides, we will not be gone long.'

Laura hesitated, running through a list of reasons and excuses not to go but suddenly dismissed them. She couldn't help but like the Countess, she was intelligent and charming, and Laura enjoyed her company. *Besides*, she told herself, *she had travelled to Munich with a measly wardrobe fitting for a grieving widow, and couldn't remember the last time she had gone shopping.*

She agreed and Emilie gave quick instructions to Heidi, who curtseyed and retrieved a coat, hat and gloves from Laura's dressing room. Emilie rushed off to gather her own coat and Laura padded quietly down the stairs to the grand foyer. Emilie joined her, chatting excitedly, leading her to a small hansom that had been parked near the stairs.

Laura climbed in and sat, feeling the carriage sway as Emilie climbed in beside her and the driver climbed onto the seat. Emilie struck up a lively chatter which Laura only half-heartedly participated in. Emilie didn't seem to mind, and interrupted her own conversation to point out the landmarks of Munich as they passed them.

The carriage drove through Karlstor and stopped on the busy street beyond. Emilie stepped out, guiding Laura into Oberpollinger, Munich's luxury department store. At once Emilie called out to the clerk who came forward to help her, leaving Laura to browse disinterestedly through the racks of ready-made dresses.

They all seemed too bright, too frilly, too silly; and Laura wondered how much she had changed from the bright, silly girl who had gone to seek love and adventure in Dalnerechensk.

'Is there anything that takes your fancy Your Highness?' Emilie asked, holding up a white silk and tulle creation against herself.

'No' she answered.

'Perhaps you did not see -' the shop clerk began, switching to French too.

'I see nothing I like' Laura said shortly.

Emilie hesitated then gave the dress to the clerk.

'Perhaps we shall find something elsewhere' she said, linking her arm through Laura's and gently propelling her out of the department store.

As the day lengthened Laura found herself growing more impatient and frustrated. It wasn't Emilie's fault, she was being accommodating and thoughtful, but Laura was regretting her decision to go shopping, and wished the girl would decide on a dress so they could go home.

'What do you think of this dress?' Emilie asked, holding up a beautiful lavender.

'It suits your hair' Laura said disinterestedly.

'I thought, perhaps, it would… suit your complexion more' she suggested, like a tightrope walker edging over the abyss below.

'Certainly not' Laura said. 'It is too garish for me.'

Emilie eyed the dress and gave it back to the shop's assistant.

'Is there nothing to tempt you? There is a rather fetching -'

'Nothing' Laura interrupted shortly, then sighed and shut her eyes. 'I am in need of hair pins' she said, the words wrenched out of her.

Emilie quickly guided her to Hemmerle's Boutique, owned by two brothers who were purveyors to the royal Bavarian Household, and renowned for the bejewelled fantasies they had created for the rich houses of Germany. The short walk to Maximillianstrasse had made Laura's feet ache, and she was short and impatient with Joseph and Anton Hemmerle, who were excitedly showing her the latest pieces commissioned by Luitpold, Regent of Bavaria. Laura selected a dozen or so seed pearl pins, leaving Emilie to haggle over the price for the credit note before her friend dragged her back to purchase the white silk and tulle she had admired so much in Oberpollinger.

Laura waited politely, but could not disguise her relief when they finally climbed back into the hansom and headed for *Schwarzschwanwald*. She had only just returned to her rooms when there was a knock on the door.

'Do not answer it' she begged, but Heidi did not understand her, opening the door for Axel.

He bowed. 'Ah Your Highness, you are back' he smiled. 'I have a surprise for you.'

He stepped aside and four people stepped into her rooms: Ekaterina and Grigory Ivanov, a woman she did not recognise, and her father. Laura cried out with an exclamation that was part surprise, part joy and part anguish, running to throw her arms tightly around him. He kissed her hair and face, tears of joy running down his cheeks.

In her brief glimpse of Luke before the tears blurred her vision she could see he was more sun-leathered than she remembered, and there were tiny strands of grey noticeable at his temples. She also saw how relieved and happy he looked, though there was a touch of unease hiding in his features.

Through a half babbled conversation she learned that he had been on a dig for a new oil well in Texas when he had received Ekaterina's worried note about the health of his daughter. Luke had immediately left for Boston and taken the first ship sailing in the right direction. Several agonising weeks later he had arrived at Varennikov Castle only to discover that Laura was no longer there.

The Ivanovs and he had then travelled to *Prinz* Sebastian's magnificent residence in Munich, arriving with luck just after he had returned from his hunting lodge. *Prinz* Sebastian had kindly received them and sent word to Axel.

Laura was suddenly aware of the woman standing near them, much closer than she should have been. She turned to eye her and watched as she curtseyed low, nervous. She had pleasant features and could have been described as pretty, though homely was more accurate. She was modestly dressed in course silk, combining just the right amount of style with humility. Laura wondered if she had studiously practised her demeanour or whether it was genuine.

Luke, aware of her curious scrutiny, looked uncomfortable.

'Laura this is Anne. Baroness Anne. Er, Lady Anne. My wife.'

'You remarried?' she gasped, hurt.

'I did send news Laura, but it must not have reached you' he said, ill at ease.

Laura turned away from his embrace, taking off her coat and trying to compose herself. Her own mother had died many years ago, miserable and ill. Luke had loved her, and there had been no one since her death. She knew her father deserved some happiness after all these years, but did not know what to make of this woman, least of all to think of her as a mother.

She gave her coat to Heidi and wiped her face, turning back to eye the nervous woman, who was now the mother-in-law of a royal. Laura was at a complete loss with what to say to her.

'It is an honour to meet you, Tsarina Vartangev' she said, mispronouncing the name as she curtseyed again.

Ekaterina winced.

'The correct title is Tsaritsa' Laura said. 'The word Tsarina does not exist in Russian. And you should really address me as Your Highness. And it is Vakhtangova, if you please.'

'Forgive me' she said, turning crimson.

They looked at each other awkwardly, and an uncomfortable silence fell, broken by the arrival of Emilie, Claudette, Helmut, Gertrude, Alexandra and Axel's nephews, greeting their guests in English. Laura gently took Alexandra and presented her to Luke, nestling her in his arms.

'This is your granddaughter, Princess Alexandra Alexeevna Vakhtangovna.'

'Beautiful' he crooned, staring at her while he wept with joy again, covering her cheeks with kisses.

Lady Anne peered over Luke's shoulder and made cooing sounds, exclaiming how perfectly adorable she was. Laura found it slightly distasteful but tried to push the feelings aside. As if sensing her discomfort Alexandra began to cry, fussing in Luke's arms.

'She is hungry' she said, gathering her to her again. 'Please excuse me.'

They bowed and curtseyed to her, slipping out the door, and she heard Axel say: *let me show you my gardens* before Heidi closed the door. By now Laura knew enough German to dismiss her and she too curtseyed, leaving Laura alone.

She sighed gratefully and sank down onto the chaise, settling back to feed Alexandra. At once she quietened and Laura smiled, stroking the soft, downy hair back from her cheek. Alexandra's eyes drooped and as soon as she was full she drifted off to sleep. Laura raised her to her shoulder and patted the wind from her gently. She leaned back to rest against the chaise, shutting her eyes too, her thoughts turning back to Anne.

She was young, perhaps no more than twenty, most certainly without children of her own. *And now a grandmother* she thought wryly. *Cooing over Alexandra as if she had some right to do so.* The thought made her angry and she pushed it away, letting the soothing feel of Alexandra breathing on her neck chase away unpleasant thoughts.

The quiet knock on her door woke her a few hours later. She sat up, surprised to see the room was dark and bathed in a muted silver. She quickly checked to see if Alexandra had woken, then righted her clothing, bidding the knocker to enter. Fredrik pushed open the door and bowed to her.

'I did not want to disturb you, in case you were sleeping' he said, quickly lighting a candle. 'Your room is cold, I will send Heidi to light a fire immediately Your Highness. Dinner is ready, would you care to join us?' he asked, lighting another candle.

'Yes of course' she said, getting to her feet. 'Let me take Alexandra to -'
'Allow me' Fredrik said, coming forward and gently taking her from Laura.

She watched him cradle her daughter in his arms, bow and leave, closing her door behind him. She took a candle with her to the dressing room and tidied her hair, eyeing the dresses in her wardrobe. They were poor, worn, drab and unfashionable; ill-fitting and as grim as wintery starvation. Her depression was beginning to lift, she could feel herself growing interested in people, in conversations and activities again, but couldn't permit herself to be happy, as if happiness somehow laughed at the cruelty of Olaf's suffering. She shut her eyes and selected a dark blue, dressing quickly.

It's so ugly! she thought as she eyed herself in the mirror. *Even the flattering warmth of candlelight couldn't make this attractive.* She quickly rummaged in the drawer of her dressing table, pulling out a pair of sharp scissors. Quickly she snipped off the thick, grandmotherly lace at her neck, cutting it down to the bodice and leaving her skin bare. *It's a shame I don't have any sapphires, or even some perfume* she thought sadly, and turned away from her reflection, joining Fredrik in the corridor.

He bowed and offered her his elbow, but Laura could not help but notice there was a sadness in his demeanour.
'What is wrong *Euer Hochwohlgeboren?*' she asked quietly.

He smiled sadly and brushed away the question, slipping into the dining room with her.

The table was rather full with Count and Countess Marbeckel, Luke and Lady Anne, Count and Countess Ivanov, Axel and his four nephews, Emilie and Laura. She was seated between Ekaterina and Fredrik, seated so close she could feel the heat of them, and their arms would brush hers as they ate. Conversations in French, German and English fluttered up and down the table and laughter soon followed it, warmed by the wine and close company.

Laura watched Lady Anne as they ate; how tenderly she looked at Luke, how attentively she listened to conversations, how nervously she would glance at her daughter-in-law.

'Axel, you have invited half of Germany to your birthday!' Ekaterina suddenly laughed, kissing her cousin's hand affectionately. 'Laura you simply *must* accompany me tomorrow! I do not have a suitable dress!'

'Of course' she said, feeling slightly guilty that she would enjoy the shopping excursion with Ekaterina more than she had with Emilie, for all that she liked the girl.

'Splendid!' Ekaterina laughed.

9

Ekaterina knocked on her door and let herself in as she sat patting the wind from Alexandra, coming to fold her arms around her friend and rest her cheek on her crown.

'You are not so pale. I am so glad to see you on the road to recovery' she said, kissing her hair. 'It was terrible, so terrible to see you so changed by all the horror. Grigory and I so feared for you.'

'I have missed you Ekaterina. I never asked you about the night of the revolt' Laura suddenly said, swivelling to look at her. 'How did you escape?'

'Anya's fiancée came riding to see us when the mob attacked the castle. He knew once they had found Aleksei they would come looking for other key ministers. Grigory and I were able to flee with some clothes and jewels. I have sent letters and telegrams to several I used to know but I have received no answer.'

'Most of them fled' Laura said absently. 'Not one of the old Advisory Council save for Ivan Gogol is in Ilich's new Parliament. They burned the throne room. They burned your beautiful house too.'

'Bricks and mortar' she said, shrugging away the tears. 'It is only a building. I am glad you and I are safe.'

Alexandra burbled and Laura kissed her head gently, handing her to Heidi who went to deposit Alexandra into Gertrude's care. Laura stood and crossed into the dressing room, agonising over her choice of dresses again.

'You must buy a new dress too' Ekaterina said, joining her and eyeing her collection with a genteel sneer.

'It does not feel right -' she said helplessly.

'I know, Emilie told me' Ekaterina soothed, coming to take Laura's hands. 'I know what you feel. When my son died I was heartbroken, and I mourned for him for a year. And as the days passed, as the grief began to cocoon itself away I was torn that I did not hurt so much, torn that I was wanting to smile and enjoy my husband, was wanting other children. It was a terrible guilt; that I should move on from my firstborn.

'It took me a long time to learn to smile and love again, a long time for that guilt to go away. There is a place in my heart that is wrapped and preserved with a strange wistfulness for him. Had I known that he would be my only child perhaps I would have mourned the rest of my days like poor Queen Victoria. Or perhaps I would have done no different, realised that Grigory loved me very much and would have done anything to make me happy again.'

She stopped and shot Laura a look.

'I shall wait for you in the foyer' Ekaterina went on, shrugging herself out of her reverie.

She left and Laura pulled on the grey silk dress, folding a warm winter coat around her shoulders and taking a fur muff with her.

'You look radiant my dear' the Countess said, linking her arm through hers when she arrived. 'Motherhood agrees with your complexion.'

'Only recently' she smiled ruefully. 'Until I had Gertrude I ran myself ragged. I cannot tell you how sympathetic I am for unfortunate mothers who cannot afford help.'

'And speaking of unfortunate mothers, what do you think of Lady Anne?' Ekaterina asked as they climbed into the carriage.

'I have not thought much' Laura admitted. 'It was such a sudden shock. What do *you* think of her Ekaterina?'

'Well, she is rather fond of telling people of her relationship to Queen Victoria -'

'Sixth cousin-in-law to her granddaughter, twice removed' they said together, with a little, mocking laugh.

'- and I have no doubt she secretly preens a little when she tells others she is mother-in-law to the Empress of Dalnerechensk' Ekaterina shrugged.

'Yet I have had some time to study her with your father, and I can solemnly promise that her feelings are genuine and sincere. She is likable and kind, not very intelligent, but knowledgeable on a range of topics. Your father is content and happy with her.

'In truth, I feel she is overwhelmed by all this. From conversations I have had with her it seems she grew up rather modestly, the only thing of worth was her title; and suddenly she is now thrust into the international spotlight as the mother to an important figurehead in European politics -'

'I could hardly say important -' Laura started to protest, but Ekaterina interrupted her.

'*Da* Laura, Dalnerechensk's defeat of Nikita's army is the Thermopylae of the modern world and it had far-reaching consequences -'

'It was hardly a Thermopylae -' she protested again.

'And did you not understand what you did with the Bodice Treaties?' she went on, using the collective name the Liberty Treaty with Russia and the secret Chamber Treaty with Germany had come to be known. 'How furious Kaiser Wilhelm was with Tsar Nicholas? How close we could have come to war? The world knows what you did Laura, how strategic Dalnerechensk is for continuing peace between the powerful nations of Europe.

'And she has become your mother. I would be daunted with you for a daughter too.'

Laura stared at her.

'Is that true?' she managed.

'*Yes* Laura' Ekaterina said gently.

Laura fell silent, mulling over her words. It had been a year ago, when she had been a guest in Marie's wedding party, that she had discovered the true market price for tin, Dalnerechensk's only export. Russia had deceived the Principality into accepting less and less for the metal, till Dalnerechensk tottered on collapse and children and old men scraped out poor livings in the mines.

Laura had been furious at Russia, and had invited both Tsar Nicholas II and Kaiser Wilhelm of Germany to negotiations for the tin, playing with the rivalry between the cousins to save Dalnerechensk from economic ruin. In order to protect the terms of the newly drawn Liberty Treaty with Russia, Laura and Kaiser Wilhelm had signed the Chamber Treaty - so named because it had been signed in Laura's private chambers.

It had promised German aide if Liberty Treaty was ever violated, in return for a renegotiated sale of tin. It had only meant to be a deterrent, a threat to stop Russia from beginning her spiral of undervaluing the tin and threatening invasion again. But as she thought she realised Ekaterina was right. Europe was drawing itself into jealous alliances and defences against each other, and Dalnerechensk stood rather precariously between Russia and the powerful new nation of Germany.

The carriage drew to a stop outside Oberpollinger again and Ekaterina slipped down, turning back to eye Laura.

'Come come, the world will not descend into war because of Dalnerechensk. It would not dare do such a foolish thing!'

Laura managed a small smile and stepped out too. Ekaterina instructed the driver in German to wait for them then led Laura into the department store, beginning to canvas the rows of dresses.

'Choose something for me Laura' she cried excitedly. 'You always have such exquisite taste.'

Laura hesitated then reached out, flicking through the racks. *Clever Ekaterina* she suddenly realised, catching herself holding a pretty blue against herself. On her own, choosing for herself, the dresses had chided her, admonished her with their colours and textures. But under the understanding that she was looking for someone else they became agreeable, beautiful; soft and beckoning. Ekaterina tutted.

'Not blue' she said, picking out a glowing cream silk. 'Try this on for me' she held the dress out to her.

'I hardly see the point if *you're* going to wear it' Laura chided, putting the blue back on the rack.

To prove that she wasn't going to play Ekaterina's game she wandered on, looking at more dresses, feeling the frustration of choice, although now she felt it because the dark dresses seemed too dreary and dull to be considered. Ekaterina disappeared into a fitting room and emerged in the cream dress, twirling for Laura.

'What do you think?'

'It is too tame for you' Laura smiled. 'You need a vivacious red.'

'Agreed! *Fraulein*, find me something risqué in red!' she laughed then went to another rack, pulling out dress after dress in vibrant colours.

Laura discovered a violet dress and gently pulled it towards her. It was plain and cut in a slightly outdated fashion. A swathe of black organza circled the top of the bodice, gathered closely between the breasts and shoulder blades but left to cascade from shoulder to elbow.

'Beautiful!' Ekaterina exclaimed, joining her so suddenly that Laura jumped. 'Go and try it on!'

'No, I couldn't -'

Ekaterina laughed and grabbed the dress, dragging them both to the fitting rooms. She pushed her in and gave her the dress, calling instructions in German to the young assistant. Laura sighed and eyed the dress then pulled it on, twisting and turning before the mirror, unsure how to feel wearing it. Finally she opened the door to show Ekaterina, who was dressed in a silk the colour of sunset.

'Beautiful!' they both said at the same time and smiled.

'We'll take them' Ekaterina added.

'Oh no -' Laura started but was hushed instantly.

Ekaterina repeated her instructions to the assistant, disappearing back into the fitting room. Laura hesitated then slipped into her own, dressing in silence.

10

The stuffiness of the ballroom had given her a headache and she had slipped away, stepping out onto a terrace. The night was brittle bright and cold; her breath tinkled in the air and she drew her arms around her protectively, sighing quietly as she felt her head clear.

Axel's birthday feast had been magnificent and the foyer and ballroom were full of dignitaries from Munich. Laura had taken a little of the wine that had been flowing, but not too much, trying to remain austere in her composure and behaviour. It was hard to do with lovely company and lively music. *When had I last danced?* she asked herself. *When had I last heard music?*

She had danced only three dances that evening, with her father, Axel and Fredrik; wondering who was watching her, wondering if she had smiled too much, if she looked too miserable. Had she talked too much? Said too little? The thinking had made her head ache and long to be free of the festivities, fighting with the part of her that wanted Fredrik to ask her to dance again.

She sighed, rubbing her temples, patting back stray wisps of her hair, feeling the tension leave her.

'Are you alright Your Highness?' Fredrik asked, joining her. He still spoke to her in French even though he spoke English well enough to Luke and Lady Anne. There was a charming hesitancy to his words when he spoke English, and some consonants were pulled into strange shapes by his accent.

'Yes, thank you' she smiled. 'I just wanted some fresh air.'

'May I keep you company?' he ventured quietly.

'That is most kind, but I shall not be long. I would not wish to detain you from such delightful festivities.'

'There could be nothing more delightful than your company' he said, moving closer, surprising her.

Fredrik leaned in to kiss her. She stepped back from his touch, looking around her carefully. Fredrik relented, stepping back too.

'You still mourn for him' he sighed quietly. 'Why do you look around you with such fear?'

She took a deep breath, looking around her again and hating herself for doing it.

'Forgive me' she whispered. 'I'm afraid... afraid I am wrong.'

'Wrong?' he blinked, surprised.

'Is it wrong of me to enjoy myself tonight, so soon out of mourning? Was I wrong to have left mourning? Have I mourned too much? Said too little? Danced too lightly? Smiled when I should have frowned, frowned when I should have laughed? I am so confused! And I worry that someone will see me, and *know* I am wrong, and then I will be punished...' she trailed off, sniffing loudly.

Fredrik fished out his pocket handkerchief and handed it over. She thanked him quietly and dabbed at her eyes, looking around when Lady Anne joined them on the terrace.

'There you are Your Highness' she said, bobbing a quick curtsey. 'Are you unwell?'

'No' she said, folding the handkerchief and giving it back to Fredrik, who bowed. 'Please excuse me, I am tired' she continued. 'Give my regards to your uncle, and wish him many happy returns. I will retire until tomorrow.'

They bowed as she left and she slipped upstairs to her quiet rooms, wishing she had let Fredrik's lips touch hers before she had stepped away.

11

Laura woke late and dressed quickly, heading down to the nursery. Many of Axel's birthday guests had departed in the last four days, and Laura was glad to be without their company, unsure how to act with so many strangers watching her. She stopped in surprise when she saw Fredrik sitting in a chair with Alexandra, feeding her from a bottle.

'Good morning Your Highness' he smiled.

'What are you doing?' she asked sharply. 'What are you feeding her?'

He looked surprised. 'Cow's milk. She was fussing, and Gertrude thought she really should be weaned, so I volunteered to feed her -'

'Gertrude does not make that decision!' Laura snapped, cutting Fredrik off. 'I am her mother, I will decide what is best for my daughter!'

'Of course, but Gertrude is experienced -'

'I *don't care!*' Laura shouted, shocking Fredrik. 'Alexandra is *my* daughter, I am the Tsaritsa of Dalnerechensk, Alexandra is *heir* to the *throne*, she is not some stupid -' she stopped herself.

'Some stupid Baron's baby?' Fredrik finished coldly.

Laura shut her eyes, fighting with the misery, confusion and anger.

'I did not mean that' she said, swallowing down the lump in her throat. 'I will not have my daughter taken from me. How will she know who her mother is?'

She stopped talking and buffed hard at the tears, surreptitiously looking around her again. Fredrik put aside the bottle and stood. He handed over his handkerchief, soothing Alexandra as she began to grizzle in protest at having her meal interrupted.

'I will instruct Gertrude to recommend to you any changes to the *Prinzessin's* routine but that the decision is yours alone, will that make you happy?'

She sniffed and nodded.

'Of course I regard Gertrude's experience; I did not mean that I didn't. I cannot bear to think of her so cold and aloof from me as my school acquaintances regarded their mothers! I could not bear being a spectator as someone else cleaned her, soothed her, fed and taught and raised her! They could force me to give her away; I would rather tear out my heart than that!'

'No one will ever take your daughter from you' he promised. 'I understand how strongly you feel for her. She is beautiful.'

Alexandra burped, spitting up a milky mouthful. Fredrik laughed, using the cloth tied around her neck to wipe the mess from his jacket, handing her to Laura in order to clean more effectively.

'Shall we go to breakfast?' he smiled, closing the nursery door.

She smiled and used his handkerchief to sponge away some more mess from his fine jacket.

'I must finish feeding Alexandra' she said gently.

'Ah, perhaps I will change. Join us when you have nursed' he smiled and bowed, taking the handkerchief with him.

Laura composed herself, slipping into the room next door and settling down to finish feeding Alexandra. When she finished she handed her back to Gertrude, opening her mouth to say something, but shut it again and headed down to the dining room. The table rose and bowed to her as she joined them, calling good morning to her. They spoke English now the company was more intimate, and Laura greeted them, sitting between Gustav and Ekaterina. A servant came forward and poured her some tea while Lady Anne asked after Alexandra's wellbeing.

A servant entered and bowed to Axel, presenting him with a silver tray on which several letters were stacked. He took them and grasped the pretty letter knife, slitting open the first and scanning it quickly.

'Ah, my sister reached home safely and thanks me for inviting her to my birthday' Axel told them, opening other letters and reading snippets of information out loud, stopping when he came to the last.

'*Prinz* Sebastian has written to you Your Highness' he smiled, handing over the thick card already slit open for her.

She unfolded it and another letter fell out. She instantly recognised the red wax seal. It was incised with a stylised ИР - the Russian initials for Ilich Rukavishnikov. A quick read of *Prinz* Sebastian's letter told her Ilich's note had arrived from Varennikov Castle a week ago and he had forwarded it to the home of his young cousin. The letter concluded with an apology and some well-wishing for his goddaughter.

'*Prinz* Sebastian sends his regards and apologises he was not able to join in your birthday celebrations as he is to spend some weeks in Paris' she said, breaking the seal of Ilich's letter.

'I love Paris' Lady Anne said. 'Such a romantic city' she added dreamily.

Laura gasped, going pale.

'What is it?' Ekaterina asked, worried.

'Ilich writes that Dalnerechensk is grateful for the news of the birth of my daughter, but adds that I must bring her to Dalnerechensk so the people can see her.' She threw down the letter. '*Must?!* How dare he think he can order me!'

There was an uncomfortable silence round the table.

'Perhaps Princess Alexandra should be shown to her subjects -' Axel began.

'I don't want to go back there!' Laura wailed, trying hard to keep herself in check.

There was another uncomfortable silence then Ekaterina said in Russian:

'Aleksei once told you it was not what you wanted that was important. This is more important than what you want and she is Vsevolod's heir, true ruler of Dalnerechensk.'

Laura stood so quickly her chair rocked, forcing the table to stand too. She said nothing and fled up to her room, shouting at Heidi to leave. Ekaterina followed her, closing the door behind them.

'I don't want to hear it -'

'But you must' Ekaterina interrupted firmly.

'I am only a ghost there! I have no power! I don't want to be there knowing that they are dead and the people do not want me -'

'Come, I know you do not think that' she said, taking her hands to still her. 'The people still love you, of that I am sure.'

'But what good can I do Ekaterina? I signed sovereignty to Ilich, I have no power, I have no heart. Tsar Constantinovich once said a man with no heart is not the man to be running a principality -'

'Laura' she said gently. 'Your heart is broken, but not gone. You still have it, or you would not have been so angry at Ilich's letter.'

Laura sighed, sniffing loudly. 'I am frightened of going back Ekaterina. Everything there; the castle, the streets, the woods; everything reminded me of faces that I would never see again; the old tsar, Aleksei, you and Grigory, Anna and -' she stopped, unable to go on.

'I know' Ekaterina soothed, folding her arms around her. 'I will go with you. Grigory and I both. I should like to see my home again.'

'But he was the Treasurer of Dalnerechensk - I couldn't ask you to go -'

'And I am telling you we will go' she smiled, stroking back Laura's hair.

She sighed again, wiping her eyes.

'What am I to do Ekaterina?' she asked finally.

'Come come Laura, you had two of the most powerful men in Europe eating out of your hand. You cannot tell me someone as cunning as you cannot outwit a peasant' she smiled. 'I told you that you would enjoy politics.'

'You said sex was power and power was politics' she said, smiling too.

'And I'm not sure which will give you the most satisfaction' Ekaterina teased and Laura laughed, long and loud till tears were rolling down her cheeks and she was holding the sides of her corset in case she split it. Ekaterina laughed with her, the unease and misery and frustrations melting away with their mirth.

At long last their laughter faded and they lay on their backs on the silk rug of Laura's chamber, staring up at the ceiling.

'I am glad that you will be with me Ekaterina' she said finally. 'I felt quite lost and alone without you.'

'I am here now dear' she said, rolling over to kiss her cheek.

Laura grinned and kissed her too, then rolled to her knees and sighed.

'It must be time to feed Alexandra again' she said, standing and stretching, arching her back.

Ekaterina stood and followed Laura to the nursery. She heard voices from the small room where she fed Alexandra and saw Fredrik sitting in the nursing chair, Alexandra in his arms as he held a bottle for her, chatting amicably with Luke and Lady Anne.

Laura couldn't stop her face twisting in distaste. Lady Anne was bent over Fredrik's elbow, cooing and waving Alexandra's arms, making silly, vacuous faces and babbling asinine words, blowing raspberries at her. She wondered how Fredrik could stand it.

'She gets bigger and bigger every day!' Ekaterina exclaimed as they stepped in, leaning close to Fredrik to see the baby.

'Gertrude says she is healthy and strong' Fredrik said proudly, setting aside the bottle. Alexandra mewled in protest, and Laura leaned down to kiss her, lingering, glad that Lady Anne had retreated the moment she stepped in the room.

'Any more care and attention and I will have no need of Gertrude' she smiled. 'You make an excellent nursemaid *Euer Hochwohlgeboren.*'

His eyes met hers, and held them.

'You are too kind' he murmured.

'Your Highness' Lady Anne started nervously, interrupting them. 'Forgive me if I am too forward, but Luke has told me so much about Dal - Dal-nere-chen-sk' she stuttered 'that I would - that is, we would - like to... accompany you when - if - you return there' she stopped and flashed Laura a timorous smile. 'As your mother, perhaps it would be less painful if I -'

'I hardly see how a stranger could alleviate my pain' she interrupted coldly.

'Laura!' Luke said sharply.

'I am sorry Father, I wish you all the happiness you deserve, but I do not know this woman and she is not my mother.' She turned back to the crumbling Anne. 'You may accompany me to Dalnerechensk but please do not presume that you will be of great support to me. The Princess needs feeding, please leave.' She turned and gathered Alexandra from Fredrik's arms.

Out of the corner of her eye she saw Ekaterina make a motion for them all to leave, and she heard the soft rustles of cloth which meant they had bowed or curtseyed to her back. She waited until the door closed behind them before relaxing, seating herself in the chair that was still warm from Fredrik's body.

12

Laura sat at a small table in her parlour, nervously tapping an empty ink pen on a blank sheet of paper. She had been trying to write a letter to Ilich, to tell him she wasn't coming, to admonish him for ordering her; to tell him she *might* be on her way but had no intention of letting him know when - but sighed as she knew she couldn't do that. She was the Tsaritsa, and that meant pageantry. Pageantry could not be mobilised with little notice, she knew she had no choice but to write and tell him when she would arrive. She hated the thought she was doing as he had told her.

A quiet tap on her door gave her a welcome distraction and Heidi announced Gustav's arrival in her chamber. He greeted her, bowing low.
'Am I late for my lessons?' she asked, surprised.
'No Your Highness, I am early, because I wanted to seek your approval.'
'Oh?' she asked, raising her eyebrow.
'You see, I am very fond of botany' he said, presenting her a bound book of meticulous notes and detailed drawings. 'And I would very much like a letter of recommendation from you to go and study the flora of Dalnerechensk.'
'These are beautiful Gustav' she said, admiring his drawings. 'You have great skill.'
'Thank you, Your Highness' he said, a pleased flush of pride darkening his cheeks. 'Has a comprehensive study been made of Dalnerechensk's plants?'
'I don't know' she said, closing the book and handing it back to him. 'I will not write a letter of recommendation Gustav, as it seems I must go back' she sighed ruefully. 'You will accompany me there and stay as my guest for as long as you wish to remain.'

'Thank you, Your Highness' he beamed, bowing deeply again. 'It is my dream to one day be *the* authority on particular plants. Perhaps you would like to see my specimens and laboratory?'

'That would be very interesting' she said honestly and Gustav grinned a little wider.

'I shall collect Kurt, our lesson will be in my laboratory' he said, bowing and rushing from her, almost dancing with excitement.

Laura smiled and put aside her letter, collecting the slate and chalk she had taken to using in her lessons with the brothers. She opened the door to follow him downstairs and almost collided with Luke, his hand raised to knock on her door. They eyed each other uncertainly, knowing that the following conversation was going to be difficult.

'May I come in?' he asked finally.

She stepped back and quietly instructed Heidi to leave so that they would be alone.

'I'm sorry for my words yesterday -' she started but Luke held up his hand for silence.

'We are strangers, aren't we' he said finally, quietly. 'I remember so clearly the girl with pudgy cheeks and messy hair - the girl who found ever more ghastly pests in the Texan wilderness she let loose in our tents on dig sites... That little girl I kissed goodbye on the steps of Lady Ramkinson's finishing school.

'She never really came out again' he said, swallowing down the lump in his throat. 'It was a woman, beautiful and poised and cultured and - and not the girl I remembered. I sometimes heard her in those early letters, but she faded away and grew so distant...' he stopped, blinking back the tears.

'I admit, I hardly know you Laura, and I regret most fervently ever sending you away, but I still love you and I am *proud*, so proud of you. Perhaps I cannot comfort you in this difficult time, perhaps we are too estranged; but I would like to be there if you ever decide you could still be the girl who loves me.'

Laura threw her arms around him, sobbing uncontrollably. Luke folded his arms around her, stroking her hair. Gustav returned, knocking excitedly, but stopped and left them in privacy. Laura sniffed loudly, wiping her nose on her sleeve.

'I remember the tents in Texas' she said finally. 'Life seemed so much simpler then' she sighed wistfully. 'I still am the girl who loves you daddy' she swallowed hard. 'I hated the school; I couldn't understand why you had sent me away.

'I told you so in my letters, but they were unseemly and Lady Ramkinson punished me. I was terrified of her, we all were. Every mistake, every indiscretion, every little thing deemed unseemly was severely punished. We learned to hide away our true feelings, to lock away the parts of us too rebellious or too weak or too precious; the parts of us that would not survive the school…

'But after so many years of pretending and fear and - I hardly know myself anymore, I could not find that little girl I put away for safe keeping. I am a stranger to me too.'

She buffed away the tears and sniffed loudly. Luke kissed her hair, cradling her against him.

'I am sorry darling, I truly am' he whispered, kissing her again. 'I had no idea.'

They stood in silence as the tears ebbed, as they tried to find the way back to the comfortable love they had known before.

'I did not mean to be so cold to Lady Anne' Laura said finally. 'But I loved my mother, and one simply does not automatically assume the role of another.'

'Yes I know' he said. 'She said last night she felt she had really blown it with you. Anne may be clumsy, but she is trying.'

'I know. I am trying too Father; but it is difficult. Perhaps we shall agree to be cautious and unassuming. I would like to know her better. For your sake.'

'I am glad' he said producing a handkerchief and mopping her tears away. 'We are here to support you Laura, in any way we can' he said, dabbing away some more moisture. 'But now you must go, I fear I have made you late for your lessons.'

She managed a watery smile and kissed his cheek, wiping her eyes as she left her rooms. She eventually found Gustav and Kurt over a game of checkers in Axel's smoking room. They jumped up when they saw her, coming to inquire if she was alright. She smiled and said she was, asking Gustav to lead her to the laboratory.

He smiled, his enthusiasm returning, and he guided her to the kitchen, stepping out into the cold day. Beside the kitchen door, attached to the side of the mansion was a small green house, the windows dusted with ice crystals. Beside it was a brick extension with stairs leading down to a door in an alcove piled with snow. This was Gustav's laboratory, part annex, part cellar, and as a result it was quite cold inside.

Laura, who had never seen a laboratory before, found it difficult to make sense of what she was looking at. The roof was, like some highly regimented witch's larder, hung with many bushels of dried herbs, their stems gathered and knotted together with string, a small paper tag attached to each one with its Latin name precisely written in Gustav's exquisite copper plate script. The far wall, in the dark recesses of the cellar, held many jars of specimens arranged along metal shelves, and a long work bench. On its scarred and bubbled surface sat several small cardboard boxes, each with a small wad of white cotton. Nestled on top of the cotton were shrivelled leaves or wizened berries, pressed and faded flowers or chips of strange rocks. Opposite this collection that seemed more at home in a disreputable apothecary, under the high windows, stood a bench littered with tools, medical instruments and glass containers that looked like the wares of an amateur glass-blower with incurable hiccups.

Laura shivered and Gustav quickly shrugged off his coarse coat, draping it around her shoulders. She thanked him, and he led her to the table where strange bottles and tubes were arranged along its length. He picked up several and explained what they were, what function they performed, and what plants he was currently distilling, pointing out the process as they made their way along the table.

Kurt followed them disinterestedly, poking at Gustav's specimens, swirling little bottles full of liquid, picking up dried herbs and sniffing each while Gustav took them off him, arranging them back in the cardboard boxes they had come from.

Laura listened dutifully to their lesson, writing the sentences in a clear, neat hand on the slate, becoming more and more aware of the scent emitting from Gustav's jacket.

'What is the delightful cologne that you are wearing?' she suddenly interrupted.

He blushed, embarrassed and pleased at the same time. 'Just a little concoction of mine' he said, then showed her where he was distilling perfume oil from plants known for their scents. 'At the moment it is very rudimentary, I am working with leaves and bark, but I am hoping come Summer I will have a range of flowers to work with.'

'I am afraid, Your Highness, that I have to cut this lesson short, I can no longer feel my fingers.'

Laura laughed and returned his jacket, following him back to the house. In the warm kitchen Gustav held his hands over the fire, rubbing them together briskly. Laura sat in a hard chair beside him, watching Kurt as he poked aimlessly around the kitchen, lifting up copper moulds and turning all the copper pots on the dresser so their handles pointed the other way.

'Tell me Kurt, what is it that you will be?' Laura suddenly asked. 'Gustav will be a famous botanist, and you...?'

He blushed. 'Well, I have a great passion for the arts' he said. 'And I hoped one day to be a patron of the theatre, perhaps even owning my own.'

'Ah yes' she smiled wistfully. 'I do miss the theatre. Dalnerechensk has no theatre or arts to speak of -'

'Then I will come to Dalnerechensk and open the first one!' he cried, becoming excited. 'If Gustav can draw his flowers I can build a theatre!'

So that was the reason for his moodiness during the lesson she realised. Kurt knew Gustav was going to Dalnerechensk and wanted to go too.

'I would be delighted for your company there, but only if your uncle approves.'

'He will approve' he said excitedly. 'I'll go and ask now!' he bowed quickly and rushed off.

Gustav laughed quietly.

13

Laura lifted the oil lamp a little higher, then pulled a tightly bound package out of the wardrobe where she had secreted it weeks ago. She took it to her bedroom, shutting the door behind her and sitting on her bed. She placed the oil lamp on the table beside her and stroked the package sadly. It was wrapped in a rather grubby oilskin, the same oilskin that had been folded around the Bodice Treaties, keeping them dry and safe as they had fled into Russia. A coarse string was fastened around it, and her fingers found the knot, gently tugging it out. She pulled away the oilskin and unfolded the soft cloth inside it, lifting the book onto her lap.

It was a rare illuminated manuscript, bound in rich black leather. It was a detailed history of Dalnerechensk, commissioned by Tsar Petrovich, Tsar Constantinovich's great-great-grandfather. It was the only copy, *the* authority of the Principality, the Doomsday of Dalnerechensk. It had been the last book she had been reading to the old tsar.

Beautiful though the book was, it was not the reason why she had taken it from Dalnerechensk. Secreted between the thick parchment pages were the documents she had taken from Tsar Constantinovich's vault; secrets and inheritance she had wanted to protect from Russians and revolutionaries alike. Carefully she flipped the pages, teasing out the faded and brittle documents, setting aside the book again.

Several of the documents were bonds, worth a million pounds and at least three hundred years old. She set them aside, they were Alexandra's inheritance, and with them she placed her marriage certificate. She glanced over the death certificate for Aleksei's mother, laying it with the bonds, and added the death certificate of Tsar Constantinovich's brother, *Velikij Knjaz* Radomyr, who had taken his own life just three days after Olaf's secret abdication.

She read through Tsar Constantinovich's three wills again; the first leaving the Principality to his younger brother, the second naming his first born Alexander Andrei Stephanovich heir and his brother as Lord Protector until Alexander had reached eighteen years old. The third was written about the time of Alexander's abdication, and named both Aleksei and Alexander as joint heirs to the Principality, though Aleksei was to manage Alexander's half until he was fit to rule in his own right or married and produced a male heir.

She stroked the third will sadly, mulling over the words. She hadn't known when she had married Aleksei that he had only inherited half a Principality. She wondered if it would have mattered. It certainly didn't matter now; Alexandra was the heir to all of it. Ilich couldn't deny her that, even if he could deny it to Laura.

She set it aside and her fingers fell to the photograph, her eyes filling with tears. Olaf's face looked out at her, youthful and carefree, happy and confident. It radiated from him, and his blonde hair glowed with sunlight caught in the strands. She stroked his face and kissed him, as she had many times before, her fingers straying to the circle of discolouration.

She knew what it was, and what it said, without having to turn the photo over anymore. It was his abdication, written in shaky, uncontrolled script; signed by Alexander, Aleksei, Tsar Constantinovich, *Velikij Knjaz* Radomyr and Nicholas Riminov, Tsar Constantinovich's oldest and most trusted minister of the Advisory Council. Her fingers stroked the wax seal on the back of the photo, still searching Olaf's face. It was Tsar Constantinovich's personal seal, and it had caused the faint circle of discolouration on the photo. She kissed the smiling face again and hugged it to her breast, picking up a much folded letter.

Olaf had written it to her their last night together. While she had slept, before Nikita's army had attacked Dalnerechensk, Olaf had written this and left with it the key to Tsar Constantinovich's secret vault, leaving her with the secrets of the Principality and the inheritance she deserved. It was written in French, uncontrolled and shaky, and the words ached with emotion.

She pressed that to her breast too, rocking with her misery. He had been her quiet pillar of strength, her friend and confidante, and eventually her lover too. She could not bear to think of his fate, disgraced and left unburied; the poor mad Prince of Dalnerechensk. She was frightened of returning there, surrounded by friends, and yet so terribly alone too. She understood how dreadful it must have been for Aleksei; so young and thrust into politics, surrounded by people yet alone with his decisions, that dark smudge of rumour hanging over him, waiting to see if he would crack like his likable, charismatic brother.

What had made Olaf abdicate? What terrible thing had driven him insane and made him turn away from all the privilege, from who he was? *Perhaps the responsibility, it was not easy to be Monarch of Dalnerechensk.* But she had felt his quiet strength; he could have easily managed the burden. What tragedies had the Vakhtangov family faced to drive Olaf from his birthright?

She reluctantly laid the photo and the letter on her bed, placing the letter on top of the photo to hide that handsome face from her. She wiped her eyes, sitting back to think carefully. The sensible thing to do would be to leave these papers safely out of reach of Ilich and his Parliament. She didn't trust Ilich, despite his competent handling of the Principality's affairs.

If she returned to Dalnerechensk with these documents would he confiscate them if he found them? Would he take the money and deny it to her, as he had denied her the contents of Aleksei's will? Would he connect the dots between Olaf and Alexander? Would he understand that the man he hung for a traitor was really his sovereign ruler? What would he do to her because she knew the truth?

She shut her eyes then, trying not to tremble. She would have to protect herself again, leaving the documents behind. *But where could she leave them?* She couldn't risk them falling into a servant's hands, who might dispose of them, unaware of what they were. She would need help to hide them.

She opened the beautiful pages of the book again, sliding the documents carefully between the pages, making sure no tell-tale corners or edges poked out. She hesitated then put the photograph in too, her fingers hesitating over the folded letter. At last she decided she couldn't be separated from the last remnant of Olaf and closed the book, wrapping it carefully back in the soft cloth and the oil skin, tying the coarse string around it again.

She slipped Olaf's letter into the drawer of her bedside table and picked up the package, padding through the quiet house with a candle to Axel's private rooms, knocking softly on the door. He was still awake, and dressed. 'Your Highness' he said, surprised.

'Forgive me for intruding at this late hour' she said, dropping her eyes when she realised Fredrik was in his rooms, dressed in a night shirt and robe.

'Of course Your Highness. Come in' he said, closing the door behind her.

She set the candle down on a table, folding the book to her tightly, wondering what Fredrik was thinking of her late night visit to his uncle's private rooms.

'I have come for your help. I find myself in a situation that is rather … delicate' she said quietly.

She saw Axel glance at Fredrik, and read the question in his eyes. She flushed and swallowed down the hot embarrassment, pushing on quickly.

'Forgive me *Euer Hochwohlgeboren*, this is a matter of secrecy and discretion, you must take your leave of us' she told Fredrik.

He eyed them both, bewildered, but bowed and headed for the door. Axel followed him, murmuring something quietly before bidding him goodnight and closing the door. He then turned back to Laura, careful and keeping his distance, aware of what his nephew was feeling.

'I apologise for the awkwardness of this moment' she said, her cheeks dark with a pretty blush. 'This could not wait for the morning.'

'I will assist you in any way I can' he said, still careful.

She held the book out to him then changed her mind and clasped it back to her chest, struggling with how to explain herself.

'These cannot go back to Dalnerechensk' she said finally. 'If they do, if they find them -' she stopped, shutting her eyes. 'They cannot go back, and yet I am afraid to leave them here too' she looked at him, frightened.

'I see' he said quietly.

'Will you help me?' she whispered.

'Of course Your Highness' he said, coming forward to guide her to his small writing desk.

Gently he took the package off her and placed it carefully on the leather blotter. For an instant she worried that he might open the package and read the documents inside. She knew he could not read Russian, but still the fear rose up in her. Instead he pulled open a small drawer in the desk and retrieved his personal seal and a stick of red wax. He held the wax into the candle flame and allowed it to drip over the knot of the coarse string, dabbing a large daub of wax onto it, securing it to the oil skin. He pressed in his seal and let it cool, watching the nervous princess carefully.

'I have a secret vault, it will be safe there' he said quietly, putting the wax and seal away.

'Thank you *Euer Hochgeboren*' she said, looking relieved and worried at the same time.

'It is late Your Highness, and we are leaving quite early. You should rest.'

'Of course, you are right' she agreed, but still hesitated.

Finally, reluctantly, she tore herself away from the documents she had protected for so long and slipped out of his rooms, holding the candle before her as she made her way back to her bed.

14

Laura woke, aware of the bustle in the house. There was a rude rap on her door and Heidi pushed it open, laying out Laura's travelling clothes with a small hint of insolence. She curtseyed shortly and left without a word, shutting the door hard behind her again. Laura knew why she was so upset. Gertrude was going to Dalnerechensk and she was not. That meant that she was also out of a job, as Axel had no further use for her. Laura had promised to write a letter of recommendation for her which would guarantee her another position shortly, but it had not appeased her.

She sighed and pushed back the covers, stretching. She dressed quickly, filled with a nervous energy, and headed to the nursery, greeting Gertrude and Claudette quietly. Gertrude lifted Alexandra out of the crib and brought her to Laura, handing her a bottle as well. Laura sat on the chair in the chamber next door and coaxed the rubber nipple into Alexandra's mouth, sitting back to wait out her breakfast.

Her breasts felt uncomfortably full, she wondered if she should breast feed her to relieve the discomfort, and wondered when her milk would dry up. But Gertrude had insisted that she no longer breast feed, and ashamed of her outburst and aware of how little she knew about motherhood she had acquiesced.

There was a quiet tap on the door and Emilie joined her, calling a cheery good morning as she ushered in livery servants, instructing them to pack away the cloths, towels and other accoutrements that the children would need on their long journey.

'I hope you don't find us too forward Your Highness' she said, switching to French. 'Kurt and Gustav were so enthusiastic about their visit, and of course Countess Ivanova has often spoken so fondly of Dalnerechensk -'

'Not at all' Laura said gently. 'I welcome you all with me.'

Since Kurt and Gustav had announced they would be travelling with the Ivanovs and the Asantons to Dalnerechensk the rest of the von Schmidt household had found one excuse or another to accompany them too. Laura had been surprised but was glad that her friends would be with her, glad that she would not have to say goodbye to them so soon.

She raised Alexandra to her shoulder and patted the wind from her, giving her back to Gertrude to see to her toilet. Emilie followed her to the dining room for breakfast where the rest of the household sat, many of them wearing their travelling coats already. Kurt greeted her excitedly, bouncing out of his seat to pull back a chair for her. She thanked him, almost amused, but sat beside Fredrik in the chair Axel had pulled out for her, disappointing him.

Fredrik greeted her quietly, aware of the anxious effervescence in her actions, despite the early hour. She noticed how difficult it was for him to meet her eyes, but when he did there was nothing but kindness there. He could not bring himself to think ill of her, even if she might deserve it. She gave him her hand and let him kiss it, and the warmth of his fingers stirred an even stranger agitation in her.

She pulled away and they ate quickly, aware of how eager her travelling companions were to begin. She could not feel their excitement, only a manic kind of listlessness. When they rose to see to their travelling trunks Ekaterina took her hands to still her, looking at her young friend carefully. Laura tried to smile for her, but couldn't quite make her face co-operate.

'I'll be alright Ekaterina' she said softly. 'I'm just...' she trailed off, unsure

44

how to express what she was feeling and shrugged instead.

'I know my dear' she sighed, and Laura saw the ghosts of fear in Ekaterina's face too.

'We won't stay long' she promised in a rush, stepping aside to let the porters carrying her travelling trunks past.

Ekaterina said nothing and followed her outside where four *petite dilegences* – coaches designed for long distance travel - stood in the driveway. Porters were hurriedly stacking travelling trunks in the luggage racks and pushing warm rugs into the carriages to ward off the cold of a fading winter. Laura tucked her coat round her tighter and balled up her hands inside her fur muff, wishing she could relax.

Axel, Kurt and Gustav climbed into the first coach; Karl, Emilie, Luke and Lady Anne into the second. A small part of Laura was glad she would not have to make awkward small talk with Lady Anne on the long journey and held Fredrik's warm hand as he helped her into the coach they would share with Grigory and Ekaterina. The last coach held Gertrude and Claudette, Helmut and Alexandra, and two livery servants of Axel's: Jan and Hermann.

No one stood on the steps to wave them off and Laura couldn't shake the strange foreboding she felt.

'Are you alright, Your Highness?' Fredrik asked finally.

'Yes' she said, but didn't sound convincing.

'Perhaps you would allow me to occupy you with some more lessons in German?' he suggested, pulling a slim volume bound in red leather out of his jacket pocket. 'Ekaterina tells me you read very well in foreign languages.'

Laura shot Ekaterina a look.

'Are you playing a trick on me?' she asked.

Ekaterina looked confused then realisation dawned and she burst out laughing, quickly telling Fredrik the trick Nikita had played on her, giving her a book of erotic poetry to read. Fredrik flushed.

'I would not play such a trick' he said, embarrassed. 'But it *is* poetry, by Goethe. Are you familiar with his work?'

'I cannot say I am' Laura said, taking the book from him.

The German script was much easier to read than Cyrillic and she was soon reading clearly, falling naturally into the rhythm of the poem. Ekaterina sighed happily.

'You read wonderfully well' Fredrik said as she paused to turn the page. 'It sounds like German is your natural language!'

She blushed and continued to read while the pretty lake of *Schwarzschwanwald* dwindled into the distance behind them.

15

The train passed into the garrison village of Tcherepnin and blew its whistle, as much to clear the tracks as to announce the arrival of the royal party to the city of Dalnerechensk twenty kilometres away. Beside Fredrik Ekaterina was pointing out the sights of the village, explaining that Tcherepnin was the first settlement built by Vsevolod in Liberty Valley.

'Look at all the people!' Kurt exclaimed, tugging Fredrik's jacket.

The train was moving slowly through the village and the tracks were lined with people, waving and cheering. Some waved flags of the Republic, but many waved the royal standard, craning their necks to see inside the carriage, pushing forward as close as they dared to the moving train. Kurt and Gustav threw open the windows and leaned out, waving. The crowd cheered, and several handkerchiefs were tossed in the window from hopeful girls in the crowd.

Fredrik glanced at Laura. She was sitting in the middle of the carriage, as far away from the windows as she could, sitting straight and tall, her eyes closed, her hands clenched tightly in her lap. On the long trip she had often sat like this, almost vibrating with the effort to stop shaking. She had been brittle and snappish, cold and aloof, passionate and weepy. Ekaterina had often taken her hands, arguing with her in Russian, or held her tightly, as if they were afraid to let go of each other. *How much is she suffering now?* he thought, his eyes stealing back to the press of faces.

The view was momentarily blocked as the train rumbled through Dalnerechensk Gate and onto the snowy fields below the city of Dalnerechensk. In spite of himself Fredrik leaned closer to the windows to see more clearly. The defensive walls of the city gleamed in the late morning sun and soldiers stood like a colonnade atop them. Rising above the snow-dusted rooftops of the town were the glowing fortified walls of Dalnerechensk Castle, green and white banners of the Republic flying from the watch-towers.

Ekaterina faltered in her narrative and fell silent, reaching out to take Grigory's hand tightly. The carriage momentarily darkened as they passed under Vsevolod's Gate and the train began to slow further as it approached the station. The whistle blew again and there was an answering shout from the crowd. On the platform Fredrik could see armed guards, some mounted and some not, holding back a huge press of people. It was difficult to gauge the mood of the crowd; there was excitement, but also hesitancy. It was expectant, and very very careful.

In front of the station house was a low box platform, draped in green and white material. On it stood the members of Ilich's Parliament, with the Head of State himself in front of them, standing behind a large microphone. Beside the platform, mounted on horseback, was Peter Kamanin, who had retained his position as Chief Strategist after the Battle of Liberty Valley. His green coat - when compared to the old black uniforms, draped in gold braid and trimmings - was plain, decorated with a single medal and the ensigns that denoted his position.

The train chugged ponderously to a stop and hissed, the blast of steam enveloping the platform before curling away into the bright blue day. The crowd grew noisier, waving flags and straining for a better view, calling out to each other and jostling for position. Ilich announced the arrival of the train, welcoming the Tsaritsa back to Dalnerechensk, and his voice crackled from the loud speakers attached to a hastily erected pole on the station roof.

The door to the carriage opened and Grigory stepped down onto the platform. A wave of silence rippled over the crowd then it began to murmur again; not exactly hostile, but not exactly welcoming. Grigory, clearly uncomfortable with the attention, quickly turned, raising his hand to help down Ekaterina. The crowd cheered, calling out to her and she smiled and waved, blowing kisses to them.

As each left the carriage they were greeted by a roar of approval from the crowd. Luke turned to offer his hand to Laura and she appeared beautiful and radiant, dressed in a warm, green silk, ever mindful of her public persona. Those who had been in the carriage with her not moments before were stunned at the change in her. She smiled as the crowd screamed their welcomes, waving and blowing kisses, calling out to her people. Only Luke felt the tremble in her hand, and he marvelled at her ability to seem far more relaxed than she felt.

She turned and took her daughter from Gertrude, holding her in a way that both supported her and presented her to the crowd. The delighted roar was a solid wall of noise that slammed into them. Alexandra had been crying before Gertrude had handed her over, but her frightened mewling was lost in the jubilation. Laura bounced her once or twice to try to soothe her, still waving to the crowd. Finally she took Luke's hand again and stepped down to the platform, moving aside so that the servants could exit the carriage too.

Several open carriages that had been waiting in a side street next to the station were now driven onto the platform and stopped so the Royal party could be escorted to the castle. Luke, Lady Anne, Karl, Emilie, Helmut and Kurt were invited into the carriage that Laura climbed into, surrounding herself with family and children in a way that she knew the Dalnerechenskers would approve. Behind her the rest of the party and parliament climbed into waiting carriages, the mounted guard moving to take up positions around the procession.

Laura waved and called greetings to all who lined Vsevolod's Way, Alexandra sitting on her lap and continuing to scream as they wound their way slowly to the castle. The careful expectancy of the crowd was now gone and they cooed and waved their handkerchiefs at Helmut and Alexandra, bowing as Laura passed by them. She dared not turn around to see Ilich's face, riding in the carriage behind her, as he had spent months encouraging the populace of Dalnerechensk not to bow to the Monarchy. But he had been fighting against four hundred years of proud traditions and a deep respect for the bloodline of Vsevolod. One revolution could not overturn that.

Vsevolod's Way narrowed into the S-bend that had prevented the castle grounds from being breached in both battles for the Principality and they passed under the narrow portcullis into the courtyard before the castle. Laura forced herself not to look at the stables and gathered Alexandra up, lifting the hem of her dress to step down from the carriage. She took the hand of the carriage driver, noticing how low he had bowed when he had opened the door.

'Roman?' she asked, surprised.

'Yes Your Highness' he said, straightening up.

He had grown a beard since she had last seen him and was nearly an inch taller, looking so much older than she remembered him.

'It is good to see you again. I trust you are well?'

'Yes Your Highness. Thank you Your Highness' he smiled, reaching up to help down the others in the carriage.

Ilich's carriage arrived, containing the rest of the von Schmidt family, Ivan Gogol and Luka Nevsky, Ilich's deputy and most trusted friend. Roman trotted off to help them down and Laura rocked Alexandra gently, watching the carriage containing Parliament members and the Ivanovs arrive. They looked distinctly uncomfortable, and Laura guessed it hadn't been a pleasant ride to the castle.

There was a rumble of wheels approaching from the back of the castle and an enclosed carriage swung into the courtyard. Axel's livery servants, Gertrude and Claudette stepped down, coming to see to the needs of the babies, beginning to unload the luggage on the roof of their carriage. A second carriage with the rest of their luggage rolled into the courtyard. Both had used Castle Street, the utility street, away from the procession.

'Welcome home' Ilich said, climbing two steps of the castle and turning to gesture broadly to them, as if welcoming them into his own home. 'I have aired rooms and the nursery for you' he went on, 'and of course you may have the Tsaritsa's rooms back.' He beamed.

'Lady Anne will be most comfortable there, as will my father in the rooms

48

opposite. I shall require rooms on the third floor' Laura said sweetly, aware that Ekaterina was quietly translating the exchange for the rest of the party.

There was a shocked gasp from the Parliament at her words and Ilich's face was priceless. Laura had to stop herself from grinning.

'Surely you mean -' he started.

'I mean exactly as I spoke Ilich' she said severely.

'They are very important rooms!' Luka interjected.

'And Lady Anne and my father are important to me' she answered. 'I wish for lodgings on the third floor.'

There was a pause but Ilich was astute enough to realise this was not a request. He recovered brilliantly and bowed low in a slightly affected way.

'Of course *Velikaja Knjaginja*' he said, gesturing to the soldiers that stood on guard at the top of the stairs to open the doors.

They saluted, as he had taught them, then pulled open the heavy oak doors. Laura inwardly seethed as she climbed the steps. Ilich had called her by her old official Russian title, knowing it was his way of trying to regain control. It had been no secret that Aleksei's Advisory Council had fought over what to title her when she married him; she was a common wife, and they had tried to avoid elevating her too far while trying to avoid insulting Aleksei. In the end they had compromised, calling her "the Prince's Wife", a title fitting for a woman married to a *Tsarevich* who was not the *Tsesarevich* - the heir.

She knew why they had resisted. That understanding had grown since she had learned of Alexander Andrei and the tragic secret of the Vakhtangovs. Alexander had been loved by Dalnerechensk, he was confident and popular, handsome and slightly roguish, though never arrogant; and had known with absolute certainty from birth that while both he and Aleksei were sons of the Tsar, he alone was the *Tsesarevich*. Aleksei's official title was *Velikij Knjaz*, Grand Duke; a title that had never been discarded even when he became Prince Regent when his older brother had disappeared.

They had resisted calling her Tsesarevna *because they resisted the thought of Aleksei - awkward, unlikable Aleksei - as their* Tsesarevich, *she thought. If they had called him* Tsesarevich *it would have meant that Alexander Andrei was really gone, a thought none of them could face. And so they had waited, like England for its King Arthur, and the rumours and stories had grown: of a mad prince, a dead prince, - a ghost prince.*

The two soldiers bowed as Laura passed by and an amused smile touched her lips briefly when she saw Ilich's look. He strode stiffly into the castle, heading straight for the stairs. Laura followed him, her quick political astuteness telling her there was another reason why he called her Prince's Wife. *The old tsar used to call me* Tsarevna: *daughter, she thought. And his affectionate title had often been repeated by his ministers, especially Nicholas Riminov and the other, older members. Olaf had also affectionately called her* Tsesarevna - her breath hitched as she thought of him and she blinked rapidly, stopping in the wide entrance hall, turning away from the party to gaze at the empty stone walls where the tapestries had once hung.

She had never asked him why he had called her that. She had thought at the time he called her "heir's wife" because it should have been her official title, and he was not the only one to call her that. In the months since learning the truth she often wondered if he had called her that to further cement in his mind that Aleksei was the heir; that he had given up the throne to him. And she had often wondered, as his love for her grew, if he had called her *his* wife...

She shut her eyes tightly, swallowing down her emotions and forcing herself to finish her thought. Tsesarevna *was not just the title for the heir's wife, it was the title for the* female *Heir Apparent*. She knew deep in her heart that she was not *officially* accepted as Tsaritsa of Dalnerechensk, but the idea had been planted in the minds of Dalnerechenskers long ago, and would be very hard to dislodge. *Especially now* she thought. *Especially now, since they know of the Bodice Treaties, especially now, since Russian money was pouring in for the tin they mined - especially now, since she had done what Vsevolod had done and repelled a stronger, invading army.* She was not the flesh and blood descendant of Vsevolod himself, but perhaps that didn't quite matter now in the eyes of the Dalnerechenskers. In any case she was mother to his heir, and *that* mattered.

Ilich touched her arm gently, breaking into her train of thought. She looked up at him, saw the masked concern there, and quickly handed him an explanation for her upset.

'I miss the tapestries' she said. 'They were beautiful and vibrant. We sacrificed so much to defend what was ours.'

Ilich smiled a sad, gentle smile and tucked her hand into his elbow, leading her towards the stone stairs. *He's much kinder when he thinks I'm being a silly seventeen year old girl* she thought ruefully, but let him lead her up the stairs, past the first floor which housed the Parliament Chambers and offices of state, to the second floor. He stopped before the door to the Tsaritsa's room and pushed it open gently.

'I had it restored' he said quietly.

Laura eyed the large sitting room that was the Tsaritsa's private retreat. It had been ransacked in the revolution, and every single piece of removable property had been taken: chairs and settees, silk rugs, mirrors and drapes, even the gilt rococo moulding had been chipped from the walls. But here the room stood, recovered and renewed, down to the fine details that she remembered. That this room should look so ordinary, so unaltered, offended her. It had no right to be as it always had, to be so unaffected and quickly recovered from the violent changes she had undergone.

Would I wake up one morning and think - even for a tiny moment - that I might go riding with Olaf today if I slept in this room? she wondered, and then felt an overwhelming sense of gladness for her contrary and obstinate demands.

'These rooms are beautiful' Lady Anne whispered, awestruck. 'I could not in good conscience take rooms that are rightfully yours -'

'I could not sleep one single night here' she interrupted her. 'You will do me a great service to take these rooms. I shall sleep on the third floor, where the *Velikaja Knjaginjas* have always slept.'

She caught the grin in Ekaterina's eye and forced herself not to smile too. Ilich had not understood the English exchange, his face blank as his eyes darted round their faces, looking for meaning. Laura removed her arm from his, steeling herself for the next shock, not wanting the shake in her hands to give her away.

She turned and opened the doors opposite the Tsaritsa's rooms, where Aleksei had once slept. This time she was surprised at how different the room looked, and she realised his rooms must have been smashed beyond repair. The low colonnade that had once divided the room in half - on one side the prince's bed, on the other the marble fire surround and the place where the court had stood to watch the Putting To Bed Ceremony - was now absent. The fire surround was smaller and less ornate than she remembered, and the bed that stood in the room was different too.

The frescoes and rich wood panelling that had once adorned the walls were all gone; it was now wallpapered in a rich hunting green. Even the fresco on the ceiling, the chubby putti and seraphim looking down on her that she had been so embarrassed about on her wedding night was gone, painted over with a soft white gloss. She glanced towards the dressing room but the door to the room beyond was shut. She had no doubt it looked completely different too.

'All the rooms were restored as much to their original condition as we could, except this room' Ilich said, but did not offer any explanation as to why.

'I'm sure my father will find them adequate' she said.

'More than adequate' Luke said, looking around the room.

The party turned and Ilich led the way up to the third floor, opening doors and ushering guests into rooms. Laura, who had been trailing in their wake, suddenly opened a door and stepped into a room.

It was dusty, and the furniture was covered in white sheets. It looked undisturbed, as if it had been unlived in for many years. She peeled back a dust cloth and looked at the chaise underneath it. It was mahogany, and upholstered with deep blue velvet. A quick peek under another dust cloth told her that all the furniture was matching in colour and elegance, and well placed in this bright room.

Brocade curtains framed the tall windows that stood each side of the fireplace. The carved marble surround was wide and imposing, and the wood panels that ran two thirds of the height of the walls glowed. Above the wood panels were painted frescoes of Ilya Muromets, the greatest of all the legendary *bogatyrs* - medieval knights-errant of Kievan Rus.

She crossed the room and pushed open the door to the dressing room, eyeing the dust covered bath tub and the draped furniture then crossed to the bedroom and peered in.

'This room has not been aired -' Ilich started.

'Is there a reason why it remains in such a state?' she asked as she crossed to the window.

'No.'

'I will have these rooms' she said softly.

'As you wish' he said, as if tired of her. 'I will send someone to air the rooms and make it ready. I will also send you a maid servant to -'

'Anna Vasnetsova' she said quietly. 'No other but her.'

Ilich started to protest but then thought the better of it and closed his mouth firmly, turning to address the remainder of the party.

'The nursery is this way' he said shortly, and led the way to the rooms, leaving Laura alone.

She sighed softly, casting her eye over the view from the window. She had chosen this room because it did not look down over the stables, nor did it look down over the private gardens of Tsar Constantinovich where she had often walked with him. Instead it looked out over the courtyard in front of the castle, and over the wall to the city of Dalnerechensk below, and beyond that to the garrison village of Tcherepnin.

Once her view from the Tsaritsa's rooms on the second floor had been of the large wall and the watch tower, and beyond it the distant horizon. But here on the third floor she could see the houses and shops that had been obscured, and to her right rose the watch tower closest to Vsevolod's Gate. It held the Tcherepnin Beacon, the bright light that, when lit, summoned troops from the barracks in the village. She approved of the view, it was busy and captivating. *I will be able to see the markets at Harvest Moon* she smiled.

There was a knock on the door and it was pushed open by three soldiers. One saluted, one bowed, the third saluted and bowed, confused as to which was appropriate, making Laura laugh.

'Salute to the Head of State, bow to me' she said, amused, and the three soldiers bowed again.

'We have come to air the rooms Your Highness' said the saluter.

'Very well. Remove the dust cloths and open the windows' she said.

She left the three hurriedly folding the white sheets, dust fountaining into the air, and slipped along the corridors she remembered so well to the nursery.

She had only seen it once before, the night of the revolution, when she had gone looking for Alexander Andrei to assuage her curiosity once and for all. Her candle had been burning low, all she had seen were the dust covered lumps and humps of toys and furniture in the gloom. In the daylight she could see the small ante chamber was pretty and airy, a place where a tsaritsa could sit comfortably while nursing a baby.

An exquisitely carved rocking horse with real hair stood proudly beside a padded nursing chair. The fireplace was covered with a beautiful wrought iron surround, and a gilt clock with a large face stood on the mantelpiece. Scattered around the room were child sized pieces of furniture; a table and four chairs, six school desks, a large chalk board supported by an easel. Beautifully crafted tin soldiers stood to attention in ranks that covered the top of a sideboard, one that had begun its life in another part of the house and moved to the nursery when it had become too battered and scratched to remain where it was.

Laura crossed the room and pushed open the door to the nursery proper, shutting her eyes briefly. The room beyond was large, bright and airy. To her surprise there were several small beds in the room as well as two cribs and a rocking cradle. Gertrude and Claudette stopped chattering in German and dropped curtsies to her, folding their hands behind their backs.

'It is beautiful' Claudette said, nodding to the room as she brought Alexandra to her. 'And she has finally stopped crying.'

'So I see' she smiled, carrying her to the nursing chair and seating herself comfortably.

Alexandra burbled at her and Laura smiled, taking the bottle that Gertrude handed her and sighed contentedly while Alexandra drank. From this seat near the window she could see the sleepy river that ran through the valley floor, and further to the trees that adorned the eastern flanks of the western range. Somewhere further north, hidden from her view, was the village of Ladozhskoye, where the Ivanovs had once lived.

It was a peaceful view and she sighed again, letting herself unwind, her muscles relax after weeks and weeks of nervous tension. Gertrude and Claudette went back to their chatter, unpacking the clothes and equipment they had brought with them, storing them inside the large armoire. Laura's respite was short, the door was pushed open and Kurt stepped into the nursery, babbling excitedly in German to Gustav. Laura managed a smile when she saw Fredrik and Emilie step into the room behind them.

'Ah my friends, I trust you have found all your rooms to be adequate?' she asked, setting the bottle on the small table near the nursing chair.

'Beautiful' said Emilie dreamily, collecting Helmut from the nursery and kissing his cheek.

'Take us exploring!' Kurt cried, wiggling with enthusiasm.

'Tomorrow afternoon' she said, repositioning Alexandra to burp her.

'But -'

'Kurt.' Fredrik spoke his name quietly, but there were harmonics in it that brooked no disobedience.

Kurt looked unhappy but bowed respectfully. The moment was interrupted with the appearance of Ilich at the door.

'I trust everything is to your expectations?' he asked, eyeing the room.

'Does your Parliament meet tomorrow Ilich?' she asked.

'Yes, they meet every week day' he answered.

'Good, I shall like to address them. Have you prepared rooms for my nurses and *Burggraf* Axel von Schmidt's livery men? I believe castle servants used to sleep in the attic rooms.'

'They did, and there are beds prepared for them' he confirmed.

'And what securities have been put in place for my guests and myself?'

'I'm sorry?' he asked, taken aback.

'Guards, Ilich' she said. 'What measures have been taken to secure the castle? Simply locking the door because no one was living in the castle will not …' she trailed off, noticing how uncomfortable Ilich was beginning to look. '*Is* someone living in the castle?' she demanded.

'Yes' he said. 'I am.'

They watched each other carefully, masking their true thoughts and feelings from the other. But Laura was better at it than Ilich. *I just bet you were living in Aleksei's rooms too* she thought, seething, though her face betrayed nothing of her anger.

'I see' she said coldly. 'And what arrangements did you make for your protection?'

'Soldiers are stationed as they have always been at the gates to Castle Street and Vsevolod's Way. Several patrol the walls and castle grounds while a number stand guard inside the castle itself. The gates are shut and portcullises are lowered each night and raised and opened each morning. Guards are now armed with rifles and all have had vigorous training on how to use them. Is that enough security for you *Velikaja Knjaginja?*'

Laura was surprised, it was much more than the Royals had ever used before. *How much of this is needed?* she wondered. *How uneasy are you with your subjects Ilich?*

The tense mood was interrupted with the arrival of Luka, who saluted.

'Dinner is ready, *Velikaja Knjaginja, Glava Gosudarstva*' he announced.

'That is one tradition we have kept' Ilich said grudgingly. 'Parliament takes all their meals here, like the court used to.'

Laura stood and called Gertrude to her, handing a happily burbling Alexandra to her.

'Very well, I shall dress and join you shortly' she said then translated for her friends as she headed out the door.

16

'You look beautiful.'

She turned to eye Fredrik, handsome in his dinner dress, his eyes not quite able to meet hers.

'I remember that dress' he went on, hesitant and careful. 'You wore it to the theatre in Debrecen. -'

'It has been a long day *Euer Hochwohlgeboren*' she interrupted softly.

'Forgive me' he said, stopping, dropping his eyes.

Something in Laura relented and she folded her fan, deciding to slip away from the crowd of ministers that had stayed after dinner to talk to the new guests.

'Perhaps you would like to accompany me. I doubt we will find many portraits, but we will possibly find some ghosts. Besides, my rooms are still musty, I should like to give the dust more time to settle.'

'As you wish' he smiled, bowing slightly.

She turned and stepped out of the dining room and into the wide entrance hall of Dalnerechensk Castle.

'There once hung three tapestries of Vsevolod here' she said quietly. 'They had been stitched by Agnessa, the second wife of Vsevolod, and the wives and daughters of the court. They were taken down to the underground river, to muffle the passage of the soldiers moving between Dalnerechensk and Tcherepnin to repel Nikita's army. They were all torn to pieces' she said sadly. We collected what we could and dried them, storing them away, but we could not save them.'

She looked up at the stone walls that seemed so cheerless now.

'Perhaps I can make replicas, I think it would be a project I could enjoy' she mused out loud, but didn't say she knew how it would improve her standing in Dalnerechensk if the people knew she was devoting her time to the memory of Vsevolod.

'I would like to think you would have people to help you, Your Highness' Fredrik said. 'It would be a lengthy, lonely task to undertake on your own.'

She agreed. 'Perhaps the wives and daughters of Ilich's Parliament might like to help. It might help endear them to the people.'

'Forgive me, but I cannot help but feel there is some - animosity...' he trailed off, uncomfortable.

'There is' she sighed quietly. 'Vsevolod's name means *lord of all*, which should tell you how much he is revered here, like a saint, a saviour. He was only a rich nobleman when he and fifty families fled the slaughter of Novgorod, the campaign that gave Ivan the Terrible his grisly reputation; but he saved them, and they made a common man a tsar. I do not think Dalnerechensk likes to see their tsar a common man again.'

She stopped suddenly, taking a careful look around herself, frightened that someone might have overheard her. *Don't be stupid* she chided herself. *Ilich is a peasant, he doesn't speak French.* But then a deeper, darker part of her whispered: *are you so sure?*

She turned away from Fredrik, opening her fan and waving it half-heartedly while she collected herself again. Her eye caught the door to the left wing of the castle and she pushed it open, heading into the gloom beyond.

'Wait a moment Your Highness' Fredrik said and lit a candle, holding it up for them.

'They burned this wing in the revolution' she said as they stepped into the fire stained corridor. 'But the fire did not do as much damage as it did to the West Wing of Varennikov Castle. It used to house a ballroom, and the throne room.'

She stepped through a door frame that had been left gaping in the wake of the fire. The room beyond was dark; all the windows had been smashed and boarded up. The wooden dais that had once housed the ornate throne was now just a pile of blackened rubble, and the gilded throne was gone, no doubt chopped to pieces and robbed of all the precious jewels and metals that had made it. But in the middle of the room was a wooden, unassuming chair, seemingly placed with great reverence.

'Vsevolod's throne' she said quietly, touching it gently. 'So they hadn't destroyed it.'

She had expected the royal canopy in the dining room would be gone; but she had also expected that Ilich would have been sitting in Vsevolod's chair at the dining table. She had been surprised to find the chair missing, and Ilich sitting on one of the same dining chairs that his Parliament sat on. She stroked the old wooden chair gently again, feeling how smooth and polished it felt.

'Ilich takes my husband's rooms but doesn't dare take Vsevolod's throne' she said quietly. 'They hated him.'

'Why did they feel so strongly?' Fredrik asked quietly, his voice sounding loud beside her.

They hated him for bankrupting the Principality, for forcing the value of the rouble down. They hated him for the children that died in the mines, hated him because he was not his likeable brother. They hated him because he was mad…

Her thoughts all rushed together and she shut her eyes tightly against them, pressing her lips together to stop them coming out. *If only he had told them!* she wailed, the rage welling up inside her again. *If only they had waited one more day,* none *of this would have happened!*

But darker thoughts were rising up inside her too. *There were soldiers in the courtyard that night when he had dragged her out of the castle; soldiers and servants who had seen what he had done to her. There were the rumours and the tales the maid told of Aleksei's chamber, of the blood they had to clean up…*

She turned, blowing out the candle and buried her face in Fredrik's jacket. She felt his chest hitch in surprise then his arms came round her, pressing her to him.

'Laura' he whispered, his voice husky with anguish and want, pressing her tighter to him when he felt her shaking.

For a moment she hovered on the brink, wanting to press passionate kisses to his lips, to pull him down to have her on the sooty floor, but the old fear had not gone and she turned away, wondering if the shadows hid men that could see in the dark, men who would whisper to Ilich…

'Forgive my moment of nerves' she said quietly. 'I believe my rooms have aired sufficiently.'

She left him, hoping she wouldn't walk into a wall as she tried not to blunder her way out of the dark room. Quickly she rushed up the stairs to her room and shut the door harder than she needed to, leaning against it with her eyes shut.

The wail made her open her eyes quickly and Anna threw herself at her feet, hugging her legs. Laura sank down and hugged her tightly, crying with happiness to see her again.

'Your Highness' Anna sobbed. 'I thought I would never see you again! I missed you so terribly!'

'And I missed you' she sobbed, brushing back Anna's hair to look at her carefully. 'Help me undress, and tell me everything!'

Anna smiled through her tears and helped Laura to her feet. As she unpinned her hair and brushed it she told Laura of her small wedding with Mikhail three months earlier, and how she had found domestic work in Luka Nevsky's home. As she unbuttoned her dress and loosened her corsets she told her how glad the Principality was that they had an heir, though they had wanted a boy, and although they wanted her to be Vsevolod's descendant they didn't want Aleksei to be her father.

She took off her chemise and washed her carefully, telling her how faint the scars from the whip were now, how nicely they had healed. She brought Laura her nightdress, telling her that the Principality was generally reserved with Ilich's government; they liked some aspects of it, but could not help but remember how he had once bayed for royal blood. They didn't quite trust him, but they did like the new projects he had undertaken.

Anna stopped talking and hugged Laura again. It was a breach of protocol, but Laura knew that Anna had earned it; as they had fled from the revolution into the forests of Russia Anna had become more than just a servant. She had put her life in danger for Laura, and she would never forget it.

'What does Dalnerechensk say about my guests?' she asked.

'That they are handsome, and have stirred many a wagging tongue' Anna said ruefully.

'Anna?' she asked quietly. 'What do they say of me?'

'They say you look happier' she said, shutting her eyes. 'They say how sad you looked walking the Avenue of Heroes, and they bless your return. They say you have brought a man to be your husband back with you.'

'Do they want me to marry again?' she whispered.

'*Da*, they want a boy, but...' she trailed off, biting her lip.

'But?' Laura pressed.

'But they want him to be Vsevolod's heir, and he won't be, not without his blood. Sorry Your Highness.'

'A monarch does not just have to be a man. Many women have presided over important reigns: Queen Elizabeth, Queen Victoria, Catherine the Great!' she cried, frustrated.

'Dunno Your Highness, Dalnerechensk has always had a tsar.'

And that's the crux of the problem right there Laura thought sadly. *This proud, traditionalist community has always had a tsar, and he has always been Vsevolod.*

She sighed and Anna folded down the fresh sheets on the bed. Laura sat and swung herself in, letting Anna tuck her in gently.

'I'm glad you're back Your Highness' she said softly. 'Dalnerechensk is glad to have you back.'

'Thank you Anna' she mumbled, shutting her eyes.

She heard Anna blow out the candle by her bed and pad across the room but was asleep before she heard her close the door.

17

Laura had risen late and breakfasted alone in her new rooms, slightly ashamed of her behaviour with Fredrik last night. She had to be careful, there were wagging tongues and gossips, traitors and spies; just as there had been before. Perhaps even moreso now. She did not want to see Fredrik dragged into political intrigue, to have them smear his name as they fought to keep Vsevolod's bloodline pure.

She shut her eyes and sighed, letting Anna dress her in white silk and pin her hair up with emeralds she had borrowed from Ekaterina. She tried to get her thoughts in order, she was going to see Ilich's Parliament today; the first time she had paid any real attention to them since the terrible aftermath of the battle for Liberty Valley. She was unsure if she held any real loyalty from them.

Finally she stood and eyed herself critically in the mirror one last time. She hoped Ilich's ministers remembered the girl in white atop the castle walls, the shock of the Bodice Treaties still fresh in their minds, the horror of Nikita's army on their doorstep reminding them of what she had done, how much she deserved what she was going to ask for now.

She padded down the flights of stairs to the first floor, heading along the corridor past Aleksei's and Grigory's old studies to the Advisory Council, now renamed Parliament Chambers. There were two soldiers standing outside the door, a clear indication that Parliament was already in session. There were some comical half bows, half salutes as she approached then one pushed open the door for her.

The council turned in surprise when she stepped in, and there were some subtle looks at Ilich before they stood to greet her. There were some half bows, some nods of the head, one or two salutes; at least some form of respectful recognition. Only Ilich made no move. Anna had told her they had moved out his belongings as they moved in Luke's, and she wondered briefly where he had spent the night to make him so sour this morning.

Maksim Yegorov and Lev Dostoevski were in the room, wearing the white sashes that proclaimed them as ministers of Ilich's government. Laura couldn't stop her moment of surprise showing but she quickly schooled her features back into a smile. *I did not see them at dinner last night* she noted, walking to the head of the table. They had either been spies for Ilich before the revolution, or had thrown in their lot with them to maintain their positions of wealth and power.

Ilich's look soured further but he acquiesced and she sat in his chair, motioning for the other ministers to sit too. There were some quick reshuffling of places so Luka and Ilich could remain at the head of the table too, Lev and Maksim bumped down to the seats at the bottom of the table. Laura filed that bit of political musical chairs away for careful analysis later.
'I have come, gentlemen, as there are some issues I wish to raise with you, but first I must give to all of you my most sincere apologies.'

There was a surprised murmur at her words. She let it die down, noticing who looked at who, and the information contained in those exchanges.
'In those terrible days following the deaths of Tsar Constantinovich and Tsar Stephanovich, and the horrific repel of *Knjaz* Rurik's army, I was not as supportive, nor as involved, in forging a new world for Dalnerechensk as I should have been' she said, and watched them leap to reassure her that

they had understood her pain. 'I therefore solemnly vow to devote all my energies to the Principality again' she went on, and saw the look that crossed Ilich's face.

'Firstly, gentlemen, is the disrepair of my home' she continued and heard them exclaim in surprise. 'The castle is not -' Lev started but Laura cut him off.

'It is the home of the monarchs, and I am Tsaritsa of Dalnerechensk -'

'That is not *de jure* and it is barely *de facto*' Maksim interrupted haughtily.

'It is, nevertheless, *de facto*' she said calmly. 'The castle will be a royal residence henceforth -'

'It has been the home for the Head of State these past few months, and you cannot just -'

'I think you will find that was also not *de jure* and barely *de facto*' she interrupted coldly. 'The castle is, and has always been, a royal residence. The Head of State will find other suitable lodgings worthy of his standing. The Revolution claimed many properties through eminent domain. Pick one.' She glared hard at Maksim.

'The castle is to be repaired. The left wing has been left in a bad state and it is unknown how this has weakened the overall integrity of the structure. I do not think I need to stress how this government will be viewed if we allowed such a potent symbol of Dalnerechensk to collapse.'

'It will not be a throne room again' Ilich said quietly. He was shaking in anger.

'Indeed. It will be the new Parliament Chambers, and will retain the throne of Vsevolod for presiding monarchs to use when they sit in parliament.'

There was silence and stillness around the table, except for Ivan Gogol, who was frantically scribbling down the minutes of the meeting. She plunged on relentlessly.

'A flag bearing the coat of arms of the Vakhtangov family will fly from the battlements to indicate that the royal family is in residence when we stay at the castle -'

'You cannot do this!' Ilich shouted, leaping to his feet. 'You have no authority here! I forbid this!'

'I signed over sovereignty Ilich, I did not surrender the Monarchy' she said. 'The Monarchy still exists, ratified and recognised by this government and you will do me the courtesy of respecting my position, if not for what I did; if not for the Treaties I forced Russia to sign; if not for the better life I gave this Principality; if not for the army I repelled as Vsevolod had once repelled; then you will follow the protocol and observances that honours the family he established!'

She stopped, breathing hard from her passion. No one moved, even Ivan's pencil was still. She shut her eyes and swallowed down her heated demeanour, composing herself again.

'As such, you will call me *Tsaritsa Tsarstvuyushchaya -*'

'*Nyet*' Ilich said quietly. 'You cannot rule in your own right. You were only the common wife of a prince -'

'Do you think the people will see it that way?'

'*We* represent the people!' Lev sneered, casting a lofty eye around the room.

'Only recently' Laura said levelly, which earnt a smirk from Luka and Ivan Gogol, who did not like the two new additions from the old Advisory Council. 'And if so, why does the Head of State live in the trappings of the Monarchy and station so many guards to stand between himself and those you speak for?'

Ilich glared at her and she knew she had hit a rather sore spot from the reactions of the rest of the ministers.

'You signed over sovereignty to us, Your Highness,' Luka started but she interrupted him.

'Under duress.'

'*What?!*' Ilich shouted.

'I was sixteen and in shock from all that I had endured. Any who know me and know what I did will say that I was taken advantage of in the settlement -'

'Whatever will be said, the fact remains that you are not the blood of Vsevolod' Luka said. 'Dalnerechensk has never been without his blood on the throne, and never without a tsar.'

'My daughter is his blood' she said quietly.

Luka caught Ilich's eye urgently, and Laura knew they would sorely like to put their heads together and whisper some vital agreement between the two of them. She was glad they were sitting on opposite sides of the table.

'If I might make a suggestion' Ivan started quietly, then cleared his throat uncomfortably. 'It is unlikely that sovereignty will be reversed, with all due respect Your Highness' he said, dropping his head to her. 'You cannot be *Tsaritsa Tsarstvuyushchaya* without sovereignty, and not without Vsevolod's blood. But no one will argue that Aleksei didn't rule Dalnerechensk in his own right, as Crown Prince, and no one will argue that you were not his wife. Perhaps the title *Vdova Tsaritsa*, styled Your Majesty, would be acceptable to all.'

Dowager Empress she mused. She could see them thinking it over, and were finding it acceptable. She decided not to push her luck with any more insistence. She had laid the seeds, they would think of nothing else for the next few hours at least. She did not blame Parliament for not wanting to give up power. If they did there was no guarantee that the needs of the population would not be disregarded again.

'There is Piotr Grigorevich Vakhtangov' Maksim suddenly said.

Laura went cold. Maksim was finding it hard to conceal his glee at her reaction. There was a storm of protest from the ministers.

'He is thirteen!'

'He is ill!'

'He is male' Maksim finished firmly.

'I have not heard that name before' Laura said carefully.

'He is descended matrilineally through *Tsarevna* Varvara Igorevna, sister to Tsar Petrovich, Great Great Grandfather to Aleksei' Ivan quickly explained. 'He is descended from Vsevolod' Maksim went on. 'If the Monarchy must be male, why not him?'

There was silence and the words *yes, but…* hovered over the heads of all there. Laura felt their attention slide back to her. *She had written the treaties* she heard them thinking. *She had come back to warn them of Nikita's army, when she might have known what would have happened to her, what* we *might have done to her…*

And then there was a deep feeling of shame.

'I think' Luka said quietly, 'that this issue is too large to answer today. Perhaps we should leave this for now, and examine this again in the future.'

'Agreed' said a minister, and the motion was quickly passed.

Ilich cleared his throat, looking as if what he was going to say had been tortuously wrung out of him.

'Perhaps you are right, Your Highness' he said carefully. 'It would not do to have the Head of State, who represents the democratic sovereignty of this nation, so removed and surrounded by the trappings of the Monarchy. Therefore the castle is deemed a royal residence, to be maintained and financed by the royal family, and no minister will reside here unless explicitly asked to stay by the royal family, as a guest.'

He glanced at Luka who nodded. The rest of the ministers agreed and the decree was noted down in the minutes.

Laura was satisfied by the outcome, but had been shocked to realise there were still male Vakhtangovs, possibly with stronger claims to the throne than she. Maksim had shaken her, as no doubt he had designed to do, and she vowed to track down all Vsevolod's descendants.

Parliament broke up and they stood, bowing to her before taking their leave. *At least we'll have no more of this silly bowing and saluting confusion* she thought, calling Peter Kamanin back to her. He bowed and stood waiting patiently.

'I did not thank you, nor commend you, for your brilliant tactical repel of Nikita's army' she said. 'For all that I claim, I do acknowledge it was through your efforts that Dalnerechensk was saved. This expression of my gratitude is long overdue, yet no less fervent and heartfelt.'

'Thank you, Your Majesty' he said, bowing again. 'Had I not been forewarned I could not have done what I did.'

'You will of course receive my thanks publically as well, and the titles of *Graf* and Knight of the Order of Vsevolod.'

Peter looked surprised, then emotional. He bowed low again, shutting his eyes.

'God bless the Tsaritsa' he said thickly.

'Rise, Peter Kamanin, *Graf* of -' she stopped. 'Well, forgive this moment of embarrassment, you will have lands with your title, but as yet I do not know what they are' she said, and he laughed, straightening up again.

Laura rose from her chair and came towards him.

'I called you back also for the security of the castle. I wish for a new detail of guards to ensure the protection of my family and guests. The gates will no longer be closed; the portcullises will no longer be lowered at night. The Monarchy will rely on the respect that it has always received from its subjects' she said, and saw him smile in approval. 'This detail will be called the Guards of the Order, and fall under your personal jurisdiction. The guards will be of your choosing and of a number that you deem necessary to effectively secure the castle and royal family. They will be volunteers, and their loyalty to me must be paramount.'

'Of course Your Majesty' he said, and Laura could see him already crunching numbers and personalities.

'Thank you, *Graf* Kamanin' she said, dismissing him, and he bowed again, taking his leave.

She stood too and went to the nursery to check on Alexandra, hoping she had done enough to secure her the throne.

18

By three o'clock that afternoon the Principality was abuzz with rumours and gossip. Women stood by their garden gates and asked each other if they were true, announcing and denouncing all sorts of wild stories. Children ran back and forth in the streets, scattering dogs and cats and toys, bickering like their mothers, spreading the tales further and further afield.

Laura, the von Schmidt family, Luke and Lady Anne, Ivan Gogol, Luka Nevsky and Yuri Drevin, another fresh faced minister in charge of public works, had gathered in the courtyard of the castle ready for the excursion into town Laura had promised Kurt. Six Republican soldiers had been drafted as an escort and the ministers looked distinctly uncomfortable at how few there were. Alexandra burbled in Laura's arms, chewing on her fist and blowing dribbly bubbles.

'Should you not leave her here, Your Majesty?' Luka asked again, eyeing the soldiers.

'No' she said simply. 'The *Tsesarevna* will be shown to her people.'

I managed to say that without flinching...

Luka said nothing and the soldiers took up positions around them as they began to leave the grounds.

Both Yuri and Ivan spoke French and they took up a running commentary on the improvements that had been made to the infrastructure of Dalnerechensk: telegraph wires linking the six villages and hamlets together, better drainage of streets, and plans for an improved sewage system. They showed the party the new school that had been built, and explained the alterations that had been made to the hospital.

As they talked they walked the length of Vsevolod's Way, and Yuri pointed out the bullet-scarred damage to buildings that was still being repaired. Crowds had gathered around them on the street, and children skipped in and out of the soldiers, poking the ministers rudely and babbling to the von Schmidts in Russian. Comely girls pushed themselves to the front of the crowds, smiling coquettishly at them, waving handkerchiefs they dropped in their paths.

One small boy tripped over an untied shoelace and landed heavily, skinning his knees and began to bawl. Laura crouched down and fished out a handkerchief she was never without, dabbing away the blood on his knees and wiping away his tears with her thumb.

'Where is your mamma?' she asked him kindly.

He looked around wildly and began to cry again when he couldn't see her. Laura wiped his tears and kissed his cheek, helping him to his feet.

'What is your name?' she asked him, stroking down his hair.

'Igor' he sniffled, eyeing the burbling baby in her arms. 'Is she yours?'

'Yes' she smiled. 'She is *Tsesarevna* Alexandra Alexeevna Vakhtangovna'

'She doesn't look mad' Igor went on, with all the innocence and subtlety of children. 'Mamma said she would be mad because the prince was mad, but she doesn't look mad.'

Laura smiled tightly, but Igor didn't notice. 'Perhaps you might see your mother in the crowd if you walk with us a little while' she said, straightening up and taking Igor's hand.

The party set off again, Igor trotting along with self-importance beside her. Laura forced herself to concentrate on Ivan's words as he continued his description of the reformed education system, and how many children were in school now that they did not have to earn a living in the mines. Igor spotted his mother and raced off, stopping to drop a jaunty little bow at her before running to boast how he had held the *Tsaritsa's* hand. Laura managed a smile for the group at the garden gate and they curtsied as she passed, craning their necks to see the baby.

Laura's arms grew tired and she hitched Alexandra uncomfortably, beginning to regret that she had not put her in a pram or something else to show her off to the public of Dalnerechensk.

'Give me my grandchild' Luke said quietly, taking Alexandra from her. 'Your arms must be very tired by now.'

She resisted the urge to shake her arms out, spying a small plaque above a shop door, one that proclaimed the business had often been patronised by the royal family. Surprising the party she pushed open the door, stepping into the jeweller's shop.

It was quite small, and very sombre. Great polished cabinets stood along the walls, and the long wooden counter top was covered with black velvet. Not a speck of dust or lint clung to the velvet, and Laura wondered briefly which poor servant had to clean it. Ornate gas lamps lit the room and made the merchandise - displayed elegantly on black velvet busts - sparkle and wink as she moved past them.

Three surprised people stood in the room, a young couple who stood arm and arm and a small, neat man with a fussy little beard and spectacles, caught in the motion of presenting them with a small gold ring. All three turned and bowed to her, while the fussy man turned and called for someone secreted in the back of the shop to see to the couple.

'Your Highness, it is an honour to have you in my humble shop' said the fussy man, his Russian slightly accented, as he came to greet her personally.

'Your Majesty' she corrected and waved away his apology. 'I understand from the plaque above your door that you have made items for the royal family before?' she asked.

'Seven necklaces, a tiara, nine rings and four sets of cufflinks, I believe' he answered, bowing deeply.

Laura was mildly surprised that he could remember each item, but a man so meticulous in his appearance was hardly going to forget his works of art. She stepped closer to the counter, admiring the way each necklace was presented in just the right angle to catch the light.

'Have you worked with enamel before?' she asked, noticing that there was nothing on display that showed he had.

'Yes Your Majesty, both myself and my son, Paul -' he gestured to the boy standing near the couple '- are skilled at working enamel.'

She smiled. 'I have established an honorific order, the Order of Vsevolod, and require an enamel medallion to signify it. Something appropriately heraldic, but unassuming, like the man himself. Do you think you could design something fitting?'

'It would be an honour Your Majesty' he said, beaming.

'Good. Present yourself to the castle in three days with several designs, I will take a great interest in its development.'

He bowed again and Laura smiled at the couple, who were frozen in place, staring at her. They remembered themselves enough to bow again as she left and joined the ministers who stood on the street outside the shop, decidedly uncomfortable with waiting for her.

Alexandra burbled and waved a slobbery fist at her. She smiled and kissed her head, wiping her small hand with another handkerchief.

'Your Majesty?' said a small voice behind her.

She turned, surprised to see Paul standing behind her, his hat clasped in his hands and nervously turning the brim round and round.

'I was in Unit E' he said, plunging on. 'My brother and I, we were in Unit E.'

Laura carefully braced herself. Unit E had been the small contingent of men who had lined the barricaded street of Vsevolod's Way, first in the line of fire when Nikita's men had breached Vsevolod's Gate and entered the city.

'Peter was wounded' he went on, in a curiously leaden voice. 'A bullet hit him in the shoulder, but he fought on for you. And when it was over, he was at the feast at the castle. I wasn't, I was on guard duty with the Russians, but he told me about it. Told me how you kissed his cheek and thanked him personally, asked him if he hurt, and he had said it was only dull. He told me it hurt, but it was all the better just for one kiss and word of gratitude from you.

'He died last year, pneumonia' he said. 'But he never forgot your words or your kiss and he said if you called Dalnerechensk again, all those you kissed would come running. But I think he was wrong Your Majesty. I think if you called again, *all* would come running.' He stopped talking, nervously twining his hat round and round ceaselessly.

Laura swallowed carefully, marshalling her words, then gently kissed his cheek.

'Thank you, Paul' she said quietly. 'The courage, loyalty and valour that your brother and others showed were what saved Dalnerechensk. You could not have better embodied the spirit of Vsevolod and the vision that made this Principality great. I am proud, and I am honoured, that I could but just kiss the cheek of those men.'

Paul dropped to his knees and took up the hem of her gown, kissing it while tears poured down his cheeks.

'God bless you Tsaritsa Stephanovna' he said. 'God save the Tsaritsa.'

The jeweller appeared in the doorway and gently helped his son to his feet. Laura saw his bottom lip wobble slightly and he bowed to her. Alexandra chose this moment to begin grizzling and wiggling impatiently in Luke's arms. Laura turned and gently collected her daughter, kissing her cheek.

'We should return, the *Tsesarevna* requires a nap' she said, and began to lead the way back to the castle. 'We will continue a tour of Dalnerechensk tomorrow, perhaps this time by carriage so we can see the hamlets too.'

The party bowed and fell into step behind her.

19

Laura sat, watching ruefully as Lady Anne struggled to stitch the border of the tapestry. She was trying to be kind, it wasn't Lady Anne's fault she had been brought up without learning how to embroider or sew anything, *but how difficult is it to stitch a straight line?* she despaired. She glanced at Ekaterina, who was bent over her work, biting her lip in fierce concentration, or perhaps in effort not to laugh.

Laura sighed quietly and picked up the drawings, studying them carefully. It had been a busy few days as she had thrown herself fervently into her new projects. Peter Kamanin had had more volunteers than he would ever need for the new guard for the *Vdova* Tsaritsa, and had quickly set up new stations and patrols within and around the castle. New uniforms had been designed, and an order for material and tailoring had been quickly dispatched.

She and Luke had toured the tin mines, the first time she had been back since the great cave-in that had killed sixteen people. Luke had spoken excitedly about the machinery that would increase the output, tutting over the primitive pickaxe and shovel method they were still using. Laura had translated his ideas and comments to an astounded Overseer, who had fast developed a strong liking and respect for Baron Asanton and had promptly told him so. Luke had laughed, something Laura noticed he was doing much more of these days, and had suddenly promised to buy the machinery he had been describing, a proposition that had surprised the miners, and they cheered for his generosity.

In those busy days Laura had also sought out Fedor, who had found work as a teacher in the new school and implored him to take the role of Head of Castle Staff. His usually unemotional demeanour had vanished and he had clasped her hands and kissed them, thanking her with a thick tongue and tear-brightened eyes. Ilich had admonished her for her blatant nepotism, but Laura had explained that Fedor had been Tsar Constantinovich's personal attaché, and as such knew most about the day to day running of the castle, the processes and ceremonies, and - most importantly - where everything was kept.

It was Fedor who had found in the library the beautiful, meticulous copies of the tapestries, bound in a book of crumbling leather. Gustav had painstakingly copied the images in faithful detail, and these copies were what they were using to re-stitch the Vsevolod tapestries. Fedor had also found a Royal Standard, somehow over-looked in the destructive days of the revolution, and it flew proudly from the roof of the castle.

Laura rubbed at her eyes and inhaled deeply, tilting her face up into the warm sunlight. Fredrik sat in her chambers, reading aloud Edmund Spencer's *Faerie Queene* for the women with her. Emilie and Ekaterina had been delighted at her project and had not hesitated to offer their needles to the task. Lady Anne had shyly offered hers, and so had Tatiana Yegorovna, Maksim's daughter and Aleksei's mistress.

Laura was surprised that Tatiana should want to help, and had quickly deduced that she had either been sent by her father to spy on any conversations, or that the two were so alike in their thoughts she had come on her own instruction. Ekaterina had quickly taken Lady Anne aside, had whispered to her of the care needed around Tatiana, and Lady Anne, terrified of saying anything that might hurt her daughter-in-law, had remained almost silent as they stitched.

Laura shut her eyes. She could not forget the hurt of Aleksei's affair; how he had stationed soldiers outside his rooms to bar her from her own husband. Even as they had grown cold and distant, even as his jealousy and bitterness had grown, she had always tried to be a good wife. To know that he had spurned her for a former lover had been a betrayal that had broken her heart.

It had cut deeper to know that it was legal. The tsars of Dalnerechensk were entitled to bed who they liked, their *droit du seigneur*. Their wives were merely property, possessions that ensured Vsevolod's blood flowed from father to son in a recognised and indisputable tie. Once an heir was born a tsar could put aside his wife, her duty fulfilled.

Would it have mattered so much if his mistress had been anyone other than poisonous Tatiana? she wondered. It was no secret that Tatiana had once been considered for Aleksei's wife. Laura finally understood now that Aleksei had not married her because she did not come with a large enough dowry. Or perhaps because he knew of Maksim's ambitions? she mused. Father to the tsaritsa brought a whole wealth of power and prestige. Grandfather to the next tsar brought even more. Especially if they all knew the tsar was mad…

Maksim had once come to her with a document to reverse the law of propriety, the law that barred illegitimate children from claiming the throne. He had wanted any fruitful union from Aleksei's affair to gain considerable power. He had also signed a petition to declare Aleksei mad, and Laura had no doubt he was the mastermind behind it. Perhaps Maksim had not been a Parliamentary informant in the uneasy days before the revolution she thought. It was no secret how he despised commoners. He and Lev had trimmed their sails to the new political winds and had joined the cause only to preserve themselves. It was a wonder Ilich had let them.

Behind her Fredrik paused in his reading and sipped at a goblet of wine. 'Your High Well Born, you read spectacularly well in foreign languages!' Tatiana spoke up in English, flashing him a coquettish smile. 'Tell me, have you ever had the pleasure of reading Alexander Pushkin?'

'Only in translations, *Mademoiselle* Yegorovna, and I am told the language suffers most appallingly in them' he answered.

'Oh terribly!' Tatiana cried. 'I have read several of his works in English, French and Russian, and can only marvel at how poor other languages are at capturing the essence of a Russian word! And their attempts at the translations of Russian verse - well, it can only be described as butchery!'

'Travesty!' Fredrik smiled. 'I have often wondered, as I had once had a few short hours to read an English translation of Goethe's *Faust*, whether the insipid nature of the words were the fault of the translator, not the language itself. I can attest, reading such writers as William Shakespeare and Victor-Marie Hugo, that English and French, in their mother tongues and mother contexts, have a beauty and a power all their own, and are in no such way diminished through any deficiency in the language itself.'

'Surely we cannot lay the blame solely at the feet of the translators!' Tatiana cried. 'These men know the languages well, but cannot find an accurate word, or rouse the equivalent feelings in the poetry!'

'Perhaps they are constrained to poor choice by meter and structure' Fredrik smiled.

'Ah, perhaps you are right' Tatiana simpered. 'When a word is in a context or a structure alien to it, or is merely selected because it performs a role, it can only be a poor shadow of the true word, and a mockery of the magnificence of its meaning.'

Ah, so there are your fangs, you poisonous viper! Laura thought, using a few choice words in the privacy of her own head.

'Perhaps mere words are poor tools' said Lady Anne dreamily.

The company stopped, surprised, as almost an hour had lapsed since she had last spoken, and she was now gazing at the frescoes of Russian knights in armour, a far-away look on her face.

'I always thought words were to language as notes are to music. Anyone can make a tune, a melody; but once caressed by a master those notes do for them what they will do for no other. Perhaps words, when touched by the genius of Shakespeare, remain altered; impressed and changed by the man who manipulated them, as if they are imbued by a divine meaning that goes beyond mere letters and order. How could a mere translator translate that? A concert hall pianist cannot translate the orchestra, even if the tune sounds the same.'

She suddenly stopped talking and blushed, aware of her ramble.

'Lady Anne you astound me!' Laura laughed. 'But let's have no more of this literary critique. Your High Well Born, please continue to read of St George while we stitch another medieval knight, surrounded by the stories of Ilya Muromets!'

'Of course, Your Majesty' he smiled, taking another sip of wine to soothe his throat.

Laura busied herself over the stitches again, her mind churning away inside her. Tatiana had no doubt acquired her father's distaste of commoners on royal thrones, her veiled remark had made that clear enough. Just how much she would be involved in her father's schemes Laura could only guess.

Her mind slid back to Piotr Grigorevich Vakhtangov. She had a vague recollection of being introduced to a nephew before her wedding, but she had met so many relatives and friends and ministers and acquaintances that she could not in all honesty say what he looked like. She had thought, from passing comments and a large number of people referred to as Aunt, and not many by Uncle, that Aleksei's extended family was comprised - if not solely then by a large majority - of women, a fact that seemed to be supported by the documents Fedor had shown her.

It had been difficult for her to follow the pages and pages of family trees, as children were written down by their given names, and it wasn't always clear which male child had become the Tsar. Some family trees had included mistresses and their offspring; others had included the family trees of the spouse. Some included titles, others did not; the whole mess making the task of discovering any other male relatives as difficult as unravelling a Gordian knot.

What was clear was that Aleksei had no siblings save Alexander Andrei, so there were no immediate claimants to the throne save for her daughter. Laura had sometimes wondered if Olaf had ever had children out of wedlock, but he had never mentioned it, and she had tried not to think about it. His father, Tsar Constantinovich, had only one sibling: *Velikij Knjaz* Radomyr, who had committed suicide without marrying or fathering a child.

In fact, she had to go back to Tsar Alexandrovich, Aleksei's grandfather, to find siblings that had produced children. He had had three siblings, but only his younger sister, Maria, had had children: one son and two daughters, all of whom had female only descendants. She had been surprised by how many of Aleksei's ancestors had died young or childless, but Ekaterina had told her it was customary for Russian princesses, unmarried or widowed by a certain age, to end their days in a convent. Laura hoped they wouldn't try to send her to a nunnery.

All in all she had discovered that the family tree, as far back as Vsevolod himself, yielded only six male relatives alive today, of which Piotr was one.

All of them had very weak claims to the throne; there was not one direct line of male descent from Vsevolod except for the one that had died with Aleksei. That realisation had hit her hard, and she wondered how many others realised what she had: that Vsevolod would never again live reincarnated through his blood; that all kings after him would only be watery, faint dilutions of the once potent bloodline.

She rubbed her eyes again, distracted. There was one strange entry of family trees that was repeated nowhere else, a mention of Tsar Vasilievich the Third, son of Tsar Radomyrevich and a date of 1735. Everywhere else he had been recorded as Vasilievich the Second, a silly mistake that seemed out of place in the meticulous record keeping of Dalnerechensk's royal line, and one that had made her spend over an hour searching for descendants that didn't exist.

A knock on her chamber door interrupted Fredrik's reading and one of the new guards stepped in, bowing low.

'Yosef ben Michael Grünbaum to see you, Your Majesty' he announced.

'Send him in' she said, trying to remember where she had heard the name before, realising that she had heard too many to easily identify these last few days.

The guard bowed and the neat little jeweller stepped into the room, bowing to her.

'I have bought some designs for the medallion Your Majesty' he said, presenting the large leather satchel he had with him.

'Grünbaum?' Fredrik spoke up. *'Sind Sie Deutsche?'*

Yosef looked at Laura, slightly confused.

'You have a German family name, His High Well Born was curious as to whether you were German' she smiled, beckoning him closer.

He looked very uncomfortable suddenly.

'It was a name my ancestors adopted in the late seventeen hundreds when they lived in Sighișoara. They brought it with them when they moved into Russia, and then to Dalnerechensk, Your Majesty' he said. 'I have the designs, would you care to see them?'

'Of course. Excuse me, my ladies' she said, standing and moving away from the sewing, beckoning him to a small writing table near the window.

Yosef bowed as he presented the leather satchel to her. Laura took it and unfastened it, pulling out a few sheets of paper, trying to ignore how Tatiana had started her flirtations again.

The first sheet displayed a crest and coat of arms. The shield was flanked by two rearing animals, a lynx and a greyhound. A plumed helmet sat in profile atop the shield, and a banner rippled down the sides and underneath, transcribed with a Latin motto. The shield itself was the rich blue of Dalnerechensk's royals, and a white stag reared in a stylised manner. A label at the top of the shield indicated the crest belonged to the first born son.

'That is Vsevolod's family crest, Your Majesty' Yosef explained. 'The Lynx is a symbol of liberty, vigilance, forecast and courage; while the greyhound is a symbol of courage, vigilance and loyalty. The blue is a symbol of truth and loyalty, the white stag a symbol of sincerity and peace, a man who will not fight unless provoked. The motto means "I serve with honours"' he finished.

Laura held it up to the light, admiring the simplicity and the beauty of it, catching sight of the design for the Order of Vsevolod underneath. She could see it had incorporated elements of Vsevolod's old family crest and the new one he had established when he had fled into the valleys of Dalnerechensk, his old titles stripped away from him. A green fesse divided the blue shield in two. The white stag occupied the top half, and the black watch towers occupied the bottom. The Lynx and the greyhound were now gorged with a crown, and the helmet above the shield had been replaced by Vsevolod's simple crown. The small banner unrolled under the shield with the Russian motto ЗА ЛЮБОВЪ И ОТЕЧЕСТВО.

'"For Love and Fatherland"' she read out loud.

'I believe it is similar to the motto for The Imperial Order of St Catherine the Great Martyr' Yosef explained nervously.

Underneath was the sketch for the medallion itself. It was slightly oval in shape, featuring a gorged, rearing stag on a blue background. Rays of diamonds emanated from the medallion in the shape of a cross. A silver bar hooked the medallion onto a green ribbon that bore the Cyrillic script for *za lyubov' i Otechestvo*, written in silver thread.

'The rays symbolise the cross, but also the mountain daisy, the symbol for Dalnerechensk, and you wore them in your hair for …' he trailed off nervously, aware of her silence. 'The medallion can be worn on a sash or a ribbon, depending on the rank of the wearer…' he trailed off again.

'Your skill and your foresight are a credit to you' she said, smiling faintly. 'The medallion and the coat of arms for the Order are perfect. However, it will not do to have the motto for the Order of St Catherine on a Dalnerechensk medal. This Order is specifically chosen for their loyalty to me and their dedication to duty, much like the most respected Swiss Guard. Their motto is *Acriter et Fideliter: For Courage and Loyalty*; traits they are renowned for, as well as their noble sentiments. One only needs to look at their valour in the Sack of Rome and the defence of the Tuileries Palace to understand why.

'To be loyal to me is to be courageous' she said, and wrote ЗА ВЕРНОСТЪ neatly under the banner for the Guard's coat of arms.

'*For Loyalty*. When will these be ready?'

'How many do you require?'

'Two, for now' she mused.

'One week' he promised. 'My son and I will both work on them.'

'Excellent.'

Laura stood, handing the papers to Yosef. He quickly pushed them into the satchel, clearing his throat self-consciously.

'I have something that belongs to you, Your Majesty' he said nervously.

Quickly he reached into the satchel and pulled out a piece of rolled velvet. He untied the strip that held the roll firmly closed and unrolled it. The black diamonds sat winking up at her from the table. Laura gasped, sinking down to the chair again.

'The Tsaritsa's lucky black diamonds' she whispered.

'Yes Your Majesty. They were brought to my shop where I obtained them for the purpose of returning them to you.'

Laura reached out and fingered the jewels gently. She had worn this necklace when negotiating the Bodice Treaties. Aleksei had given them to her, in a rare moment of tenderness in those last few days, just before she had entered the Advisory Council to negotiate the treaties, explaining that they were his mother's favourite piece of jewellery, given to her on the birth of her first son.

'Oh how lovely!' Tatiana suddenly exclaimed, appearing beside Laura. 'At least now you will have *one* necklace to wear! Your Majesty, we have grown bored with stitching and Spencer! I have invited Lady Anne, Countess Ivanova and Baroness von Schmidt to ride through the Hunting Forest with me, as we do not wish to intrude on matters of business. And of course Baron von Schmidt must come as chaperone!'

'How terrible that such a tapestry is not of interest!' she smiled, being careful not to let it twist in a nasty way, though Tatiana was intelligent enough to hear the insult in it. 'But of course His High Well Born must chaperone you.'

Deliberately she slid off her wedding ring and handed it to Yosef.

'It is all that my daughter has of her father' she said. 'Please recast this as you wish for my daughter. Oh dear, Tatiana, do not let me delay you, least this business quite ruin the day. Thank you, dear friends, for your company!' she called as they stood and bowed to her, leaving the room.

She let herself smile as the door closed behind them, aware of how Fredrik had looked at her, then turned back to Yosef.

'A necklace, perhaps, some earrings' she shrugged dismissively. 'Embellish the gold as you choose with a precious stone or two.'

'Yes Your Majesty' he bowed. 'My son, Paul, asked me to present this mere token to you, for remembering his brother' he said, pulling out a blue roll of velvet from the satchel.

It unrolled to reveal a lovely necklace of diamonds, sapphires and emeralds set in silver.

'It is beautiful' she smiled, lifting it from the velvet so it caught the sun and sparkled.

Quickly she called Anna over to fasten the jewels around her neck and to bring a hand mirror so she could see their effect. They lay in a gentle cascade of finery, but didn't cluster, giving the impression of wealth but frugality too.

'I will require a crown' she suddenly said. 'A coronet perhaps. Vsevolod's crown is plain and unassuming, I shall require something more feminine. It will not do to have a monarch without a crown.'

'Yes Your Majesty. Will you require a sceptre?'

'No. But perhaps some more jewels in future. Thank you, you may go.'

He collected up the satchel and bowed to her, walking backwards to the door, trying not to trip on the abandoned silk for the tapestry.

20

Alexandra burbled *mmmm, mmamm, mmamma* as Laura carried her down to the ground floor, wondering if she was saying her first word. *It certainly sounded like mama* she thought to herself. It was still early but the castle was busy with servants rushing in and out of the left wing with pails of soapy water and scrubbing brushes. She stepped into the wing, following the sounds of talking and activity to the throne room.

At once the noise stopped and an army of servants rose, bowing to her. She smiled and called good morning to them, while Alexandra blew bubbles. A man with a sheet of paper in his hands came to her, bowing low again.

'The fire has not damaged the structural integrity of the castle, Your Majesty' he said, then introduced himself as: 'Petrovich Kamanin, architect. Would you care to see the plans for the new Parliament Chambers?'

'Your father is Peter Kamanin?' she asked.

He saluted. 'Yes Your Majesty' he beamed.

'Then I am honoured to make your acquaintance, and would be delighted to see the plans. Please, proceed with what you were doing' she smiled at the rest of the servants, and followed Petrovich to a table near a window that had the boards removed from it.

'Excellent' Laura smiled, eyeing the neat drawings, liking how the room looked grand but austere, like a small cathedral. 'Has Ilich Rukavishnikov approved of these drawings?'

'Yes Your Majesty' he said. 'Even the dais that is to be constructed.'

There was a flood of light as boards were removed from another window, and a maid set to work scrubbing the sooty coating from the sill.

'Tell me Petrovich, have you ever wanted to design and build a theatre?' she asked.

He looked surprised. 'It had not crossed my mind, Your Majesty' he said. 'Does Her Majesty want a theatre?'

'It has been a long time since I've been, and I had thought that Dalnerechensk was sadly lacking in an entertainment such as this. I have heard that picture theatres are the coming thing for public performances, and I think Dalnerechensk might embrace a new entertainment.'

'Pictures?' Petrovich looked perplexed.

'Moving pictures' she smiled. 'I have never seen one, but I imagine it would be something almost magical.'

'Indeed' he said, trying not to sound as if he thought she was barmy. 'Do you want just a picture theatre?'

'No, a traditional theatre for ballet and operas too, with a screen or a separate room for moving pictures. Do you think you could build or renovate something for this purpose?'

'Of course Your Majesty' he smiled, bowing.

'Good. Would you mind a protégé?' she smiled. 'Young Kurt von Schmidt is fascinated by the arts, and did express to me his desire to be involved in the patronage of arts in Dalnerechensk.'

There was a brief hesitation. 'It would be an honour, Your Majesty.'

Alexandra burbled, shaking a tiny hand at him.

'Do you think she is saying "mama"?' Laura asked as Alexandra started her *mmamm*-ing again.

'I'm honoured to have heard the *Tsesarevna's* first word' he beamed, calling out excitedly to the servants. '*Tsesarevna* Alexandra has said her first words!'

They applauded, cooing and calling congratulations. Laura kissed Alexandra's head, slightly embarrassed, and now could not retract it if she was wrong. So she said her goodbyes and left, heading across to the dining room.

Parliament stood and bowed when she entered the room and she took her seat next to Luka in the centre of the table, noticing that Ilich was absent. Fredrik smiled and brought her some breakfast, inquiring after her health and Alexandra's.

'I believe people think she said her first word this morning' Laura said.

'Really? What was it?' he asked, pleased.

'Mama' Laura blushed.

'That's wonderful!' Ekaterina cried, and the news was passed on in Russian to the others in the room.

'Anna, will you send for a bottle from Gertrude for Alexandra?' Laura asked, sitting her daughter on her knee and sipping her tea.

She noticed Fredrik's glance at her now bare finger as he sat again and she turned politely to Luka, aware that she hardly knew him. She could not remember seeing him before Ilich had taken power, and had not seen him during the defence of Dalnerechensk against Nikita's army. She wondered if he had had any interest in politics before Ilich's bumbling take-over, then thought he hardly had the right to admonish her for nepotism.

'Tell me, Luka, how did you come to be interested in politics?' she asked.

He was quiet, then said carefully:

'I was angry and bitter. But I was ignorant and foolish' he shrugged. 'When I think of us, so full of hatred and desire for revenge, and - and the things we said...' he trailed off. 'It makes me ashamed, and humbled, and earnest to fulfil a promise that perhaps I shouldn't have made.'

Anna returned and handed Laura a bottle. She thanked her absently, turning back to Luka.

'What promise was this?' she asked innocently.

'A better life, higher wages, to make those who starved us to this point pay' he stopped short and lowered his eyes. 'We were so *sure*' he said quietly. 'So *sure* of ourselves, so sure Aleksei was mad and doing it deliberately...' he trailed off again.

'We were going to smash open the treasury, to shower the gold from the castle walls, to -' he stopped again. 'We had no idea' he sighed. 'Had we have known, we wouldn't have -' he broke off.

'Perhaps' she said quietly. 'But it is done now.'

A silence fell between them.

'Perhaps,' he started uncertainly, 'perhaps you might join me riding today' he said. 'I know you were most fond of it before.'

She shut her eyes briefly, so briefly it was only a blink, then accepted, dreading the thought of going to the stables. She had not been there since they had arrived in Dalnerechensk.

'Excellent, I shall send word to Ilich, he will not need me in Parliament today.'

'I could not detain you from you duty!' Laura started to protest but he waved it off.

'We did you a great disservice Your Majesty' he said. 'I feel it is only right for Parliament to court the Monarchy again.'

The little, political flirt reminded her of another, which seemed so far away now.

'Ilich once mentioned that he was married, but I do not think I have ever met his wife.'

Luka's face stayed carefully blank, as if he had been expecting this inquiry for a long time.

'She is presently visiting her sister, who is holidaying in the Caspian. I believe it is an extended stay.'

'Ah, perhaps Ilich should write to her and inquire as to her return. Perhaps she might like to stitch Vsevolod's tapestry with us. So far I am yet to convince the wives of the Parliament. Perhaps your wife…?'

'I am not married, Your Majesty' he smiled, then stood and bowed. 'If you will excuse me, I will see to my apologies and will meet you shortly in the stables.'

Alexandra finished her bottle and Laura raised her to her shoulder to burp her.

'*Euer Hochgeboren*' she smiled at Axel, switching to French. 'Would you care to accompany Luka and I riding in the Hunting Forest? I would be most delighted for you and your nephews to join us.'

'We would be delighted' he accepted. 'Both Fredrik and Gustav speak highly of it.'

'Where is Gustav?' she asked, looking around. 'I have not seen him for many days.'

'Neither have I, Your Majesty' he grinned. 'Since you so kindly provided him with a secretary that spoke French he has been gone all the hours of daylight, and when he returns he is exhausted but so content and joyous.'

'I am glad' she smiled. 'I will put Alexandra in the nursery and join you shortly.'

She rose, causing the table to rise at her departure and headed back up to her rooms on the third floor. She pushed Alexandra into Gertrude's arms with a quick kiss on her head and smiled at the guard outside her door, who saluted. Inside she quickly pulled on a new riding habit and smoothed back her hair, slipping out to the courtyard before the stables. She stopped just before they came into view, dreading the sight that would greet her.

She tried to compose herself as best as she could then marched resolutely towards them. Her first surprise was the stable groom was still only a boy, one she recognised as the Ivanov's groom. Her second surprise was that the groom was the only change. Olaf's Russian Blue Olenka lay curled up in the sunshine, her tail twitching as she dreamed; the scent of hay and horses hung in the air, and the stables were full. Even the hook that Aleksei had hung her from to punish her the night of the revolution was still there. She turned away sharply from it, her breath catching hard in her throat.

'Your Majesty?' Axel asked, concerned.

She turned away from the little group that had just joined her, calling the boy to her.

'That hook is to be removed at once' she said, her voice trembling.

He bowed, terrified. 'Yes Your Majesty' he quavered. 'Only -'

'Only what?' she snapped sharply.

He bowed again, nervously wringing his hands in his shirt.

'Only we need it' he whispered. 'For the horses and carriages and...' his voice faded away.

She shut her eyes, her emotions twisting hard in her.

'Roman!' she called, knowing that he had followed her to the stables.

Quickly he rushed to her and saluted.

'See to it that that hook is removed' she said, and knew she didn't have to explain which hook, as he had been in the courtyard that night. 'Install a new one so that the groom can perform his duties.'

Roman saluted again then headed off to relay orders at a few guards patrolling the grounds.

'Rise and see to the horses for my guests' Laura said quietly, and the terrified groom raced off, bringing out horses that jinked nervously in his grip.

The grey stallion that Laura had been given as a courtship present was still there and she stroked its nose gently, letting it nuzzle her, surprised that it still remembered her after her long absence. Luka boosted her up and she watched as Roman mounted, looking splendid in his new uniform: the royal blue jacket with three black stripes on his cuffs which signified his rank of *Sotnik*, smart black pants and the green sash worn across his chest from the left passant to the right hip.

Fredrik rode up beside her, inquiring quietly in English if she was alright.

'Forgive me for saying so, you have acted somewhat strangely' he said apologetically.

'I am alright' she said quietly. 'And it only seems strange when it is removed from context. How did you enjoy your ride in the forest with my sewing party?' she smiled, changing the subject.

'It was pleasant enough' he said dismissively. 'Tell me, how - how well - acquainted - with *Mademoiselle* Yegorovna are you?' he looked uncomfortable.

'She was my husband's mistress, and daughter to the minister that despised me the most in the Advisory Council' she shrugged, noting his horrified look. 'The vilest rumours came from her. Let me guess, she hinted at one or two unsavoury things while you were riding together.' He blushed and she smiled humourlessly. 'She is simpering coquettishly at you as she is aware of my affection for you' she went on, scratching the stallion between the ears, a blush coming up in her cheeks too.

She turned her horse away, noticing the party was mounted and ready to leave the castle grounds. Roman rode in front and she followed, smiling and waving at the people who called out to her, with much more enthusiasm than she remembered. The sullen resentment for the monarchy had melted away in the wake of the Bodice Treaties and the repel of Nikita's army. She wondered if - even in a small way - it had to do with the knowledge that

Aleksei was dead.

They left King's Gate, the northern most city gate, and headed towards the Hunting Forest on the slopes of the East Valley. It had once been the private retreat of the monarchs but Ilich had declared them public property following the revolution. It had triggered an avalanche of hunting as people sought fresh meat to ease the rationing and the hunger, the legacy of the poor price Russia had paid for tin. The forest had been stripped of her animals in the greatest cull the Principality had ever seen, and now they were virtually silent.

Axel, Fredrik and Kurt chatted quietly together as they rode, Fredrik pointing out the sights to his kin that Ekaterina had pointed out to him earlier. Laura listened to Luka talk about the improvements to the roads they hoped to make now that the thoroughfare from Dalnerechensk through the forest to Kalach was public, and Roman rode silently behind them, keeping watch.

'I would like some private recreation' Laura suddenly said. 'I enjoyed riding in the forest because I could not be observed, and I was away from the slander and gossip and lies. It is a terrible thing to always be in the eyes of people, and have them judge you.'

Luka fell silent.

'But I do agree with you, it was difficult to maintain a thoroughfare from Kalach when the only public road went to Tcherepnin. It is sensible to leave the Hunting Forest road open, and perhaps will encourage more people to settle in the small hamlet.'

'I do not think Ilich will agree to a private forest -' Luka started.

'Perhaps he will agree to restricted rather than private.'

'Restricted to the Royal Family only?'

'Perhaps' she said. 'Perhaps royals and ministers' she shrugged. 'I'm sure there are times when you wish that you could have moments to yourself, when you are not subject to the intense scrutiny of the public.'

There was a flicker on Luka's face, brief and fleeting, but in it Laura read all she wanted to. *So Ilich and his Parliament were unsure of their place in the Principality. They may be providing some much needed upgrade to the infrastructure, but they had been despised at the time of the revolution.*

'Your Majesty!' someone called, waving. 'God bless the Tsaritsa!'

Laura looked, and saw striding down the road towards them from Kalach was Paul, Yosef's son. She called back a warm greeting.

'And how fares you this fine day?' she smiled.

'It is fine indeed, and I have no complaints' he grinned, bowing as he reached them.

'And what brings you to the Hunting Road this morning?'

'I have been to see my brother's widow in Kalach' he said. 'My nephew is growing fine and strong!'

Laura was caught off guard. There was only one family that lived in the hamlet of Kalach, a farmstead where the fleeing royals had hidden for a few short hours the night of the revolution. Laura had been in her nightclothes, and the farmer's wife had given her a dress, one her daughter wouldn't need as she was now married...

She half stammered some commiserations and some farewells, nudging her horse further along the road and lapsing into thought. It was some time before she noticed that Fredrik had ridden up beside her. She gave him a sheepish smile.

'Might I enquire into the tolerance of the people of Dalnerechensk?' he suddenly asked.

She blinked at him, surprised by the odd question. 'Vsevolod led fifty families away from persecution in Novgorod, I would imagine that Dalnerechenskers are very tolerant. Why do you ask me such a question?'

'*Herr* Grünbaum is a Jew.'

She laughed, astounded. 'Good Lord, how did you discover that?'

'He said his family took the German name of Grünbaum in the late seventeen hundreds when his family lived in Sighişoara. Countess Ivanova kindly translated his words for me. I believe it is a town I know as Schäßburg, in the Austrian Empire, and I know that in seventeen eighty seven The Austrian Empire passed a decree requiring an official family name for Jews. Until then they had patronymic names, known as: such and such, son of such and such. I believe the word is "ben" for "son of"' he said. 'He did introduce himself as Yosef *ben* Michael Grünbaum.'

'Well I never' Laura said, smiling.

'I only ask as I know you must be mindful of your public persona, and there are those that hold Jews in ill regard.'

'That is true, and those that hold me in ill regard. Perhaps they are the same' she smiled.

Fredrik looked embarrassed.

'Forgive me, I did not mean -'

'Do not fear, *Euer Hochwohlgeboren*, I only jest. Thank you for your kind thoughts of my public persona.'

They were interrupted when Gustav burst out of the trees, his hair tousled, the knees and elbows of his clothes muddied, the front of his coat dirty as if he'd often wiped his hands there. He had a few leaves grasped in his hand and was waving it, wildly excited.

'*Filipendula vulgaris!*' he cried, charging down to them, his harassed looking secretary hurrying after him. '*Sehes du* Fredrik! *Es ist wunderbar!*'

He saw the rest of the party's amused expressions and quickly composed himself, brushing at the dirt on his clothing.

'I'm sorry, Your Majesty' he said, smoothing back his hair. 'This plant, *Filipendula vulgaris*, has great medicinal properties -'

His enthusiastic lecture was interrupted with a shout. The party turned to see two soldiers riding frantically towards them. Out of the corner of her eye she saw Roman's hand fall on the rifle he had slung over his shoulder. The two riders pulled up shortly, their horses stamping and snorting.

'Your Majesty, you must come back!' one cried. 'Your mother!'

'What?' she cried, frightened.

'Your father sent us for you!' the second cut in, short of breath. 'Quickly!'

Laura didn't wait for any more news but spurred her horse back to the castle, hearing the others fall in behind her, struggling to keep up with her. People scattered out of her way as she galloped along Castle Street, the stallion's hooves sparking on the cobblestones. She yanked hard on the reins and dropped to the ground, turning the horse loose, unmindful of anything but the desperate need to find her father and Lady Anne.

She burst into the castle and raced up the stairs, calling out for her father, aware that Roman was trailing behind her. She could hear wailing coming from Aleksei's old room and burst in, crying out wildly.

Lady Anne was standing by the window, wailing loudly, and Luke was trying desperately but fruitlessly to comfort her. Ilich suddenly appeared behind her, a telegram in his hand.

'We just got the news this morning' he said apologetically.

Laura snatched it and read it. Axel, Kurt, Gustav, Fredrik and Luka crowded into Luke's rooms, worried looks on their faces.

'An earthquake has destroyed San Francisco' she said, the telegram fluttering from fingers that couldn't feel anymore. 'There are fires raging out of control.'

'My God, how terrible' Axel said softly. 'Does Lady Anne have any family in San Francisco?'

'It would appear so' she said, then gently herded the von Schmidt family, Roman, Luka and Ilich out of the room, closing the door on Lady Anne's wailing. 'They should not be disturbed in this time of grief and mourning' she went on. 'We shall endeavour to find what information we can.'

'Yes Your Majesty' Luka said, bowing slightly.

She shut her eyes and turned away, unsure what to do. She hardly knew Lady Anne enough to give her comfort, and to her shame, was slightly annoyed with her wailing. Instead she left them and climbed the stairs to the nursery, where Alexandra lay on a sheepskin rug, learning to roll herself over.

21

One week later a new telegram had arrived, and Laura had made a public announcement and a small prayer from the walls of the castle, aided by a new microphone, the speakers turned towards the crowd gathered on the village green. Dalnerechensk was pleased to hear that Lady Anne's family was safe, though homeless, and their thoughts and prayers were with those who had not survived.

She had sat twice more in Parliament, listening to their discussions, listening to Petrovich Kamanin's application for the abandoned grain warehouse nearest the city centre to be transformed into a theatre. Ilich and Luka had been surprised, but agreed, and another teacher who spoke Russian and French was employed as Kurt's translator for the enterprise. Maksim had made a snide aside to Lev about having to close the new school if all the teachers were used for the queen's pet projects.

The valley was growing warmer as the days had passed, and lush new shoots were appearing in the castle gardens. Laura, Ekaterina, Tatiana, Emilie and Lady Anne had taken the silk tapestries across the pretty stone bridge that spanned the river near Dalnerechensk and had spread blankets on the ground, stitching in the warm sunshine. Near them sat Gertrude and Claudette, mindfully watching over Helmut and Alexandra as they played together, waving their arms and legs and laughing.

Kurt stood on the banks of the river, gloomily skipping stones into it, bored and unwilling to partake of the more refined pursuits of reading aloud or drawing, as Gustav and Fredrik were doing. Laura watched him as she paused to rethread her needle, feeling sorry for him. There was no one his own age to befriend, and none who spoke German. She wondered briefly if Piotr Grigorevich spoke French, and made up her mind to ask Fedor how the boy was doing.

Kurt briefly perked up when he saw Karl strolling down towards them and ran to the stone bridge to meet him. Karl greeted him warmly, stopping to admire the view of the fortified town from the bridge. Laura had to admit it was an impressive sight. The walls were amber in the midday sun, and the snow had melted away to reveal dark green grass. The river was full of ice melt, bubbling and gushing round the rocks, rushing into the wide moat.

It had been rediscovered during the defence of Dalnerechensk, a wide, deep and steeply sided ha-ha that redirected the river to flow around the city walls. Some time ago the moat had been mostly drained, semi filled in, boarded over, covered with turf and forgotten. Ilich had decided to return the moat to its original design, which meant re-digging the channels from the river, and building bridges for the roads and railway lines that had been undermined.

Laura smiled as Emilie stood, greeting her husband warmly as he joined them, bowing to Laura.

'Good day *Euer Hochgeboren*. Have you come to join my sewing party?' she teased.

He laughed, ruffling the hair of his little brother.

'Dear me no Your Majesty, I have come to rescue Kurt from it' he grinned. 'Though he might not appreciate the rescue.'

'I will!' Kurt cried.

'I have delayed his education too long and he will be fourteen soon. I believe it is time to send him to Göttingen University.'

Kurt fell quiet at that, his face clearly struggling with mixed emotions. Karl laughed to see the disappointment, and said something soothing in German, taking his wife's hand.

'But I have one small bit to cheer you' he went on. 'The Intercalated Games began a few days ago in Athens, and I have had an invitation from *Onkel* Kristin to join him. He quite recommends them, and has asked to see his godson.'

Emilie glanced at Laura. 'My pleasure for Athens would be dampened with the sadness of leaving Dalnerechensk and the dear friends I have here.'

'But of course you must go' Laura smiled. 'And hurry back, I shall miss you terribly!'

'When do we go?' Kurt asked excitedly.

'Tomorrow, and we shall be but three weeks' he promised Laura.

'I'll go pack!' Kurt cried and raced back to Dalnerechensk.

Laura watched him go, aware of the looks that Karl sent Fredrik and Emilie. *So they were all going* she thought, and quickly pushed down the pang she felt at the thought of Fredrik's absence.

'You will of course stay for the banquet tonight' she asked.

'Of course' he assured her.

Ekaterina sighed dreamily. 'It has been such a long time since we had dinner and dancing' she said. 'We used to have it very night before -' she stopped, their eyes turning to the newest member of their sewing circle.

Nineczka Rukavishnikova was a woman permanently in the airs of her own importance and displeasure. Her small, mean mouth was twisted down at the corners and puckered so tightly in furious and put upon displeasure that looking at her reminded Laura of an anteater with bad indigestion. She was thin and ungraceful, her fingers stabbing at the tapestry, irritated with a task and people she saw as beneath her. Laura secretly wondered if she was behind the revolution, and had sent her clever and quick-tempered husband to do her will.

'- before poor Tsar Constantinovich passed away' Ekaterina finished, rallying magnificently.

'It is hard to think he has been gone nearly a year' said Zarya Drevin, sister to the Minister for Public Works, and was shushed rudely by Nineczka, even though she had not understood the French conversation completely.

Laura's thoughts turned to the final days of his life, lying crippled from a stroke or a heart attack in the hay of a milk cart, unable to get a doctor for him as they had fled into the night. He had lasted two miserable days while the rain had poured down, and they had dug his grave with their bare hands, burying him in his nightshirt and Laura's shawl, a hastily removed bracket from the milk cart as a make-shift Sword of State. Despite the pretty setting they had found it was still demeaning and insulting for a tsar to lie with no proper tomb.

She stood up quickly.

'If you will excuse me, ladies, I have a few things I must do before the ceremony tonight' she said and left, aware that Roman was following at a discreet distance.

Peter Kamanin had made him *Sotnik* - captain - of the Vsevolod Guards, and since then he had taken it upon himself to act as her personal guard, shadowing her whenever she left the castle. It reminded her of the earliest days in her marriage to Aleksei, when Fedor would shadow her at Tsar Constantinovich's request.

'Roman?' she called, stopping suddenly.

'Yes Your Majesty?' he asked, quickly coming to her side.

'Where do they bury the tsars in Dalnerechensk?'

'In the mausoleum in the Macherna cemetery' he said.

'Show me.'

'I suggest we get horses Your Majesty, it is a bit of a walk.'

Laura agreed and they returned to the castle stables. She noticed the hook had been replaced with another, newer hook, and in a different place. She mounted her stallion and waited for Roman to mount then trotted down Castle Street.

She stopped when they reached the Avenue of Heroes, the new road that branched away from Castle Street and led to the Northern Border, lined by the graves where they had buried those fallen in the defence of Dalnerechensk. She dismounted and gave her reins to Roman, paying her respects to each man who had died, all the way to the wall.

Nikita's army had camped here she recalled, gazing at the empty fields of Russia on the other side. His cannon had destroyed this section of the wall and men and weapons had poured through, intent on the destruction of Dalnerechensk. Stone masons had designed pretty arches and two of the cannon sat in them, carefully orientated so the concrete-filled barrels pointed at the central gap and not at Russia or Dalnerechensk.

Russian graves lined the wall outside Dalnerechensk, a small plaque dedicating the resting place for the soldiers was affixed to the wall, carefully worded so as not to glorify an enemy of Dalnerechensk. Inside the wall, at this new border crossing was a guard post, and a tall tower called the North Beacon, which housed a bright light to be lit when a guard saw any enemy approaching from Moscow and St Petersburg.

She greeted the guard at the post who saluted her, standing stiffly to attention. She made some comment that commended his attention to his duty then quietly left, heading slowly back down the avenue, taking the reins from Roman again.

He mounted wordlessly and followed her to Miner's Way, the street that headed up the western flank of Liberty Valley, past Ladozhskoye to the mining village of Macherna. At Ladozhskoye she paused on the road. The black stained ground where the Ivanov house had once stood was visible even from here, even after all this time. Since their return Ekaterina and Grigory had lived in the castle as Laura's guests, but she wondered if they would ever rebuild their house; if they still wanted to belong to the Principality that nearly cost them their lives.

She decided not to investigate the ruins of the once beautiful house, to wander in the gardens where Aleksei had made love to her, and she turned her horse quietly onwards to the pretty village on the ridge in a reflective mood. In the main street of Macherna was a large crowd, watching a man on an upturned beer crate, who was waving his hands and shouting at the crowd.

A strange feeling of *déjà vu* crept up on Laura: the moment, the stance, the crowd; brought to mind the evening she had snuck into the bar dressed in disguise and heard Ilich denounce the Monarchy. Roman rode up beside her but she reached across, laying a hand that trembled only slightly on his arm. The crowd did not look happy with what the man was saying.

'It is a travesty!' he protested. 'If there must be a monarchy, and I do not say this lightly, there should be none at all, but if there *must*, then it cannot be her!'

The crowd booed and jeered, but one or two looked thoughtful.

'Do you know who he is Roman?' she asked quietly.

'Seryeshka Shcherbakov, Nineczka's brother' he answered, his distaste for the family clear in his features.

'All I'm saying is what good could she do?' Seryeshka went on hotly, shouting over the growing opposition. 'I would rather have some stupid, mad, sick boy on that toilet than a hermaphrodite, foreign *Sooka!*'

Laura clutched Roman's arm tightly, stilling him.

'Did I kiss your cheek?' she asked.

Silence radiated outwards and Seryeshka swivelled towards her, his face drained of colour and his eyes rolled so far back in his head they appeared white.

'What?' he croaked.

'Did I kiss your cheek?' she asked again.

'No, he hid in the cellar!' cried a woman, who Laura guessed was either his unhappy wife or a vindictive neighbour.

The crowd roared with laughter and cruel comments, pouring scorn and derision on him. Laura held her hands up, quieting down the crowd.

'I too was in the cellar of the castle' she said, but the crowd interrupted her.

'You were on the walls, my son saw you!' one cried.

'You were fighting right alongside the men!' another cried.

'I wanted to' she smiled. 'But *Sotnik* Prokofiev, with rather more sense than I, ordered me to the castle -'

'Where you made pies for us!' a man with one eye shouted.

'Where you cracked that bastard Rurik on the noggin with a rolling pin!' shouted another.

Laura had done no such thing, but the rumour that she had gave her some small satisfaction.

'Yeah?' Seryeshka sneered. 'Well he cracked hers on her headboard first!'

There was a hiss of in-drawn breath, but before the crowd could turn into a mob soldiers arrived, spreading out to quickly take control of the situation. Seryeshka was arrested, his hands roughly tied behind his back. There were some subtle looks at Laura, wondering what she was going to do or say, but she wisely ignored the arrest, turning to the crowd to answer Seryeshka's question.

'What good could I do?' she asked quietly. 'I could give you a defence of this beautiful land that Vsevolod would have been proud of. I could give you the Bodice Treaties; recognition from Russia and support from Germany. I could give you higher wages and deer meat to alleviate the hunger. I could give you a woman who so loves this land and her people that I would lay down my life beside yours to save it. And I could give you a daughter of Vsevolod, a legacy and a lineage!'

The crowd cheered, but she could see not all of them were, and some looked distracted and thoughtful as they applauded. Her heart sank a little, though she didn't show it. *Bloody men and their bloody chauvinism!* she thought angrily, smiling and blowing kisses to the crowd. *Why does it have to matter so much? The world was changing; there were temperance and suffrage movements worldwide. Britain's tiny colony in the South Pacific, New Zealand, had already given women the right to vote last century, and the Grand Principality of Finland, part of the Russian Empire, had granted women the right to vote* and *stand for election, which meant they could end up with a female prime minister. So could we* she added, *if Ilich ever decides to hold elections.*

She waved goodbye to the crowd, nudging her stallion through the throng, heading past the village, Roman following close behind her. She called back to him for directions to the cemetery and headed through the pretty pines, in the opposite direction to the path that led to the mine.

The Macherna Cemetery was the only one in the Principality, a place where princes and paupers had been buried alike. Laura dismounted and tied the stallion's reins over a low branch, stepping through the rusted metal gate. The large mausoleum for the Vakhtangov family dominated the centre of the cemetery, the plots laid out in square patterns around it. Laura walked quietly through the garden of headstones, aware Roman was still shadowing her.

Someone had spent a lot of time and money crafting the marble mausoleum. It was the size of a small house, styled in the elegant lines of a classical temple. A carved base relief of the Vakhtangov Coat of Arms was mounted above the doorway. A wrought iron gate barred entrance to the crypt, though Laura could see into the dim chamber beyond. A large marble casket stood in the centre of the room, topped with an effigy of a stone knight. Carved into the end of the casket closest to the door was the name ВСЕВОЛОД. Around the sides of the crypt were smaller marble caskets, and some large black urns stood in niches that had been cut into the walls.

'Roman?'

'Yes Your Majesty?'

She turned away from the graves to look at him carefully.

'Why does it matter so much that the monarch has to be a man?'

He looked uneasy.

'If I can speak honestly Your Majesty, it is because the bloodline of Vsevolod was the one constant thing in the Principality, and that matters now, more than ever. There was a *revolution*, and suddenly everything is different. There are peasants in a Parliament, new uniforms, new laws, new colours…

'The monarchy is all that is left of the old ways, and even then it is changing. A woman, and a daughter…' he trailed off again. 'The people love you, Your Majesty, but they want the monarchy to stay the same.'

Laura bit her lip. 'Will they ever accept me Roman? Will they ever accept my daughter on Vsevolod's throne?'

He shrugged, helpless. 'I don't know Your Majesty.'

She sighed quietly, looking back at Vsevolod's large sarcophagus.

'You cast a long shadow, most revered father' she sighed. 'Come then, Roman, I have a speech to write. I will return to the castle now.'

He saluted and fell into step behind her.

22

Laura stood at the altar in Dalnerechensk's cathedral, wearing a white silk gown. Across her body lay the green sash that tied the medallion for the Order of Vsevolod at her hip, the blue enamel vibrant against the silk, the diamond surround winking in the light of thousands of candles. At her throat she wore the strands of sapphires, emeralds and diamonds that Paul had given her and she wore the new crown she had commissioned.

There had been a ripple of murmurings as she had stepped out of the carriage, ripples that had preceded her into the cathedral, the only place big enough to hold this ceremony. The whispers had made the cathedral sound like a cote of roosting pigeons, and there had been rustlings as people craned to see and turned to pass on the gossip. It had whispered that she was wearing Vsevolod's crown, that she was wearing the heavy ermine mantle of state, that she was carrying the golden sceptre of Royal Authority. It had whispered back that it was not Vsevolod's crown, but something finer and feminine, and it had watched her as she had walked the nave, Ekaterina carefully holding the thick fur for her.

She stood at the altar and spoke of the Defence of Dalnerechensk and the honour that each man deserved, spotting the scowling pair of Shcherbakov siblings beside Ilich Rukavishnikov. She let her gaze pass over them and alight on the von Schmidt family, noting the reserved expression on Fredrik's face with some surprise.

A fanfare started as she finished and heads turned to see Peter Kamanin, handsome in the blue uniform of the Vsevolod Guards, march solemnly along the nave. At his hip was the dress sword from his old Palace Guard uniform. He was wearing all his decorations from his previous post, and the simple medal that Ilich had presented to him which commemorated the battle. He reached her and bowed low before her, remaining bent till the fanfare stopped.

Fedor stepped up to the altar, holding a cushion on which rested a plain sword. It was Vsevolod's sword, nicked and scratched, the leather of the hilt so worn and ancient it was like teak, and impossible to tell where the edge of the strips overlapped another. Laura grasped it, commanding Peter to kneel before her. With great ceremony she laid the sword on his shoulder, announcing him as Peter Kamanin, *Graf* of Pavlodar.

It had been a farm at the southern end of Liberty Valley, abandoned decades ago and used as free grazing land for the alpine cattle owned by farmers who lived close to Pavlodar. It had been absorbed into the various properties and lands that the crown had owned in Dalnerechensk many years ago, and Peter would need to rebuild the house as the small farmstead was crumbling beyond repair.

Laura placed the sword reverently back on Fedor's cushion and waited till he presented her with the second Vsevolod medallion that she had ordered. Peter rose and she pinned it gently to his left breast, under his impressive medals, biting her lip slightly in concentration. He bowed deeply again, taking the edge of the ermine robe and kissing it.

The cathedral broke into applause and he rose, managing the difficult walk backwards down the stairs, bowed in respect to Laura. He then turned to present himself to the crowd and his soldiers leapt to their feet, calling out *bravo* and other cries of recognition and approval. The fanfare started again and Laura stepped sedately down the steps, aware that Ekaterina had fallen in behind her to hold up the heavy robe.

She took Peter's arm and they walked the length of the nave and got into a waiting open carriage at the foot of the stairs, feeling the *déjà vu* of her wedding day sit uncomfortably in her heart. She smiled and waved to the people that called out to her, waiting for Ekaterina and Ilich to join her in the carriage. Roman closed the door and quickly mounted, riding in the procession behind the carriage, keeping a close eye on the crowd.

The air was slightly chilly and she shivered, pulling the robe tighter around her, thankful that it was only a short ride to the castle. The ballroom, she knew, was still being repaired, and although it was now weather proof it had none of the decorative finery it should have had. Instead the dinner and reception would be held in the dining room, and as such had to be kept to a small affair.

It hadn't been difficult. She had sent courteous telegrams to all the living relatives of the Vakhtangov family and had received polite and cool declines or no reply from most of them. A number of telegrams had also been sent to Ilich's ministers, and the more socialist members of the party had sent back chillingly civil refusals. The end result was a mixture of unimportant royals and unimportant ministers, soldiers and foreign guests. She wondered what they would all talk about.

Music was already floating out of the dining room when they stepped into the wide foyer. Anna quickly took the heavy mantle and sceptre from Laura, bundling them up and carrying them to her rooms. She brushed away a few stray strands of fur from her neck and shoulders, patting her hair before slipping her arm into Peter's and leading him to the dining room.

There were a few people inside who had not been at the ceremony: two ancient sisters, spinster third cousins of Aleksei; his elderly first cousin once removed Elena, and her huge squabbling brood of thirteen daughters, some with squabbling daughters of their own; and his frail third cousin once removed Varvara, grandmother to Piotr Grigorevich, and married to Maksim Yegorov's uncle. Beside her was eleven year old Anna, the consumptive-looking sister to Piotr, who looked as if she had been dragged from her sick-bed to attend.

They rose as Laura entered and bowed creakily. Laura wondered if it were the bones in their knees or their corsets that made so much noise and she waved them back to their seats, heading with Peter to a place of honour that had been set beside hers for him. *They may be old and unimportant* she thought, *but they are all watching my new crown like vultures!*

The musicians struck up again, and the room began to fill with people from the cathedral. Laura watched them as they ate, noticing how they took surreptitious looks at her crown, and how out of place the soldiers looked. When the meal was cleared away she stood, causing the room to rise too. She curtseyed to Peter, who bowed, then took her hand to lead her down to the area reserved for dancing.

She let herself relax as the evening wore on, and noticed how many times the charming von Schmidt family asked Nineczka to dance despite their many kicked shins and trodden toes. She caught sight of Ekaterina's grin and realised her friend had played a trick on Nineczka, who was famous for her dislike of dancing. She bit down a smile, noticing how several others were trying to do the same thing.

She spotted Kurt with Anna Vakhtangovna and noticed how animated his face was as they talked in French, and how charmingly she smiled at him. Laura smiled, but it cracked slightly when she saw Fredrik laughing with Tatiana, her arm tucked into his elbow. Quickly she turned her attention back to Luka in time to catch:

'- and we thought it might be a good idea for the Revolution's anniversary.'

She blinked, caught off-guard. Luka was watching her with a slightly worried expression. It grew even more worried when she didn't respond straight away. *A year* she thought, slightly surprised. *Has it really been a year? Tsar Constantinovich has been dead nearly a year!* And then a small part of her whispered: *Your husband has been dead a year…*

'Forgive me, I did not mean -' Luka started but she waved him off.

'Why do you think it would be a good idea?' she asked, rallying from her inattention magnificently, hoping he would reveal what he was talking about in his explanation.

'Well, we want to show that we are forward thinking,' he started uncertainly, carefully not stating the long held belief of monarchy being backwards and stuffy, 'and we have heard great things about wireless telegraph. It could greatly improve communication in emergencies, and provide news readings…' he trailed off. 'We thought perhaps we could have a demonstration for the anniversary, and a reading of an account of Vsevolod's life, to show that we uphold the traditions and the persons sacred to the Principality' he finished, looking at her carefully.

'It sounds interesting, I should like to hear a transmission' she said almost absently, curtseying when the dance finished.

Luka bowed and she turned away, calling an end to the evening's proceedings and thanking them all for coming.

The soldiers were the first to leave, saluting her and their commander then marching single file out into the night. Laura stood in the foyer and farewelled each of her guests as they left, noticing how Nineczka limped and hung onto Ilich for support. Peter Kamanin bowed deeply and bid her good night, and she waved the carriages goodbye on the doorstep, her breath frosting in the night air.

Quickly she slipped inside and the soldiers on duty closed the doors, locking them against the cold. She listened to the castle settling down for the night, watched as the musicians headed towards the kitchens for their supper or their pay, then climbed the stone stairs to her room, greeting Anna quietly.

'Do you have a foot bath or some other small basin?'

'Yes Your Majesty' she smiled.

'Good. Go and fetch it and then come with me' she smiled, waiting till her servant had arrived back with the bath.

She led the way to Fredrik's room and knocked on the door. He answered it, his jacket gone and his hair loose about his face.

'Your Majesty!' he said, surprised and bowing low.

'I could not help but notice how many times you danced with Madame Rukavishnikova and how many times you winced, though it were a good number less than were merited' she grinned. 'I have brought Anna, who is excellent in ministering to sore feet.'

'How very kind of you, please come in' he smiled, opening the door for her to step through.

Her gaze travelled sadly over his trunks, which sat already packed in the room.

'I shall miss you and your family while you are in Athens. You must promise to write to me' she said, turning to watch Anna place the footbath on the floor and enter his dressing room for water.

'I promise Your Majesty' he said.

She looked around the room again, feeling awkward, wanting to blurt out what she knew she couldn't.

'Well, Anna will minister to you and return to me afterwards' she said, translating to her servant, who curtsied. 'Sleep well and *bon voyage Euer Hochwohlgeboren*' she said finally and left, heading quickly back to her room.

Inside she cursed herself quietly and then brushed her hands over her face to calm down. It had been a silly gesture, she had no idea what she intended by sending Anna to him, only wanting to find some excuse to be in his company again tonight. *And how handsome he is in the firelight, with his blonde hair loose!* she thought, shutting her eyes dreamily.

She shook herself then began to unpin her hair, shaking it out to ease the tension in her scalp then set about taking off the medallions and jewellery she was wearing. There was a quiet tap on the door and Anna slipped in.

'He sent me away' she said by way of explanation. 'I think he was rather embarrassed. He did give me this to give to you' she said, handing over a small box tied with a ribbon.

Laura untied it and pulled the lid off, aware that Anna was craning to see into the box too. Nestled under a layer of tissue paper was an emerald necklace, decorated with tiny pearls. Anna gasped then quickly helped Laura fasten it around her throat, bringing a mirror for her to see.

'Beautiful' she sighed dreamily. 'Emerald sits well on your skin Your Majesty.'

'Thank you Anna' she smiled, unfastening it. 'Now help me undress, I feel as if Nineczka has spent all evening standing on my toes too!'

Anna giggled and knelt to pull off her shoes.

23

Maksim threw down the newspaper on the table in Parliament Chambers, slamming himself into a chair. The headline shouted *Did I kiss your cheek?* in the largest, boldest font the typesetters had.

'This is intolerable!' he shouted. 'This cannot go on! You have to do something about this!' he spat at Ilich.

'What do you want me to do? Tell her: Stop making people like you?' he snapped, skimming through the article, wincing at the mention of what his brother-in-law had called the Tsaritsa.

'You can tell her she cannot marry Fredrik von Schmidt!'

'Why? Do you have a brother you'd like to introduce her to?'

The temperature lowered by several degrees in the room and ministers looked at each other carefully.

'She has said that the wireless telegraph is a good idea' Luka said, changing the subject. 'She would like to hear a demonstration -'

'He is only a *baron*' Maksim interrupted. 'A rich German, nothing more' he sneered. 'And he will become our *Tsar!* he shouted. '*Tsar!* Is that any quality of man to lead a country?'

'Be mindful of your company Maksim' Luka snapped. 'And do not forget Vsevolod himself was only a rich Russian -'

'Don't patronise me -' Maksim started, but the ensuing fight was interrupted with a sharp cough from Yuri.

'It must be said,' Lev started, 'that there are some factions who do not wish to see her as Tsaritsa, even as *Vdova*, and it is not just Maksim and myself that feel this way. Many of the Vakhtangov family feel she is too common for them. But,' he went on reluctantly, 'it may not be easy to remove her, she has become immensely popular since the Revolution, and if this government deposes her I fear an equally incensed mob will over-throw democracy and vie for autocratic monarchy again.'

Maksim shot him a glance and he stopped talking.

'The monarchy is now redundant' Ilich said wearily. 'Why should it matter who she marries?'

'It matters because of Vsevolod's blood' Ivan sighed, setting down his pen. 'Europe has fought for years, opposing and deposing thousands of kings and emperors, but Dalnerechensk has had one unbroken family since she came into being. One intact lineage; more than just her ruling family but Dalnerechensk itself. We all know that gentlemen, all school children know that.'

'Yes, but -' someone started.

'*Tsesarevna* Alexandra -' began another.

'Is just a baby' Luka cut in. 'She is no potent symbol of personality that people can rally around. Perhaps the people might accept a daughter of Vsevolod on the throne, but she could not rule for another eighteen years, and that is a long time. If the *Vdova* Tsaritsa remarried, what would happen if her next children were male?'

'They would not become tsar, you know that! Why ask such a stupid -'

'Because it isn't' Luka cut off Ilich. 'She has practically re-invented herself as Vsevolod, defender of Dalnerechensk, repeller of rebellious Russian invasions, punisher of Russian greed, saviour of the poor and suffering. She is spoken of in revered tones and compared more and more to Vsevolod each day. She is also young, witty, and highly attractive. It is unconscionable that she remain unwedded and unbedded. She will have more children, gentlemen, and they may be boys. It is bad enough to have a woman on the throne, but do you want men without the blood of Vsevolod to sit in his place?'

'It might not be so bad' spoke up another minister. 'After all, we do have a *new* Vsevolod.'

He coughed uncomfortably under their looks.

'Come come' snapped another. 'We spent years organising this! *We overthrew the monarchy! Vsevolod's bloodline!* Did the things we say and swear by then mean nothing now? There was to be no more blood, bad blood, *mad* blood, and now you are all squabbling about how to keep her on the throne?!'

'What about Piotr Grigorevich?' Maksim reminded them.

'What if he married *Tsesarevna* Alexandra?'

'Don't call her that!'

'He is thirteen years her senior!'

'What if he married the tsaritsa?'

'He is just a child!'

'She is a mere few years his senior, she is only seventeen -'

'And he will grow into a man soon enough' leered another. 'If he is anything like his father, may he rest in peace, then -'

'*Are you all completely mad??*' screeched Maksim. '*Get* rid *of her!*'

Ilich glared at him. 'We will not be ordered by you!' he thundered. 'We are *not* your servants! How dare you sit there with your titles and wealth and dare to *presume* to -'

'If you care not for my wealth Ilich you have only to say and I will stop funding your projects' Maksim said icily.

A thick, embarrassed and uncomfortable silence fell in the room. It was interrupted when the door was pushed open to admit Laura. She eyed the room carefully, aware of the tense atmosphere.

'Forgive my lateness gentlemen' she said, closing the door behind her.

'This is Parliament, *Velikaja Knjaginja*, not your privy council -'

'Nor your servants' she interrupted coolly, indicating that she had heard at least the last few sentences uttered in this room. Ilich wondered briefly just how much she had heard.

'We did not expect to see you today, Your Majesty' he said, suddenly drained.

'I have said my farewells to the von Schmidt family, and I have a pressing issue to raise with the good members of Parliament.'

Ilich wiped his mouth, and silently pulled out a chair for her to sit in. She sat and motioned for the other ministers, who had hastily scrambled to their feet when she had entered, to sit as well.

'I was kindly reminded last night that the first anniversary for the revolution is approaching and that Parliament has in mind some festivities and a public demonstration of a wireless telegraph to show Dalnerechensk a bright new future. We cannot deny that even the monarchy is affected by these changes, perhaps accepted, perhaps not.'

Again Ilich wondered just how much she had heard of their discussion before entering, wondering if she was listening at the keyhole.

'It is in my interest, and in yours, that I make this next suggestion. Tsar Constantinovich died two days after the revolution in Russia, and he lies in a grave in foreign soil. He was a man that Dalnerechensk loved, and it is a terrible thought that he is so far away from us.

'I suggest, gentlemen, that this Parliament announces that they are going to retrieve the body of Tsar Constantinovich and lay it to rest in the Vakhtangov tomb. A sincere and reverential laying to rest of the old man, the old ways, will speak in favour of this new Parliament, this new way forward.'

Ilich had to admire her artfulness. *No wonder they forgot she was only seventeen when she thought in circles like this* he smiled. And he could imagine just what effect that would have in Dalnerechensk too: a respectful goodbye to the old ways, a celebration of a new way, new technologies, new roads, new entertainment…

'And what about your husband?' Maksim interrupted. 'I notice you were not sending us out to look for him!'

'I do not know where his body is' she said quietly, shutting her eyes. 'Perhaps once he may not have deserved a grave in Dalnerechensk, but he was also once loved by you, once loved by me' her voice faded away to a whisper. 'He may still be alive.'

'Do you believe that?' Ilich asked, folding his hands carefully. *Do you fear that?*

'No' she said, then cleared her throat of the lump. 'No I believe he is dead, and I don't believe we will find his body, not after this time.'

'Do you think you could find Tsar Constantinovich's grave again?' Yuri asked.

'Possibly, but I do not intend to go traipsing through Russian forests looking for it. Anna and Fedor are needed by me, but Anna's husband Mikhail was Aleksei's servant and with us in Russia, he will assist the party to find the grave again.'

'Very well' said Ilich, eyeing his ministers. 'All those in favour of finding Tsar Constantinovich's body and bringing it back to Dalnerechensk?'

All hands went up.

'Then it is to be organised immediately and the party should set off as soon as possible. Was there anything else you wanted Your Majesty?'

'No. Are there any issues that need my attention?'

'There is the succession crisis…' mumbled Lev.

'I see. And would you kindly explain exactly what the crisis is? The Vakhtangov line did not fall with the death of Aleksei as once feared and Alexandra is the bloodline of Vsevolod. Is the crisis because she doesn't have a penis?'

Luka coughed hard to cover his laugh and even Ilich's mouth twitched. Lev glanced at Maksim and shuffled his feet.

'These are changeable times, gentlemen' she went on. 'You have a Head of State and a Parliament that I have faith in. The voice of the common man is represented here, as is the voice of the nobility and the monarchy. The authority of law and justice and rule comes not from just one anymore, but from all of us, and so it is not as important that the highest office be filled with the highest man. The voice on the throne speaks for the history of the blood and the Principality, and for the interests of the royal family. I dare say that a woman can speak for those. What woman would not speak for the honour of her family and her home?'

Ilich glanced at Luka, aware of the way he gazed admiringly at Laura, and had to marvel at the clever way she had turned around several of her most emphatic detractors. By styling herself as a mother, the monarchy's mother, *their* mother; meant that she would forever cement her importance to them in their minds. No self-respecting man would ever disrespect his mother.

She rose causing them to rise too.

'Good day gentlemen' she said. 'Thank you for your kind assistance.'

They bowed and she bowed back, slipping out of Parliament Chambers, closing the door behind her. She paused by the door, in the pretence of rubbing a lash from her eye and heard Maksim say:

'You must do something!'

'No' Ilich answered. 'I will not overthrow the Monarchy again.'

Laura smiled and slipped up to the nursery.

24

'*How big?!*' she gasped, astounded.

'Thirteen inches!' Anna giggled. 'At least that's what they say.'

Laura's mind boggled and she glanced at Ekaterina, who was the only one sewing with her today. The pretty Hungarian was in peals of laughter, her hands on her corsets to stop them splitting.

'But he is a holy man!' she gasped. 'How can they know that?'

'Well, they *call* him *starets*,' Anna went on, a word Laura knew that meant 'elder', a title used for monk-confessors. 'It is said that he was also a pilgrim to Greece and Jerusalem, and that he may be involved with the *khlysty* -'

'*Khlysty?*' Laura asked, glancing at Ekaterina.

'It is a banned religious sect in Russia' she explained, sitting up. 'They renounced the Orthodox priesthood, veneration of saints and all the holy books, claiming they could communicate directly with the Holy Spirit. But it is claimed they have orgiastic rituals and indulge in flagellation.' She switched to French to add: '*Khlyst* is Russian for whip, and *khlysty* is a corruption of their proper name of *Khristovovery*, or *Khristy*, Christ believers.'

'And he is accepted in high Russian society?' Laura went on, astounded.

'They say he is a drunkard and a buggerer, often fornicating with prostitutes' Ekaterina added.

'He is not accepted by all, but is very popular with women -'

'I can't imagine why!' Ekaterina interrupted and doubled over in stitches

96

again.

'How can this man be so revered by the tsaritsa?'

'Rasputin can cure her son Alexei through prayer and laying hands on him when he has his bouts of illness' Anna explained.

'Perhaps you should invite him to Dalnerechensk Your Majesty' Ekaterina giggled. 'I've been troubled by a terrible affliction, and could do with some holy hands on me.'

'A terrible thing that you have not consulted our fine physicians' Laura scolded.

'Ah do not fret my friend, I am fine. I only want to see it. *Him*' she corrected theatrically and doubled over again.

Laura tried not to laugh but Ekaterina's giggling was infectious and soon she was holding her sides to stop them from splitting too. She managed to get herself under control and wiped her eyes, sighing quietly. There was a knock on her door and Fedor stepped in, bowing to them.

'Forgive my intrusion Your Majesty, I have come in regard to some pressing business.'

'Come in Fedor, and what business do you bring?'

His eyes flicked to Ekaterina, who read in them the private nature of their discussions.

'Farewell Laura!' she cried, leaping to her feet. 'I shall ride immediately to Russia and salvation at the hands of a holy man!' she laughed, running out of the room.

Laura smiled and Anna stuffed her handkerchief into her mouth to stop from laughing.

'Anna, take the afternoon off and go see your husband before he leaves' she said, motioning for Fedor to join her at her small desk. When the door clicked closed she turned to him and asked:

'How much money do I have left?'

He blinked then answered 'about four thousand roubles. Ilich was paying you a modest sum that accumulated while you were away, but the cost of the repairs to date and the jewellery have used up nearly eighty percent.'

'What do you suggest Fedor? Ilich still refuses to hand over the contents of Aleksei's will.'

'I believe that is because he has no personal wealth to speak of, or perhaps it is because -' he faltered, then plunged on '- because perhaps it was written long ago and does not name you as beneficiary.'

'I see' she said quietly.

'You must tell the ministers that if they wish to have their own chambers, regardless of whether it is in your home or not, then they have to contribute some funds towards it, and begin to generate some personal income Your Majesty' he said. 'Do you have stocks you could trade, bonds to cash in, personal wealth to earn interest from?'

She paused, thinking briefly of the million pounds hidden in Axel's secret safe. *I could do with that money now* she thought bitterly. *What made me think I could do without it?*

'No I do not' she said. 'Perhaps I could invest a portion of the four thousand roubles.'

'If I may, Your Majesty, I would recommend no more than forty percent to be used in any investment schemes, and the purchase of some stocks -'

'Fedor, you handled all of Tsar Constantinovich's personal affairs didn't you? Is there some wealth that he left that could come to my daughter?'

He looked uncomfortable. 'He personally owned about a million pounds of bonds. There were the family estates that he managed, but his last will left them jointly to Aleksei and Alexander Andrei. There is no death certificate for either of them, and so it is doubtful that the estates will be released to you, at least, not for several years of legal wrestling that will cost you the remainder of your money and a good portion of what you might get.'

Laura sighed quietly. 'Bring me the newspaper then, and advise me.'

He bowed and quickly retrieved the newspaper from the chaise lounge, bowing slightly as he handed it to her.

For the next hour they discussed and compared prices of bonds and investments, stocks and company profits till they were interrupted with Roman announcing the arrival of Luke. Laura quickly concluded her time with Fedor, instructing him to cautiously invest in the two companies they had identified. He bowed to her and then to Luke, leaving them alone.

'Come for a walk with me' he said, leading her down to the castle gardens.

She walked beside him quietly, watching him suck on his lips absently, the way he did when he was thinking deeply.

'What is it Father?' she asked quietly.

He stopped and turned towards her, taking her hands and looking at her carefully.

'Your heart truly is in this place my dear' he said. 'This is your home now. I know you never really had a home, just the dig sites, and the school...' he trailed off. 'But this is your home, and you seem happy here. Are you happy?' he looked worried.

'I am happier than I have been in a long time' she smiled gently. 'It was difficult at first, it is still difficult some days, but I grow a little less hurt each day.'

'I am glad' he said quietly. 'We have been with you these last two months and have watched you grow happy, and smile more...' he trailed off again. 'But Lady Anne and I, we long for our home now. I've come to tell you it is our intention to leave soon, unless,' he stopped, looking at her carefully. 'Unless you can think of some reason for us to stay...?' he faltered, searching for an answer.

'I would like you to stay' she said quietly.

'I know my dear' he said, squeezing her hands gently. 'But if there isn't any reason to stay, then I guess … we can't stay' he finished lamely.

He's asking if there's going to be a wedding any time soon she thought, the flush coming up in her cheeks.

'He is a fine man Laura' he pressed. 'Honourable and charming, kind and generous.'

'Yes, he is all those things, and he will make a fine husband, probably even a fine tsar' she said. 'But things aren't easy Father' she sighed.

'They never are' he smiled sadly. 'But you must choose Laura. What is more important? What the people want or what you want?'

'It isn't as simple as that' she sighed.

'Eventually it is' he smiled. 'You will see that one day Laura. I hope for his sake and yours that day is not too far off.'

They walked in silence for a moment, each lost in their own thoughts. Laura stopped to turn and look up at the window where the Advisory Council had once met. It was here in this garden she had looked up and seen Aleksei watching her, unable to take his eyes off her. He had loved her once, she had known it and had felt it. She shut her eyes, looking away.

'When will you leave?' she asked quietly.

'Within a week or so' he said. 'We hadn't made any definite plans in case we needed to cancel them' he smiled sadly again.

They passed the small fountain, the little icicles dripping steadily from the rim of the bowl onto the path.

'Will you be alright Laura? I don't want to think of you stranded here again…' he stopped, biting his lip hard. 'When I think about what could have happened to you…'

'But it didn't' she soothed him, letting him hug her to him. 'And I had friends to help me. I have friends to help me now too, but the revolution is over, there is no danger to me anymore. All I fear now is Tatiana's terrible tongue' she grinned.

Luke wiped away his tears and kissed her head, pushing her back to look at her.

'If there's anything we can do for you Laura, you only need to ask.'

'Thank you Father' she smiled. 'I could do with a loan.'

'A loan?' he looked surprised.

'Come, perhaps we should talk in my rooms' she said, looking around to see if anyone was listening.

She tucked her arm into his elbow and adroitly propelled him back to the castle.

25

Laura rose and stretched, stepping into the bath Anna had prepared for her. Her servant's eyes were red from crying and she sniffed occasionally as she gently washed Laura's back. Laura shut her eyes, forcefully willing her thoughts not to go sliding back to Olaf again. *A year* she thought miserably. She had busied herself so much to avoid thinking about him, had worked hard at not letting the memories come too close, but the preparations for the recovery of Tsar Constantinovich's body reminded her too strongly of two other bodies she could not lay to rest.

She had read his letter again last night, pressing it to her lips and sobbing quietly, muffling the noise with the corner of her comforter. His words; these last tender things he said to her; brought back the memories of his voice, the feel of his breath on her skin, his quiet strength, the reassuring knowledge that he was always there. She had come to depend on him so completely for her happiness in Dalnerechensk that she didn't ever think she could be happy here without him.

But that wasn't quite true anymore a small part of her had whispered in the quiet hours of the morning. *There was no terror here anymore; no fear of a rebellious and resentful population, no ailing, aging husband to suspect her of cuckolding him, no manipulative snake to twist her round in a silly infatuation. And there was a man, a kind and courteous, gentle man…*

She was sure he loved her. In the night her memory had played that quiet, yearning want in the way he had whispered her name, held her in the darkness of the ruined throne room. In one moment all their courtly pretences were gone, all the watching eyes were gone, the strict social constraints of etiquette stripped away to let their feelings bubble to the surface. It had only been a moment, so small and fleeting, but it lived forever in her memory.

She wondered if Fredrik played that moment over and over in his head, then wondered why he had seemed so distant the last few days. Naturally he had been kind and impeccable, as always, and yet there was a reservation that Laura had sensed, a careful layering of civility between his feelings and his actions. *What had been said to him to make him so careful? Who had said it to him?* It was clear that his family looked to him for guidance in all things, even his young uncle. But Axel had a clear and level head, and knew when advice for his young nephews was needed.

Had Axel told him something? she wondered. *What could he have said?*

She sighed quietly, shutting her eyes. *There were so many things he could have said* she reminded herself. *No doubt there were hundreds of little rumours and whispers about her again, and no shortage of wagging tongues to pass them on. Seryeshka had voiced the darkest one of them all.* Whore. *What could she do in the face of that? It was true.* But would Fredrik believe that of her? She doubted it, he could not bring himself to think ill of her. *So what else could it have been?*

She rubbed her eyes, trying to clear her head. *But this was Dalnerechensk after all* she sighed unhappily. *There was only one thing it boiled down to. It was a morganatic match. Their first tsar had only been a rich noble, with less personal wealth than Fredrik had, and yet the bred-in-the-bone snobbery of the citizens found it somehow beneath them now to have a mere baron even considered for the throne.*

Perhaps it hadn't been Axel after all she thought glumly. *Perhaps Ilich had gone to him, or someone else had said something.*

She stood suddenly, surprising Anna, and stepped out of the bath, wrapping a towel around herself.

'Are you alright Your Majesty?' Anna asked, worried.

'Hm?' she asked distractedly. 'Oh, yes, Anna' she smiled sheepishly. 'Only, it's a year…' she trailed off, knowing that she didn't need to explain anymore.

She turned away, wiping the moisture from her skin, busying herself with finding a dress to wear.

Anna helped her into it, shooting surreptitious looks at her distracted demeanour. Laura thanked her absently then sat at the dressing table while Anna combed out her hair and pulled it expertly into a coif, pinning it in place with pretty pearls.

Laura rose and slipped along to the nursery, greeting Gertrude quietly, wondering how isolated she felt now that she was stranded here without Claudette, any of the von Schmidt family, or the two livery men, Jan and Hermann, that Axel had brought with him. Gertrude brought Alexandra to her and she sat in the nursing chair, talking in her hesitant and limited German to her while she fed her daughter.

Gertrude seemed grateful for this small chance to talk to someone and be understood, and Laura knew how she felt, though Ekaterina had been invaluable for her fluency in French and English. She couldn't imagine how lonely it must be without someone you could talk to. *When Kurt and Gustav come back I must ask them to continue my German lessons* she thought. *Or perhaps I could ask Fredrik…*

Alexandra burbled, pushing away the bottle. Laura stroked the fine wisps of blonde hair on her head and kissed her, handing her back to Gertrude before heading down to the dining room.

She ate disinterestedly, pushing the food around her plate, only half aware of the conversations around her. Ilich and Luka shot each other a look, wondering if the anniversary was bringing back the strain of those days; her imprisonment in the tower and the terrible aftermath of Nikita's attack.

'Your Majesty?' Luka finally asked. 'Would you care to go riding in the forest today?'

She blinked, and he could see she was unhappy with the idea, but she agreed, rising from the table to put on her riding habit, meeting Luka and Roman in the stables. She shut her eyes tightly, trying to ignore the sights of the stables without Olaf, trying not to breathe the smell of the hay.

Quickly she mounted and trotted down Castle Street without waiting for the others, pushing her stallion into a fast trot, trying to outrun her thoughts. It wasn't long before she heard hoof beats catch up and slow to keep pace with her. She turned sharply into the forest, making the stallion snort and stumble. She ducked under a low branch, shutting her eyes against the memories and was slapped in the face by a pine branch.

She could hear Roman and Luka calling out to her but she urged the stallion faster, changing direction again. The stallion shied under her distracted handling, prancing uncomfortably at the strangeness. She ducked under another branch, catching sight of a frayed and worn piece of rope looped around it as she did. She hauled tightly on the reins, bursting into tears and put her face in her hands.

Luka's arrival beside her was what stopped the bullet from hitting her. It smashed into his shoulder, spinning him in the saddle and knocking him to the ground, making him cry out in shock and pain. Roman cannoned into her as the rapport echoed around the forest and bore her to the ground, protecting her body with his, one arm around her, the other holding his rifle firmly, his eyes scanning the forest for the assassin.

Laura's heart was knocking painfully in her chest and she gasped for air, twisting to see through the thick ground foliage. Luka groaned beside her, writhing on his back to look at the expanding red stain that was spreading down his arm. Roman shouted suddenly, and there were answering shouts in the forest, the sounds of two people hurrying through the undergrowth.

Roman suddenly got up, shouting at the two hunters, who had dropped to their knees, wringing their hands in horror when they realised they had nearly shot the tsaritsa. Laura sat up, surprised by the agony in her side and pressed her hand there, turning to look at the hard, knobbly tree root that she had fallen onto. Luka cried out again, sitting up, cupping a hand over the wound. She turned back to look at Roman who was still shouting at the hunters, who had raised their hands and begun wailing, prostrating themselves repeatedly.

'Can you ride?' she asked Luka urgently, pulling him to his feet, wincing at the pain in her side.

'I think so' he panted, and Laura helped him to mount, grunting with the effort.

Quickly she swung up onto the stallion and took the reins from Luka, telling him to hang on to the saddle tightly. Roman swung up into his own saddle, shouting at the hunters to turn themselves in and raced after Laura, who led Luka straight to the hospital, aware of how much blood he was losing.

She clattered to the cobbles, helping Luka down, hearing Roman jump down and come to assist her. He staggered between them, crying in pain, and they helped him into the hospital, calling for Doctor Pushkin, who quickly came to their aid. Luka was taken from them and rushed into an operating theatre while Pushkin called instructions over his shoulder to several nurses trailing in his wake.

Laura shut her eyes, realising that she was shaking and took a deep, unsteady breath.

'Did I hurt you, Your Majesty?' Roman asked, worried.

'I landed on a nasty tree root' she said, and realised she was crying.

'In here' Roman said gently, leading her into an empty room and shutting the door.

Her knees felt weak and she held his arm tightly, shutting her eyes in the shaky aftermath of shock.

'It would have killed me' she said, eyeing him.

His finger brushed a line through the air across her chest. 'Through your heart, through your lungs' he said quietly. 'Or maybe through your throat...' he pointed, his finger millimetres from her skin, so close she could feel the heat and she shivered. 'You would have been dead in less than ten minutes.'

She turned away and sat on the narrow bed, shaking as the tears threatened to spill over again. Roman sat quietly beside her, handing over his handkerchief silently.

'Find someone to send word to Ilich, and to his family' she said quietly. 'Then stand guard outside, only admit Doctor Pushkin.'

'Yes Your Majesty' he said then stood and let himself out.

Alone in the small room she pushed his handkerchief into her mouth and sobbed, the sight of the rope round the branch rising up in her mind like a black and terrible tide. *Had they hung him there?* She could barely bring herself to think the question. *Poor poor Olaf...*

It was Roman's raised voice that roused her some time later. Quickly she sat up, groaning at the pain she felt in her stiff side and listened carefully. She could hear Ilich and Roman in a heated argument and quickly slipped to the floor, grimacing as she limped towards the door, quickly brushing her cheeks free of the tears before opening it.

Both stopped and eyed her, bowing shortly.

'Are you alright Your Majesty?' Ilich asked, stepping into the room despite Roman's attempt to stop him.

'Yes, I am fine. How is Luka?' she asked, her voice husky from crying so long.

'Doctor Pushkin has just emerged from the surgery. It went well, and he will recover provided no infection sets into his bone.'

'That's good to hear' she said, wincing as she moved too sharply and hurt her back.

'Have you been seen to Your Majesty?' he asked, concerned.

'No, it is a mere bruise' she said, waving away his concern and wincing again.

Ilich turned to Roman and ordered him to find Doctor Pushkin then closed the door, gently guiding Laura to the bed again. She sat and sighed quietly, relieved that Luka would be alright. She still couldn't quite believe the miraculous escape she had just had, how close she had come to death.

'On reflection, Your Majesty, I agree with your assertion that there is a need for a restricted section of the forest for the use of Royals and ministers, and suggest that Parliament should enforce a ban on hunting too.'

She laughed then quickly stopped, gasping at the sharp stab of pain in her side.

'Your Majesty?' he asked, concerned.

'It's cutting me!' she cried, tugging uselessly on her dress. 'Take it off! Help me get it off!'

There was a flicker of embarrassment on his face then he quickly began undoing the buttons of her dress, tugging it open. Laura winced as each movement twisted the sharpness in her side.

'Corset!' she cried, and Ilich struggled with the ties, apologising each time his movements caused her pain.

He dug out his sharp pen knife and slit the strings, folding open the corset. Laura groaned and Ilich saw one of the bone supports for her corset had snapped and stabbed her, piercing through her chemise that was now bloodied. Quickly he untied the strings and opened it then gasped, eyeing the mess of scars.

She turned away quickly, pressing her clothes to her chest to stop them revealing her to him, a hot flush in her cheeks. She shut her eyes at the horror she saw in his face.

'Would you be so kind as to inquire how long Doctor Pushkin will be' she snapped coldly.

He dropped his eyes then bowed. 'Yes Your Majesty' he said, turning to open the door.

'Don't -!' she started urgently then stopped. 'Don't tell anyone' she whispered.

Ilich hesitated then pulled open the door, almost colliding with Roman. The soldier's hands tightened on his rifle when he saw his mistress half disrobed and distraught, and shot Ilich a look that could have destroyed civilizations. Doctor Pushkin stepped past them both and shut the door, turning to the tsaritsa.

Quickly he ministered to the minor cut on her side, glancing over the old scars with a professional eye. *Three were recent, about a year old* he mused, and the whole Principality knew about the whipping Aleksei had given her in the courtyard the night of the revolution, which had probably given Tsar Constantinovich his heart attack. *These others were older, much older, perhaps childhood scars* he concluded. He was not given to speculation in his line of work, but he, like everyone else, had heard rumours about disfigurements and the particular reluctance to dress assisted by servants.

'I will need to come regularly to change the dressing' he said when he was finished, stepping back and folding his hands the way he always did when giving his prognosis.

'Very well' she said, trying to be distant, as if she wasn't half naked with another who knew about her scars. 'When will Luka be fit to leave the hospital?'

'A day or two, with strict bed rest' he assured her. 'His prognosis is good.'

'Can I see him?' she asked quietly.

'He is still resting, and has not woken from the chloroform' he answered. 'He will be groggy for a while yet.'

'I would like to see him' she insisted. 'Wait for me outside.'

'Of course' he bowed, letting himself out.

Laura shut her eyes tightly, forcing away the embarrassment. She pulled off her ruined corset and managed to button her dress closed again, feeling the material chafe her tender side. She rolled the corset tightly and briefly considered leaving it behind in the room, but instead she tucked it into her elbow, as if it were a parcel or a purse. She hesitated only briefly before opening the door, gesturing for Pushkin to lead her to Luka's room.

'This way please' he gestured, and headed along the corridor.

Roman fell into step behind them quietly, and the doctor opened one door to a small room, stepping aside politely to show the tsaritsa in.

Luka lay in a white bed, a white bandage wrapped around his shoulder and chest, the starchy sheets pulled up to his shoulders. Every once and a while he groaned sickly.

'Is he in much pain?' Laura asked.

'I dare say some' Pushkin said nonchalantly. 'But it is the effects of the chloroform that make him sickly. It is terrible stuff, we will probably go back to using ether, it is not as toxic, despite the side effects.'

Luka groaned again, and his eyes fluttered open, gazing unfocusedly around the room until they came to rest on Laura. He coughed and tried to sit up, but Laura pushed him back gently, soothing him. Luka was in no state to protest, and shut his eyes against the headache.

'See to it that he gets all the care he needs Doctor Pushkin' she said. 'And when he is well enough to be taken home I wish him to come to the castle where he will find excellent care until he is healed.'

'Yes Your Majesty' Doctor Pushkin bowed.

Laura eyed Luka again, wondering if he was still awake, then turned and headed back to the castle. Roman led the horses by the reins, walking at a discreet distance behind the pre-occupied tsaritsa, who was still carrying the rolled up ruined corset in her arms. He eyed the people that shot her curious looks, and wondered what they would be saying at garden gates, whispering in Parliament Chambers.

The guards on the gate to Vsevolod's Way saluted as they passed, trying to eye the tsaritsa while staring straight ahead. Roman glared at them then led the horses to the stables, looping the reins on the hook before rushing into the castle, not willing to let her out of his sight too long. But despite the short time she was nowhere to be found and he cursed quietly, going to stand uselessly outside her doors.

26

Fedor coughed subtly, bringing a tray to her on which were several letters of business, already opened. Laura cast a disinterested eye over them, playing distractedly with the corner of the tablecloth that covered her small writing desk.

'Anything of interest Fedor?' she asked, feeling as if she were a bad actor in a terrible play.

'There is an invitation to the coronation of Haakon the Seventh, elected King of Norway' he said.

'Elected?'

'Norway and Sweden dissolved their personal union last year, and a referendum found they were still in favour of a monarch, so they elected King Haakon from those who had claims to the throne.'

'Why is he inviting me? Does he want to marry me?'

Fedor paused. 'He is already married, to Princess Maud of Wales, youngest daughter of King Edward. They have a son, Crown Prince Olav. I believe the invitation was sent to the monarch of Dalnerechensk, not, as such, to you personally.'

'Why?' she demanded. 'Dalnerechensk has been ignored in all of Europe's affairs.'

'Yes Your Majesty' Fedor said soothingly. 'But she has, recently, become central to some important affairs in Europe, namely -'

'The Bodice Treaties' Laura sighed. 'Nearly start a war and suddenly all of Europe wants to wine and dine you. Very well, are there any other invitations in there I would not have previously received?'

'As a matter of fact, there is an invitation to King Alphonso the Thirteenth's wedding, for the thirty-first of May.'

'Ah yes, "The happiest and best loved of all the rulers of the earth"' she quoted dryly. 'King of Spain from birth, as I understand. What is he now, twenty?'

'Yes Your Majesty, and marrying Princess Victoria Eugenie of Battenberg. She has recently been elevated to Royal Highness so the marriage will not be seen as morganatic.'

'Another of Queen Victoria's grandchildren' Laura mused. 'That woman must be the matriarch of Europe.'

'Quite so' Fedor smiled. 'Shall I accept the invitations on your behalf?'

'No' she said, pulling at the table cloth again. 'I have no desire to be reminded of weddings at this time. And Norway is too far away.'

'The trip can be made easily in time Your Majesty, it is not until June -'

'No' she said again, sharply.

'As you wish Your Majesty' he bowed and an awkward silence fell between them.

'Any other business?' she asked finally.

'Doctor Pushkin has given his consent for Luka Nevsky to be discharged. He will be arriving shortly, and there are rooms aired for him.'

'Good' she responded absently.

'The machine that your father so generously bought for the mines has been assembled. There will be a small opening ceremony this afternoon that you and Baron Asanton will attend. -'

'I wish to be left alone' she interrupted, suddenly tired.

Fedor eyed her worriedly, then bowed and left. Laura picked disinterestedly at the table cloth then pulled an inkwell towards her, dabbling her pen distractedly into it, trying to put her thoughts in order. She was trying to write a letter to Fredrik, torn between writing something scandalously saucy, something weepy and accusatory, or something civil and polite, and could not begin any of them.

She pressed her pen in a flurry of thoughts then scrunched the paper even before the ink was dry, flinging it into the fire angrily. Several more followed and she stood, striding around her room, fussing so agitatedly with the lace at her cuff that she tore it.

She turned suddenly and flung open her doors, startling Roman. She stamped along the hallways and let herself into the rooms Ekaterina and Grigory shared without knocking.

'Laura, what is it?' Ekaterina asked, seeing the state of her friend.

'Are you going to rebuild your home or not?' she demanded.

Ekaterina and Grigory shared a glance, then Grigory closed the door against the ears of the castle. Ekaterina came to take her hands.

'We are undecided' she said gently. 'This is your home Laura, and they have accepted you, but we barely dare to go out, they still hold us accountable for their grievances, and someone brings us little notes of hate...' she trailed off, her lip trembling.

'Why have you not told me?!' she cried, horrified and angry.

'It is nothing to trouble you with' Ekaterina said quickly.

'Who is bringing them, your maid?' she demanded.

'I do not know' she said helplessly. 'But please Laura -'

'They cannot do this!' she shouted and flung open the door again, rushing past a bewildered Roman, despite Ekaterina's attempt to stop her.

Ekaterina, Roman and Grigory followed her as she stormed down to Parliament, pushing open the doors roughly. The ministers jumped quickly to their feet, surprised by her sudden entrance. Ekaterina took her hand but she shook her roughly off.

'You must issue a pardon to all the members of the old Advisory Council' she said. 'Or do I need to remind everyone that the Bodice Treaties were acquired by the old government, and not this one?'

'How dare you burst in here, a child in a tantrum, and demand things of this government as though we were some genie to grant your wishes!' Ilich snapped.

Laura paled, and let Ekaterina grab her hands again, squeezing them tightly in the face of Ilich's fury. For just a moment she saw him again, ranting on the bar top, young and full of fire at the indignities the Principality faced on a daily basis. *And one of them was his belief in an arrogant and pampered monarchy* she reminded herself. *How I must seem so like them now.* Beside her Ekaterina was hurriedly explaining the notes.

'*I don't care!*' Ilich thundered. 'A discipline matter within the staff of the Royal Household is not a matter for governmental policy! We will not be ordered by anyone on what to do! This is a democratic representation of the citizens of Dalnerechensk, and it will not be told what to do by a monarchy anymore -'

'When are your elections?' Laura asked suddenly, interrupting his tirade.

'What?' he stopped mid-rant.

'You know as well as I do this government was not elected. You cannot be a truly democratic representation of Dalnerechensk without their vote in you. If you continue this government without an election you will be no better than a tyrant. Or a monarch' she added dryly.

'She has raised a valid point' Maksim said quickly, and Ilich shot him a glare that had more to do with the hour of haranguing for Parliament to put Piotr Grigorevich on the throne than her argument.

Ilich looked carefully at Laura, but she had been surprised by Maksim's quick support, and he knew they could not have secretly come up with this between them beforehand. Indeed, Maksim will not support her in any venture, no matter how beneficial the results for him may be. *That man would cut off his own nose to spite his face where she was concerned* he reminded himself.

'We cannot truly be the voice of the people without, as the *Vdova* Tsaritsa points out, the people's support' Maksim went on, and Laura saw his astute political wheels spinning rapidly.

'Forgive me, Ilich, Ministers of Parliament' she suddenly said. 'I did not mean to come as a child in a tantrum, only I was outraged at the treatment of my friends in my own household. I thought it a matter that could be addressed by Parliament: forgiving the old Council would be a gesture towards the unity of this new order -'

'And would you magnanimously pardon this Council for its treason?' Maksim sneered. 'Forgive the purse strings, forgive the rebels and skip off into the sunset holding hands to live happily ever after?'

Laura shut her eyes, close to losing control. Ekaterina squeezed her hand tighter and took the initiative, seeing how distressed she was.

'I should very much like to see you skip into the sunset Maksim' she smiled. 'I don't know what would make more noise, your knees or your heart!'

There were a few chuckles, which helped to lower the tension in the room. Laura sniffed quietly.

'Forgive my intrusion in such a rude manner' she said, wiping her eyes. 'I have been - at a loss and distracted these past few days. It is a terrible time for me.'

'I understand, Your Majesty' Ilich said quietly, coming to reassure her. 'We understand how difficult this must be for you.'

'Thank you' she said, and bowed to them. 'I will take my leave, forgive me for my tantrum.'

She turned and fled up the stairs to her rooms, shutting the door hard against Roman. Ekaterina pushed open the door and watched as Laura flung herself down on her chaise lounge.

'Why are you so agitated my dear?' she asked, coming to take her hands.

'Fredrik has written to inform me that he is having a wonderful time in Greece, and perhaps he might extend his time there *and* travel on to Rome. That would not be so bad if I had not seen this!' she grabbed a screwed-up newspaper and thrust it at her friend.

Ekaterina took it carefully and unfolded it, smoothing out the wrinkles and fitting the ragged edges of a long tear back together, immediately guessing the truth of Laura's distress when she saw the picture in the society pages.

Fredrik stood in front of the Athens Opera House, resplendent in a fine suit. Beside him stood the beautiful lyric soprano Lilia Bellagio, radiant and sensual, her arm tucked through his elbow. Even through the grainy, black and white image of the newspaper photo Ekaterina could see the subtleties of her body language and the glow in her face.

'Ah yes, I had the pleasure of seeing her in an opera last year, such a beautiful voice, and so sweet and charming.'

'You're supposed to tell me she is a vicious mule and Fredrik is only smiling for the photograph' Laura sulked.

Ekaterina put aside the ruined paper.

'Oh Laura, I am truly sorry my dear' she said, sitting beside her and folding her arms around her.

'Someone said something to him!' she burst out, then rushed on, her words tripping and tangling around each other as she poured out her fears and her heartaches.

Ekaterina was quiet when she finished, letting her young friend cry on her lap. Laura snuffled, wiping her nose, hating how emotional and raw she felt. At long last she sat up, rubbing away the tear stains on her cheeks.

'I don't know what to do Ekaterina' she mumbled.

'Don't fear' she soothed. 'He will not fall in love with Lilia, I know my cousin well. She is beautiful, but she is rather - innocent, like a kitten' she smiled. 'Fredrik is clever and witty, he will delight in a wife that is cunning and vivacious and intelligent. Lilia can sing well enough to make angels weep, but she is not you.'

Laura managed a smile, and buffed some more tears away. A knock on the door interrupted them, and Roman ushered in Doctor Pushkin.

'Good morning Your Majesty' he bowed. 'Luka Nevsky is now resting in one of the rooms in the castle, and is under strict instructions not to exert himself' he announced. 'I have come to check the progress of your small wound.'

'Of course. Do excuse us Ekaterina' she said, ushering her friend to the door.

'As you wish my dear' she smiled. 'And do not trouble yourself, I am sure of my convictions.'

'Thank you Ekaterina. It is a great comfort' she said, their eyes saying more than civility allowed them to.

She closed the door and turned back to Doctor Pushkin.

'Please make haste, doctor, I have an appointment in Macherna to keep.'

'Yes Your Majesty' he bowed, and opened his medical bag.

THE NINE WEEK KING

27

Ilich knocked politely and the door was opened by Anna, who dropped a curtsey when she saw it was him.

'Good morning my lord, please come in' she said, carefully balancing the tray with one hand and stepping back to admit him into Luka's rooms.

She led him across the pretty sitting room into the bedroom beyond, where Luka was propped up on a multitude of cushions and reading the newspaper in bed. Anna placed the tray on a small lap table and placed it over Luka's legs.

'Thank you Anna, that will be all for now' Ilich said and closed the door behind her.

Luka eyed him, holding up the newspaper, the heading shouting *Elections!*

'Trust me, it was not my idea' Ilich said. 'And now it seems it has been leaked by Maksim.'

Luka didn't question the source. Parliament was fully aware of Maksim's lofty ambitions, and his overt actions to acquire more power. An election would serve him well. Head of State would be a nice stepping stone on the road to the Monarchy.

'Do you think she realises the danger in an election?' Luka asked quietly.

'She is somewhat distracted and erratic at present' Ilich said. 'But no doubt when she puts her pretty head to it she will understand all the implications. I fear for Dalnerechensk with Maksim at the helm. He will block any attempt to work with her - at least we are working with her.'

'What are we electing? A new Head of State? There is technically only one party -'

'Not for long' Ilich pointed out. 'Maksim and Lev will form a new party, and they have the support of the Boyars and the large, rambling Vakhtangov family. Their popularity will quickly grow, if not because they believe in his policies, but because they oppose the tsaritsa and us. They have immense influence.'

'Do you truly believe he will win?' Luka asked, eyeing him.

Ilich shrugged, running his fingers through his hair.

'How is your arm?' he asked instead.

'Painful' he winced. 'The tsaritsa is convinced I saved her life, she even wrote to my mother. The card is now framed and displayed over her mantelpiece. She might even bring herself to think about forgiving me for being a traitor' he managed a weak smile.

Ilich smiled too.

'And how is your stay in the castle?'

'Glorious. She is kind and attentive, but don't think saving her life will make her pathetically eager to make me the happiest man alive.'

'Do you have any influence with her?' Ilich asked quietly.

'None. But give me time' he promised.

'Luka' he started. 'You are my oldest friend. Do not lose your head over this.'

Luka looked away.

'Thank you for your concern my friend' he said quietly. 'I will do my best to hold onto it.'

There was a knock on the door and Roman announced Laura to the two men in the room.

'Ah Ilich, I thought I would find you here' she smiled. 'Please let me extend to you the courtesy that I have granted Luka's family; to come and see him as you wish.'

'That is most kind Your Majesty' he said, bowing slightly.

'How fares you today Luka?' she asked, stepping closer to the bed.

'I mend Your Majesty, I mend' he smiled. 'Thanks to your sweet attentiveness.'

'It is kind of you to say so' she smiled. 'But I must, alas, deprive you of your company. I wish to show *Glava Gosudarstva* his new Parliament Chambers, they are almost complete. There will, of course, be a grand unveiling when they are finished, and I hope that you will be able to see them then.'

'God willing' he smiled, then avoided Ilich's eyes.

They took their leave of Luka and made their way down to the foyer of the castle where the rest of Parliament was waiting for them. They bowed when Laura appeared and followed her to the newly repaired Left Wing.

'My lords' she smiled, stepping into the large, empty ballroom. 'Petrovich Kamanin assures me that the seamstresses are working hard, and that the draperies for the windows will be ready by the end of the week' she gestured to the large, unadorned panes of glass. 'I have been assured that this window design is modern yet will not detract from the style of the room. The large mirrors along the opposite wall make the room bright and beautiful' she went on, smiling slightly as she imagined what the room would look like full of people, with the missing chandelier replaced and glowing, with music and the mirrors reflecting her and Fredrik dancing together.

'The upholsterers will have a number of seats available, and the chandelier is arriving this afternoon, which will be winched into place tomorrow. I will hold a ball to mark the opening of the new Parliament Chambers, to which you and your families are all invited' she went on, smiling at them.

There was quiet, appreciative applause and she led them towards the throne room, now the new Parliament Chambers.

'I trust you will find these rooms adequate for both state and royal occasions, including ceremonial observances' she said as she led them into the room.

Petrovich Kamanin had designed a room with a central aisle that led to the dais on which sat Vsevolod's throne. The stone walls above it were bare, but it would be hung with the royal standard of Dalnerechensk, or maybe some other tapestries that would suit the room, and the floor would be carpeted with something rich and green, the colour of both the Republic and the Monarchy.

The long room itself was lined on each side with beautiful wooden desks, though the chairs to sit with them had not been delivered yet; and at the top of the aisle, before the dais, was a thick mahogany table, broken and held together with metal brackets. Every man in the room knew what it was: Vsevolod's dining table, which had been smashed by a cannonball in Nikita's attack. Now, repaired and covered in the flag of the Republic, it sat at the feet of the throne, positioned to adjudicate the debates of the ministers.

The room was designed so that the Parliament could take sides to debate issues while Ivan could sit between the two at Vsevolod's table, jotting down the proceedings. But when no issues were in need of debate, Parliament could meet in committee around the table, as they had so many times before. It was also no trouble to carefully carry the table to the side and leave the aisle free for pageantry processions. Laura could see that the majority of the ministers approved of the new rooms.

'What will you do with the old Parliament Chambers?' Yuri asked, admiring the fine wood grain of the desks.

'A small private dining room' Laura answered. 'For those times when I wish for a more intimate dinner.'

A quiet cough from the doorway drew the attention to Fedor, who looked deeply uncomfortable.

'Forgive this intrusion Your Majesty, Ministers, I have terrible news' he said. 'Piotr Grigorevich is dead.'

There was a shocked silence, and out of the corner of her eye Laura saw Maksim and Lev begin nonchalantly heading towards each other with determined looks on their faces.

'He passed away an hour ago from complications of influenza. I am terribly sorry to bring you this news.'

'This is dreadful news' Laura said. 'In light of this gentlemen, perhaps Parliament should not meet today.'

'Agreed' Ilich said, eyeing the hushed whispering of Maksim and Lev disgustedly.

'Please stay and council me' Laura said, turning to Ilich as the ministers bowed and began to take their leave.

He waited silently, eyeing her as she crossed carefully to the door, closing it after Yuri bid her a quiet goodbye. She sighed, shutting her eyes, and leant her head against the door. After a while she heard Ilich pad quietly across to where she stood.

'Vultures' she sighed quietly.

'Your Majesty?'

'They didn't even feel sad' she said, turning to face him. 'As soon as they knew he was dead they were plotting the next puppet for the throne. Another Vakhtangov to wed Tatiana; to tie him tighter to the throne.' She sighed and shut her eyes tightly again, putting her hands over them. 'I am half afraid he will decide to pursue a courtship with me to get the throne, except he despises my breeding, or lack thereof.'

She shuddered involuntarily, and wrapped her arms around herself, squeezing carefully.

'So Ilich' she said quietly. 'Who else can they marry?'

'I don't believe there is anyone else' he said, leaning against the door beside her. 'There are only -' he stopped, recalculating sadly. '- five. Three are married already, one is widowed and old enough to be Maksim's father, the last is most certainly not interested in marrying a woman.'

'So that means he will be ruthless in his pursuit of *Glava Gosudarstva*' she concluded.

'I gathered he would be ruthless anyway, but now perhaps there would be an element of, how should we say, desperation?'

'I do not wish to quarrel with you anymore Ilich' she said softly. 'I will need your support, and you mine, in the attacks that will come.'

'I know' he said gently.

'Forgive me, it was a moment of anger, I did not mean for this to happen' she whispered.

Ilich looked at her gently.

'Those same words were on my lips a year ago' he said then sighed, shutting his eyes. 'My hand has been forced in this matter, I will announce a date for the elections in June.'

'I suggest that you and I embark on a number of undertakings together to improve our standing in the Principality' Laura said.

'I don't think you need much improvement' he smiled. 'You are more popular now than you were when you arrived beautiful and sixteen, ready to give Dalnerechensk their next heir.'

'And I have done that, only they are not so happy with the gender I produced' she sighed.

They fell silent, each of them lost in their own thoughts.

Laura shut her eyes, trying to force a wedge of calmness through her thoughts. Beside her, close enough that she could hear him breathing, was a man she still had mixed feelings for. She still remembered the fear she had felt, dressed in disguise and sitting in the pub, watching him rant on the bar top against the monarchy. She still wondered, even now, if he had been searching for her in the castle that night, if he had been beating down the door while they had fled into the underground river.

This man had arrested her on her return, and had sent Olaf to a lonely spot in the forest, and put a rope around his neck for treason. She was still unsure where she stood with him, and was pretty sure he was still trying to convince himself that Dalnerechensk had no more need or want for the monarchy.

And yet… she thought quietly. *And yet he admired her, and looked to her for the subtleties of protocol when it was beyond him.* There was a kindness in him, a resoluteness, and the wellbeing of Dalnerechensk was never out of his thoughts. It was not for the first time that the likeness between Aleksei and Ilich had struck her. *But Aleksei's kindness had only been seen by so few people, the public had never seen him as she had seen him.*

How on earth had Ilich come to marry Nineczka?

'Your Majesty?' he asked softly. 'Did you find where the distressing notes were coming from?'

'Yes, a maid, and she is no longer employed here. Fedor saw to it.'

There was a quiet knock on the door and Roman opened it, his eyes lowered in the manner of someone wishing he wasn't about to deliver bad news.

'Your Majesty' he said thickly then cleared his throat self-consciously.

'Yes?' she asked, watching him struggle to speak with a sinking heart.

'They have returned' he said, his chin wobbling.

She didn't need him to elaborate to understand the reason for his distress. She picked up her skirts and rushed out into the courtyard.

Mikhail stood beside a cart that was covered over with a thick canvas tarpaulin. Behind him two men stood with their hats in their hands, clearly affected by the ordeal of digging up the body of the Tsar. Laura rushed over to the cart, flinging back the coverings. Quickly Mikhail took her hands, stilling her.

'He's not here' he said quietly, pulling her gently but firmly away. 'We set the casket to lie in state in the cathedral.'

She turned and headed towards the castle gates to Vsevolod's Way but Ilich took hold of her gently and firmly.

'Tomorrow we will hold the public ceremony for him' he soothed. 'We will give him the dignified goodbye he truly deserves.'

She shut her eyes and agreed silently, letting Ilich guide her back into the castle. Carefully and gently he led her up the stairs to the second floor, knocking on the door to Luke's room. Lady Anne opened the door and gasped, pulling her trembling daughter into her arms.

'What has happened?' she cried in English.

Laura opened her mouth but stopped when she saw the travelling cases open in their room, and a maid who was folding Luke's shirts. She closed her mouth and composed herself carefully.

'I regretfully must inform you that the search party has returned with Tsar Constantinovich's body. There will be an official funeral ceremony for him tomorrow, I do hope you will not be leaving before then' she said, and managed to sweep out of the room before Luke could call her back.

She rushed on to her own rooms, shutting the door firmly, jumping when she turned around to see Nineczka, Zarya Drevin, Tatiana and two other women in her rooms. They rose and curtsied to her, holding on to the edges of the tapestry they were stitching. Anna, fluttering nervously by the fireplace, gave her an apologetic look.

'There you are Your Majesty, isn't it terrible!' Tatiana cried, dabbing a little theatrically at her eyes with a handkerchief.

'We have come to comfort you in this distressing time of grief' Nineczka simpered and Laura stamped down on her emotions hard.

'That is very kind and thoughtful of you, but I do not believe stitching the tapestry is a fitting occupation for me right now -' she started.

'Of course, we could talk -'

'It would be callous -'

'We could not leave you without comfort!' Tatiana cried.

'I wish to spend this time in prayer' she tried desperately.

'How kind and blesséd!' Nineczka cried. 'We will pray with you!'

Laura looked at them carefully, realising she was not going to be left alone. And she understood why. They were watching her, calculating, measuring. They would count every tear she shed, every silence, and say she was hard-hearted not to cry for the misfortunate death of a poor boy, or that she was false and theatrical for a boy she barely knew.

'How kind' she said quietly, and led the way to the small chapel in the castle.

It was up near the attics, dusty and faded through many years of disuse. Laura knelt on one of the prayer cushions and clasped her hands in front of her chest, aware of the smirking looks that Nineczka was shooting at Zarya over her head. Laura ignored them, starting to whisper a few of the scriptures she knew off by heart. Her small gathering of conspirators knelt with her, whispering along with the prayers or starting their own quietly.

As she whispered Laura cast her eyes towards the small window above the little stone altar, eyeing the way it framed the beautifully wrought cross that stood on the altar, lighting the ivory and making it glow. The rest of the chapel was austere stone, designed solely for focusing the mind on the holy miracles despite the discomfort to the body.

As the minutes dragged by their knees began to throb, and Laura noticed Nineczka and the other two women were beginning to fidget and shift uncomfortably. She finished her recital of the scriptures and crossed herself, then clasped her hands and started again, keeping her face carefully composed.

Who were those two women? she wondered as her mouth worked on automatic. Her mind quickly spun through the names and the faces she knew, wondering where she had seen them before. *They were familiar* she mused. *I have met them before, but perhaps only briefly, and possibly not recently. At my wedding?* she thought. *They did carry themselves with more bearing than most of the minister's wives.*

And then it struck her. The woman sitting to the left of her was one of Elena Petrova's daughters, and the one on her right was another cousin, possibly a Konevna? The Vakhtangovs had sent spies as well as the Parliament. She finished her second recital and crossed herself again. Nineczka rose, grimacing, but Laura clasped her hands and began again, aware of the discomfort in the other women. Nineczka hesitated, half dropped to continue praying, but then crossed herself and swept pompously out of the room.

One by one the women left her, till only Tatiana was left, grimly muttering scriptures, her hands clasped so firmly to control their shaking that her knuckles were white. But Laura had spent many more years training herself to ignore her pain and discomfort as a student at Lady Ramkinson's ghastly school that Tatiana was no match for her endurance. Finally she left, fuming silently, and Laura finished her prayers, getting to her feet gingerly.

To her surprise the women had not left, and were hovering near the chapel door, watched over by a distrustful Roman. Though her knees ached she glided lightly along the corridors, aware that they were all falling into step behind her. Laura despaired, she had thought her prayer trick would get rid of them, but as she approached a familiar door another plan quickly formed in her head.

She stopped at the door to the nursery and opened it, stepping into the chamber beyond. The women gasped.

'The curse!' Zarya said quietly.

'You stepped into the nursery before!' Tatiana said, accusation dripping off her tongue. 'You were seen by the head of the night staff!'

'It is true I was seen by her, but she will attest that I could not have stepped into the nursery room as she was standing in the doorway at the time' she said as Gertrude brought Alexandra to her, noticing how reluctant the women were to come into the room, and a large part of her rejoiced. 'As you can see, Natasha's curse had no effect on me' she smiled, kissing her daughter's head.

Tatiana raised her foot to step over the threshold and hesitated, and Laura felt like bursting into song. All of the women were childless, and the threat of Natasha's curse kept them from even stepping into the small parlour. She could see Tatiana's quick mind working; Natasha's curse was for tsaritsas, not for any other noble lady, and in her hesitation Laura read the expectation that she would be tsaritsa someday.

'Ladies I thank you for your support but now I must nurse my daughter. Roman will kindly escort you.'

The soldier saluted and began to herd the women down the stairs to the foyer. Laura rocked her daughter quietly, watching as they shot glances back at her, distrust and anger twisting their features. Laura waved then gently closed the door over, sinking down wearily onto the nursing chair.

'*Guten Arbend Ihr Magistät*' Gertrude said eagerly, handing over a bottle of milk.

Laura greeted her quietly, beginning a halting conversation with the poor stranded servant, wondering whether she should hire a Russian nanny and send her back to her family.

But who could she hire? she wondered. The role of raising royal children was usually given to a member of the extended family, of noble birth and blood ties, which created a problem for Laura right then and there. It would be unthinkable to hire someone without impeccable credentials for the important task of looking after the future tsaritsa of Dalnerechensk, but unconscionable to ask any Vakhtangov member to do so - she would fear too greatly for her daughter to have her in the hands of those that wished her ill.

For the time being it was safest to keep Gertrude as her nurse, though she did feel guilty for her isolation in this small room in Dalnerechensk. *I must take her out into the Principality; she should see more of this beautiful country* she mused, and tried her best to give the woman the company she was starved of.

28

The soft click of the door opening surprised Roman and the tsaritsa slipped out, dressed in a warm coat and hat. Quickly he fell into step behind her, checking the gilded clock in the dark corridor as they passed. It was twenty minutes past one. She looked around when she heard his footstep behind her but relaxed and continued her quiet descent through the sleeping castle.

Roman didn't have to ask her where she was going, and managed to grab a warm coat from the small cloakroom as they stepped out into the quiet night. Their breath puffed away as they slipped past the guards on the gate, Roman murmuring where they were headed to them, gripping his rifle tightly as he eyed the moonlit streets for any sign of danger.

They reached the church and padded up the stairs, pulling open the door and closing it against the crisp wind that whispered through the streets. Laura hurried down the nave to the quire, where the royal standard of Dalnerechensk was draped over a long pine box. She sprawled forward, and Roman rushed over, thinking she had tripped, but she stayed pressed against the casket, great sobs wracking her.

He hesitated, wary of laying a hand on the monarchy, as the offence carried a punishment that he was unwilling to risk; but was torn by the misery of the tsaritsa. *She was only a girl after all* he told himself. *And she had not been able to grieve for him properly, surrounded by those who watched her constantly: anti-royalists, the remnants of the Vakhtangov family, the spiteful Shcherbakov family.*

He pulled his handkerchief out of his pocket and pressed it into one of her hands, wanting to leave his hand gently on her shoulder or arm to comfort her. He wondered if her other servant, the one she had gone riding with so often, had ever had to comfort her like this; wondering if she had filled the forest as she was filling the church with the sounds of her misery.

Out of the corner of his eye he saw the door to *Episcop* Yeltsin's apartments open and the doorway darken as the priest poked his head out into the church to see what the noise was. Then very quietly he closed the door again and Roman let out the breath he didn't realise he had been holding. He stole a quick glance at the tsaritsa but she hadn't noticed the small intrusion.

His eyes drifted back to the doorway, eyeing the deep shadows in it. *Was the door still open slightly?* he wondered. *Who else was spying on her? Would they go rushing to Parliament, to Maksim, and whisper gleefully of her misery and her solitude in this lonely hour?*

He knew how carefully she was watched, how she barely had any time to herself, how firmly she had to hold her emotions in check in case someone saw her and used it against her. A small part of Roman was proud that she trusted him enough to show this great emotion in front of him, but another part of him was worried that he had witnessed this moment of weakness.

He shut his eyes briefly, his thoughts turning to the frightening few minutes he had experienced a week ago. He had woken in the darkness of the barracks in Tcherepnin where he slept when he was not on duty in the palace, the muzzy uncertainty of waking torn aside by the solid feel of a gloved hand across his mouth and the thin coldness of a knife against his throat.

A voice had whispered to him, offering him a huge sum of money to betray the tsaritsa's confidence, to pass on her secrets and her indiscretions. *Did she write in a diary?* it had asked, misting on his ear unpleasantly, and smelt strongly of garlic sausage. *Did she keep personal papers in a safe in her rooms? Had she taken a lover? Baron Fredrik von Schmidt? Who was the father of her daughter?*

The questions had dragged on in his silence, then the voice had whispered where to go if he accepted the proposition, and had vanished so suddenly and so completely it had surprised him. Quickly he had jumped out of bed and fumbled for a lighter, cursing the time it took to get a candle lit. By the time he had flung open his door to check the corridor and pushed back the shutters at his window he knew the chance of finding the voice's owner was gone.

He had not been able to sleep again, and had gone two hours early for his shift outside the tsaritsa's doors, the fright gradually giving way to anger. The bribe had sickened him, an affront to his professional and personal integrity. But as he sat here now, listening to her cry, a more worrying thought was growing. *There was more than one way of getting information out of a person* he shuddered. *Torture, for example...*

He wasn't sure what he would say under torture. *Would he remain stalwart? Would he confess all that he knew? Would he invent lies or speak rumours as truth to end the pain?*

He was lost in his own horrific thoughts and didn't realise that her sobs had gradually quieted and stopped until she lay her hand gently on his arm. 'Thank you for your handkerchief Roman' she whispered. 'If you please, I will keep it and return it when it is clean.'

'Of course Your Majesty' he said, distracted.

'What is wrong?'

He shut his eyes, unwilling to tell her, but sighed and finally confessed when she pressed him.

'I was offered a - a bribe' he said, the taste of the word sickly on his tongue. 'To spy on you. I refused.'

'I know. You should accept.'

Roman blanched, aghast.

'Never!' he almost shouted.

'Do you know who offered you the bribe?' she asked, motioning for him to keep the noise down.

'No!'

'Or what they will use it for?'

'No.'

She eyed him quietly.

'I want to know those things' she said. 'Secrets are the currency of power. Accept the bribe. Donate it to the hospital if it makes you feel better. Find out what you can, and tell me.'

'And what will I tell them?' he asked, uneased by the conversation.

'A mixture. Some truths, some lies; some rumours that they should already know' she shrugged.

'I am unhappy with this Your Majesty' he said reluctantly.

She smiled then. 'Your loyalty to me is unquestioned Roman. You would not have been made *Sotnik* of my guards if it was. But I need you to do this for me.'

He screwed his eyes up tightly and turned away, torn between his feelings. She patted his hand gently.

'Don't decide now Roman, think about it' she begged. 'And walk me back to the castle, while it's still dark. They'll be coming to prepare the funeral procession to Macherna soon.'

He agreed silently and stood, wincing at the stiffness in his legs. He reached down and Laura took his hand, wincing as she stood too. She dusted off her dress and patted her hair distractedly, slipping her hand through his elbow as he led her down the nave. They both eyed the door to *Episcop* Yeltsin's apartments, but it was resolutely shut, and they were both glad Laura's tears had not been watched by the priest.

The morning was still cold and dark, but the outline of the Eastern Mountains was picked out against the silver of the coming dawn. The streets were still empty, and they made their way quickly to the castle, nodding to the guards on the gate as they passed. Roman opened the castle door for her, following up the stairs to her room.

'Thank you Roman' she whispered, then closed the door against him, crossing to the dressing room to wash her face.

The water was cold against her skin and revived her, despite her lack of sleep. She patted her face dry with a soft towel and turned to her wardrobe, pulling open the doors quietly. The black dress she had worn for so long was too shabby for an important state occasion, so Anna had been sent to purchase a new one, and a hat with a veil to match.

Carefully she undid her coat and her dress, letting them slip to the floor. With a bit of uncomfortable tugging she managed to tighten her corsets into a more shapely bind then pulled on the rich sable dress. It made her face look pale and she quickly pinned up her hair, perching the hat on top and pulling the veil down over her face.

'You look beautiful, but very sad' Anna said quietly, stepping into the room.

Laura managed a gentle smile and gave Anna leave for the day so she could watch the procession, stepping out into the corridor to greet Roman.

'Do you have a part in the procession today?' she asked quietly.

'No Your Majesty' he answered. 'Commander Kamanin has stood down all the night watch of the Order for it.'

'I have one favour to ask of you' she said, dropping her eyes. 'Alexandra's nurse Gertrude will be given permission to attend. She will take *Tsesarevna* Alexandra with her. Protect my daughter Roman.'

He saluted. 'Yes Your Majesty.'

Peter Kamanin arrived in the corridor and bowed low when he saw the tsaritsa. He was wearing the smart uniform of the Order of Vsevolod, the green bow of his knighthood pinned to his chest, the enamel medallion hanging from it. At his side was an ornamental sword, the jewels catching the weak dawn light.

'Good morning Peter' she said softly while beside her Roman saluted his commanding officer.

'Good morning' he said, bowing again before acknowledging Roman's salute. 'Most of the ministers have now assembled in the castle entrance; we will proceed to the cathedral soon.'

'Very well' she said, taking the gloves and lace handkerchief that Anna handed to her as she headed past to get a good view of the procession.

Carefully she tucked the handkerchief up her sleeve and pulled on the soft black kid gloves, smoothing her veil absently. Peter followed her down to the entrance where Laura stopped in surprise. The ministers of Ilich's Parliament were there, splendid in their unfussy green uniforms with the white sash across their chests; but so were the old ministers of Aleksei's council, wearing the smart black uniforms trimmed with gold and medals, the blue sashes across their chests; huddled together away from the Parliament and eyeing them uneasily.

'Nicholas!' she exclaimed, seeing the eighty-three year old minister, sitting in a wicker wheel-chair and heaped with blankets.

Quickly she rushed over and took his hands, kissing both his cheeks.

'I did not think I would ever see this council again' she said, stepping back to eye the others.

They smiled timidly, though their smiles cracked slightly at the edge. She took each of their hands, noticing how the fingers trembled in her grip, how gummy each of their dry lips felt when they pressed them to the back of her hand. Laura wondered how deeply they feared for their lives standing here in the castle they knew well. *But the respect for the Tsar was too great* she added quietly, stepping back so Peter Kamanin could direct her to her place in the funeral procession.

In the courtyard before the castle was a mounted guard, dressed in the simple green uniform, without the white sash. There were many open carriages belonging to the Vakhtangov family, who sat inside, beautifully dressed in furs and coats while the chaos of organisation went on around them, like rocks in a spring stream. Laura eyed the milling crowds as Ekaterina appeared beside her, taking her hand out of a sable muff to link through Laura's elbow, her white hand disappearing into the fur again.

'You look beautiful' Ekaterina whispered, eyeing the heads in the coaches that refused to look in their direction.

One small girl was looking in their direction though, sandwiched between the crepey, ancient cousins of Aleksei, her face so pale and rent with grief it struck Laura right through her heart.

'Poor Anna' Ekaterina sighed. 'Piotr Grigorevich's funeral is today too, but her grandmother insists she is in the funeral procession.'

'What about her mother?'

'Died giving birth to her. And her father died when she was four. She's been raised by a succession of older and older aunts and her grandmother ever since.'

'I never thought the Vakhtangovs were so tragic' Laura said. 'I mean, you told me the family had suffered great tragedies, but ...' she trailed off.

'But you were happy, and were planning your wedding' Ekaterina smiled sadly.

'Your Majesty?' Peter asked quietly, appearing beside them. 'We're ready for you.'

She smiled sadly and unlinked her arm from Ekaterina's, climbing into the open carriage with her father and Lady Anne. Peter bowed and swung into the saddle of his horse, snapping orders at his soldiers that were low in volume but still managed to carry across the whole courtyard.

A mournful reveille sounded from a lone trumpeter atop the castle walls and the procession began. Peter Kamanin led the column of mounted guards who fell in behind him in neat rows. At the head of the procession was the old palace guard, then the carriage that held the tsaritsa and her family. Behind them were the carriages of the Vakhtangov family, then those of the old Advisory Council. The middle carriage held Nicholas Riminov, Ivan Gogol, Maksim and Lev, the ministers from the old that had found their way into the new. The carriages holding the new Parliament members and the mounted soldiers of Ilich's new army brought up the rear.

The procession was so long that the mounted army had not even left the castle grounds when the palace guard arrived in front of the cathedral. Slowly the Vakhtangovs and Parliament disembarked and climbed the steps, silently filing into the pews. Laura shut her eyes quickly, but the sight of Tsar Constantinovich's coffin struck a fresh stab of pain through her. It had been draped with white cloth embroidered with his personal coat of arms, surrounded with bouquets of white roses and lilies; the mountain daisies of Dalnerechensk scattered at the feet of the coffin.

She shuffled into the pew beside her father, collecting up the small prayer book to stop her hands from shaking. It took nearly half an hour for all the dignitaries to arrive, and the cathedral filled with the silent rustlings of grief. *Episcop* Yeltsin, in all the official regalia of his station, delivered a poignant but lengthy service, tears rolling down his cheeks as he shared his boyhood memories of the beloved tsar.

He blessed the coffin several times, sprinkling it with holy water, reciting prayers of protection over the body. The congregation murmured *amen* at the conclusion of the ritual and Laura rose, causing them to rise with her. Griping her small prayer book and a damp handkerchief she ascended the stairs to the altar, kneeling briefly so *Episcop* Yeltsin could make the sign of the cross above her head. She bent to kiss the coat of arms on the coffin then turned to face the full cathedral.

She swallowed thickly and coughed to clear her throat, aware that every single head in the Vakhtangov family was bowed down to snub her. She cleared her throat again and began to speak, aware of the pageantry of state occasion and the intimacy of the emotions, and managed to strike a perfect balance between the two. She let her tears fall behind her veil as she finished, and walked sedately back to her seat, the rest of the congregation sitting too.

Ilich then stood to speak, and Laura was surprised with the poor oration. Ilich had powerful rhetoric, she had seen it for herself on many an occasion, yet here he seemed awkward and dithering. *Perhaps he was diminished under the weight of pageantry and history* she mused quietly. *Perhaps he was guilty…*

Ilich's speech stuttered to its end and the soldiers of the Tsar's old Palace Guard came forward, taking their places on either side of the coffin, ready to carry it out to the waiting bier. *Episcop* Yeltsin raised his staff and led the slow way down the nave, the royal family of Dalnerechensk falling in behind him.

Outside in the soft sunlight soldiers stood in ranks, keeping back the crowd from the church. As the coffin emerged they saluted, coming to attention in a precision movement, as if an order had been shouted that only they could hear. Two black horses stood harnessed to the bier at the foot of the stairs, tall black plumes rising from their harnesses; and the Old Guard carried their tsar down the stairs, placing him gently on the wooden cart.

Laura dabbed at her tears and took her place in the procession that would wind its way on foot to the cemetery atop the western flank of the valley. *Episcop* Yeltsin led the way, his staff raised high before him. The bier followed, the reins of the two horses held firmly by a black-robed priest, his face hidden by the cowl. Laura walked behind the coffin, at the head of the chilly Vakhtangov family, flanked by Luke and Lady Anne. Behind the family came the Palace Guard and the Advisory Council, then Ilich's new army and Parliament. Between the two was Nicholas Riminov, oldest member of the old ways, pushed in his wicker wheelchair by Ivan Gogol, once the youngest of the old Council and one of the oldest in the new Parliament.

The road from the church all the way to the gate at the cemetery was lined with the citizens of Dalnerechensk, standing in silent rows, watching the last of their royal family walk slowly past. The road was strewn with freshly cut bouquets of mountain flowers, and the steps of the procession crushed the heady smell into the air. It reminded Laura of her wedding day, and she shut her eyes against the hurt, stumbling on an uneven cobblestone.

Luke caught her arm quickly and she regained her footing, thanking him quietly. He looked worriedly at her but stayed silent, ready to catch her if she stumbled again. She didn't, even though the procession took over an hour to reach Macherna, mainly up-hill. Most of Aleksei's ancient and frail relatives were visibly suffering by the time they reached the marble mausoleum.

The soldiers carried the coffin from the bier and laid it in the tomb on one of the quickly vacated marble plinths. *Episcop* Yeltsin blessed the tomb and the coffin again, sprinkling holy water over the pall bearers to purify them. Six soldiers from the old guard and the new army took up positions of respect around the tomb, Peter Kamanin himself taking up guard point at the entrance. The slow procession walked past them, paying their final respects to the tsar.

Laura was glad to see the carriages discreetly tucked behind the fence to the cemetery, waiting to cart the family and ministers back to the walled city. Her ankle was throbbing dully from walking all the way to the cemetery and she carefully climbed into a waiting carriage; Luke, Lady Anne and Ilich climbing in with her. Four mounted guards took up position and followed them as they left the cemetery.

They did not follow the main road back past Ladozhskoye as it was choked with people coming to the tomb to pay their respects. Instead the carriage rode west towards the hamlet of Davostok; a collection of three houses and a mill; the westernmost settlement of Dalnerechensk. The condition of Miner's Way this side of the Western range was as poor as ever, as it was only used by the families that lived in Davostok and the guards that changed posts by the border crossing.

They sat in silence, feeling the carriage jolt uncomfortably over the ruts and potholes as it swung south, following the line of the low stone wall that marked the boundary of Dalnerechensk. Laura shut her eyes, trying to block out the sight of this little visited part of Dalnerechensk. She had seen it twice before, once in her marriage procession, following the same route they were now; and once as she had led Olaf back to the Principality, trying to beat Nikita's army who were approaching from the North.

She sniffed loudly, pressing the handkerchief to her eyes. *The hand he had offered her to climb over the wall was one of the last times he had touched her, and it was only hours after climbing the wall that she had been arrested, and hours after that that Nikita had attacked, and hours after that that Olaf was dead.* Or maybe he was dead before Nikita had attacked. She never knew when he had lost his life. She never knew where, or what had happened to his body.

She sniffed again, but her tears had been spent in the dark hours in the church, and what followed now was just the trickling aftermath of the deluge. She knew it was making everyone in the carriage uncomfortable; Anne who couldn't be close to her daughter-in-law, Luke who was estranged from her, Ilich who was constrained by protocol and etiquette.

Lady Anne winced as they bounced over a particularly nasty jolt and pressed her hand to the small of her back, reaching out with her other to take Luke's, shooting him a veiled, worried look. He squeezed her hand gently, leaning over to press a kiss on the back of her fingers. Laura looked away, eyeing the trees of the mountain flank as they crossed back into Liberty Valley, emerging many miles south of Tcherepnin.

The valley was eerily empty. No one tilled the farms here; the building site where Peter Kamanin was erecting a grand home on his new lands stood abandoned. The garrison village of Tcherepnin, with its rows of barracks dissected neatly by the iron rails, was silent and ghostly in the sunshine. Laura shivered and folded her hands tightly in her lap, dreading what the city of Dalnerechensk itself would be like.

It had been dark when we returned she remembered. *The Tcherepnin Beacon had been lit, the only light in the city it seemed. The riot had emptied the streets, which were humming with tension and fear.* She didn't want to see Dalnerechensk empty again, so she sat with her eyes closed all the way to the castle. Ilich took her hand gently to help her down in the courtyard and she thanked him absently, being careful with her tender ankle.

She nodded to the guards at the door who saluted her, and slipped up the stone stairs to her rooms. She took off the hat and veil, noticing that Anna had not returned and wondered if she had gone to the tomb too. She placed her hat on the chaise lounge and headed to the nursery, calling out to Gertrude. There was no answer and she pushed into the small parlour, eyeing the empty nursery beyond.

An uneasy feeling settled over her and she found it hard to dislodge, even when she told herself that Roman was with them and would die to protect her daughter. She shook herself hard, telling herself that she was worried for nothing, and quickly made her way to Luka's room.

She let herself in quietly in case he was asleep, checking around for his maid. But he was alone, his head tipped back on the pillows, a sheen of sweat on his forehead and cheeks. She quickly went to his dressing room, filling a shallow bowl with water and brought it back with a strip of linen. She dipped it into the cool water and gently began to sponge away the discomfort from his forehead. He stirred and opened his eyes.

'Ah, Your Majesty' he said faintly, pleased but a little surprised. 'How was the procession?'

'Beautiful' she said sadly. 'And terrible. It seems there are no people left in Dalnerechensk at all.' She carefully sponged his cheeks and he took the cloth from her gently.

'Please, you do not have to wait on me.'

'It is no trouble' she smiled. 'I also find myself without a maid at present' she stopped, reminding herself she didn't have a nurse or a daughter at present either. She shook the thought away, but the unease didn't leave.

'Besides,' she went on, 'I thought the socialists thought no man was better than another' she smiled again.

'Yes' he said. 'But you are a woman…'

She paused at the inflection she heard in his voice then smiled it away.

'So is your maid Luka, and even a tsaritsa is only the property of her husband.'

'Dalnerechensk always did have some old fashioned laws' he said quietly.

She dropped her eyes and folded her hands carefully.

'Luka -' she started, but the knock on the door interrupted them.

It was a gentle knock, a knock that didn't want to wake a sleeping man. The door clicked open quietly and Ilich stepped in. He bowed slightly to her and closed the door behind him.

'Ah my friend, you are awake' he said, bringing a chair from the small table for Laura to sit on. He then brought a second and sank gratefully onto it, pulling the seat quite close to the bed.

'Have you seen Anna?' Laura asked him, anxious.

'No Your Majesty. She is probably still in the crowds visiting the mausoleum. You spoke very well at the funeral.'

'Thank you' she said, trying to mask her worry.

'Doctor Pushkin has given me permission to leave my sickbed tomorrow, and I should very much like to join in the celebrations' Luka said.

'That is good news, though you must not exhaust yourself celebrating' Ilich chided.

'And these are emotional days, we must take care that we are not crass or careless in these times' Laura added. 'Tomorrow is the anniversary of the revolution, but we still must mourn for Tsar Constantinovich. It would be too crass to drink and dance and make merry.'

'We will announce a public holiday for tomorrow, and perhaps the wireless demonstration for the day after' Ilich soothed.

'Tsar Constantinovich died the day after that' Laura said, shutting her eyes. 'There must be a marking of that anniversary too, perhaps a small candlelight ceremony on the town green. And the repel of Nikita's army five days after that.'

'Ten days' Ilich corrected.

'Pardon?' Laura blinked.

'You returned to Dalnerechensk thirteen days after the revolution Your Majesty' Luka explained, shooting Ilich a worried look. 'You were in Russia nearly two weeks.'

Laura blinked, taken aback, and fell into reflection, worrying her lip with her teeth. *I could have sworn it was only a few days* she thought. *Tsar Constantinovich died on the second day, and we were prisoners of* Knjaz Rurik *for three days, and there were those two beautiful nights with* - she stopped herself. *That was it. Where had the rest of the time gone?* she wondered helplessly. *Wait, it rained for three miserable days, we dug the grave in the rain…*

And then we found the cave…

Three days, it must have been she mused. *Three days with Nikita, three days with*

-

'Three days' she said out loud.

'It was much longer than that Your Majesty' Ilich said gently.

She shut her eyes. 'We will hold a torch lighting ceremony in the Avenue of Heroes' she said, pushing through the wall of rising emotion. 'And then we will open the new Parliament Chambers, with a ball. I trust by then Doctor Pushkin will allow you to dance' she smiled shortly at Luka then rose, causing Ilich to rise too. 'If you will excuse me gentlemen, the hour is getting late and I am tired.'

'Of course Your Majesty' Ilich bowed. 'I do hope you sleep well tonight.'

She smiled shortly again and nodded to them, letting herself out of the room.

It was indeed getting later, and she went quickly back to the nursery, her concern growing when she saw it was still empty. She crossed to the window by the nursing chair and looked vainly for her returning servant. But it was no good, the window looked out over the river, and the window in her rooms looked out over Vsevolod's Way. Anyone returning from Macherna would come via Castle Street, the back entrance to the castle. She paced the room and went back to the window, still searching though she knew it was in vain.

Stupid! she shouted at herself. *Stupid stupid! You sent her out with only a nurse and one soldier, one tired from his night shift!* The icy cold dread suddenly filled her. *What if he's lost her? Something must have happened!* She raced to the window again and stood on her tip toes to see more, then tore herself away, trying to be rational, trying to push away the rising panic.

Roman will be with her she told herself hysterically. *Roman won't let anything happen to her.* She paced the room again then yanked open the door, determined to race along the line of pilgrims to Tsar Constantinovich's tomb until she found her daughter and knew that she was safe.

She rushed down the stairs, glancing along the corridor of the first floor and stopping in shock so quickly that she stumbled and nearly tumbled down the rest of the stairs. Roman stood in the gloom at the far end of the wing, where Aleksei's private study had once been. *What is he doing there?!* she cried silently. *Is Alexandra there? Why would Gertrude have taken her there? What's going on?* Then the icy dread turned into a solid lump on her backbone. *He's hiding. He's hiding in the dark, he's lost my daughter! Where is my daughter?! What is he doing sneaking around by Aleksei's office?!*

'Roman!' she cried, but her voice was so strangled with panic it came out as a dry croak. 'Roman!' *And he's ignoring me too!* her thoughts screamed wildly as her panic burst forth. '*Captain!*'

He stopped. And he turned. Laura took a deep breath, her horror crystalising the world around her.

'*Guards!*' she shouted. 'Who are you? Where is Roman?!'

The man in the *Sotnik* uniform whipped the hat off his head, coming closer, stuttering and stammering as several guards surrounded him.

'I found the uniform' he was stuttering. 'I found it. I thought I would try it on, I thought I would see if I could get into the palace, I meant no harm' he burbled in terrible dread.

'What is it?' Ilich and Luka cried, running down the stairs to meet her, the latter dressed hastily in a robe.

'How did you get in here?!' Laura shouted.

'I salute, so they can't see my face' he said, demonstrating then shrugged, embarrassed.

Shaking, Laura turned to the nearest guard. 'Arrest him' she said.

Soldiers moved in and Luke quickly joined them, asking what was wrong. A burble made Laura look around then cry out in anguish and relief. Gertrude was coming up the stairs with Alexandra in her arms, and both of them looked happy and unharmed. A grubby servant was following them, and Laura blinked hard before realising it was Roman, dressed in ragged clothes, his face and hair dirty.

She rushed down the stairs and yanked Alexandra into her arms, hugging her so tightly to her that she began to wiggle and grizzle uncomfortably. She kissed her over and over, pressing her tightly to her as the guards hustled the imposter down the stairs and out into the courtyard.

'Where was you?' Laura asked in German, fright and tiredness and lack of knowledge of the language making it difficult to express herself clearly.

Gertrude cooed and clucked in a soothing way, waving her hands and babbling excitedly in German, most of which Laura didn't understand at all. She glanced at Roman and read in his expression that he understood a good deal more than what Laura did.

'Alexandra *bliebt mit mich heute nacht*' Laura stuttered, cutting off Gertrude's talk. 'Alexandra's crib is to be moved into my parlour' she said to the others in general and carried her daughter back up the stairs to her rooms. 'Roman see to it that you get your uniform back and report this incident to *Graf* Pavlodar, then personally explain to me how that man got your uniform.'

She slammed her door and sank down onto the chaise lounge, pulling her daughter close to her. Alexandra's small face nuzzled into her neck and she felt the hot mist of her breath on her throat. She shut her eyes in relief and exhaustion, cradling Alexandra's tiny head on her shoulder.

A timid knock announced the arrival of the crib, but Laura was unwilling to let her go just yet and shut her eyes, trying not to fall asleep despite how heavy her limbs felt. Gertrude eyed her worriedly as she set the crib down, aware that the tsaritsa was angry with her but didn't exactly know why. *It is too late for explanations now* she told herself. *In the morning will be better.* She curtseyed and left, closing the door carefully behind her.

Alexandra snuffled quietly on Laura's shoulder, nuzzling unconsciously against her warm throat. Laura squeezed her eyes tighter, the tears welling up behind her lids. There was a soft sound by the fireplace and she opened her eyes quickly, fear pushing the tears away again.

Luke stood at the fireplace, wiping the tears from his eyes.

'Daddy?' Laura asked.

'You spoke very well at the funeral' he said, swallowing down the lump in his throat, and Laura heard that hidden note of jealousy, that she had been so close to the man, that she had called him Father. 'Countess Ivanova was good enough to translate for Anne and I.' He wiped away some more tears. 'Will you say such eloquent things when I -'

'No!' she cried, getting to her feet and rushing to him. 'No how could I? I would not be able to speak for misery!'

Luke folded her in her arms and kissed her forehead, sighing quietly, then kissed Alexandra's head too.

'Anne is pregnant' he said quietly. 'She wants to have the baby in America, close to all her family. If we delay much longer she won't be able to travel.'

Laura blinked, unsure how to feel about this news, and was a little guilty to realise she really didn't care that much. *I must be just too exhausted and drained to care* she told herself hurriedly, and said: 'That is great news; and terrible news too.'

Luke smiled sadly and kissed her forehead again.

'I'm sorry to bring you the news so late, perhaps I should have left it for the morning' he mused, stifling a yawn. 'Get some rest, and put Alexandra to bed, you both look exhausted. It has been a long day.'

'Yes Father' she said dutifully, but knew she couldn't go to bed until Roman had explained himself.

She opened the door, aware that Anna had still not returned, and the feeling of concern and unease grew a little more. There were six soldiers stationed outside her door instead of the usual one and further down the corridor, at the head of the stairs they could see Peter Kamanin and several more soldiers, who he was directing to various parts of the castle.

'There are lots of guards about tonight' Luke noted absently, and Laura realised he didn't know what day it was. She decided not to tell him, to avoid worrying him.

'Perhaps it is a shift change' she murmured, bidding him goodnight and watching him slip down the corridor to the stairs, watching the soldiers salute him as he went past, and Luke awkwardly acknowledge it.

She closed the door and hesitated, but Alexandra was growing heavy so she placed her in the crib, folding the warm blankets over her. She then pulled a chair close to the crib and sank into it, placing one hand inside to reassure herself of her daughter's presence, and liked the way the little fingers curled around one of hers unconsciously.

There are *a lot of guards* she thought as she listened to the faint sounds of them going about their rounds, and the creak of the floorboard outside her door as one of the guards shifted his weight. *Is Peter Kamanin just being cautious or is something going to happen?* she wondered worriedly. It wouldn't surprise her if the more militant socialists of the party tried to oust the monarchy by force again tonight. *Maybe the Vakhtangovs would oust me and blame the revolutionaries* she thought darkly. *Maybe Maksim might try and blame both the Vakhtangovs and the Revolutionaries.*

Nobody wants me on the throne...

The little, self-pitying thought was interrupted with a knock on her door. It opened and Peter Kamanin stepped in, saluting smartly despite the late hour.

'Forgive my intrusion Your Majesty' he said. 'I know you don't have a maid, Anna has sent a note. She will be with her husband tonight, and regrets the inconvenience that this might cause you.'

Laura looked away. *Anna feared what might happen this night too* she told herself. *She knew what terrors Russia had held, she had been there in the misery of it all.* Laura didn't blame her for not wanting to go through it again. *And* a small, dark part of her whispered, *this time we might not be so lucky, this time we may not get away...*

'Are they going to kill me tonight?' she asked, not wanting to look at him, to see the truth written on his face.

'No Your Majesty' he soothed. 'We have heard no whispers of any unrest or demonstrations planned. *Glava Gosudarstva* has forbidden it. -'

'He was not exactly in control last time' Laura interrupted, looking at Peter.

'It will not happen' he said so confidently that she was instantly soothed. 'And even if it does we will be so forewarned that you will escape unharmed.'

'Into the tunnel? Are there soldiers stationed in Tcherepnin by the door to the reservoir? They know about the tunnel now -'

'Indeed they do Your Majesty, and indeed there are soldiers stationed outside the reservoir. But they don't know about the cellar I had flooded when we redug the moat, nor the boat I have there waiting to ferry you away should anything happen.'

Laura looked surprised then smiled. 'That is genius *Graf* Pavlodar, Vsevolod should have thought of that.'

Peter was hard pushed to control the pleasure of that illustrious compliment and saluted her smartly.

'Thank you Your Majesty' he beamed. 'We are prepared for any eventuality. Do not worry yourself, and get some sleep, it has been a trying day. I will be downstairs in the foyer if you need me.'

She thanked him and dismissed him, hoping that Roman would not be much longer, as she was feeling increasingly wearied. But he knocked the instant that Peter laid his hand on the doorknob and quickly saluted both of them. Laura noticed he was dressed crisply in a clean jacket, though his pants looked wrinkled and worn.

'Come in Roman' she said, keeping her voice stiff and formal. 'Good night *Graf* Pavlodar.'

Peter hesitated only briefly before bowing and closing the door behind him. Roman was radiating nervousness and still stood saluting her.

'At ease soldier' she said gently. 'What happened?'

'I was watching her, like you asked me to' he started, lowering his arm. 'We were standing close to the cathedral while the ceremony was happening inside, and a man in the crowd bumped into Gertrude. He said something which must have been an apology, but it was in German -'

'German?' Laura interrupted, surprised.

'Yes Your Majesty' he said. 'Gertrude instantly began talking to him, and they had quite a conversation, though I am sorry I can repeat none of it to you -'

'Who was this man?' Laura demanded.

'I don't know Your Majesty' he shrugged. 'But he was - odd.'

'In what way?'

'He seemed - odd. Out of place' Roman shrugged. 'I can't explain it.'

Laura eyed him, irritated.

'Go on' she prompted.

He paused. 'I only looked away for a second Your Majesty, I swear I did' he said. 'But when I looked back she was a good way away, being hurried away by him. I ran after them, but there were all these people in the way, and I know he was keeping an eye on where I was. The uniform, it stuck out so much...' he shrugged helplessly. 'I stole some laundry and changed quickly in an alley, I knew which way they were going so I knew I would be able to find them again... I'm sorry Your Majesty' he said.

'Where did they go?'

'A house; a grand house' he elaborated. 'He led her straight in the front door, but I went round the back and snuck in. They had tea' he shrugged. 'In a parlour, and there was someone else present. I couldn't see who it was through the keyhole, I could see Gertrude, and a little bit of the *Tsesarevna's* dress, but not the man, or who the other was.'

'He must have been a *boyar*' Roman burst out. 'The man that took Gertrude. He was not dressed like one, but he was, I'm sure of it.' He stopped and Laura arched her eyebrow. 'The other man did not speak German' he went on. 'So the boyar translated for him, and for her when he wanted to know something.'

'And what were they discussing?'

'You, Your Majesty' Roman said uncomfortably. 'They were rather - candid.'

'Tell me *exactly* what was said Roman' she demanded, rounding on him.

'They asked her exactly how old *Tsesarevna* Alexandra was, and when you had given birth to her. They asked what your feeding routine with her was, whether you used any - potions or - herbs or - anything like that' he stopped embarrassed. 'Whether you had taken anyone into your confidence. She talked very openly, but nothing was scandalous, she didn't know the answers to a lot of the questions, and they couldn't press her because they were just having a nice little chat, you know, she had someone she could talk to who spoke her own language, and wasn't the master nice? Wasn't it so eccentric of him to be so interested in the gossip of servants and so on.' His voice took on a slightly mocking tone.

'The *Tsesarevna* began to cry then, and Gertrude said she should be getting back, so they promised to take her back in the coach. She came back with the German speaker. I hitched a ride on the coach but they didn't know I was there.'

'Were you seen?'

Roman hung his head. 'I must humbly beg for forty roubles' he mumbled. 'I was seen when I was listening at the keyhole, and I promised the maid forty roubles to keep quiet.'

'That is a small fortune indeed' she said. 'You did offer far too much. A sum of fifteen would be more appropriate when you are caught listening at keyholes again.'

Roman blushed 'I'm sorry Your Majesty' he mumbled.

'And you must take more care where you leave your uniform.'

Roman's blush deepened. Laura sat in the chair again, placing her hand back in the crib to stroke Alexandra's soft hair.

'Do you have any idea who either of the men were?' she asked quietly.

'No Your Majesty.'

'Could you find the house again?'

'Yes Your Majesty' he said firmly.

'Good. These men are members of Parliament or the Vakhtangov family, or highly influential with them. They have played an open hand, they know it will not take me long to figure out who they were, and what they know from that meeting. It is a source they cannot use again. Perhaps this open blunder was a feint for some more devious discussions. They may be those behind the man that tried to bribe you, but again, perhaps not' she fell silent from her musings, the weariness pressing on her. 'What did you tell *Graf* Pavlodar?' she wanted to know.

Roman stifled his yawn. 'That I had lost my uniform while spying.'

'That perhaps was not the wisest move' Laura mused absently. 'He is downstairs. Please ask him and six other guards to join you here.'

Roman saluted and hurried off, returning shortly with the assembled guards Peter could spare. They saluted her, looking alert and slightly worried. Laura bid them to stand at ease then turned to Peter, whose careful face betrayed nothing.

'*Sotnik* Prokofiev has disgraced the uniform of the Order of Vsevolod and was unmindful of its duty to the Royal family. He is relieved of command for two days and his pay reduced to two thirds its current rate for one month.' Roman's mouth fell open in shock. Laura went on to address the remaining guards, ignoring Roman. 'You know what day it is. These men are to stand guard inside this room, and frequently relay information from other guards in the castle. Goodnight.'

She turned and strode into her bedroom, closing the door against the soldiers who had saluted again, and whispered to the silent room:

'I'm sorry Roman.'

29

Alexandra's cries woke her around midday and she grumbled loudly, pushing back the covers and pulling on a robe, determined to give her back to the nursery as soon as possible. Six soldiers were still in her rooms, one holding Alexandra and cooing softly, two others bent over his arms and waving a tassel from the curtains to try to stop her crying. They stopped, a little embarrassed, and saluted her quickly, the soldier holding Alexandra keeping his arms around her and lowering his head to make the salute, nervousness caking his face.

'Forgive me Your Majesty' he swallowed. 'She was crying; we didn't want her to wake you.'

'She is hungry' she smiled, taking her daughter from him and waving away the salutes. 'Thank you for your dedication to the happiness and security of the monarchy' she went on. 'Please send Anna and Gertrude to me, and see *Graf* Pavlodar to resume your duties.'

They saluted her again and filed out, closing the door quietly behind them. Laura sat down on the chaise lounge, Alexandra nuzzling hard at her. But it was no good, her milk had dried up, and Alexandra cried in frustration, her little fingers tugging at the front of her nightdress. Laura rocked her gently, stroking her soft hair and whispering soothingly to her.

She had been too afraid to sleep and too exhausted to stay awake last night, and she had gotten just enough sleep to feel as if she had had none at all, but couldn't fall asleep again, and was not looking forward to the day's activities. But she was grateful for these quiet moments alone with her daughter, even if she was fussing and hungry.

But it was over too soon, interrupted by a timid knock on the door and Anna stepped in, a little nervous for her breach of duty last night.

'I am sorry Your Majesty' she said quickly. 'I had to be with him -'

'It's alright Anna' Laura soothed. 'I know. Find me something suitably dignified for today, there is a lot to do.'

Anna curtsied and scurried off to do her bidding, coming back to answer the second knock on the door. It was Gertrude with a bottle and a feeding rag, looking subdued. Laura beckoned her over and took the bottle, tipping it up for Alexandra. She eyed Gertrude as she handed her the rag, wondering if she should tell her how dangerous her actions had been. *He spoke German to her* she reminded herself. *The only person with a fluent command of the language that she had encountered in this tiny place.* Laura wondered, if put in the same position, whether she might have done the same thing. *Probably not* she sighed. *I have more political savvy than Gertrude, and I know what is at stake.* It had been a cruel hand to play, as she doubted she would see her new friend again.

She gave her instructions to take the crib back to the nursery then rose and carried Alexandra with her to her dressing room where Anna had laid out her clothes for her. With Anna's help she dressed in a rather sombre blue and sat at her dressing table for Anna to pin her hair up. Alexandra finished her bottle and smiled a gummy smile at Laura, who laughed and kissed her nose.

She stood and headed to the nursery to deposit her into Gertrude's care then descended the stairs, greeting Luka as they arrived at the dining room door together. His arm was supported in a sling and he bowed to her, wincing slightly.

'Good morning Luka, it is nice to see you up and about. Is your shoulder mending well?'

'Indeed, and no sign of infection' he smiled.

'That is good to hear' she said, stepping into the room.

Those already seated at the dining table stood as she entered and bowed to her. She took her place at the table and waved them back into their seats, watching as Ilich came towards her, followed by a nervous little man, who was twisting his hat round and round in his hands.

'Your Majesty, may I present to you Jurek Titov, who will be conducting the wireless exhibitions this afternoon.'

'I am pleased to meet you' Laura smiled while he bowed low. 'How does it work?'

At once she regretted her question. A torrent of information flooded past her, wherein she only caught random words like alternator transmitters, sine waves, rotary-spark, amplitude modulated and electromagnetic radiation. At the end he stood waiting expectantly, watching the effect his mini-lecture had had on her.

'How fascinating and technical' she smiled. 'And what message in Morse Code will you transmit for us?'

'No no, not Morse Code Your Majesty' he corrected hurriedly. 'Audio. I have produced audio transmissions, though they are relatively weak.-'

'Has that been done before?' Ilich interrupted, astounded.

'I do not believe so' he smiled. 'I thought perhaps this first transmission might be a reading of a passage from the Bible, or perhaps music.'

'Music? How delightful!' Laura smiled.

'Would Your Majesty care for a private demonstration?' Jurek asked, hopeful.

'Of course. Fedor -' she stopped looking around for him, a flash of guilt overcoming her. *He had been with us in Russia too* she reminded herself. *Where had he been last night? Had he been as frightened and worried as Anna had been? As she had been? Where was he now?*

But all this passed in a moment, with barely a falter in her words, as she spotted him close by, as he always was.

'- can arrange matters with you. I trust you will not need to erect an antenna on the castle roof?'

'No Your Majesty' he smiled and bowed again while Fedor guided him out of the dining room.

Laura began to eat the small course placed in front of her, her gaze drifting over the other diners. She noticed with some trepidation that there were only ministers seated at the table, none of the usual court detritus had dared to show their faces today, not even the unimportant and lecherous Vakhtangovs.

With the arrival of the second course her thoughts turned to the rest of the day. Parliament would not meet because of the holiday Ilich had declared but she knew a good number would be out and about, making their presence felt, talking to the common man, and every other political manoeuvre that would help paper over the cracks the revolution had caused. It would be a good idea for the royal family to be out talking to people too.

She stopped, suddenly feeling very lonely. Fedor would be busy with Jurek Titov, Roman had been temporarily banished from her side, and the charming von Schmidt brothers were still absent. *I will take Grigory and Ekaterina* she thought in a rush of passion. *They are my friends and I want them to walk unafraid through their city again.* She had heard the guards whispering information to those in her sitting room last night. There had been guards stationed outside the Ivanov's door too, and there were mixed feelings for that duty.

She put down her fork halfway through the second course, listless and without any appetite. She dreaded the thought of this public performance, how careful she had to be to strike the right balance between the solemnity of public grief and the casual, friendly engagement with her subjects. *But I must do this* she told herself firmly. *For Alexandra, and for the Vakhtangovs I loved...*

She had read the paper, when? *Yesterday? Or the day before?* she mused. It seemed so distant now. An anonymous informant had hinted of the divides within Ilich's party, at the contesting feelings of respect for the monarchist institution that some of the members held. The article had bemoaned the loss of Piotr Grigorevich; and Aleksei and Tsar Constantinovich too; mourning the loss of the male line of the Vakhtangovs. But it had - *to their credit* Laura supposed - begrudgingly approved her efforts to re-establish the credibility of the Monarchy in the Principality.

The anonymous contributor had called for a referendum Laura reminded herself. *A vote on whether the monarchy should continue in this country.* The thought of it worried her. The Monarchy had survived two Russian armies, a plague and economic meltdown in her long history; and yet now it might so easily be swept aside by a small stroke of a pen. *Over what?* she thought testily. *Over some misguided hate? Over the fact that her daughter was, in fact, female?*

Perhaps she could remind the people that whilst she may be a woman it would not be so forever. The sons of Vsevolod would sit on the throne again. *That was a stirring thought* she mused. *I must remember to use that line. Perhaps I should write a letter to the newspaper* she thought, her mind turning to the new technologies. *Perhaps soon I could use the audio transmitter of Jurek's to speak to each citizen, reminding them that things do come full circle again...*

A polite cough behind her brought her out of her musings.

'Jurek Titov has set up his transmitter, Your Majesty' Fedor said quietly. 'He will demonstrate it when you wish to see it.'

'Very good Fedor' she smiled. 'I shall see it now. Ilich, Luka, Father, Lady Anne; would you be so kind as to join me?'

'Of course, Your Majesty' they bowed, and followed her to the empty room that has once housed the Advisory Council.

30

Roman stood in the centre of a line of five Vsevolod Guards lining the back of the platform. It had been erected that afternoon at the end of The Avenue of Heroes, before the Northern Wall and the new border crossing, draped in the green of the Republic and the Monarchy. The tsaritsa, *Glava Gosudarstva*, Luka Nevsky, *Episcop* Yeltsin and Maksim Yegorov, who had weaselled his way into the ceremony somehow, stood before the guards on the platform. Down the avenue, at the foot of each grave, stood an unlit torch, and two paces back from it stood a soldier at attention, a burning brand held before him.

The avenue was thronged on both sides by Dalnerechensk citizens, standing still and silently. Fathers had hoisted small children onto their shoulders; mothers stood close by their daughters. Some carried candles, some others carried flags, but they didn't wave them. All eyes were fixed on the line of orange fire slowly rising up the eastern tips of the mountains, cast by the setting sun.

Roman eyed the back of the tsaritsa as she stood before him on the platform. She was wearing black again, veiled in respect, but wearing the crown she had had made to hold it down in the gentle breeze. He was trying to stop his thoughts from sliding back over the last two weeks, trying to stay focused on the ceremony, but he couldn't help himself.

He had been furious with her for docking his pay, for his public humiliation when he had only been doing his job, *and had come up with quite a creative way to follow them so that* Tsesarevna *Alexandra had always been in his sight* he thought. *Nearly always been in his sight* he corrected himself. Her ungrateful dismissal of his actions had made him wild; wild enough to find himself heading down the street where he knew to meet his midnight visitor. He had had his hand on the door of the run down tavern when it had occurred to him that this was precisely the reaction she had intended to provoke in him.

He had hesitated then, and a scruffy patron barging out had startled him, causing him to retreat back the way he had come. And as he had thought about it on the way back to the barracks, her punishment had really been a blessing in disguise. She had given him two days to recuperate after his lengthy shift, a luxury he would not have had before.

But he had hated the way they looked at him he reminded himself, trying not to fidget uncomfortably in the ceremony. *Everyone had gossiped, everyone had seen him without his Sotnik jacket, everyone knew he was being paid less than a corporal for a month...*

Everyone *had known*. Which might have explained why, four nights ago, he had woken again with the hand across his mouth and breath misting unpleasantly on his throat. *The voice had whispered to him again, but it had sounded different, more wheedling.* He couldn't be sure if it was the same man or not. *He didn't stink of garlic sausage this time, but that was proof of nothing* he thought.

He had not had a chance to talk to the tsaritsa until two days later, on a rare riding excursion. Baron Asanton and Lady Anne had left that morning, sorry that they could no longer delay their departure as the risk to Lady Anne's health would have been too great. But there had been some welcome news for the poor tsaritsa, the train that had taken her family away had also brought back a familiar face: Gustav von Schmidt.

Laura had cried out in surprise and pleasure, and had embraced him warmly, eagerly looking for his brothers. But Gustav had returned alone, presenting the apologies of his brothers and uncle, and only those who were looking for it saw her brief disappointment. She had smiled and had returned to the castle with him, and over a long luncheon they had talked of their activities in the weeks they had been apart.

Then, unable to contain himself any longer, Gustav had begged to go riding, to continue his catalogue and study of Dalnerechensk's flora. Roman remembered thinking at the time she had not been hesitant to agree, and probably relished the thought of some time away from the public's eye. And so he had accompanied the tsaritsa and her German friend into the Hunting Forest that was once again private property, had listened to them talk together in French and examine the flowers and leaves of the forest carefully.

Gustav's Russian secretary had joined them in the forest then, and Gustav had bowed and left the tsaritsa, rushing off to scramble and crawl through the undergrowth. The tsaritsa had then turned her horse further on into the forest, and Roman had followed her silently, listening to Gustav's French instructions fading away behind them. Still they had ridden on, until they had reached the falling remains of the Northern Wall, no more than a foot high in some places. The tsaritsa had stopped then, and dismounted, had sat on the low stone wall and eyed him expectantly.

He had dismounted and saluted, feeling awkward. She had waved it away, watching him carefully.

So you have been offered another bribe she had said.

Yes Your Majesty. They will make me Commander of the Army under the New Regime he had told her. *They sounded more… well, they sounded different this time. I'm not sure if it's the same person. They talked about how demeaning it was to be stripped of command, and how it would never happen to me again. They promised me a title too, and more land than just an abandoned farm. Sorry Your Majesty.*

Do not apologise she had smiled. *And have you accepted?*

He had fidgeted. *No Your Majesty.*

There are only three things that they can offer a man to make him break a vow: wealth, power, and women. Perhaps you should accept when they offer you me.

His mouth had fallen open in surprise then, and even the tsaritsa had blushed at her words. She had coughed and rushed on with an explanation: *In classical times when a regime was overthrown the wives and daughters were married off to loyal servants and soldiers because it was supposed to be demeaning* and she had stopped, as she had seen the look on his face; that hot, pink feeling of embarrassment growing between them. *Not that it would be demeaning to marry you* she had babbled on, clearly aware that she should have stopped talking, that pink cloud surrounding them and lying stickily on their skin.

On the platform Roman shifted uneasily, the memory making his skin feel hot again. *A tantrum* the midnight visitor had called her actions. *A lover's tiff.*

And therein had been that subtle, quiet bribe he thought, blushing. *To have her as a lover, a mistress. Though as a wife she would be his property, and would have to do what he wanted.* It was a thought to make any man weak.

Don't dally too long Roman, she had said, standing from the wall and fussing with the bridle of her stallion. *Or they will think you incorruptible, and move on to someone else, who may not be so loyal to me.*

As he fought to control the blush in his cheeks Roman became aware of a sound that had been there for a while, but had only just registered in his ears. Dalnerechensk was singing; gently, quietly; the sound filling the valley like spring fog while the cold stars glowed above them. Peter Kamanin gave the command to light the torches and two rivers of fire lit up, flowing towards the city of Dalnerechensk.

It's beautiful Roman thought, listening to the national anthem in the dark. *She certainly knew how to deliver pageantry. And that's what we'll all remember, the lines of fire that led from her to the castle, lit up against the twilight sky as if it had been set alight again.*

Episcop Yeltsin stepped down from the platform and Laura followed, Luka, Ilich, Maksim and the soldiers falling in behind them. *Episcop* Yeltsin made the sign of the cross over each and every grave as they made their slow way back to Castle Street, to where Peter Kamanin stood at the junction of the two roads. When Laura reached him he saluted, and she pushed back her black veil to kiss his cheek.

Roman resisted the urge to touch the spot on his own cheek that she had kissed a year ago. He had been in the small unit that had gone to Tcherepnin through the tunnel, had stood on the walls of the garrison village and fired shots down into Nikita's army between Dalnerechensk and Tcherepnin, sandwiched between the two Dalnerechensk units that had boxed them in.

Basil Barad had been right beside him the whole time, his childhood friend; who had noticed how ineffectual they were on the walls, how they couldn't help but hit their own citizens in the mêlée, how they were too far away from the push into Vsevolod's Way to do any good. It had been Basil who had given the order to open the gates, to put bayonets on their rifles and close up the box, to push the Russians tighter and tighter together.

They had become separated in the battle, and he had gone bloodied and wearied to the palace without him. He had seen that look of horror on the tsaritsa's face, how strained she had been by the blood and the misery and the pain. It had been the next day before he had known that Basil had been killed. He had spent days at the foot of his grave, and had seen the poor tormented tsaritsa walking the Avenue of Heroes alone, hiding away in her mind from the horrors she had endured. As he watched her now, walking slowly back to Dalnerechensk, he wondered how close she was to hiding away again.

There was no question that she was strained he told himself. *Even with the return of Gustav von Schmidt she had no family save for her daughter, and even the irrepressible Countess Ivanova had faded away in the aftermath of the revolution, hiding away inside the castle and careful, oh so careful, how she spoke to the new Parliament Ministers.*

They wound their way silently through King's Gate and up Castle Street, passing through the back gate of the castle near the private gardens of Tsar Constantinovich. The tsaritsa said her quiet thank yous and goodbyes and Roman followed her to take guard outside her door again. He wondered if he should ask her if she needed anything, or if he could do anything for her, as he knew she had already dismissed Anna for the night.

But she shut the door quietly against him, and as he stood there noiselessly he could hear the sounds of her moving about in her rooms. He sighed quietly, settling in for his four hour vigil outside her door, quickly rubbing his face to check for any stray tears or dirt.

After a while he became aware of another sound from her rooms; the quiet hitch of breath, the low moan of the agony of heartbreak. He shut his eyes briefly, wondering how many more times he would listen to her cry herself to sleep. *She was only a girl* he told himself. *She was younger than he was, and weighed down with the burden of Monarchy, without friends and supporters, without the knowledge of who was plotting against her…*

I have to accept the bribe he concluded, though the gall rose in him to admit it. *I'll go tonight, once my shift is over.*

And now that he had made up his mind he found the hours crawling by and his impatience growing. The soft sounds inside the tsaritsa's rooms gradually faded away but he didn't notice, consumed with his thoughts. *What would he tell them?* he wondered. *Would they expect information from him right away? What if he had dallied too long?*

He sighed quietly and shifted his weight. As much as he liked his job he couldn't wait for his replacement to come, and rushed off when he finally arrived. He headed at a quick trot to the barracks at Tcherepnin, changing quickly into the grubby clothes he had worn whilst spying and hurried back to the tavern in Dalnerechensk.

He hesitated at the door but pushed it open and slid inside, sitting in a shadowy corner, looking carefully around the bar. There were not many patrons, and all of them were ignoring him. He ordered a drink and sat back quietly, looking over the people who were near him. They would shoot him furtive glances every now and then and it made him uncomfortable to see them whispering.

There was a young couple kissing in a booth, and three old men sitting near the fire singing *Kalinka*, conducting the song with their glasses. There was the waitress that brought him the drink, and a man lugging barrels up from the cellar and stacking them behind the bar. There were no other people in the tavern, no one who could have been his sinister visitor. He hunched back even further into the shadows, feeling disappointed.

Perhaps it is the wrong time he wondered, checking his pocket watch. *They might not be here, they might not be coming.* He tucked the watch into his pocket again and scrunched his shoulders back against the wall, trying to get comfortable. The old men finished the song and began again, still conducting their harmonies with their drinks. *Beautiful maid, dear maid, please fall in love with me…*

After three hours he gave up, tired from his long wait and frustrated it had been uneventful. *Maybe I'm too late* he thought despondently as he made his way back to the barracks. *I can only hope that I haven't left it too late, that they haven't found someone else who –*

The thought was interrupted when he was grabbed from behind and pushed hard into a darkened doorway. The gloved hand mashed his lips against his teeth and the strong arm pushed him hard against the stone wall, the body forcing him into the shadows.

'Do not cry out' the voice whispered, misting on him again.

Hello Mr Garlic Sausage Roman thought drily.

The pressure released him a little, and the hand was taken away from his mouth.

'Well?' the voice demanded.

'I have decided to –'

'Clearly, or you would not be here' the voice interrupted peevishly. 'What do you have to tell me?'

'I think –'

'Think?' he spat. '*Think?!* What you *think* is of no use!'

'She is in love with Baron –' Roman stuttered, but was interrupted again.

'Come come, that is obvious! You are of no use if you can only state the obvious! You, who stand guard outside her door all night! Who goes into her rooms?'

'No one!' Roman cried, beginning to feel panicky and ashamed that he knew so little.

'Has she taken a lover? *Who is the father of her daughter?!*'

'I don't know!'

'When will you?'

'I - I don't -'

'Then you are of no use whatsoever.'

'*She cries herself to sleep!*' he yelped, and instantly regretted it. There was silence behind him. 'I don't know why. I could, I could -'

The pressure released him and he took a shaky breath.

'Who am I talking to?' he asked quietly. 'I want to know who I'm -' he turned around and stopped.

There was no one there. He lunged out into the street, searching wildly around him but it was deserted. He clenched his fists as tears of rage and shame pricked at his eyes. He had betrayed the tsaritsa, and had no information to give her in exchange. He felt soiled. He hung his head and slunk back to the barracks.

31

Laura sat in the nursing chair, rocking Alexandra as she drank, watching as Gustav strode towards the Western flank. His secretary trotted after him, his arms full of paper and specimen jars. Every now and then she saw him halt in his hurried gait and bend down, scooping up an item that had fallen to the ground, only to stop a pace or two later to scoop up another. She smiled and stroked Alexandra's hair, noticing that she was fussing more than usual and her skin was warm to the touch.

'Gertrude?' she called, worried. 'Is she sick?'

The nurse came and looked at her, confused. Laura put her hand on Alexandra's head again, eyeing Gertrude worriedly.

'*Sie ist Warm*' she stuttered in her limited German.

Gertrude came over and felt her head and cheeks then poked a finger into her mouth, running it along her gums. Alexandra grizzled and wiggled away from the touch.

'*Zahn*' Gertrude announced, tapping her own teeth to emphasise what she meant.

'*Sie ist sehr Warm*' Laura said, eyeing Alexandra as she fussed and pushed away the bottle, beginning to whimper.

Gertrude did her best to explain that babies get fevers when they teethe and it wasn't something to be too concerned about. Laura wasn't convinced, and wondered if she should ask Doctor Pushkin to take a look. *I cannot help but worry* she told herself, biting her lip. *She is too important…*

Alexandra's whimpering turned into tears and Laura hugged her, wondering what she could do to stop the pain. Before she could ask Gertrude there was a knock on the door and Luka pushed it open, dressed, with a white sling supporting his shoulder.

'Forgive my intrusion Your Majesty' he said, bowing. 'Ilich has asked me to respectfully request your presence in Parliament today.'

'He does? What could he want me for?' she asked, surprised.

'I could not tell you, only that it is a matter of grave importance.'

Laura hesitated. 'Alexandra is ill, she is teething -'

'It is a natural part of growing Your Majesty' he soothed. 'She will be safe in the capable hands of your nurse.'

Laura eyed Alexandra, stroking her head while she squirmed away, her tears gaining momentum. She kissed her, lingering, then stood, handing her to Gertrude.

'Very well. I shall dress and join you shortly' she said and Luka bowed as she slipped past him.

Laura worried at her lip absently as she headed to her rooms, passing the guard at her door with a brief acknowledgement. *He's summoned me* she thought as Anna helped her dress in something sombrely regal. *This can't be good news.* She chewed her lip again, turning this way and that in the mirror. She debated wearing her crown again, to remind them exactly who was in charge, but decided against it in case she was over-reacting.

She eyed herself one last time then took a deep breath to steady herself. She left her rooms again, heading down to the new Parliament Chambers. Luka and Ivan were waiting outside the doors for her.

'Forgive us Your Majesty, Maksim has forced the issue' Ivan said apologetically.

This really can't be good news she worried, but kept her face calm and carefully blank. Luka opened the door, wincing slightly at the effort and essayed a quick bow as she stepped past him. The ministers who were already inside, seated at the beautifully carved desks that lined the central aisle, rose to their feet and bowed as she made her way to the dais. Ilich was standing at Vsevolod's table and bowed to her as she passed him, not looking very perturbed.

She seated herself and motioned for the ministers to take their seats again, keeping her back stiff and straight. Ivan took his place at Vsevolod's table and quickly set out the date on a piece of paper, ready to jot down the minutes of the day. Ilich called Parliament to order then Maksim rose, brandishing several editions of Dalnerechensk's newspaper.

'My esteemed colleagues' he began, slipping out of the desks and striding to the centre of the aisle. 'I take it that several of you read the article in this morning's edition? It has been a growing concern in the populous, gradually growing larger since the return of the *Velikaja Knjaginja*' he stopped. 'Excuse me, *Vdova* Tsaritsa' he corrected himself.

He lay the papers on the desk in front of Lev and Laura didn't miss the smile of encouragement Maksim's lackey gave him. He turned, addressing the whole Parliament.

'These are changing times gentlemen. I have seen the old ways die, have seen Vsevolod's line wither and die. They were men we admired, respected; men who we sadly - wistfully - remember in the downfall of their house.' He stopped, aware that some of the ministers were shifting uneasily.

'The old ways have died, gentlemen' he went on, raising his voice. 'And this new blood, fresh and vibrant, has taken up the baton from where it slipped from weak and unmindful fingers. The Government of Dalnerechensk is changing; the technology and infrastructure, politics and indeed the very culture of our people are changing.'

He pointed to the papers he had put on the desk.

'But our people want us to change more' he went on quietly. 'When you committed to this, gentlemen, you swore no more blood. You promised the people they would not have to submit to the Monarchy's will, to the outdated and backwards view of the world any longer. But now they ask *why have you not done as you promised?* To allow this mockery to continue, this hollow institution, undermines *everything* you ever stood for. *Everything.*' He slammed his hand on the bench to emphasise his point. 'I move that we abolish the institute of the Monarchy once and for all.'

Parliament erupted, shouting and fist waving across the aisle. Ivan tried to write the objections and counter-arguments raised but gave up, tossing down his pen in the swirl of the cacophony. It took several minutes of banging on the wooden desks and shouting for order to restore peace again. 'Make no mistake gentlemen there is no Vsevolod there' Maksim went on, red faced and waving his finger at the ministers. 'Oh yes, you may think that she saved Dalnerechensk, but not when it counted, not when there were Russian troops at the city gates - I will be heard!' he shouted as he was interrupted again. 'No then, *then* it was men, and our military leaders, our strategists that repelled the Russians. There was no Vsevolod that time gentlemen. *We* did it! She said it herself, the spirit of Vsevolod lives in all of us here who are descended from those men whose very blood and sweat saved Dalnerechensk. Vsevolod could not have saved her without the Dalnerechenskers themselves!'

'Vsevolod's bloodline has failed!' Lev shouted wildly, jumping to his feet. 'There's nothing but silly petticoats left!'

'But there is precedent' Yuri Drevin interrupted. 'Elizabeth the First and Queen Victoria - God rest her soul - Catherine the First, Anna, Elizabeth -'

'Queens regnant, every one of them' Maksim sneered. 'Not some foreign bride on a throne -'

'There is precedent for that too' Yuri snapped. 'Catherine the Second -'

'Ah!' Maksim shouted in malignant pleasure, as if someone had jabbed him with a pin. 'Yes how well to compare *Velikaja Knjaginja* to her! Both poor, and married to unlikable men; surrounded by rumours of illegitimacy. We cannot discount how strongly our citizens feel for her indiscretions. And, it is said, they both have a strong liking for stallions -'

Laura slammed her hands down on the arms of her chair, rising to her feet in one violent move.

'*Enough!*' she shouted as the ministers fell into silent bows. '*How dare you speak so slanderous in my presence!*' she continued, her face burning with embarrassment, well aware of the rumour that Catherine the Great's death had been caused by a stallion falling on her during a sexual act.

'Forgive me, I was unmindful of my tongue -'

'Indeed. And your shameful words reveal your fallacious nature. You would do well to comport yourself with decorum and honour at all times' she snapped, swallowing down her fury as best she could.

'I apologise wholeheartedly for my slander' Maksim said, his lips tight.

Laura eyed him, wishing she could slap him hard enough to make his teeth rattle. Her hatred and anger twisted like smoking nests of snakes inside her, roiling in her guts, rising in her throat like thick black bile.

'Ivan' Ilich said quietly. 'Please note in the minutes that Minister Maksim Yegorov was fined four hundred roubles for breaking the Slander law.'

There was a mutter in the ranks of ministers.

'I will bear that as good and fair punishment' Maksim said. 'But I cannot in good conscience let this matter rest. The people have called for a referendum, an official poll as to whether Dalnerechensk should discard the Monarchy or not. I feel it is only fair to give them what they want.'

'No' Laura said.

'Your Majesty -' Lev started.

'It is true that I am poor, and foreign' she interrupted. 'It is true that I am not descended from the line of Vsevolod's house. But my husband shared his body with me -' she blushed.

'He may have bedded you but that does not make the blood of Vsevolod flow in your veins' Maksim interrupted. 'A pot, once seed has been planted, does not become the flower too.'

'And when I swore my body to my husband I swore it to that of Dalnerechensk too' Laura went on coldly. 'I love this land and her people, and I swore to do all I could for it, to lay down my very life that I hold precious for it should she but ask me -'

'And your patriotism for your adopted home does you credit, but it does not disguise the fact that you are *not her true daughter*' Maksim finished. 'You are a foreign woman, and what comes after you is a woman. Who will she marry? What children will she have? What children will *you* still have?'

Laura was surprised and momentarily thrown. Maksim used the pause to turn and address the ministers again.

'It is a growing concern for our populous. I do not ask you to revolt again, I only ask that we allow their voices to be heard on this matter. They may decide to keep the Monarchy, they may decide to dissolve it. *But their voices will be heard gentlemen.* Is that not what you stand for?'

Laura tried hard not to clench her fists but the rest of her was strung tightly with rage. She could see the effect Maksim's words were having, how uneasily they shifted and cast their eyes over their neighbour, to read in their faces the doubt and guilt too. *They're going to vote my crown away!*

The panic made her cry out for their attention. They turned to look at her and she swallowed, trying to push down the rising fluster.

'My lords I beseech you! Yes, I am a woman, perhaps too poor and humble to sit where I do, yet I wedded a son of Dalnerechensk, a son of Vsevolod; and I grew that blood in my womb and gave you a daughter, a mother for his new sons. I will do my best to raise her to that most worthy name, and I will find for her a husband from the families that can claim Vsevolod's blood too. I swear to you in this mighty place of justice and law and righteousness that Vsevolod's sons will sit on his throne again. God grant you the wisdom to choose now for your sons, and your sons' sons.'

There was silence when she finished speaking. Ilich cleared his throat and called for a vote. Laura shut her eyes so she wouldn't have to see how many hands were raised, how many of her ministers wanted her gone. Ilich and Ivan both counted, put their heads together and consulted quietly. Laura opened her eyes again, realising she had missed an opportunity to see just how they felt, information she could have done with. But all hands were lowered and all eyes were looking expectantly at Ilich.

Ivan and Ilich reached an agreement and Ilich turned to his Parliament.

'The motion is carried by two votes. We will put the referendum to the people.'

There was a smattering of applause, and Laura could feel their eyes sliding to her. *I won't give them the satisfaction of seeing me run out of here upset* she told herself fiercely.

'So be it. I will bind myself to the will of my people' she said, and sat back on her throne, letting her features settle into an expression of thoughtful attentiveness while the ministers went on with reports.

Inside she was seething. *I should have worn the crown after all* she thought. *Or at least the lucky black diamonds.* She couldn't bring herself to look in Maksim's direction. He was puffed up and silently crowing with his accomplishment, one step closer to ousting her from power. *Oh it had been masterful!*

There was no doubt in her mind that the anonymous voice in the newspaper was Maksim. *This could only be to stir trouble* she mused, beginning to chew her lip again. *Maksim does not want me on the throne, but surely he does not want the Monarchy abolished? His family is related to the Vakhtangovs, his uncle is married to Varvara, Piotr's grandmother. He wants this crown, this throne. He could have ruled through a poor, sickly child king. And assumed power at his sudden, untimely death -*

Her thoughts crashed to a halt in horror. *Surely he could not have - could he?* Piotr had been sickly and weak, he could only have died young, but - *what if he had not died fast enough?*

I think I need a food taster she thought, then realised that Parliament was looking at her. *They've finished* she realised and stood, watching the way they bowed as she made her way along the aisle to the doors. She tried to ignore how Maksim's back barely bent at all.

That - that snake! she seethed as she quickly made her way up to the third floor, rushing into her rooms and slamming the door behind her. *Either way he wins* she thought angrily. *He'll abolish the Monarchy and win the elections, ending up in power as Head of State, possibly calling on his weak connection by marriage to eventually seat himself on the throne. Or he will keep the Monarchy, and find a way to rid himself of her, and take her place with some concocted coup on the throne.*

That - that -

She was at a loss with what to call him. She wanted to scream and yell, but there were ears outside her door and tongues that would pass on what she said. She seized up a pillow from her chaise and smothered her face, swearing into it all the vile words she could remember from her childhood, all the curses she had heard those rough and ready workers of her father's utter on the dig sites in Texas.

She paced and cursed, then flung aside the cushion to rush into her dressing room to don her riding habit.

She stopped, her knees going weak and she clutched at her doorframe for support. Behind her the flung pillow knocked over a crystal vase and sent it shattering onto the rug.

She sank to the ground in a half swoon, the agony gouging its deep channels of grief and despair in her again. *She had wanted to go riding, to see Olaf...*

She was so in need of him. She ached with longing for him. She missed his strength, his quiet comfort, the way she confided in him. She had trusted him completely, unashamed of sharing her fears and secrets with him. *I have no one now, no one I can trust. I need you Olaf!*

Unaware of what she was doing, blinded by misery, she crawled into her bed chamber, her hand seeking the drawer of her bedside cabinet and deftly pulling out the secreted letter. She sat with her back against her bed, great sobs wracking her as she unfolded the letter and pressed it to her face, trying to breathe in the now vanished scent of him from the parchment.

She missed the feel of his hands, rough from ten years of work in the stables, how strong and how delicate they were at the same time. She missed the feel of his body against hers, in hers…

She pulled the paper away from her face. Her kisses and tears were beginning to smear and dilute the ink, the folding and refolding causing the parchment to weaken and fail in the creases. It was the last little piece of him, and she was beginning to lose that too. *All I have left of him to touch, and yet touching it will destroy it* she moaned to herself, pressing it tightly to her chest and wishing it would grow arms to hold her back.

I will lose everything here…

'Your Majesty?' Roman whispered, knocking softly on her door.

Laura rolled away, pushing the letter into the drawer sharply, wiping her tears away quickly.

'Yes Roman, what is it?' she asked, keeping her voice level.

'Forgive me for my intrusion' he started.

She rose, wiping the rest of her face quickly.

'It's alright' she said, turning to face him, managing a smile she didn't feel.

His face betrayed nothing yet she knew he had seen the letter. A small stab of fear and guilt shot through her. She knew he couldn't read French, and he would not rifle through her drawers in search of it, but would he tell his mysterious benefactor of its existence? Perhaps she should tell him not to mention it. *But that will only look as though I have something shameful to hide* she thought. *I should not worry, he will only say what I tell him to say.*

All this passed in a moment.

'*Episcop* Yeltsin has requested to see you' Roman said. 'He is without. Shall I send him away?'

'No, admit him.'

He bowed and ushered the bishop into her parlour, then resumed his newly begun duty outside her doors.

'*Episcop* Yeltsin, to what do I owe this unexpected pleasure?' she smiled.

'The pleasure is all mine, Your Majesty' he answered, bowing low. 'I have heard of your devotion to prayer of late' he smiled. 'It does lift my heart so to hear that. Yet you have not come to confess.'

Laura looked at him carefully. *Whose side are you on?*

'I enjoy the solitude and the comfort of the words' she said. 'I am out of habit of going to confess, as your predecessor did not encourage it.'

'No, he did not' *Episcop* Yeltsin agreed sadly. 'It must be said that I am not the man that *Episcop* Vasily was.'

'Indeed' Laura said.

Episcop *Vasily had been a drunken avarice, if I remember rightly* she thought, but did her best not to let the thought show. *And he had deserted Dalnerechensk when the revolution had happened, leaving the people without spiritual comfort in that frightening time…*

She eyed *Episcop* Yeltsin thoughtfully. *It was a brave man who stepped forward in a moment of crisis* she mused. *Or a highly ambitious one. I don't know if I can trust you.*

'Perhaps you might like to see the changes I have made? I could hear your confessions then' he went on.

'I should like that' Laura smiled, though would never admit it to the half honesty of it.

She crossed to her dressing room and gathered her coat, wondering where Anna was. A small part of her was glad that she had not witnessed her breakdown, and though she was sure her eyes were red from the bout of tears *Episcop* Yeltsin had not noticed. *He also couldn't see the shards of the vase all over the floor from where he was standing* she realised, and was grateful for that too.

She returned, pulling on her coat, careful that it was the rich blue of the Monarchy, and ushered the priest out of her rooms. Roman fell into step silently behind them, and a quick summons had five more soldiers as an honour guard when they left the castle grounds.

Laura was glad they were on foot, and she made a point to smile and talk with everyone who spoke to her. It meant that the walk to the cathedral took over an hour and a half but *Episcop* Yeltsin didn't seem to mind, blessing people as they moved on.

They reached the cathedral and the *Episcop* led her to the gated entrance to the bishop's apartments at the side of the church. In Vasily's time they had always been shut and bolted, and Laura was glad to see the gates now stood open, and the courtyard inside bustled with lesser brothers of the order, unloading barrels and boxes from a cart, stacking them neatly inside a large storeroom.

'We are organising the tithes' *Episcop* Yeltsin explained as they stepped through the gates. 'Your escort will not be needed inside this holy place.'

Five of the soldiers saluted and remained outside but Roman stepped into courtyard, following Laura stubbornly.

'*Sotnik* Prokofiev is charged with my personal safety, he will come with us' she said, moving on to inspect the tithes.

The brothers stopped what they were doing and bowed as she approached, keeping their eyes lowered. *Episcop* Yeltsin joined her and explained where the tithes came from, where they would go, how much would end up in Russian markets, how much would be kept to feed the poor come winter. Laura listened to it all, approving of the calculations and the destinations, letting him usher her into the apartments.

She was struck by how barren and bleak they looked. She had never been inside them before, but knew that *Episcop* Vasily had lavished art and tapestries and carpets in his apartments until its sumptuousness rivalled the palace itself.

'Were the apartments ransacked after *Episcop* Vasily deserted his post?' Laura asked, moving closer to the small fire to warm her hands.

'I believe that the properties he owned were' *Episcop* Yeltsin confirmed. 'But the cathedral apartments were not. The fineries that were not the personal property of the church were sold off shortly after the new government came to power.'

'Who sold them, you?'

'Yes Your Majesty.'

'And who bought them? Who could afford such luxuries?' she wanted to know.

'I believe Minister Yegorov purchased the bulk of the items' he said. 'The money from the sales was given to help build the new school.' He was beginning to look worried. 'Does Her Majesty not approve?'

'It is a good deal more austere than it was' she said, rubbing her hands. 'And it is good that the church can no longer be accused of wastefulness and gluttony. Yet there are expectations of pageantry required of you, whether you approve of them or not. You are the spiritual leader of Dalnerechensk, the people expect to see you represent God's majesty here on earth.' She stretched her hands out to the fire again. 'Besides that, there are practical implications as well. It is cold enough to light a fire in here, and the weather has been mild. Your health will suffer come the winter. At least put rushes or something on the floor to alleviate the chill if you would not have the carpets back.'

He smiled. 'Wise words Your Majesty. I shall look into something suitable.'

'Forgive me for saying *Episcop* Yeltsin, but I do not recall that you were ever *Dyakon* Yeltsin, I believe the position was held by *Dyakon* Arakcheyev?'

Episcop Yeltsin looked embarrassed and coughed uncomfortably.

'It is true I was never a *dyakon*, only a *svyashyennik*. *Dyakon* Arakcheyev still holds that position' he explained reluctantly.

Laura was surprised, as she had thought the job of bishop would have gone to Deacon Arakcheyev once *Episcop* Vasily had deserted, rather than a mere priest, and said so. *Episcop* Yeltsin looked wretched then.

'Perhaps in other circumstances he would have, Your Majesty' he said. 'But his position did not automatically assume the bishop-hood with *Episcop* Vasily's - departure. Authority is passed directly from God down to bishops through the laying on of hands. It was started by the apostles and is a physical and historical unbroken link, an essential element in the conferring of bishop-hood.'

'And *Episcop* Vasily laid hands on you?' she asked, astonished.

'Yes.'

'Why?'

He dropped his eyes. 'Because I caught him fleeing.'

Laura pressed her lips together. She could just imagine the scene, and how the priests might have felt with their spiritual leader fleeing in fear of his life. She could just see the panicked laying on of hands, and wondered if it was even done properly.

'We argued' *Episcop* Yeltsin continued, sounding hollow. 'I tried to hold him here, to tell him that we needed him, to fear no man, but he wouldn't. He lay hands on me. It was witnessed, by none other than *Dyakon* Arakcheyev and two other *svyashyennik*, who had been drawn by our words.

'And then he was gone. I wanted to offer to lay hands on *Dyakon* Arakcheyev but I knew in my heart he would refuse. They were afraid; I could see it in their eyes. We heard that they had murdered the royal family, had murdered ministers and were looking for anyone else in authority. If anyone were to die it should be me, to leave better men to guide Dalnerechensk in the aftermath. But of course no one did die, and for that we thank God.

'I know I am unworthy, perhaps unsuited, for bishop-hood; but I will bear it with God's grace and guidance.'

He turned and opened the side door that led from the apartments into the nave of the church, ushering the tsaritsa through. She placed her hand against the wall of the stone chapel to the side of the door as she did so and was shocked by the heat.

Of course, the fireplace she realised, remembering how Vasily had boasted of it, pointing out which chapel was kept permanently warm by its heat. Too late the memories came flooding back.

She had gone to the bar that second time, and had taken refuge here in this chapel with Olaf...

It had been warm with Vasily's roaring fire behind the stone they leaned against. Olaf had slipped his arm around her, to hold her while she rested her head on his shoulder. He had called her Your Highness, *the first time he had ever called her that, and warned her not to go back to the pub again.*

The first time he had touched her... had held her...

'Ah yes, Natasha's chapel' *Episcop* Yeltsin said, breaking into her thoughts. She realised with some horror that her reverie had been so deep she had been unmindful of her company and had reached out, tracing lines on the door. 'It is very beautiful, would you care to see it?'

Laura managed a sad smile, shutting her eyes.

'I have had my fill of death and mausoleums' she said quietly.

Episcop Yeltsin looked embarrassed and flustered, and quickly hurried to the lectern to make ready for her confession. Laura was glad of the momentary solitude to compose herself but reined her relief in sharply when she heard Roman's footsteps behind her. *You are never alone* she told herself angrily, and tried hard to turn that tide of longing in her.

She made her way to the large icon of Christ on the cross that hung beside the lectern. *Episcop* Yeltsin stood in front of it, his hand resting on a gospel book and a blessing cross that lay on the lectern. She dutifully venerated the book and cross then laid her thumb and first two fingers of her right hand on the feet of the Christ icon, as she knew the Orthodox had to do.

As she knelt *Episcop* Yeltsin read an admonishment warning her to make a full confession, holding nothing back. She shut her eyes and clasped her hands together, carefully marshalling her thoughts. *The Russians believe that a confession is to God, the priest is only a witness and a guide* she reminded herself. *But what will he witness? And what will he tell others?* She couldn't tell the truth. But she couldn't lie. She took a deep breath and began to speak.

When it was over *Episcop* Yeltsin placed his stole over her, and his voice trembled slightly as he read the Prayer of Absolution. Laura rose when he finished, wiping her eyes a little sheepishly.

'Rest assured Your Majesty, God has heard your words and will comfort you' *Episcop* Yeltsin said with a wobbly smile.

She thanked him and took her leave, trying not to look at Roman as he fell into step behind her, surreptitiously wiping his eyes on his sleeve. She paused at the door, taking a moment to ensure her face was clear of tears, wiping her eyes again.

She stepped out, smiling at the people who had gathered to see her, noticing that Peter Kamanin was waiting beside a carriage at the foot of the stairs. Four mounted Vsevolod Guards stood in position around it, and the five members of the guard she had left with stood in a row behind the carriage. Peter Kamanin bowed when she emerged, and the nine soldiers saluted.

'Roman?'

'-s?' he asked then coughed, embarrassed. 'Yes Your Majesty?' he tried again.

'Check your pocket watch. What time is it?'

He fished it out quickly. 'It is nearly six, Your Majesty.'

I'm going to be late for the first ball to be held in the renovated ballroom she thought, and hurried down the steps. Peter extended his hand to help her inside then leapt up to the driver's seat himself to rush her back to the castle, helping her down when they arrived.

She thanked him absently and slipped upstairs, checking in on Alexandra. She was sleeping, and Gertrude said she had been for nearly six hours. Laura bent over the cradle and kissed her gently, smelling the whiskey Gertrude had rubbed on her gums to numb them. Her fever had not abated, but the nurse promised that there was no ill. Laura hesitated then sighed and slipped back along the corridor to her rooms. Her legs were already tired, but there were hours still of dancing and feasting to mark the grand opening of the new Parliament Chambers.

The second session – the first proper one – in the new chambers and I had to give my crown away she thought sadly.

For a moment she wished that Aleksei could still slip into her rooms and massage her feet, could still talk so shyly and awkwardly with her, could still look so roguishly handsome in the firelight. She had loved those small moments of tenderness with him, had loved him for his insecurities and his weaknesses. But he was gone now, and she could not have those moments again.

She sighed softly and pushed open the door, glad to see that the broken shards of the vase were now gone and a new one sat on her small table, filled with fresh flowers. She smiled softly and went to her dressing room where Anna was smoothing down the evening dress Laura had picked out.

32

'Who is he Roman?' she breathed.

He had not heard the door click, so silently had she turned the handle, and only the feeling of space behind him before she spoke alerted him that she was there. He turned his head so she could hear his soft answer better. 'The German Boyar.'

I thought as much she mused silently. She had noticed Roman's stiff reaction when Maksim had introduced his cousin - a well-connected merchant prince who lived in Ekaterinburg - as they met at the entrance to the dining room. *He had recognised him, but he could not have said what he knew then.* So she had slipped away to dine, and Roman had gone off duty. She had to wait, whiling away the night with polite small talk and dancing until three in the morning, when Roman came back on guard, to be absolutely certain.

He was insanely rich she reminded herself, *dealing in silver, gold and precious gems mined from the area around Ekaterinburg. As rich as Maksim was he would need a vast fortune to run a political campaign. Knjaz Sergei Uvarov had been brought to Dalnerechensk to bank roll his bid for power, and to weed out her secrets, one way or another.*

'Is he the man that bribes you?' she asked.

'No' he answered, then amended it because he couldn't lie to her. 'I don't think so. At least, he is not the man in the pub.'

Laura fell silent again. She highly doubted the man Roman met in the pub would be the prince, he possibly wasn't even the one that the man he met reported to. She shifted uncomfortably on her sore calves, chewing her lip thoughtfully.

Knjaz Sergei Uvarov was handsome in his own way, imposing and commanding in his demeanour, and better than his cousin at hiding his disdain for her. He had been polite and conscientious in his discussions with her, graceful in his dancing, but there was always something unspoken and distasteful in the curl of his lip, in the glint in his eye.

She shifted again, trying to ease the ache that was becoming unbearable.

Why had they revealed themselves now? Had they truly used up their advantage in talking to Gertrude? Had they not gotten the information they wanted from her? What other plan had they set in motion? Did they have any other plan?

The ache in her legs was too much to stand in the one place any longer and she stepped out, heading to the nursery, feeling her legs wobble unsteadily under her. She heard Roman close her door quietly and follow her. She had only gone a few steps before she realised her mistake. She reached out and clutched at Roman's sleeve, feeling his strong arm catch her under her elbow.

He helped her back into her sitting room, gently guiding her to her chaise lounge. She sat and groaned, massaging at her tired legs. Roman saluted smartly.

'Permission to retrieve Anna to see to your feet?'

'She has gone home for the evening' Laura smiled sadly.

She tucked her feet up and rubbed at her calves, noticing how nervous Roman looked. *He's worried about being in my rooms with me* she thought as she rubbed, wishing that she did have Anna with her. *There was no reason why she could not dress herself when needed, and no need to have someone waiting on her hand and foot, sleeping in the servant's rooms above to arrive at her beck and call whenever she felt like it. And Anna was married now, to a man that held no position in the household anymore. She should have the right to go home to her husband.*

It did make it difficult when, in the middle of the night, she needed things that a tsaritsa should not get for herself. Instead she sent Roman to find a foot bath, and down to the kitchen to heat kettles of water over the fires that never went out. He was smiling faintly when he returned, placing the bath of water on the floor at her feet.

'What do you find so humorous?' Laura asked.

He sat on the floor at her feet. 'When I was a boy I would sit like this by my mother, and she told me the story of The Secret Ball. Do you know it?'

'No I do not.'

'Would you care to hear it?'

She smiled and said she would, dipping her toes carefully into the steaming water. It was pleasant so she rested her feet in the bath, leaning back comfortably on the chaise.

'Once there were twelve daughters of a king' Roman started. 'They were each more lovely than the last, and they all slept together in a room that was shut and bolted each night, but each morning when the doors were opened all their shoes had been worn to pieces, as if they had been dancing all night, yet none of the princesses were tired in the morning.

'Finally fed up with the cost of replacing their expensive shoes and the mystery of how they had gotten worn out, the king promised that the person who could discover their secret would marry the daughter of his choice and inherit the kingdom after the death of the king. But, if they could not discover the cause in three nights, they would forfeit their lives.

'Many tried; princes, and kings; but none could discover their secret. They slept in an antechamber, and the princesses' door was left unbolted and open, yet every night the suitor would find their eyes growing heavy until they could not keep them open, and could not discover why the shoes were worn out. All of them were executed.

'Finally it came to be that a lowly *Graf*, noble but needy, was out walking near the palace when he happened upon an old woman. She begged some food from him and he shared the meagre meal of bread and cheese he had brought with him. For his generosity the old woman gave him an invisible cloak and told him that if he wanted to discover the princesses' secret he should not eat or drink anything that they gave him.

'He thanked the woman and took great heart, proceeding directly to the palace and announcing to the king that he was here to solve the mystery of his daughter's shoes. He was received courteously by the king but the daughters made fun of him for his poverty, all except the youngest who gave him fine clothes and spoke with him kindly.

'Later that evening, when he was resting in bed in the antechamber beside the princesses' room, the eldest daughter came to him and offered him a goblet of wine. Remembering what the old woman had said, the *Graf* took it and pretended to drink it by turning his face to the wall and pouring out the wine into his bed. Then he shut his eyes and pretended to fall asleep. The princesses laughed when they heard him snoring, and they pulled on pretty dresses and their new silk dancing shoes.

'Then the eldest daughter touched a secret spot on her bed, and it moved aside, revealing a staircase down into an underground kingdom. As the last princess disappeared into the ground the *Graf* leapt to his feet and threw on the invisible cloak, following them.

'At the bottom of the stairs was an avenue of trees, along which the princesses were walking. The closest trees had twigs of silver, so beautiful that the *Graf* could not help but collect a twig. As they walked further the trees had twigs of gold, and he collected another piece. The last trees had twigs of diamonds, and again the *Graf* collected a twig, stowing them all carefully in his pocket.

'At the end of the avenue was a lake with twelve little boats drawn up on the shore. In each boat stood twelve princes, ready to ferry the princesses across the lake to a wonderful palace. The *Graf* quickly got into the boat with the youngest princess and watched as they danced all night with the princes, finally going back to their room when their shoes had fallen to pieces on their feet.

'For two nights he followed them, and on the third night he bought back a cup from the kingdom, presenting it with the twigs he had taken the first night to the king. The princesses had no option but to confess the truth of the *Graf's* story when presented by the evidence. The king then asked the *Graf* which of his daughters he wanted to marry.

'My mother would always pause in her story and ask me: Which should he marry? The eldest, because he himself is not young? Or the youngest, because she was kind to him? Then she would say to me, Roman, it is neither here nor there who he married, they may have been companionable, or kind or beautiful, but they were deceitful and willingly sent men to their deaths to keep their amusements.'

'I was wondering if you had worn out your dancing shoes too.'

'Am I deceitful Roman?' she teased.

He blushed. 'I did not mean that -' he started, but she waved it away, lifting one foot out of the bath to wiggle it experimentally, testing the tension in her muscles.

'Your Majesty?' he started, biting his lip. 'Did you mean what you said in confession? Forgive me, I did not mean to listen in, and the bishop came to my barracks especially to admonish me for eavesdropping - but, did - did you mean it?'

Do you miss the poor mad prince was hovering on his lips, but he did not speak them.

'Only I didn't know he was ever kind' he rushed on, babbling. 'We only ever heard stories, and you've cried yourself to sleep so many nights -' he stopped, clamping a hand across his mouth to shut himself up.

The blush came up in Laura's cheeks.

'You can hear that?' she asked, embarrassed.

Roman nodded, blushing too, keeping his hand firmly across his mouth. Her blush deepened.

'Please don't cry Your Majesty' he begged. 'I didn't mean to, I told them you cried yourself to sleep -' he shut his eyes. 'I'm sorry. It was horrible to say that to them.' He shuddered.

'Who were they?' she asked, diverting her emotions away from the embarrassment. 'What do they look like?'

Roman hung his head. 'I did not see them' he mumbled. 'I'm sorry, I panicked, but I will try to find out who they are, I swear Your Majesty.'

'When you do, tell them I have come into a large sum of money recently, and that there are a million pounds of missing bonds from the old tsar's safe.'

Roman gasped. 'You did not -'

'No of course I did not. I made some money in shares in various companies, and nowhere near a million pounds. But Tsar C-

Constantinovich did have over a million pounds that Parliament cannot account for, and they disappeared around the time of the revolution. Compress those two facts together and you have something seditious to tell your benefactor. I will confirm it by purchasing a large number of jewels in the next few days.'

'Your Majesty?' he asked, his words coming close to interrupting her. 'Do you not mind them thinking this ill of you?'

'Yes Roman, I do' she said quietly.

Carefully she lifted her feet out of the bath and padded the excess moisture onto the carpet before she rose wobbily to her feet, covering her yawn.

'Thank you for the bath, and the story Roman' she smiled. 'But it is time for you to resume your duty outside my doors, and I must try and sleep' she smiled sadly again. 'Goodnight' she whispered, and slipped into her bedroom, leaving Roman to close her door and take up guard again.

33

Laura woke and stretched, rising from her bed. Anna greeted her quietly, pushing back the drapes at her windows when she stepped into the parlour. She called a greeting back, ignoring the foot bath that was still sitting on the floor by her chaise. Anna followed her to her dressing room and helped her out of her nightdress, pulling on a corset and lacing it firmly. Laura fidgeted while she waited for her dressing to be complete, hurrying out while Anna chased after her, fastening the last of her pins in her hair.

She was glad to feel her calves did not hurt so much this morning and she skipped lightly on them as she hurried to the nursery, anxious to see how Alexandra was doing. Gertrude smiled when she arrived, and Laura could hear Alexandra's gurgles as she lay in her crib. Laura stood in the doorway and thrust her arms forward for the nurse to deposit her daughter into them.

Alexandra smiled, burbling happily when she saw her mother, and Laura planted kisses on her soft head, sitting in the nursing chair, catching sight of a flash of a small white tooth in her mouth. Laura smiled, and took the bottle from Gertrude, settling down to nurse, grateful that Alexandra's fever was gone.

She looked up at the quiet tap on her door and smiled when Luka bowed.

'Good morning Your Majesty' he smiled. 'I came to congratulate you, last night's ball was a resounding success.'

'Good morning Luka' she smiled, adjusting her grip on the bottle.

'How curious that she has blonde hair' he mused out loud.

A warning sounded in Laura's mind and she smiled, being careful to keep her attitude light and flippant.

'My mother had blonde hair, as did late Tsaritsa, I believe' she said. 'Perhaps she will look more like her Grandmother' she smiled, stroking her hair again. 'I would like that, The Countess has such poise and grace in the portrait in the library. Many people have told me she was very beautiful.'

'She was' he answered, as if he were conceding a point. 'Alexander Andrei looked very much like her.'

The name on his lips startled her, and there was a flicker in her eyes that Luka missed, as he was staring intently, critically, at Alexandra, and the words he was thinking were loud enough to hear. Alexandra finished her bottle and flashed Luka her white tooth in a gummy smile, declaring proudly:

'Mama!'

Laura laughed and kissed her again, wiping away Alexandra's drool on a soft cloth. Instead of handing her back to Gertrude she took her with her as she headed back to her rooms, excusing herself from Luka's company. She sighed then dabbed perfume behind her ears before carrying her daughter out into the busy market on Vsevolod's Way. Roman and another of her personal guards escorted her, their uniforms bright and highly visible in the gay crowd.

People called out and curtseyed as she passed, cooing at Alexandra, who sat alert and watchful on her hip, burbling happily and waving her fists. Laura spoke to as many as she could, striking a gentle balance between sombre gravitas and friendly approachability.

In the distance, near the train station, she could see a wagon, draped in flapping bunting, and four people stood in it, two of them unfurling a large canvas banner. The royal blue flags piqued Laura's curiosity and she headed towards it, noticing that people near the wagon were distributing bright leaflets to those gathering around them.

The banner unfurled completely, revealing the name: *The Principle Party*, and the poles supporting it were secured to the sides of the wagon. Laura recognised Tatiana, smiling and charming, handing out leaflets and chatting amicably with a man dressed in a bloodied butcher's apron, who looked bashfully at his feet and clutched a leaflet in both hands before him, as if it were a shield.

Maksim has wasted no time she mused sardonically. As surprised as she was to see Tatiana mingling with commoners she realised it made sense. *Tatiana is clever and savvy, and can be sweet and attentive too. Aleksei must have seen something in her to have taken her as his mistress.* Laura brushed the thought away quickly, stopping Alexandra from tugging at the lace of her bodice. *Maksim will need a woman to compete with an Empress* she consoled herself.

She turned away as Maksim and his cousin climbed into the cart, calling for attention from the crowd. Laura did not doubt the speech would be lengthy, clever and persuasive, and she had no desire to see the effect it would have on her people.

Instead she turned into a side street and soon found herself walking along a wide, pretty road, lined with many a stately home. Roman suddenly coughed, his eyes fixed on a large manor. Laura eyed him curiously, then followed his gaze to the house, guessing what he couldn't say. Knjaz *Sergei Uvarov had led Gertrude here…*

'What beautiful fretwork!' she exclaimed, catching Alexandra's hand from her bodice again. 'Who owns this architectural marvel?'

'Vasilievich Chekov' said the other guard. 'But it has been empty since the revolution.'

Alexandra grabbed at her lace again and tried to stuff it into her mouth, beginning to grizzle at Laura's continual attempts to thwart her. Laura ignored Roman's steady gaze on her, quickly moving on. *He is not mistaken* she told herself. *He followed Gertrude here, and someone* is *living in this house.*

Fed up and foot sore Laura headed back to the castle, depositing Alexandra into Gertrude's care, heading to her rooms to change her wet dress.

Through her windows she could see the crowd had doubled around Maksim's wagon, and she could hear the applause from her parlour. She hugged herself suddenly, shuddering; then turned away, instructing Anna to send for some musicians to drown out the cheers.

34

Roman shifted, uncomfortable on the hard bench seat, nursing the dregs of his beer. He had been waiting for four hours, and was due back at the castle in just over forty minutes. He wondered if it was one of the men here, or if someone sent a runner to tell Mr Garlic Sausage he was sitting and waiting.

He sighed then drained the remainder of his beer and dropped some coins on the table, pushing out into the early evening, squinting against the glare of the setting sun. He rolled his shoulders quickly, setting off at a sedate pace, his hands swinging casually by his sides.

He was ready for the attack from behind when it came, ducking and twisting out of the grasp of the assailant, shoving him forcefully into the doorway he had been propelling him towards.

'Leave off, leave off!' he shouted, wiggling in Roman's grip, managing to free himself and turn around. 'You're not supposed to see me' he hissed, rubbing away the blood from his nose and fingering his lip gently.

'I will know the man that I am traitor for' Roman said, eyeing him distastefully, and was shushed quickly.

The man before him had no features that were remarkable. His hair might have been described as blonde or brown, his eyes possibly blue or brown, of average height and weight. He had no jutting jaw, no hooked nose, no prominent brow, no scars or blemishes that would identify him readily. *Had he been in the pub all that time?* Roman couldn't remember. He was utterly forgettable.

He rubbed his nose again, shooting him a testy look.

'Well?' he snapped. 'It better be worth it this time.'

'Who are you?' Roman demanded.

'That's not how this works soldier boy, and don't even think of asking who I report to. I would not tell you even if I knew.'

'You have not paid me for the last information -'

'It was not worth it' he said irritably. 'Come come, I grow tired and I am sore pressed to have done with you' he grimaced at his pun, fishing out a gold coin he held up for Roman to see.

'I heard tell a million pounds of the tsar's inheritance is missing, and she has purchased a lot of jewels lately' he said, surprised by how much easier he found this, despite his distaste at the lie.

The man mused, flipping the coin up and catching it again, wondering if this was worth the money he had been instructed to pay.

'And one other thing' Roman added, hesitating. The coin stopped flipping. 'When I came on duty the night Parliament opened, there – there was a man leaving her rooms.'

'Who?'

'I did not get a good look at him -'

'What time?'

'Three in the morning -'

'Did you see him again in the castle?'

'I – no – I couldn't tell -'

'How many indiscretions has she had?'

Roman stopped trying to answer and glared at him. The coin flipped again and he snatched it out of the air, pocketing it quickly, catching a whiff of garlic as he did so.

'You haven't given me -'

'I have given you enough' he snapped and headed off quickly, wondering if he would have time to wash before he was due on duty.

35

The spring days were growing warmer and the Principality was ripening with flowers and leaves. The gypsies had come to Dalnerechensk, travelling down the Avenue of Heroes and setting up camp between The Avenue of Heroes and Miner's Way, their bright tents reminding Laura of Nikita's army camped on their borders. There were grumblings from the population, but it wasn't until their dogs began to dig up the graves for the bones they smelt within that Laura was forced to send soldiers to clear them off the land.

After the gypsies had come a delegation of Bishops from St Petersburg, to officially sanction the Bishophood of *Episcop* Yeltsin; and following them an ambassador from Tsar Nicholas II, to renegotiate the Liberty Treaty.

Laura was glad the stuffy little man was not as handsome as *Knjaz* Nikita Rurik had been, and was far too old to even remember what flirting was. She was also glad that, despite Russia's own deepening economic crisis, she was still prepared to pay the original price she had negotiated for tin. The new negotiations were a mere formality, and over in half an hour, though the ambassador stayed in Dalnerechensk for nearly a week.

She sighed ruefully as she sat on the bank of the river, watching the carriages of the departing Bishops wind their way along the Avenue of Heroes. She was sure one of the horses had lifted its tail and defecated near a grave.

Ekaterina paused in her stitching and her eyes followed Laura's gaze but she said nothing and bent her head over the tapestry again. Nineczka snorted distastefully but said nothing as well, yanking her needle through the cloth and shooting Zarya a withering look. No one was going to say it, but Laura knew what they were all thinking. The Avenue of Heroes was sacred ground for Dalnerechenskers, and it was being disturbed with all the traffic that had driven over it recently. Laura wondered if it would only increase now that families were coming to pay their respects for sons laid to rest at the Russian Border; if those curious about the Principality continued to arrive.

Something would have to be done.

She winced slightly as Nineczka yanked savagely at her thread, puckering the material around her badly stitched geometric design, and wondered if she would have to unpick everything she had done again. She knew why she was in such a bad mood. Somewhere in *Episcop* Yeltsin's private apartments he and a small army of brothers from his order were counting the results of the referendum to keep the Monarchy.

A preliminary poll by Dalnerechensk's newspaper had a little over half in favour of retaining the crown. But their readership was still small and exclusive, and despite a growing attendance at the schools many of the population still could read very little. The ballot papers had had little pictures on them, and beside them a square for people to make their mark with the official charcoal sticks.

Laura bent her head over the tapestry again. *Half in favour.* It was promising, but she could still lose her crown today. *Such a quiet coup; a revolution of pens. How terrible writing could be!*

She glanced at Gustav, who sat at this moment with a drawing box on his knees, his pencil caressing the likeness of Dalnerechensk's national flower, the mountain daisy, onto a thick parchment, twisting a freshly picked specimen in his fingers, watching the way the sunlight shone on the petals.

In the distance a horseless carriage came into view, the very first to arrive in Dalnerechensk, slowing only briefly to negotiate the rather narrow gap in the Northern Wall before motoring down The Avenue of Heroes.

'How amazing!' Zarya cried, watching the horseless carriage approach. 'Who on earth drives that?'

'*Knjaz* Sergei Uvarov' Tatiana burst out with an excited tremble she found difficult to repress.

Laura was surprised at the shudder. *Is she…? No, surely not!* she thought hurriedly. *She could not be in love with her father's cousin. Could she?* Laura eyed her, noticing the hungry way she looked at the car. Another glance at the horseless carriage told her that there were two people inside, and she could not tell who either of them were.

Another scheme she told herself. *Their alternative plan, in case they could not remove me from power with the referendum. Whoever is in the carriage will be someone to help Maksim find some other way to snatch power from the government and the crown.* She suddenly stopped herself, realising how spiteful and paranoid she was sounding, even in her own head.

Perhaps she could be in love with Sergei Uvarov she conceded. *He was attractive, in his own way, and rich and powerful and widely connected and respected in Ekaterinburg. And let's face it, there are not that many eligible bachelors left in Dalnerechensk.* She suddenly felt sorry for Tatiana. Most of the old ministers had left the Principality already, and taken their families with them. As powerful as some commoners were becoming, they were still commoners, and would not appease the snobbery of her father.

She must be very lonely Laura suddenly realised. *Almost everyone she knew has gone, including the friend she was once inseparable from: Natasha Chekovna.*

'Forgive me, Tatiana, I do not think I have asked about Natasha' she said, watching the way the annoyance at the comment flickered over Tatiana's face before her features settled into something like a smile. She tore her eyes away from where the horseless carriage had disappeared into the city of Dalnerechensk.

'She is married, and living in Paris now' she answered casually, her attention diverted by the five horseback riders that had made their way along the river bank towards them.

Laura eyed the riders with apprehension. *They have not come from the cathedral* she noted, as they had ridden for some time along the river bank as they approached, from the southern end of the Principality. *They are also hardly likely to be ministers. Is this some new bold attempt at assassination? Dear God, I really am paranoid!* Roman shifted slightly, standing up straighter, and Laura was comforted to see she was not the only one nervous at their approach.

The riders stopped a little way back from them, and they dismounted, bowing low before her.

'Forgive our intrusion Your Majesty' one said, whipping off his cap. 'We have come from Nicholas Riminov.'

'You may approach' she said, beckoning him forward.

He took two steps then bowed again. 'Nicholas is on his death bed' he said. 'He has respectfully begged to see you before he dies.'

Laura rose sharply, the tapestry tumbling from her lap and upsetting the box of threads that was sitting beside her.

'How soon?'

'Imminently' was the answer.

Quickly she strode over to the man, taking the reins of his horse from him and boosting herself up into the saddle. Roman was following quickly behind with a curt command for another to surrender his horse.

'Lead the way' she said, and followed the boy back to a small farmstead near Pavlodar, her heart hurting when she saw the condition of the house that Nicholas Riminov was to end his days in.

She dismounted hurriedly and ran up the tangled, overgrown path, trying to avoid the edges of the paving stones where errant roots had tipped them to trip unsuspecting visitors. Without waiting to be admitted she pushed open the door, stopping briefly when the smell of the house assailed her. Death hung heavy in the air: the smell of laudanum, unpleasant excretions and the thick cloying scent of sage and flowers trying desperately to mask the stench of illness and waning life.

A woman appeared on the stairs in front of her, carrying a heavy porcelain basin she was taking care not to slosh as she walked, and Laura rushed past her, not looking in the basin and holding her breath at the same time. At the top of the stairs were three rooms, but Laura headed to the one where the smell of blood was the strongest.

I'm too late! she thought momentarily, before she saw the figure on the small bed. His eyes were open and turned towards the door. Relief flooded over his face, the corners of his mouth forcing past the grimace into a semblance of a smile. He was too weak to beckon her in, but his fingers stretched to her and she rushed to him, taking his fine hand in hers.

'Your Highness' he whispered, a tear beginning to roll down his cheek.

'Do not stand on ceremony with me Nicholas' she said, kissing the hand that felt like a child's in her own. 'Call me Laura now, please.'

'Laura' he breathed. 'Forgive me' he broke off, coughing.

Worry began gnawing at her again, wondering what he had to unburden himself with at the end of his life, what confession he must make in order to rest easy in the afterlife. *How many more secrets are there?*

'You have nothing to apologise for -' she started but stopped as he began to speak again.

'I do, I do' he whispered, the wheeze in his voice more apparent. 'We made him you know. He wasn't going to marry. Aleksei' he clarified, his voice fading away. 'We forced him to choose. We were responsible for what he did.'

She stared at him, at his wasted body, eaten by cancers and the guilt that their pressure to wed had led to Aleksei's breakdown of sanity; had led to her brutal whipping in the castle courtyard, had led to his last, violent use of the marriage bed.

'No' Laura said, kissing his hand again. 'No, I could never lay blame with you.'

'I am so sorry that we failed him; failed you' he whispered, his other hand fluttering to cover hers.

'Hush now' she pleaded, her own eyes beginning to fill with tears.

He sighed, a ghostly breath, shutting his eyes against the terrible pain, but continued to talk, his voice becoming so faint that it was impossible to make out the words, and what she could make out was beginning to ramble through various memories. Laura hated herself for robbing the man of his last few moments but knew she couldn't stay silent any longer. *He was the only one left who had signed Alexander Andrei's abdication.*

'Nicholas' she whispered, smoothing back his hair from his cheek. 'I – I found – documents' she bit her lip. 'Did you know?'

'He was a mighty buck, antlers like tree roots' his breath stopped and started in a way that might have been a silent laugh, the last memories of pride and happiness giving him some joy again.

'Nicholas' she interrupted, shooting a surreptitious glance at the door and lowering her voice urgently. 'Alexander Andrei.'

The agony of that distant upset hit him again, and he groaned against his torment.

'That poor boy' he sobbed.

'Did you know?' she hissed urgently. 'Did you know who he was?'

'That p- p- ... th...' he shut his eyes again, trying to form the word *sorry* on lips that would no longer move, on breath that no longer came.

Laura shut her eyes, pressing her lips to his hand one last time, biting down on her sobs. *How could I have done that?* she chided herself angrily. *His heart broke then, I'm sure of it. That look on his face... His last few moments on earth had been a torment...* She pressed her hands to her mouth, holding back her guilty sobs. *And I can't be sure, not completely* she further admonished herself. *I broke his heart for nothing.*

'*Dedushka?*' asked a small voice behind her.

The woman on the stairs was now back in the room, the basin tumbling from her fingers as she rushed over to her grandfather, falling to her knees beside the bed and sobbing pitifully. Laura rose, knowing she had to leave.

'I am very sorry for your loss' she said. 'He was a great friend to me.'

Somehow she managed to make her feet walk out of the room and down the stairs before her.

To her surprise Gustav was waiting with Roman outside the small, dilapidated cottage, his face lined with concern and worry, but there was a hint of admiration for her fast ride to the southern edge of the Principality; a ride he and Roman had been hard pressed to match.

'Your Majesty, is there anything I can do?' he asked, bowing slightly.

Write to your brother, tell him I need him she wanted to say, instead she wiped her face on the back of her hand and took the reins of the horse she had borrowed from where they were draped over a broken fence paling.

'Help me mount' she said, letting him boost her up to the saddle.

Roman quickly mounted too, following her as she rode slowly back to Dalnerechensk, Gustav riding closely behind him.

They heard the cheering while they were still riding through Tcherepnin, heard the noise that spilled out of Vsevolod's Gate and snowballed into the garrison village. People came out of their houses to see what the shouting was about, and Laura was surrounded by a large crowd when the ruckus turned into discernible shouts. *The votes are counted* Laura realised. *And they are in favour.*

The people near her called out and waved their handkerchiefs at her, running along beside the horses as they made their way through the village. Laura did her best to wave and smile despite her grief at Nicholas' death.

And this moment of triumph has to be bittersweet she thought as she rode into Dalnerechensk, nodding and waving sedately at the crowds. *I must still be alone; I cannot be seen unhappy for seeming ungrateful to those that voted me, I cannot triumph for seeming callous and unfeeling, and there is no one who can put their arms around me in comfort unless I want to add to the rumours that I am a whore. How much a simple human touch can mean!*

She dismounted in the castle stable yard, feeling the longing for Olaf twist slowly, savagely in her chest again, handing over the reins to Roman. 'See that the horses are returned to their rightful owners' she managed to get out, though her emotions threatened to choke her into silence. She headed up to her rooms as quickly as she dared, throwing herself down on her bed to cry loudly into her pillows, muffling the noise as best as she could.

36

Laura knelt at the small altar in the castle's chapel, her hands clasped before her, her eyes shut to block out the sight of Tatiana, Nineczka and Polina, one of Elena's younger daughters, kneeling in this small room with her. As her lips whispered automatically her mind was on other things, analysing the events of the two weeks since Nicholas' funeral.

It had been a pitiful thing, a prince's pall with a pauper's purse, and for all the power and influence he had had in the Advisory Councils of Tsar Constantinovich and Aleksei the pews had virtually been empty. Ivan Gogol had been there, and Nicholas' children, grandchildren and great-grandchildren; but no other council member had been in attendance, from the new government or the old. Laura had sat alone on the royal balcony, letting the public grief she had been unable to express earlier flow down her cheeks.

After the ceremony *Episcop* Yeltsin had seen her personally, to formally tell her what she already knew – that the people had voted in overwhelming numbers to retain the monarchy. A warm glow of gratitude and vindication had welled up in her, and did so every time she thought about the referendum. Despite their hatred of Aleksei they still believed in the institution of the Monarchy. They still wanted her as their tsaritsa.

It must have galled Maksim terribly, but not a flicker of it had passed over his face as he congratulated her on the results of the referendum. And not a flicker had passed over her features as she congratulated him on the growing support for his Principle Party. They both had been modest and deferential in acceptance of the praise, and they both had watched each other like cats over a cornered mouse.

Laura shifted slightly to ease the ache in her left knee, continuing her whispered prayers. It was quiet, and despite the presence of the

Vakhtangovs she liked it here, as it was the only place during the day that she could be alone with her thoughts, and not have to keep up a steady stream of chatter. She couldn't help but smile sardonically at the thought. *Two years ago she had been desperate for company, and now she wished they would just go away...*

Two years ago she would have sent away the likes of Tatiana she reminded herself, shifting back to ease the pressure on her right knee. She was no friend of hers, none of those who knelt with her were even remotely inclined to her. But their presence did serve one purpose: she could not have any indiscretions if she were never given the opportunity. And there was one other knowledge that gave her hope: her observers were getting tired of their fruitless vigil. *Perhaps they will soon give it up...*

She dared not think it, lest it give her a hope that would never be realised, but even as the thought occurred she knew it was a vain fantasy. Maksim's political party was gaining momentum. He was cleverly distancing himself from the revolutionaries, reminding the population of how they had bayed for royal blood, how they had wanted to abolish the Monarchy completely, and citing the recent referendum to highlight just how out of touch they were from the thoughts of the people. He was even styling himself as a supporter of the *Vdova* Tsaritsa, and, Laura supposed, would have loved to have seen her reaction to that bit of news.

She shifted her weight slightly again, semi-aware of the rustlings of her attendants as they strove to ease uncomfortable aches, as one by one they gave up and slipped silently fuming from the room. Alone at last she shifted sideways and sat on the floor, taking the weight off her knees and sighed softly, rubbing them tenderly.

Maksim was supporting the Monarchy. His party, named with a clever pun, evoked the belief in the population that it was, in turn, supported *by* the monarchy. It certainly seemed so with the large numbers of Vakhtangov women handing out leaflets and attending rallies. Even sickly Anna had been handed a bundle of papers and made to smile as she passed them out. *And I have said nothing* she thought, shutting her eyes tightly. *Because to deny my support of Maksim means I must support Ilich instead...*

She squeezed her eyes tighter and rubbed her forehead worriedly.

He sent the man I loved to hang in the forests...

She shut her eyes against the longing that rose up in her. She had dreamed of him again last night, dreamed of the terrifying river they had marched beside as captives of Nikita. She had replayed her daring, foolhardy leap into the rushing torrent, swollen from three days of miserable rain. To this day she still had no idea what had compelled her to jump in. To escape yes, but she could have drowned. *I nearly did drown* she reminded herself.

It had been Olaf who had saved her, his strong arms holding her tightly, fending off the rocks and debris as they were buffeted through the river, holding her close to him in that secretive cave beneath the overhanging bank as Nikita's men searched for them...

She had dreamed of the feel of his arms, the hardness of his body, the earnestness of his kisses. But his face had become fuzzy, indistinct, as if she were looking at him through lashes thick with tears. His hands, once so rough with ten years of manual labour in the stables, had become soft and refined, gentle and supple. They flitted over her exposed skin, the hands of a tsar, fine and commanding and *how she had responded to them...*

She had sobbed at his touch, at the ecstasy that had shivered through her as he made love to her, wrapping her arms around his neck and tangling her fingers into his hair; hair that was too silky and too long and *Fredrik's hair...* And with that knowledge she cried out and shuddered awake, cramming a pillow into her mouth so Roman could not hear her.

Laura shut her eyes, averting them from the ivory cross on the altar, ashamed of her carnal longings. She pushed aside the thought of her dream, as she had done the morning she had woken from it, refusing to entertain the fantasy.

Ilich was going to lose the elections. She knew it, and she feared it.

And yet she could not find herself supporting him, despite what she had said to him in the Parliament Chambers all those weeks ago. He reminded her more and more of Aleksei, a good man constrained by things beyond his control, made useless by economics and politics and peerage. But Maksim was right, he was no fan of the institution of Monarchy, he had once bayed for its destruction, bayed for the royals to be thrown off the throne.

And he had killed the last Tsar. Unwittingly perhaps, but he had killed him just the same.

She shut her eyes tighter, pushing the heels of her hands against her eyes, as if she could somehow stop all the things that she had seen, all the things that she knew. She may as well have tried to hold back the ocean with a stool.

Her lips wobbled with misery as her thoughts turned to her only friend, and the terrible things she had told her that morning. *Ekaterina was going to leave her.*

A sulky, childish part of her knew she could order her not to go and she would, unhappily, stay in Dalnerechensk forever. She could offer her countless meaningless jobs to fill up her time, even give her the important role of Royal Nanny, but she had stopped herself. It would be too cruel to give a baby to the friend that had lost hers, who could never have any more; it would be too cruel to keep her here when she hardly ever saw her anymore.

Ekaterina had been her confidante and her friend, her only happy lifeline when she had arrived in Dalnerechensk to be Aleksei's bride. They had been inseparable, and the vivacious nature of the Hungarian Countess had kept them in peals of raucous laughter for hours. They had returned as frightened mice to their home, and both had received very different welcomes which, without their knowing, had slid a silent wedge between them.

Laura shut her eyes tightly, rubbing them with the heels of her hands. *She is still frightened* she whispered to herself. They had barely left the rooms she had generously given to them. Grigory hadn't left at all. A maid had brought them nasty, spiteful little notes, their friends – those that were still left in Dalnerechensk – had politely declined invitations to see them. *The Revolution was not over for them yet...*

There is no happiness here, only you Ekaterina had told her that morning, and she had heard in the silence that followed a tiny, little thought. Not an accusation, not even a gentle rebuff, but a thought there nonetheless. *Your happiness no longer impinges on me.* And the guilt told her the thought was right, she hardly saw Ekaterina now, her days were filled with running a household and a Principality and her daughter and tapestry sewing and other assignations. As much as she loved Ekaterina, she no longer needed her, and her dearest friend knew it.

I have taken the liberty to write to my cousin she had told her, holding her hands gently. *To invite him back to Dalnerechensk. It is my last gift to you.*

Please stay until Fredrik comes she had begged, and they had held each other until Polina had come looking for the tsaritsa, the flock of spies following in her footsteps. She had not been alone again until now.

With a soft sigh she shifted sideways and lay on the floor. It was not comfortable, but she pillowed her head on the crook of her arm and shut her eyes tiredly, the tears squeezing out into her lashes. She let her hitched breaths fill the chapel like a whispering flock of starlings.

*

She woke some time later with a warm hand on her arm, gently shaking her. She looked up into Roman's concerned face.

'You're not supposed to touch the Monarchy' she said quietly, her voice still thick with sleep.

'The Monarchy is not supposed to cry herself to sleep on the floor of the chapel' he answered, removing his hand.

She sat up and winced at the pins and needles in her limbs.

'What time is it?' she asked, peering through the gloom towards the window, which was so dark she couldn't see the outline of the ivory cross against it.

'After three in the morning, I just came back on duty' he answered, helping her to her feet, providing a sturdy arm when she wobbled at the numbness in her legs. 'I would not have disturbed you were it not for the fact that the chapel makes a god-awful bed and I had been instructed to.'

'Instructed?' she asked, wary. 'By whom?'

'Marie Vakhtangovna, Your Majesty' he answered.

'What is so important -' she broke off, wincing as she took a step, feeling Roman's arm come around her waist to support her '- that she cannot wait for a suitable time?' she said irritably. 'Help me to my chambers then tell her I will see her presently' she continued, leaning on him until she began to feel steady on her legs again.

'Your Majesty' he suddenly said, stopping outside her door, his voice dropping. 'If there is anything, anything at all that I could do, you need only ask me, and it would be done' he dropped his eyes.

She hesitated.

'Thank you for your assistance' she said quietly. 'When you have delivered my message to Marie, return to your post outside my door.'

Roman let her go.

'Yes Your Majesty' he said, looking away as she stepped into her room, closing the door against him.

Laura blew out her cheeks then sat on her chaise lounge, taking up the sweetmeats Anna had left for her on the small table nearby. They were stale but she ate them all then went to her dressing room to clean the residue from her teeth and lips. She spent some time arranging and rearranging her hair, marvelling at how Anna seemed to make it stay in pretty shapes effortlessly. Finally she pulled it all out and left it down, after all, she should have been in bed when Marie had come knocking. She changed her dress and pulled on a warm shawl, wrapping it around her.

When she had decided that she might now grace Marie with her presence she opened the door again and stepped out, heading to the small audience chamber on the first floor. It was cold in the room, and the woman inside was still wearing her travelling cloak, though she had been waiting for several hours. As Laura entered she sprang to her feet, coming forward to meet her quickly.

'Your Majesty, I beg your forgiveness for this intrusion, but I have come to throw myself on your mercy' she said, dropping to her knees in front of her.

Laura eyed her in surprise, this was not the conversation she had expected to be having. *She's my age* she realised. *We might have been friends.*

'Stand up' she said, as kindly as she could manage in this strange moment, looking carefully at her.

She was extraordinarily beautiful, with large dark eyes and a full head of thick hair curled winsomely against the nape of her neck. She was taller than Laura, but not overly tall, and her figure was well proportioned. *I have never seen her before* she thought. *I would remember a face like that.*

'Why have you come to throw yourself on my mercy?'

'I am the great great great grand-daughter of Grigory Igorevich, youngest sibling of Tsar Igorevich.'

Laura did some quick calculations. *Tsar Igorevich was Aleksei's great great grandfather. Varvara Igorevna, whom Piotr and Anna were descended from, was his sister; together with Grigory Igorevich they made the three of the six children of Tsar Petrovich who had survived into adulthood.*

'I grew up in Izhevsk' Marie continued, 'living with my mother and aunt. I will not bore you with the details Your Majesty but we lived on her charity, and she took it upon herself to find a good match for me.'

Here her voice faltered and her eyes filled up with tears, but she swallowed it down as best she could.

'Stepan Borodin, the kindest, handsomest, most generous man I have ever known asked for my hand in marriage and I accepted. It was to be a six month engagement, so he could arrange his affairs before our wedding.' More tears fell down her cheeks. 'But then, a month ago, he came to me with a letter, demanding to know why I had called our engagement off.

'The letter was written by Great Aunt Varvara, and it told him he was unsuitable as a match for me. I knew nothing of this letter, and I promised him I had not withdrawn my consent to the marriage. But my mother said the wedding was not to go ahead, and I was to be married to Maksim Yegorov. -'

'Maksim?!' broke in Laura, surprised.

'My mother is too cowed by her aunt-in-law to refuse, and they were to excuse all my uncle's debts, but I refused, Your Majesty, I refused! Yet they came to fetch me and brought me here. Please Your Majesty! Please I beg of you, don't allow this to happen!'

'What does your father have to say?' Laura asked, eyeing her display, wondering if this was some trick devised by the Vakhtangov family, for what end she could not guess.

'He died when I was nine, Your Majesty.'

'I'm sorry.'

'It's alright Your Majesty, Vakhtangov men die young.'

That was a callously flippant thing to say Laura thought, but Marie was still talking.

'... average age is thirty seven. My father was thirty six when he died. Did you know that the oldest living monarch was Tsar Constantinovich? Sixty. Even mighty Vsevolod was only fifty eight when he died -' she stopped talking, realising she was beginning to babble.

'Why have you come to me?'

Marie blinked. 'I thought you would understand' she said, a flicker of doubt flitting through her eyes.

Laura's expression hardened. 'My dear, you are very much mistaken' she said coldly. 'I loved my husband, despite what insidious gossips have said.

My father was not bribed and I most certainly was not abducted and forced into the marriage. How could you possibly think I would understand?!' Her voice had risen to a near shout but she didn't care.

Marie dropped her eyes.

'I thought you would understand how loathsome he is' she whispered. 'He cares not for me, only his lascivious pursuit of power. He has expressed no interest, he did not even come himself to get me, he sent *Knjaz* Uvarov…' she trailed off miserably.

Laura eyed her, feeling embarrassed that she had jumped too readily at a perceived slight.

She is right, I do understand she thought, mentally smoothing away her discomfort, flicking through the memories of the Vakhtangov family tree. *Maksim's uncle is married to Varvara, making him half uncle to Anna and Piotr. Or half cousin?* she wondered. A sneaky suspicion wondered if Maksim had thought of wedding Anna, but she was too young and too sickly, far too frail for the rigours of the marriage bed. A small part of her shuddered.

Varvara Igorevna had been older than Grigory Igorevich, but was female, and Grigory's descendants would have had precedence she went on. *Yet his line too had failed to have a direct male descendant, although their ties to the crown had been strengthened through marriage to cousins. Marie's grandfather, if I remember rightly, was Varvara's brother.*

Marie sniffed and buffed daintily at her nose with a lace kerchief, bringing Laura's attention back to her.

'Did your aunt approve of this match to *Monsieur* Borodin before she received *Madame* Durova's letter?' she asked.

'Oh very much so!' Marie cried emphatically. 'She told me he was a better match than she had hoped for and was thrilled. Were it not for the money to clear my uncle's debts she might have protested -' she stopped, the colour rising in her cheeks.

'And where is *Monsieur* Borodin now? Does he know you are in Dalnerechensk?'

'Yes Your Majesty. He is in the courtyard waiting for me. He came straight away when he heard' a pretty blush at the romance of the gesture came into her cheeks and she couldn't stop the smile.

It hit Laura right in her memories and twisted her unhappily.

'How gallant' she said with a sad smile, then raised her voice to call in Roman.

'Yes Your Majesty?' he asked, saluting and accidentally knocking the barrel of the rifle that was always slung over the shoulders of the guards on duty.

'There is a cold man shivering in the courtyard. Bring him to me forthwith' she said.

Roman saluted again and rushed out. Laura headed to the small table near the cold fireplace that held a decanter of brandy and poured three small glasses, listening to Roman pass on her message to the nearest guard. *He doesn't like leaving me while on duty* she thought casually. *I wonder if it was because he was almost too late to save me once?* She shivered at the remembered sound the bullet had made hitting Luka's shoulder. *That could have been my own shoulder, my chest, my throat...*

She turned quickly to Marie, bringing her a glass that she accepted with a curtsey. Downstairs she heard the front doors open, and then the quick steps of a man cross the wide entrance hall and climb the stone steps. After a brief moment of silence in which the thick carpets muffled his approach a young man appeared at the doorway. Roman announced Stepan Borodin and he bowed deeply, almost reverently, before her.

She gestured for him to rise and approach and he did, coming to take Marie's hands earnestly. His clothing and hair were dishevelled, rumpled from travel and several days of continuous wear and his face was unshaven. His eyes were red-rimmed with worry and sleeplessness and he seemed pale at the ordeal, but otherwise Laura could not fault his looks at all. She gave him the third glass she had poured and he bowed, downing the warming drink with relish.

'Well?' she asked. 'Are you resolved, *Monsieur* Borodin, to have this woman as your bride?'

'Most ardently, Your Majesty' he swore.

She smiled sadly again.

'Very well. I think it prudent that you do not leave the castle. In the morning – at a more respectable hour' she corrected herself 'we will send for your aunt and uncle -'

'Forgive me' Marie interrupted. 'They are here, Your Majesty. I am to be wedded to Maksim in two days' time. One day's time' she corrected unhappily.

Roman knocked politely on the open door and announced Fedor, who bowed as he stepped in, fresh and immaculate despite the early hour and his hurried dressing.

'Fedor will show you to some rooms where you can rest. I'm afraid they won't be aired but I dare say you would be prepared to endure a little mustiness after this nasty ordeal' she said and they both rushed to assure her. 'When *Episcop* Yeltsin wakes for morning mass he will be summoned here to perform your wedding -'

The rest of what she was to say was cut off with Marie's cry of happiness and she threw her arms around Stepan, kissing his cheek, then let him go to grab Laura's hand and kiss it fervently.

'And of course, your uncle's debts will be honoured. I trust you will sleep well, goodnight' she dismissed them.

Fedor stepped forward and escorted them out to rooms on the second floor, their thanks and praises tripping over each other's as they left the tsaritsa. Laura smiled to herself. *So*, she *was the other figure she had seen in the horseless carriage*. It gave her no small satisfaction to thwart Maksim, and she could only imagine the thunderous reaction at the loss of his bride and firmer connection to the crown. No doubt there would be retribution for her meddling but right now she didn't care.

What a scandal that poor girl had just avoided! She would be grateful for the rest of her life for the prevention of the loss of her good name. No doubt Fedor would delicately suggest ways in which they might financially express their gratitude to her...

We might even become friends she thought, but didn't let herself hope. She stifled her yawn and blew out the lamp on the table, feeling her way across the dark room to the door. Roman followed her silently to her room, and she bid him goodnight at the door, undressing quickly and leaving her clothes on a pile on the floor. She slipped into bed and pulled Olaf's letter out of the bedside table, pressing it to her chest and shutting her eyes against the jealousy of young love.

37

Laura left the small chapel near the roof in a reflective and slightly melancholy mood. *Episcop* Yeltsin had been surprised at the early summons but had managed to officiate the short ceremony with just the right gravitas and intimacy that it required. Marie had looked beautiful in her silk gown, joyful tears making her dark eyes shimmer like moonlight on a midnight lake. Her uncle beamed as he had led her up the short aisle to her waiting groom, who had had to borrow a wedding suit from Fedor, as he had arrived in the Principality with nothing but the clothes he was wearing.

The ceremony was bereft of the grand pageantry that her wedding to Aleksei had had, yet she couldn't help but think of him, remembering how nervous he had looked, how he hadn't been able to take his eyes off her, how his fingers had trembled with desire and fear as he had slipped the ring on her finger. He had been a good man once. A good man that had broken under the strain and the burden of leadership, a break that had been savage and violent and terrible in its aftermath. But he had loved her when he had wedded her, and she missed that man terribly.

Outside the Parliament doors she collected herself and nodded to the guards who saluted her, one reaching back to open the door for her. Parliament glanced in her direction then as one man rose and bowed as she stepped in.

'Forgive my lateness gentlemen' she said. 'I was delayed on account of Marie Vakhtangovna's wedding to Stepan Borodin.'

There was a slight murmur in the ranks but there was not one flicker of surprise or anger on Maksim's face. *He knows!* she realised with a horrible certainty. *But how can that be? The ceremony has* just *finished!* She made it to the dais and sat, motioning for the members to sit too. *Marie had been in my home a total of a little more than five hours, and was wedded not five minutes ago.* How on earth *did Maksim know already?*

There is a spy in my home.

The thought made her cold. It was the only way he could have known. *Someone in my home had seen Marie or overheard our conversation last night, and reported it to Maksim, despite the early hour. Was it Roman? Had he slipped away from his post and seen his mysterious contact? Was it a maid that had to prepare rooms for the young lovers? Was it one of the soldiers on duty?*

Impossible she told herself. *They are all my Guards of the Order, hand-picked by Peter Kamanin from volunteers for their loyalty and devotion to me.*

And they think they got to Roman; the best of them, she reminded herself. *Could they have bribed another soldier too? One that neither of them knew about? Could it really be a soldier? It was not likely, but possible* she conceded. *It was more likely to be a maid or livery servant* she mused. *But who? And for what reason? Money, perhaps, or spite, or...* she trailed off. *Or a hundred other reasons that I could spend all day guessing at* she sighed.

How many people actually work for me? she wondered. *Did they work here as part of staff for Ilich? Did Fedor hire all new staff? How blindly trusting and ignorant have I been?*

'Your Majesty?'

Perhaps Fedor should carefully screen the staff, and give me a full account.

'Your Majesty?' Luka asked again, a little louder.

'I agree' she said.

He blinked. 'I beg your pardon?'

'You raised the motion as to whether *Episcop* Yeltsin and his deacons should count the votes for the election' she said, not letting the smile at his shocked response touch her lips. *It always unnerved them,* she told herself, *the way I could follow a conversation while seeming to be lost in internal thought.* 'I agree, it is a wise choice. A man devoted to the laws of heaven should be unbiased towards those that make the laws of men, and I have no doubt that *Episcop* Yeltsin is as honest as he seems.'

I don't think you can bribe him Maksim she said in the privacy of her head. *Perhaps you might be able to bribe one of the brothers drafted to do the counting, but perhaps it doesn't really matter. We all know what will happen when the polling booths open.*

Ilich declared the motion carried and Ivan noted it in the minutes, carefully blotting the paper as he wrote. The ministers began to stir, looking forward to the end of the session, looking forward to the lunch they could smell coming from the kitchens.

'My lords' Laura started, stopping them in their tracks. 'I have a motion I would like to raise with you.'

There were disgruntled rumblings but they settled back in their seats, looking at her impatiently.

'It has come to our attention that The Avenue of Heroes is becoming more frequently used, and this use is disturbing those who are buried there. I place before Parliament a motion to move the bodies from the Avenue.'

Parliament erupted with shouted opposition.

'This is preposterous!' Lev shouted.

'Hear hear!' several agreed.

'Those graves cannot be moved!' another shouted.

'Those graves are being desecrated' Ilich said softly, but his voice somehow carried over the hubbub, like it had so many times when he had spoken over the rabble in the revolutionary's tavern.

'So they must be moved?!' cried one, disbelieving.

'How?' Maksim asked. 'In broad daylight? Where everyone can see them dig up the bodies of their sons?'

'Perhaps it could be done at night…?' Yuri suggested.

'So it looks *more* like grave robbing?!'

The argument raged across the new barricades, but Laura could see it was mostly one-sided; most of the ministers were opposed to moving the bodies. *The only road we have to the North is the Avenue* she thought. *Miner's Way looped past Ladozhskoye and Macherna, meandered through the pass in the Western Range and limped its way to Davostok, losing its battle with Mother Nature. Every winter a bit more of the surface washed away, every summer a bit more wild grass poked up through the ruts and potholes. And in Russia it continued to run east, maybe all the way to the Austro-Hungarian Empire. Olaf and I followed that road for nearly three days back to Dalnerechensk and never saw it branch once…*

There hadn't been a road in Russia that led to the Northern Border, but the approach of Nikita's army had cut a swathe through the valley. The families that had followed them had beaten a rough track of sorts, which had become more and more defined in the course of a year. Fedor had told her the closest major Russian road was to their north, which was why all their visitors were chancing the short, unformed road, rather than travelling long distance on the badly degraded but existing routes to Dalnerechensk.

And now there were horseless carriages that were growing in popularity she told herself. It would make it easier and easier for people to mobilise, to come *through* the Principality instead of making a wide berth around it. *And let's face it, people will come* she thought. Dalnerechensk, once ignored and mocked, had nearly started a war, and in doing so had become a curiosity for the rest of Europe. In the last week alone Fedor had received five letters curious about the availability of accommodation suitable for the gentry.

The road traffic was going to grow, and the only way to protect the reverence for the bodies was to move them to where they would not be disturbed.

'… becoming too busy!' broke into her private musings, rising above the cacophony of the arguing ministers.

'*You cannot do it, that is where they died!*'

Laura rose suddenly, causing those who were not already on their feet, shouting and gesticulating wildly, to rise too. They broke off their harsh words, turning to face her, bowing slightly.

'Come with me' she said, and strode down the aisle to the doors, quickly pulling them open.

The guards beyond looked surprised at the parade of ministers that filed out behind the tsaritsa, as they had not heard the ceremony that usually signalled the end of their sessions in chambers. They shot each other a look of confusion, then, as they had been instructed to protect the Parliament, they fell into step behind the last ministers and followed them along into the entrance hall.

Roman too was surprised by the departure of all the ministers and quickly inserted himself into their midst, keeping close to the tsaritsa, but not so close that he might accidentally jostle her as they walked. He could hear their confused questions and disdainful comments and knew that Laura could hear them too, but pretended she couldn't.

She led them out the front doors of the castle and then around it, through the newly flowered gardens of Tsar Constantinovich, crossing the old parade ground where Roman had once performed a drill for her, so many lifetimes ago it felt now. She led them to a set of stone stairs that took them to a section of the castle walls that overlooked the village green, where royal proclamations had been made ever since the castle had been completed.

From the wall the ministers had a good view of most of Liberty Valley, all the way to the Northern Beacon, and down past the garrison village to the sprawling farmlands at the other end of the valley. They could see the tiny figures of children clinging to the tops of the trees on the ridge near Macherna, where children had always climbed trees to see two valleys at once, and they could see the large picnicking party at the Northern Border, and children climbing over the cannon in the wall.

Laura waited till all the ministers were on the wall and had had a good look at the picnickers before pointing to a street below them in the city of Dalnerechensk.

'Do you see there my lords? The inconspicuous cobble by the cart, near the mouth of that alleyway. That is where Vadim Kortnev died, struck in the neck by a wild arrow. And there, gentlemen, outside Nechayev's butchery on Vsevolod's Way. That's where Yefim Spanov died, when the barricade failed and he was dragged there by Russian soldiers who bayonetted him thirteen times. And there' she pointed to the green expanse between the garrison village and Vsevolod's Gate. 'Beside the railway, beyond the newly found moat. That's where Basil Barand died, his heart pierced with a bullet, and found curled as if asleep from exhaustion.'

She turned to face them again.

'If any ground be sacred ground those are the places, gentlemen. Those, and a hundred and twenty seven more; hidden, lost, perhaps forgotten; but not that road. They have remained there, an honoured guard protecting the new road; standing vigil, dutifully, for what we have lost.

'But they should rest now, the well-deserved rest of heroes that have served valiantly their country and tsaritsa. The road will forever bear their names, but not their bodies. They should rest beside their families, in Macherna. It is time for them to go home.'

There was silence when she finished talking. She turned and watched the families at the Northern Wall again, watched the children climb off the cannons and chase each other around the headstones of the nearest graves until a woman went to scold them.

Maksim hasn't said much she thought as she watched a boy jump boldly over the wall into Russia. Neither he nor Lev had been particularly vocal on the subject of the removal, and that made her suspicious. Outright opposition would have convinced her of the *rightness* of the move, wholehearted support would only convince her of the dire blunder it would be to exhume them. *I can tell they don't know what to do* she thought. *They are waiting to see how the wind blows and will trim their sails to it, telling everyone that was what they had thought all along.*

She sighed softly, shutting her eyes and rubbing them tiredly. *I've had so little sleep...*

'All in favour of the motion?' Ilich asked quietly.

Hands went up. Laura didn't turn to see them.

'All against?' Ilich continued and counted the hands again. There didn't seem to be as long a pause before he asked 'Any abstentions? The motion is carried.'

There was no applause or congratulations at the news, and the ceremonial close to end the Parliament session was performed on the wall. Ministers began to descend for lunch, leaving Laura, Roman, and one of the two soldiers overlooking the village green. The second soldier gave his partner a puzzled look, then left him, heading back to the garrison village barracks to change out of his uniform and go off duty.

'Your Majesty?' the guard asked cautiously.

She turned to eye him.

'Yefim Spanov was my brother' he said. 'Thank you for remembering him.'

She opened her mouth to reply and instead broke down in tears, buffing at them quickly with a lace handkerchief. The two guards stood awkwardly, feeling sorry for her and doing their best to say soothing things that just seemed to make it worse.

Laura left them quickly, slipping down the stairs to go to the nursery, to hug her daughter and feel her small arms circle round her neck.

38

'Good morning Your Majesty' Fedor said as he bowed and placed a silver tray of correspondence on the table beside her.

She put down her fork and moved her empty plate to the side, motioning that Gustav could keep eating if he chose. He bowed his head to her with a smile, used to her relaxed protocol in the morning, and buttered another slice of bread, reading over his latest notes on the flora of Dalnerechensk.

'Some more tea please Fedor' she said and picked up the top letter while Fedor fetched the teapot from the small sideboard.

Since the completion of the renovations in the old Advisory Council, turning it into her private dining room, Laura had taken all her breakfasts there, preferring to be away from the gossip of the court and parliament, tired of the spies and the intrigue that she was the focus of. The Ivanovs and Gustav had dined with her every morning, and every so often she would invite one or two guests to dine with them, taking care not to favour anyone, nor to invite anyone more than once.

'This one is addressed to you' she said, handing over the letter to Gustav.

He took it and thanked her absently, pulling the papers out of the already opened envelope. Laura selected the next letter, skimming through the business correspondence quickly, pleased to see that her income had doubled recently.

'It is from Kurt' Gustav smiled, finishing the letter. 'Petrovich Kamanin has kept him fully informed of the progress of the theatre renovations and he is pleased to see that they are nearing completion. He writes that he is studying French and law at Göttingen and they are progressing well, his professors are pleased with him.'

'That is good news' she smiled.

'He writes that he has included a letter for *Mademoiselle* Anna Vakhtangovna and begs that we deliver it for him.'

'I believe your brother is besotted with Anna' Laura smiled. 'I shall invite her for breakfast tomorrow' she added, instructing Fedor to send the invitation for her.

She read through the other letters she had received, stopping with a skipped heartbeat when she saw the familiar script on the last letter. Her fingers trembled slightly when she picked it up, and she had to pause for a moment to remind herself how to breathe. She was disappointed to see how short the letter was but caught her breath at the salutation.

> *Fondest greetings my dear friend*

it started, and Laura felt the colour coming up in her cheeks. She shot a glance at Gustav but he was happily proof reading his notes, making quick corrections in the margins of the page.

> *It is with a glad heart that I tell you I will soon be*
> *returning to Dalnerechensk. Kurt has provided*
> *delightful descriptions of the theatre's progress*
> *and I shall be returning with a wonderful birthday*
> *gift for you. I count the days eagerly.*
> *With warm regards,*
> *Fredrik.*

She read it twice through and shut her eyes at the warmth spreading through her. *He has been thinking about me* she thought happily. *He remembered my birthday is soon, he will be back for my birthday!* She couldn't think of a more perfect gift. *Dear, dear Fredrik! Such a carefully worded letter, and yet I know your feelings so clearly from it.*

She refolded the letter and put it back in the envelope, sliding it into the bodice of her dress.

'Good news?' Ekaterina asked, missing nothing.

'Fredrik will be back for my eighteenth birthday' she said, and couldn't hide the smile.

'Splendid! You *must* hold a party!' she laughed.

'A party' Laura smiled. She couldn't remember the last party she had been to.

'A ball, a masquerade!' Ekaterina went on excitedly. 'I would love to spend an evening dancing as the court used to.'

'Me too' Laura agreed. 'You and I must spend all day planning!'

She didn't add that she would welcome such a distraction, today of all days. From her window she had seen the crowds lining up outside the polling stations, their collars turned up against the chill of the morning. She dreaded what this day would bring.

Yet despite the fear of the election results, despite the coldness in the pit of her stomach of knowing that there was a spy in her home, Fredrik's letter had lit a fire in her, and she would be hard pressed to quench it today.

Maybe it would even grow and consume her until she saw him again. *I must be in love with him* she thought.

Gustav stood and bowed to Laura, excusing himself from her presence. She bid him a good day and drained the last of her tea, setting the cup on the saucer.

'... musicians and fireworks and a grand unveiling at midnight...' Ekaterina went on.

'Come Ekaterina, quickly to my chambers!' she cried. 'Before my spies arrive!' she grabbed her hands and laughingly pulled her after her, rushing up the stairs to the third floor, the two guards that had been stationed outside the dining room following them closely. 'No one is to disturb my secret conclave with Countess Ivanova, we are planning my birthday!' she tossed over her shoulder to the guards, laughing, before shutting the door hard, seizing writing materials and coming to sit on the floor beside her friend.

*

Roman saluted as he passed one of the guards on duty, heading for the gate to Vsevolod's Way. Under the thick stone rampart he stopped and stepped close to the wall, running his hand carefully over the runnel where the portcullis would descend, checking for nicks and loose chips that might jam or hinder the free motion of the iron grate.

Satisfied that there was no impediment he bent to check the hinges of the fire-hardened gate. The wood was old and cured to be tougher than steel, and had easily withstood the battering rams of Feodor, Tsar of Russia, over four hundred years ago. They had not been touched in the recent revolution, as the tsaritsa had ordered no resistance to the mob; castle guards were not to fight and kill their own brothers in that time of uncertainty and anger.

The hinges were oiled and free of rust, and the great door swung easily on them when Roman pushed it back and forth. He straightened up to check the top hinges, leaning back slightly to see them, and was brushed lightly as a man passed him, heading out into the street beyond the castle.

Roman froze, suddenly cold. *Garlic sausage.* There was no doubt about it. *He had been in the castle.*

He turned quickly, but the man was already out of sight, he had disappeared around the s-bend in the road before the castle gate. He darted out into the street after him, stopping at the top of Vsevolod's Way, searching in the busy crowds before him. Once he caught sight of the back of a man's head, average and unremarkable, and stared hard at it, trying to match that figure to his hazy recollection of the man who paid him. He couldn't swear to it, not absolutely, but there was no doubt in his mind. *He had been in the castle.*

'I don't like him very much' Anna said suddenly, appearing beside Roman.

'I wish the tsaritsa hadn't let them all visit.'

'You know him? *Who is he?*' Roman asked, a little more forcefully than he had intended to, scaring her.

'I – I don't really know him. I saw him a few times when I worked for Luka Nevsky. There was something about him, he always *felt* wrong. I wish Her Majesty hadn't let Luka's family visit him when they wished. I don't like the thought of that man in the castle.'

'Is he Luka's family?' Roman pressed. 'What is his name?'

'I don't know. To both of those questions.'

'What does he do for Luka?' he pressed, frustrated.

'Again I don't know. But whatever it is, it's questionable. Why this sudden interest in him?'

'It's my job to know who comes near the tsaritsa. I don't know what it is, but he gave me a funny feeling.'

Anna's suspicion cleared and she looked at him sympathetically.

'Luka did once mention the name Lvov. I don't know if that's him, but I never met anyone else with that name in his employment. I must go, the tsaritsa wants me to collect some things for her and I must hurry. Hopefully I won't run into him!' she tossed over her shoulder and hurried into the throngs on Vsevolod's Way.

Roman looked after her for a moment, then turned and hurried into the castle. He went directly up to Laura's rooms and pushed past the guards on duty, bursting into her apartments. She and Countess Ivanova looked up in surprise at his entrance. He paused in horror, his mouth dropping open, then saluted, trying to gather his thoughts in the awkward moment. But Laura was quicker.

'Is it time to go riding already?' she asked, feigning surprise. 'My, how time does get away from me! Please excuse me dear Ekaterina, I quite forgot I gave *Sotnik* Prokofiev strict instructions to collect me now for a jaunt riding in the forests.'

'Of course' she said, giving Laura a little, wry look. 'I dare say you are tired of making lists with me!'

'Not at all' she assured her quickly. 'My birthday shall be splendid, thanks to your suggestions!'

Ekaterina rose and dipped a curtsey then eyed Roman critically as she left. Laura eyed him too, then gave him quick instructions to wait outside while she dressed. Roman bowed and closed the door behind him, nearly hopping from foot to foot in impatience. The guards outside her door gave him surreptitious looks whilst trying to stare straight ahead, but Roman could see his behaviour was drawing attention to himself.

He forced himself to relax, to stop pacing and to take a deep breath, folding his arms casually. The tsaritsa finally emerged, dressed in her riding habit and carried a pair of gloves in her hands. Roman saluted then led the way down to the stables, ordering the boy to saddle two horses quickly. Laura waited patiently, but Roman kicked himself for his oversight. He should have gone and gotten the horses ready while he was waiting for her.

But he had been in the castle...

He couldn't get that horror out of his mind. The thought of that slimy unpleasantness near her, able to harm her...

He looked so unsuspecting.

The groom brought the horses over and Laura mounted quickly, barely glancing in Roman's direction as he mounted too. She guided her stallion down Castle Street and he followed, casting his eye over the people in the street.

'Your Majesty -'

'Not a word Roman' she said quietly and he fastened his lip smartly. There was no anger or annoyance in her voice but something in the timbre told him that disobedience would be a very poor decision.

He squirmed with impatience as they slowly rode down Castle Street, Laura nodding at those that called out to her, suddenly wishing he had his rifle with him, feeling exposed and incompetent. *Was he there at that time because he knew I was off duty? Was I not supposed to see him at all? But then, why brush against me? The gate is wide enough for a carriage, and there were no others walking through at the time. He meant for me to know he was there...*

He wiggled impatiently in the saddle but Laura was in no hurry, the reins held so loosely that she seemed to let the horse meander where it wished. At long last they made it to Hunter's Pass, turning into the private forests of the monarchs. Roman wondered if he should ride up beside her, but the trail they were following was too narrow to allow that. Laura's back was stiff in front of him, and although she made minimal adjustments and corrections to the stallion, they seemed to be turning in purposeful directions. Roman wondered where they were going. The area they were riding through was overgrown and difficult to navigate. Part of him wondered whether she was just going to ignore him out of spite.

Then, as they ducked under the drooping arms of a tree, the trail opened up into a small, pretty clearing. On their right a waterfall cascaded down a steep bank into a rounded, deep pool, the river welling from it meandering away from them through the thick trees. Roman was struck by how charming it was, green with the flush of summer and twinkling with sunlight.

Laura dismounted easily but slowly, as if she was in some dream, her eyes drawn to a particular spot in the clearing. Roman looked, but there was nothing in the grass that he could see. Before he could take a closer look Laura shook herself and rounded on him.

'Well?' she asked, and he could see she was displeased with him. He dismounted quickly, but she didn't wait for his excuses. 'How dare you!

How could you be so careless?! As if there are not enough rumours floating around about me and now they have all seen you waiting like an impatient lover outside my rooms, they all saw us riding off into the forest together, they all know that you're not on duty, did you even think what this would look like?!'

'He was in the castle, Your Majesty' he blurted out, stopping her ranting. 'The man who pays me. I didn't see his face, I can't be sure – no I am sure. He smelt the same. It was him, I know it.'

She looked stunned, so Roman pressed on:

'I may have a name for him too, Anna Vasnetsova says she has seen him before, working in Luka Nevsky's home. Lvov.'

'Luka?!' Laura cried, shocked. 'All this time I suspected Maksim -'

'At all makes sense now' Roman went on, interrupting her, half unaware of what he was doing. 'Luka said he couldn't sleep, that he would often come and talk to me, or go to the library to borrow books, and what he must have been doing was spying, and I didn't *notice*, I was so *stupid*' he railed against himself, hitting his thighs with his fists and falling into inner reflection, horror scanning through those half remembered conversations. He wondered what he had said in those easy, quiet words, wondered if Luka had read into them more than he had meant.

'All this time' Laura was saying, fuming, 'and I had invited my spies to walk right into my home!'

'Send him away Your Majesty' Roman begged.

'I cannot' she sighed unhappily. 'You have only just learned the face of your benefactor, you can't be seen to connect the dots between him and Luka in case they realise you are a double agent.'

She sighed again and looked across to the lake and Roman was surprised, and moved, by the yearning he saw there before she shut her eyes and turned her face away.

'Do you swim Roman?' she asked, and there was a tremble in her voice.

'No Your Majesty' he answered, concerned at the pain he heard.

'Perhaps it is just as well' she murmured to herself then seemed to shake away the sadness. 'It is growing dark and we must return.'

He bowed and brought her stallion, which had wandered off a little way, back to her. She waved away his offer of assistance and mounted quickly, turning the stallion back into the Hunting Forest. Roman mounted and quickly caught her up, turning back to eye the hidden entrance to the glade. Even when he knew it was there he could not detect it. Laura must have been there many times before to find it so easily. He wondered who she had been with, in that secret place, to be so moved by her memories there.

The sun had disappeared behind the western flank when they reached Liberty Valley again, and the basin was gloomy in the dusk. Silently they made their way up Castle Street and under the portcullis to the gardens of

Tsar Constantinovich. The guards patrolling the grounds saluted as she rode by, shooting each other curious looks when she had passed.

In the courtyard before the doors she dismounted and gave her reins to the stable boy, heading into the castle. In the foyer was Fedor, clearly waiting for her.

'Your Majesty' he bowed. 'Both *Episcop* Yeltsin and Maksim Yegorov are waiting for an audience with you.'

'I will see *Episcop* Yeltsin first' she said after a brief hesitation. 'I will send for him when I am ready.'

'Yes Your Majesty' he bowed again, and Laura headed up the stone steps to the third floor.

Anna poured her a bowl of cool water and Laura washed her face gratefully, glad for these few moments of respite. Anna undid the buttons of her riding habit and she stepped out of the material, using a soft cloth to give her limbs a cursory wipe down before she pulled on another dress to receive the priest. Anna dabbed a small amount of perfume on her and then Laura sent her to call in the first of her guests.

She sat on the blue chaise lounge and smiled graciously when *Episcop* Yeltsin was ushered into her room. He bowed respectfully before coming forward to address her.

'The votes are almost counted Your Majesty, but we have given preliminary accounts to the population throughout the day, and about ten percent still remains to be tallied' he said as he approached. 'But the votes stand with Minister Yegorov at fifty nine percent and Minister Rukavishnikov at thirty one percent.'

Maksim has won Laura realised. *Even if all the remaining ten percent was for Ilich he could not hope to beat fifty nine.* She smiled a little sadly.

'That is both good news and sad news' she said ambiguously and *Episcop* Yeltsin nodded. 'I thank you for the news, and bid you farewell.'

He bid her good night too and bowed, walking backwards to the door as he took his leave. Laura sighed, dreading this last interview. *I will have to smile and congratulate him, and listen to him crow...*

Anxious to get it over with she instructed Anna to call for him, layering her feelings carefully behind years of training in Lady Ramkinson's school. Maksim was jubilant when he arrived, bowing almost theatrically low in his greeting, approaching her quickly.

'Good evening Your Majesty' he smiled, and she heard the gloat in his voice. 'I have come to personally invite you to a grand ball I will be holding in honour of my appointment to *Glava Gosudarstva*. It may be a little preliminary, as I gather not all the votes have been counted, but I humbly extend this invitation in the hope that the office will soon be ratified.' He held out a gilt edged card, bowing his head as he did.

Laura murmured some acknowledgment of the invitation, thinking how sickly false humility sounded in his mouth.

'I wonder Your Majesty, if you would not devise some small ceremony to mark the occasion' he pressed, and Laura knew just what response he was hoping for from her.

'Of course' she said. 'I will instruct Fedor to do so in the morning.'

'Fedor?' he asked, surprised. 'He is but a -'

'He was Master of Ceremonies for Tsar Constantinovich and I dare say he will know of something that could be made suitable for a new Head of State.' Laura interrupted.

'Of course, Your Majesty' he said, swallowing his pride.

'I will attend the ball, Minister Yegorov' she promised. 'Good evening, you may leave me.'

He bowed slightly and turned.

'Minister Yegorov?' she asked. 'Aren't you forgetting?'

Maksim swallowed down his fury and bowed to her again, walking backwards stiffly. It was petty, but Laura made him do it. *You are not Tsar, and I won't let you forget it.*

She sighed when the door closed behind him and dismissed Anna for the night, wanting to be alone. *So my fears have come true* she thought tiredly. *I hadn't expected the invitation, maybe it's a peace offering.* She dismissed the notion as soon as it occurred to her. *I will go, but I will take care. Maksim has planned something.*

She stood and brushed back her hair, blowing her cheeks out then slipped down to the ground floor, stepping into the west wing. *I'm still paying off the repairs to the ball room, and Parliament is paying – albeit reluctantly – for the new Parliament Chambers. Have we wasted all this money? What kind of Parliament will we have with Maksim in charge?*

She pushed into the new Parliament rooms and held her breath when she caught sight of the occupant. *It seems I'm not the only one in a melancholy mood* she thought as she eyed Ilich. He was standing, jacketless, in the dark gloom of the room, his hand resting on the silk covered table of Vsevolod. He didn't acknowledge her as he should have, but seemed to know she was there.

'I thought I knew what they wanted' he said, half to himself, half to the room around him. 'I fought for what they wanted. They all said no more blood, no more family...' he trailed off and turned to her. 'What did I really create here? They all spoke against you, they all said we needed change...' he shut his eyes. 'I gave them change, and they hated me. I took away the man with the whip and they spat on me in the streets. I only wanted to do what was best for them -'

'So did he' Laura said quietly. 'You were more alike than you might think.'

He looked away, stroking the cloth again, finding the splinters and the cracks of the wood under his fingers.

'Maksim will staff the key positions with his cronies and yes-men, all those who were working, all those who could have worked will no longer have a place in the Principle's Parliament. I won't be allowed to work anymore.'
'What will you do now?'

He went on as if he hadn't heard her interruption.
'If nothing else I gave them a voice, a Parliament that would have listened to them' he lamented. 'Will that continue? I doubt it. It will become no more than what the Advisory Council was, a bunch of old cautious men frightened of losing their privileges and estates and rubber stamping all of Aleksei's whims -'
'You're a fool if you think that' Laura interrupted angrily. 'Aleksei respected the opinions and advice of his Council, and they in turn had no fear in telling him when he was being a bloody idiot. Aleksei had many faults but to think of him as some petulant child who always got his way is to fall for your own propaganda.'

'Ilich,' she continued on a softer note. 'You must stay in the Parliament. You must be the check and balance for Maksim's power.'

He sighed, weary, then removed his hand from the table. A soft tap on the door caused them both to turn to see Luka approach, bowing politely to Laura.
'I am sorry, my friend' he said quietly.
'As am I' Ilich sighed.
'If you will excuse us, Your Majesty, we will retreat to commiserate. Your words cannot comfort him tonight' Luka said, taking Ilich's arm gently.
'Of course. Good night gentlemen' she said and watched them leave the room.

She understood Ilich's bitter disappointment. All he had tried to do was about to unravel, and he knew it. She wondered what Luka would say to him tonight; would he convince Ilich to fight on or to surrender with dignity?

She sighed again, and headed for her private dining room, wondering if Gustav would be buried in his book again. *I am so tired of being alone* she thought sadly, and closed Parliament doors behind her, knowing that when they were opened again nothing would ever be the same.

39

Laura dreamed she was lying in the soft grass of the meadow by the waterfall. Her eyes were closed and she could see the patterns of the tree branches moving in the sunlight against the red insides of her eyelids. She could hear Olaf swimming in the pool beneath the waterfall, as he had the day before the revolution, the day they had been here safe and secluded when the riot had happened over the rationing of meat and sent Dalnerechensk into hiding, sent soldiers to the walls to light the Tcherepnin Beacon to alert troops in the garrisons to come to their aid.

How blissfully unaware we had been she thought, shivering at the cold touch of his wet skin as he left the water to lie astride her, his lips earnestly seeking hers. *How blissful and happy Aleksei and I had been, in this very spot…* her memory supplied, and she knew, as she had somehow known it had been Olaf, that the man making love to her was now her husband. His skin was hot with the sunlight and flushed from the hours of dancing, and his thrusts were firm, quick, and desperately earnest.

And now they were no longer by the waterfall, but in some secluded part of the Ivanov's garden, the strains of the distant party rustling like sparrows in the hedgerow, making Aleksei wild with desire and fear of discovery. The rough material of the captain's jacket scraped against her bare skin, twisting that tight knot in her harder, pushing her to that moment where she had learnt how enjoyable sex could be.

She tangled her fingers harder in his long blonde hair, feeling his hot breath mist on her throat and lips, feeling him shudder and lose control in his passion. He whispered her name, and she heard it echo in the silence of the ruined ballroom, filling the sooty air with yearning want.

She woke; trembling, sweating, aching with unfulfilled desire.

She threw off the hot covers and quickly ran across her parlour, flinging open her door and startling Roman.

'Your Majesty, what is it?' he asked, worried at her agitation.

She ignored him, pacing distractedly up and down the corridor, a worried Roman shadowing her steps but always too far away. *He would do anything for me* her mind whispered. *He had dared to touch me, he wants to touch me, I saw it in his face…*

She wondered if the Tsar's right to take mistresses extended to her.

The words were on her tongue, pressing it down, pulling her lips into a pucker, clogging her throat with the breath to speak them, her vocal chords trembling with anticipation to say them, her chest hitching against the remembered weight of him as he had lain on her in the forest, his heart knocking a frantic tattoo against hers, his breath panting as he had searched for her would-be assassin.

To feel that again she yearned, *to feel hard flesh and hot, liquid desire spurt in her again…*

There was a rustle somewhere in the castle, a murmur, a quiet word. Laura turned away, carefully glancing around her, letting her feet take her to the nursery, distracted and unsure of herself.

A bewildered Roman followed her to the parlour but did not cross into the room. She closed the door against him, avoiding looking at him, then crossed to the door for the nursery proper. She had never been in the nursery itself, too afraid of the memory of the night of the revolution, too worried that her transgression against the superstitions of the Dalnerechenskers would be reported to those who would use it against her. But the desire to see Alexandra was too great.

She pushed open the door and stepped in, stopping in shock. Luka was in the nursery, and he was holding Alexandra, his head bent over her in intensive scrutiny.

'*What are you doing?!*' she hissed, rushing over to grab her daughter.

She caught a whiff of alcohol, and realised that Luka had been drinking, probably since she had left him with Ilich all those hours ago. Even more disturbingly, he did not let go of Alexandra. Laura struggled with him, trying to pull her daughter away, unwilling to pull too hard in case she accidentally hurt her.

'Let go!' she snapped.

Luka did, but only with one hand, which he used to grip her arm firmly.

'I hear you at night' he hissed. 'I hear you moan for him -'

'Let my daughter go!' she shouted.

The butt of Roman's rifle smashed into the side of his head, sending him sprawling, and it was only pure luck that Laura managed to hang on to Alexandra, pulling her out of Luka's embrace. The violence of the action woke her, and she began to cry. Laura folded her tightly into her arms, soothing her as best as she could.

'Are you hurt?' Roman demanded, standing over Luka with his rifle raised, ready to strike another blow. 'Is the princess hurt?'

'She's fine, I'm fine' she said, cradling Alexandra and turning away from them. '*Monsieur* Nevsky, you are no longer welcome in this home. *Sotnik*, escort this man out of the castle.'

She hurried out, taking Alexandra with her, frightened and shaky.

Back in her room she sat on her chaise in the dark, rocking Alexandra to soothe her, becoming aware of a now familiar mechanical puttering from outside in the valley. *Now where could Knjaz Uvarov have gone to, to be coming back at three in the morning?* she wondered, listening to the motor of the horseless carriage echo through the silent streets, finally cutting out near the castle district.

In the silence she heard the floorboards outside her room creak as Roman returned to his post and she yawned, taking her now sleeping daughter into her bedroom, lying her down on the bed and propping pillows around her. But it was still hot with her arousal, clammy with sweat and she sat reluctantly on the edge of it, still in need of a release, twisted with the unfairness of it all.

Why could I not have had my happily ever after? she cried, her fingers pulling open the draw to the bedside cabinet and slipping inside for Olaf's letter.

Her fingers touched bare wood. She leaned over, brushing against the bottom of the drawer, then stood up and began to scrabble frantically, the cold dread squeezing her heart and lungs. She grabbed at the matches on her bedside table, her shaking hands causing them to scatter all over the floor but she managed to find one and scratch it against the matchbook.

In the flare of sudden light she saw what she dreaded most. The drawer was empty.

She yanked it out of the bedside table in the vain hope that it had somehow fallen down behind the drawer, or under it, or under the bed. But it was gone.

The light went out. Laura threw back her head and screamed.

Her parlour door burst open and she heard Roman running across it. Alexandra, woken once again, began to cry in fright. Roman burst into her bedchamber and found himself not confronting an intruder but assailed by the furious tsaritsa, who rained blows on him.

'*Did you take it?!*' she screamed, slapping him again. '*It's gone! Where is it?!*'

'You've been robbed?' he asked, bewildered, pinning her arms down to stop her attacking him.

'*My last piece of him!*' she shouted. 'It's gone, you took it!'

'No! I could never steal from you!' he cried, offended.

'It was all I have left, you gave it to them' she sobbed, her struggles and blows becoming weaker as her misery took over. 'You gave them his letter…'

'*No*' he swore, soothing her. 'No Your Majesty, I would never, *never* steal from you.'

He held her as she sobbed; a deep wrenching misery that she couldn't seem to stop, whispering soothing sounds to her, aware that anxious, curious faces were now poking into her chamber.

'Spanov' he beckoned, and the soldier saluted, coming forward into Laura's bedroom. 'Wake the nanny, get her to take *Tsesarevna* Alexandra back to the nursery. And send someone for Doctor Pushkin' he added as the soldier saluted again and raced to do as he'd been told.

Carefully he lifted Laura up and set her down on her bed, sending a maid for cold water and some cloths to minister to her, aware of the liquid feel of her night dress, the softness and the heat of her body under it. Gertrude arrived and scooped up the sobbing baby, clucking to her soothingly as she took her back to the nursery, followed into the room by

Fedor, who ushered everyone out, including Roman.

Reluctantly, one by one they left, casting dubious glances at each other and their captain. He could see what they were thinking as they eyed him, shooting each other knowing smiles as they did so. *She had screamed, and they had found him in her bedroom, with her in his arms...* It was no secret that she favoured the captain of her guard, despite the humiliating punishment she had inflicted on him. *They all think I'm her lover* he thought, as they glared at him accusingly, though there were some that looked on with jealous admiration. *They all think I was with her, giving her an orgasm that was so nerve-shatteringly, toe-curlingly, thigh-tremblingly* good *that she had screamed awake her household.*

Dear God I want to he admitted to himself. He had heard her moan in her sleep, had seen how flushed with arousal she was when she burst out of her rooms, had felt underneath her anger when she attacked him her desperate need to feel his hands on her -

No he shook himself. *She's ill, she has a fever, that's all.*

Poor girl, that's the last thing she needs he sighed, trying to fan away the sexual stirrings he felt. He wondered what had caused her frightening behaviour, the sudden anger, the tantrums, the – the *hysteria...*

He groaned silently. *Female hysteria...* he had read several translations from English medical literature that his neighbour had been studying in hopes to become a doctor. The list of causes and symptoms had been long and tedious but the treatment had all been the same: weekly pelvic massage until "hysterical paroxysm" was achieved, and more frequent application of marital duty.

There had been pictures too... and diagrams... And electric vibrating metal rods that looked suspiciously like the devices for muscular-skeletal massage in his sister's magazines...

Electricity was not widespread in the Principality yet, and he wondered if that stuffy little doctor would -

Stop it he groaned, shaking himself harder, aware that his erection was growing.

She needs a good fuck said his traitor soldier crassness. *Weekly.*

Dear God she was so damn *attractive...*

'Ask me' he whispered, pleadingly. 'Ask me, ask me, ask me...'

Spanov arrived at the top of the stairs, ushering the hurriedly dressed Doctor Pushkin to the tsaritsa's apartments. Roman saluted and stepped aside to let the doctor in, shutting the door firmly before Spanov could follow. The Private eyed him, grinning. *I wish I was doing what they all think I'm doing* he sighed.

'Stay here till you are relieved' he commanded, and headed down the hallway.

'But my patrol!' he started to protest.

'I'll do it' he snapped, running down the stairs. *And it would be a very good idea to trip and fall into the fountain...* he admonished himself and sighed, welcoming the shock of the cold wind on his face as he burst outside.

40

Despite her misgivings, she was almost excited to be going to Maksim's ball. In the week since the election she had recovered from her fever and officially sworn in the new Prime Minister with a relatively understated ceremony that Fedor had devised; one that previously had been for the handover for the office of Key Holder to the Tsar's Privy Chambers. Laura had laughed at the reference and Maksim had glowered through his moment of triumph.

Her excitement might also have something to do with the beautiful blue dress that had arrived for her that morning she thought ruefully. Fredrik had sent it ahead of him, made from the finest Italian lace and silk. Ekaterina had told her the colour was Bavarian Blue, the colour of Fredrik's homeland, and the only thing that had stopped her from wearing it to Maksim's ball was the thought of waiting to see Fredrik's face when she wore it first for him.

She thought back to when she had negotiated with Russia and Germany for the Liberty Treaty, of how she had worn dresses in their imperial colours, a careful political manipulation, and wondered what would be said when she suddenly stepped out wearing the colours of the Kingdom of Bavaria.

No, I don't need to wonder she reminded herself.

She shook herself absently, upsetting Anna, who was carefully pinning her hair into a fantastic creation, twisting seed pearl, emerald, sapphire and ruby clips into her hair; the gems arranged to look like flowers and vines twisting through her tresses. She apologised, sitting still again, smoothing down the bodice of her white dress.

Anna finished and stepped back to admire her handiwork, smiling with satisfaction before applying kohl and other cosmetics to Laura's face, pinching her cheeks to bring up a subtle colour in them. A quick gust of perfume that Gustav had given to her followed, then Anna crossed to Laura's jewel case to bring back the necklace Fredrik had given her, fastening it around Laura's throat.

'You look magnificent, Your Majesty' she smiled.

'Thank you Anna, I would not do so were it not for your talents!' she smiled too, then stood to eye herself in the mirror, turning this way and that.

The dress hugged at her curves that were still girlishly attractive and firm, despite her pregnancy and childbirth, and prettily displayed her breasts and shoulders. She pulled on her fine silk gloves and picked up her iridescent blue fan, eyeing the full effect. Anna sighed dreamily, then bid Laura goodnight, quickly disappearing through the door.

Laura smiled unhappily, wishing she too had someone to rush home to, someone to fill her bed at night. Her eyes strayed to the bedside table she could see through the open doorway of her bedroom. She had looked everywhere for the letter; in all her drawers, in her jewellery case, in the pockets of her clothes, in the little waste paper basket by her writing table, behind and under every cushion in her apartments. It was gone.

She sighed again, wondering who had it, wondering what they were doing to it. Destroying it? Dissecting the French words and reading those heartbreaking declarations, twisting Olaf's love into something terrible and shameful? She had grieved for the loss of the letter as she had grieved for Olaf, and her hot tears were always tinged with remorse. *It would not be gone if I had not brought it with me!*

She shook herself, smoothing down the dress again. There was nothing she could do about it. It was gone, and they most likely had it. *How* they got it was immaterial. Would they use it tonight to accuse her of adultery? Possibly. There was a game afoot, and – to her surprise – she was looking forward to the battle of wits, almost as much as she was looking forward to dancing again.

She looked at herself one last time then opened the door to the corridor. 'Roman?'

He saluted. 'Yes Your Majesty?' he managed, trying hard not to stare.

'You are to come with me into Maksim's home tonight. I fear some mischief.' She fluttered her fan nervously at her side.

'Have no fear, Maksim would not dare attempt assassination -' he rushed to reassure her but she cut him off, her voice clipped with irritation.

'He is no fool to murder me at a party in his own home. But it will be filled with all those whose loyalties lie with him, and he would not have invited me if there was not some humiliation he had designed, and I want – I want a face there that is loyal to me still' she dropped her eyes and fussed with the fit of her silk glove.

Then without another word she strode out into the corridor, leaving Roman to follow in her wake. In the entrance hall were six livery men, dressed in the colours of the Vakhtangov household, who Fedor was instructing in the pageantry of the evening. They bowed as she appeared, and she motioned for Fedor to continue with his lesson, collecting a fur stole that Ekaterina had lent her and draping it around her shoulders.

When dismissed, the livery men quickly saluted and rushed out to take up positions around the carriage: Two on horseback before and behind the carriage, two riding on the back plate of the carriage, and the Ivanov's groom, who Laura would always think of as the Ivanov's groom, would drive the team of four horses, their bridles and plumes gleaming in the light of the torches.

Roman mounted the lone horse at the front, and Fedor handed him the royal standard of Dalnerechensk, which he would carry as he rode before the procession. Laura was helped into the carriage by the groom before he jumped up to take his place in the driver's seat, waiting for the procession to set off.

Laura couldn't understand why she had insisted on the pageantry, it seemed silly to arrive in such splendour for such a short trip. *And the pomp and ceremony might make a higher platform to fall from with whatever degradation Maksim has planned* she thought, then waved it away.

I still am Tsaritsa, and this is a semi-official outing. Pageantry is needed she told herself, then motioned for Roman to ride out.

It took less than five minutes to arrive at the splendid, palatial home that had once belonged to Nicholas Riminov. It had been one of the most sumptuous houses in the Principality, rivalling the splendour of *Episcop* Vasily's famous apartments, second only the Ivanov home. Tsar Constantinovich had rewarded him handsomely for his services to the crown during his lifetime, and it hurt to think that he had died a beggar in a rotting farmstead instead of in the place where he had lived and served Dalnerechensk.

It hurt more to know that Maksim had all but stolen the house under Eminent Domain, purchasing it for a pittance she added ruefully.

The carriage stopped and she alighted, Roman following her as she climbed the steps, giving her stole to the girl at the door. Beside her stood an old man, who announced her name to the throng who stood in the elegant entrance hall, and she watched the bows and curtseys ripple out across the room as they all turned to greet her. Laura spotted Ekaterina, resplendent in red silk, and near her the consumptive form of Anna Vakhtangovna, draped in a royal blue dress cut too revealing for her slender figure, her cheeks pinched until they were red, like an angry blotch.

Knjaz Uvarov came forward to bow deeply and kiss her hand, offering his sincere apologies that Maksim was not there to greet her himself.

'He is, unavoidably, detained with a matter of utmost importance, but please, allow me to escort you to the glass gallery.'

'Thank you that is most kind' she said, slipping her hand into his offered elbow and hoping that Roman had the sense to follow her at a slight distance.

She had never set foot inside Nicholas' home but had heard of the glass gallery. It was a long, wide room, almost the length of one wing of the house, cut on one side with windows overlooking the sculptured grounds, decorated on the other with a wall of mirrors that made the room seem twice as wide and light. Seven expensive, cut crystal chandeliers hung from the painted ceiling, and at the far end of the gallery a grand staircase led to balconies above, and a set of wide double doors that led into the private apartments of Nicholas. *Maksim*, she corrected herself.

Knjaz Uvarov excused himself and left, and Laura accepted a glass of wine a servant handed to her. Across the room she could see Tatiana, surrounded by a group of women, all shooting veiled looks in Laura's direction.

There was a smugness in the crowd as she greeted members of the Vakhtangov family, a hostility that was palpable behind their false smiles and meaningless exchange of pleasantries.

'This is wrong, this feels wrong' Roman said under his breath, wishing the tsaritsa had let him bring his rifle.

'Go and stand by the wall, don't let me out of your sight' she said, placing the empty wine goblet on a table.

She spotted Ekaterina and her cousin Gustav and made her way to them, a sudden fanfare arresting her greeting. Maksim appeared at the top of the grand staircase, spreading his arms wide to gather in the applause of his guests and bowing left and right to the room below him.

'Ladies and gentlemen, forgive me for my late intrusion, I trust that my most honoured guest will more than make up for my neglect as your host' he said, and a ripple of murmur went through the crowd. 'It is my humble privilege to announce *Naslednik Tsesarevich* Nikolai Viktor Antonevich Vakhtangov, great-great-great-great-great-grandson, and *direct male descendent*, of Tsar Vasilievich the Third.'

'The Nine Week King' Ekaterina breathed, and Laura heard it ripple through the room in excited whispers.

'"The Nine Week King?"' she asked, confused, but there was no time to answer.

Another fanfare played, and a ripple of anticipation wove through the crowd. They moved nearer to the stairs, straining to see. *Naslednik Tsesarevich* Laura thought. *Maksim called him Heir Apparent. So that was why they were all so smug!*

He must be an imposter she thought wildly. *How could the Vakhtangovs go along with this?! I have never seen the name Nikolai in all my research, and there was no Vasilievich the Third...*

Her thoughts stopped when a man appeared from Maksim's apartments and made his way to the top of the stairs. He was young, Laura guessed about twenty-five, and handsome; dark like Aleksei, boyish and casual like Alexander Andrei must have been. He was dressed in the black military uniform of the old Palace Guard and wore all the trimmings for the highest rank of the army, bar the one designated for Commander in Chief, as only the Tsar could wear that. Under his right epaulet, and across his body he wore the royal blue sash of Dalnerechensk. Laura didn't miss the meaning of it.

There were gasps and coos, and a sudden wind with the fluttering of a hundred fans. Excited applause broke out then bows and curtseys, leaving Laura stranded awkwardly below. She didn't dare look around her, and didn't dare curtsey either. Whatever battle she had been looking forward to had not prepared her for this.

Nikolai half turned to Maksim, who bowed, then turned back to the waiting crowd in the glass gallery, beginning to descend the stairs. *He moves very gracefully* Laura noted, unable to stop herself. *And he is coming towards me* she realised, refusing to let herself fuss with her gloves or fan, to let her trembly fingers flutter to her necklace or hair.

As he came closer and she began to make out his features better, she was struck by just how uncommonly handsome he was. *He could have been Marie Borodina's brother* she thought. He was tall, but not overly so, and well-proportioned in his limbs. His shoulders were wide, his waist and hips slender. His black Vakhtangov hair was romantically curled and tousled on his forehead, brushing at his collar. His nose was straight and noble, almost classical, his brow deep and smooth. His lips were firm and well-shaped, invitingly kissable.

But it was his eyes that struck her the most. He reminded her of those tragically romantic poets that heroines were always fawning over in popular literature. There was a deep sadness in him, a tormented, haunted look she was very familiar with. *He knows real loss...*

He stopped in front of her, his eyes lowering briefly as he did. Laura wondered if he was eyeing the shape of her body, or unable to meet her gaze.

'*Velikaja Knjaginja*, may I present to you *Naslednik Tsesarevich* Nikolai Vakhtangov' Maksim grinned, eyeing them as they stood there, facing each other.

Nikolai bowed to her. It was a bow carefully calculated in height. Not so deep to show any acquiesce, not shallow enough to cause any offence, but the correct height for one royal to another. She in turn curtseyed to him, carefully calculating the bend of her knees, tilting her head forward just far enough.

'I am delighted to at last make your acquaintance' he said in English, his pronunciation so perfect she could have mistaken him for an Oxford man. 'The rumours of your beauty hardly do you justice.'

'You have me at a disadvantage sir, I have heard no rumours of you' she replied, pointing her comment at Maksim.

'Perhaps you will allow me to further our acquaintance?' he asked, half turning and offering her his elbow.

'I shall not refuse' she said wryly, slipping her hand into his crooked arm.

Behind her she heard the guests rise, heard the music start up again, heard the excited gossip fan out and wiggle around everyone; twisting them into gathering knots of scandalmongers before flinging them outwards to join other groups, commenting and laughing and watching them oh so carefully...

Well done Maksim she thought bitterly. *It was a masterful coup.*

They found themselves in the middle of a small clearing, as Maksim's guests hung back to stare at them, to whisper to each other, to wait with baited breath for each snippet of conversation, each movement, each look they shot each other.

'You speak English very well' she said finally. It was a safe topic of conversation, and she was careful to avoid calling him *Naslednik Tsesarevich*. 'Where did you learn?'

'I had tutors as a child, and I have travelled often in England' he answered.

'And your Russian is very good, your accent is charming.'

'Thank you. For my proficiency I must thank my dear friend Countess Ivanova. I am greatly indebted to her.'

An awkward silence fell again and they struggled to fill it.

'Please excuse my interruption' *Knjaz* Uvarov suddenly said, stepping in front of them. '*Naslednik Tsesarevich*, my niece Tatiana has requested the next dance from you, and I would be most honoured, *Velikaja Knjaginja*, if you would consent to my suit for the dance.'

Nikolai turned to Laura and bowed carefully again, kissing the hand she offered him. 'Forgive me, I did promise to dance with Tatiana' he said apologetically. 'Perhaps you will allow me to acquaint myself in more detail at some other time?'

'I shall look forward to it' she murmured.

'Have you ever ridden in a motorised carriage?' he asked suddenly.

'I have not.'

'Would you like to?'

She opened her mouth to refuse then stopped. 'Yes, I would' she accepted.

'Splendid, I shall call on you tomorrow morning.'

'I regret that tomorrow morning I have a prior engagement with my Parliament' she said coolly, reminding him that she was still Monarch of Dalnerechensk, despite what Maksim might have told him. *You cannot command me, Nikolai* she thought, and refused to add the word *yet* to the phrase. 'I believe I have some time free in the afternoon.'

'The afternoon then' he smiled, and Laura felt herself melt at it.

He bowed again and left, taking Tatiana's hand and leading her to the centre of the room. Laura let *Knjaz* Uvarov lead her to her place in the dance and dipped her head to her partner when the music started.

She tried to be subtle in the times she glanced at Nikolai, watching the way he danced, noticing the way people's eyes flicked between her and the prince, like they were watching some invisible tennis match. She caught sight of Ekaterina once, deep in conversation with her cousin, and seemingly avoiding looking at her.

Had she known? Laura wondered. *Nikolai seemed to be the worst kept secret in Dalnerechensk. And I was the last to know* she smouldered. *No wonder they were all so smug!*

Tatiana laughed girlishly nearby, and Laura tried to ignore it as best as she could. She caught sight of Roman, looking unhappy near the wall, and desperately wishing he had his rifle, his eyes constantly moving over the party guests for signs of trouble. *What a pity you can't shoot gossip and rumour!*

The dance ended and Laura bowed to *Knjaz* Uvarov again, fanning herself as she went to collect another goblet of wine, catching snippets of gossip as she moved through the crowd.

It's true! Male children, all the way back to The Nine Week King! ... Did you see the way he looked at her? Who, Tatiana? No! The ... So handsome, and he dances so gracefully! ... No, no wife, but he has a ... Obviously he loved her very much ... She would do well to marry... Could gain the throne, after all, she's ... It's not Aleksei's, he drowned, and everyone knew he despised her!

Laura faltered, accidentally knocking over her goblet as she set it down on the table, shutting her eyes against the hurt.

'Your Majesty, do allow me to show you the glass gallery from the balcony' Ekaterina said, curtseying as she appeared beside her.

She said nothing, following her up the staircase, leaving behind the noise and the heat of the gallery below.

'The Nine Week King?' she hissed.

Ekaterina took two more steps before answering.

'A succession crisis, in the sixteenth century, I believe' she said unhappily. 'Tsar Radomyrevich had two sons, Peter and Viktor. Peter was older, and became Tsar Vasilievich the Second on the early death of Radomyrevich, when he was about twenty seven. He was very unpopular; awkward, unsure, brusque – to the point of rudeness.' She shrugged then raised her arm, pointing to the chandelier, as if she were recounting facts about it.

'His younger brother, Viktor, was charming and confident, pleasant and astute, and the better of the two for the throne. It made Peter extremely jealous and bitter, especially when Viktor married. It was said he refused to go to the wedding, and refused to give his brother his blessing.'

'Sounds charming' Laura said, turning to look dutifully at the beautiful fresco Ekaterina was gesturing towards, becoming uncomfortable with the parallels between Peter and Viktor, and Aleksei and Alexander Andrei.

'Peter was married eventually, but remained childless. Court gossip said his wife was still a virgin seven years after they wedded. He grew more bitter and jealous of his brother's happy marriage, who by now had three sons and a daughter.

'Then Peter fell sick, with typhoid, and a rather ambitious Advisory Council member called Sergei Beria persuaded Viktor to take the throne. He did so, taking the name Vasilievich the Third, and reversed many of Peter's unpopular taxes and laws.'

'Peter survived, didn't he' Laura interrupted.

Ekaterina sighed unhappily again.

'Yes. And he was furious. He executed Beria for treason, banished his brother and all his descendants; decreed that all mention of Vasilievich the Third be expunged from every record. No one could even speak his name, so he became known as the Nine Week King, or the Banished King -'

'You're getting caught up in the romanticism of this all too!' Laura cried hotly.

Ekaterina shut her eyes, sorry for her enthusiasm. 'Forgive me Laura, I did not mean to cause offense. It *is* romantic, as no doubt Maksim hoped it would be. If Peter *had* died, Nikolai would be on the throne now.'

Her gesture down at the glass gallery managed to encompass the small crowd around the Prince.

On the throne now Laura's mind repeated. *And none of this – Aleksei, Alexander Andrei, the revolution – none of this would have happened either. I would not be Tsaritsa.*

'Why is he not?' she asked instead.

'Peter had a son' Ekaterina said simply.

'With his *wife?*' Laura asked, surprised.

'Yes indeed, though there were many rumours, ones no one dared say aloud. *One* son, their only child, Igor, who became Tsar Petrovich on his eighteenth birthday, three days after his father died.'

Tsar Petrovich, Laura realised, *was the reason why Viktor had not come back.* He too had been handsome, witty, charming, and a *very* astute politician. He had been guided in much of his young life by Litke, another clever and canny minister, who had helped him become beloved and popular with Dalnerechenskers; reversing his father's unpopular laws and taxes, building public works, and laying the first stones for Dalnerechensk's drainage system.

Tsar Petrovich had become so popular Viktor would not have been needed. *I wonder whose decision it would have been not to reverse the banishment of his uncle?* Laura thought. She could not blame the young king for being wary of his hold on the throne. Tarnished forever by the name of his father in his official title, the poor boy could not have afforded the reminder of the better alternative that had so recently held the throne.

The Heir of the Nine Week King she thought, gazing down at the handsome man. *It certainly was a romantic notion.*

'Ah Your Majesty' Maksim said, appearing behind her and bowing deeply, able to afford some acquiesce in his magnificent victory. 'Allow me to escort you to the dining room.'

Laura slipped her hand into the crook of his elbow, descending the stairs with him while Ekaterina followed behind them.

'And what is your opinion of my glass gallery?' he asked, almost crowing.

'It is beautiful' she smiled sweetly. 'I was not able to compliment Nicholas Riminov for his exquisite taste. My word!' she exclaimed, seeing the magnificent setting of the table. 'Am I not mistaken, did that beautiful centrepiece once grace the table of *Episcop* Vasily?'

You are a pirate Maksim, I will not let you forget it she thought nastily.

'You are correct, Your Majesty' he said, some tightness in his voice.

Laura smiled deeper at her small victory, but it vanished quickly when he led her around the table to the Royal Canopy. Underneath the large standard was an ornate chair; but beside it, conspicuous by its lack of ornamentation, was an old wooden chair.

Vsevolod's Throne! she gasped. *How the hell did he get that out of the castle?!* And then a terrible realisation hit her. *The throne is not intended for me. He's going to sit Nikolai on it!*

I'll sit on it myself! she thought, but Maksim had been ready for her coup, and expertly guided her descending backside onto the ornate throne, Tatiana adroitly manoeuvring Nikolai into position beside her. Maksim held the chair and gently pushed it forward behind Nikolai, who – Laura noticed – recognised what it was, but hesitated only briefly before sitting, slightly reverently, on the chair. It was a stunning piece of symbolism, and everyone, *everyone*, saw him do it.

She fumed, so incandescent she could not formulate a coherent protest, and now it was too late, Nikolai was sitting on the throne. The table filled up around her; Maksim and his cousin beside Laura, keeping her involved in a steady stream of inane chatter, while Anna Vakhtangovna was seated beside Nikolai, her creaking aunt and grandmother with her, fostering conversation between them, answering Nikolai's questions for her and parading her small accomplishments before him. Anna looked deeply unhappy, but she smiled at him after some sharp prodding from her grandmother.

Throughout the ten courses of the meal they so artfully monopolised their time that Laura and Nikolai were not able to say a single word to each other. It was uncomfortable, and obvious, and Laura was so wound up she could barely eat a thing. She was noticing something else too, another petty little slight that was carefully orchestrated to snub her.

Each time a course was served the Vakhtangovs would grow a little more impatient to begin, picking up forks before Laura did, sipping at their wine when she did not, ruder with their table manners. *Knjaz* Uvarov was even bold enough to cut his meat before Laura started, but was careful enough not to put it in his mouth without a glance in her direction.

No, not mine, Nikolai's she realised. *They are taking their cues from him, not from me.*

I wish this night was over.

It was late when the tenth course was finished and Laura was finding her company insufferable. It had taken her until the fourth course to locate Ekaterina and Gustav, almost hidden away from the centre table where she sat, far too far away to hold a conversation with them. Tired of Maksim's boorish company she rose suddenly.

They turned to look, but only three rose; Ekaterina, Gustav, and Anna Vakhtangovna, whose arm was grabbed and yanked back down into her seat by Varvara. Nikolai turned in surprise, saw Laura standing and quickly got to his feet, bowing his calculated bow again. As one the Vakhtangovs rose and bowed. *They have made their loyalties perfectly clear* Laura thought miserably, though she didn't let the humiliation show on her face. Nikolai, for his part, looked troubled and a little embarrassed.

You shouldn't be Laura thought as she looked at his handsome face again. *This is what you came here for, I am sure of it.*

Swallowing the gall that rose in her she turned to Maksim and bowed slightly, praising him for the wonderful party and thanking him for graciously inviting her.

'Surely you are not thinking of leaving already?!' Maksim cried, and she heard the taunt in his voice. *Stay, it is too early to leave, and I have more humiliations in store!*

'Alas I must, I fear' she said, wondering if she could make the excuse that she was not yet fully recovered from her fever, and beginning to feel ill again. *No, no weaknesses, not here. These are bloodhounds, and they will tear you apart.*

'Your Majesty' Nikolai started, bowing slightly, and Laura stopped, surprised. She hadn't expected to hear that title from him. Perhaps he truly was embarrassed at the slight his family had paid to her. 'I could not but help admiring you as you danced earlier this evening. Would you do me the honour of dancing with me?'

She hesitated. She wanted to refuse, she wanted to stamp out of Maksim's house, to throw herself down on her bed and sob unhappily. *But I can't* she sighed. *It is such bad form for a royal to race out of a semi-formal engagement.*

She accepted the dance, allowing Nikolai to escort her back to the glass gallery, listening to the rustle as the Vakhtangovs fell in behind them. Maksim gestured for the musicians to strike up a waltz, but no one else joined them in the dance, filling the gallery to watch the two of them together.

Their conversation was stilted and careful again, inane and unsuitable for such a momentous occasion. *We should have shouted, struck blows, smashed furniture* Laura thought, but Nikolai was civil and polite with her, his true feelings carefully hidden. He was well versed in court etiquette, and better at it than Laura.

The dance seemed endless, but when the music finally came to an end Nikolai bowed to her then turned to address Maksim.

'I thank you, cousin, for this wonderful evening, but I fear you must forgive me, I am tired from my long journey and will retire.'

As one the Vakhtangov family curtseyed and bowed deeply to him. He acknowledged their decorum, then turned to Laura again.

'Good night, Your Majesty' he said, bowing to her. 'I shall look forward to our outing tomorrow afternoon.'

'As will I' she said, and didn't know if she was lying or not.

Nikolai left her and crossed the glass gallery, climbing the stairs to the apartments. A servant opened the doors for him, bowing deeply, then closed them when the prince had stepped through.

'Goodnight, dear guests!' Maksim called loudly. 'May your journeys home be uneventful!'

He's dismissed us! Laura fumed. *Dismissed us, like we were Nikolai's court!*

At least you can go home now a small part of her said. She turned and headed towards the entrance hall, glad to be leaving even if she was being unceremoniously sent from his home, like some disgraced servant.

Maksim himself brought Laura's stole to her, draping it over her shoulders, eyeing Roman as he did so.

'Better take that young man home to bed Your Majesty' he said. 'Though I don't know how good he'll be, he's yawned several times this evening. There is nothing worse than a soldier who falls asleep standing to attention!'

Tatiana burst out laughing and quickly ran over to her friends, waving her fan to hide her merriment.

'Thank you for your words of wisdom Maksim, no doubt garnered from many, *many* years of frustrating experience!' she said, and swept out of the house.

Her parting shot gave her no satisfaction and she climbed into the carriage, impatiently waiting for Roman to mount his horse and start the procession back to the castle.

When at last they set off the tears came, tears that seemed so acidic they cut stinging trails down her cheeks, the reservoirs of dark and violent frustration in her finally overcoming her barriers of decorum. Fear and impotent rage twisted deeper and deeper into her, finding ever more black wells of anger, hate and misery.

It was all she could do to sit in the carriage, resisting the almost overwhelming urge to slam open the door and stalk home on foot, to march back to Maksim's house and slap the treason out of him, to snatch the ceremonial pike out of Roman's hands and beat Ekaterina with it. And just when she thought she might burst, the carriage drew to a halt in the castle grounds. She slammed open the door, not waiting to be escorted out and raced up to her room, practically knocking aside the guards on duty at the castle doors.

Anna had set a foot basin beside her chaise in her rooms, ready to soak her feet from the hours of dancing. With a savage kick Laura sent it crashing into the marble surround of her fireplace and a violent swipe sent the vase of flowers shattering to the floor too. A thick ceramic ewer made a satisfying mess when it landed beside the vase and six crystal tumblers knocked gilt rococo off the walls when they shattered against them. The decanter was about to follow suit when something strange caught her eye and she stopped, curiosity momentarily getting the best of her.

There was a gap in the ornate decoration of the marble fire surround. *No, more than that; there was a hollow, a space.*

Shorn momentarily of her destructive rampage she put the decanter back on the table, uncaring that it was barely balanced on the edge, ignoring it when it toppled over and landed on the rug, sloshing its sickly strong contents onto the floor.

She made her way over to the fireplace, picking carefully through a wide debris field of stray shards, noticing the large lump of a flower the footbath had knocked off the marble surround. Absently she picked it up, eyeing the minute detail carved into the three petals, then looked carefully at the fireplace.

A secret drawer, approximately twenty centimetres across, had slid out from the marble, its face decorated with carved flowers and expertly hidden by the broken outline of leaves and petals that slotted into gaps carved especially for them. So perfect was the fit that not a crack or overlap gave away the secret compartment. Six inches above the drawer was a marble flower, three petals knocked from it, revealing that the sculpted centre was not as solid as it had once appeared.

It looks like it is some kind of button Laura realised, then experimented by closing the drawer almost fully, anxious not to close it completely if this experiment didn't work. Then, when she had pushed it in as far as she dared, she placed her finger on the dimpled centre of the carved daisy and pushed. There was a click, and the drawer slid out an inch again. She smiled and slid the drawer shut completely, then pushed the button again. This time the click was louder, and the drawer slid out several inches.

She smiled then critically eyed the lump of marble in her hands, orientating it and fitting it against the flower. It fitted back perfectly, looking none the worse for her violent demolition. She wondered if she could get a mason to reattach the petals again, but then wondered if that would give away the secret compartment, or worse, accidentally glue it shut.

She eyed it again, wondering if she could attach it herself, and avoid calling in anyone else. *I wonder if this is truly secret* she thought. *It would have been useful to have known about this before, Olaf's letter might have been kept safe from prying eyes.* She hooked her finger into the drawer, testing the extent to which it would slide out, and was surprised to see the book inside it.

Unable to help herself she reached in and plucked out the book, absently placing the broken petals on the top of the mantelpiece. It was bound in leather, and looked old but in good condition. It was not embossed or marked with a title, so Laura opened it. There was a hand written dedication on the first page, in a language she couldn't recognise. *Polish?* she suddenly wondered.

She turned a page and found that the script here was decidedly different, and appeared to be a diary of some sort, written in Russian. The hand was most definitely masculine here; there were bold, firm lines almost etched into the page, whereas the dedication was in a delicate and cultured script – a woman's hand. *Could this be Tsar Constantinovich's diary?* She flipped the pages lazily, and two things happened simultaneously which made her heart stop.

A lock of blonde hair, tied with a black ribbon, dropped out from between the pages and fell on the floor, and as her gaze followed it, out of the corner of her eye, she caught near the bottom of one page the name Alexander Andrei. Quickly she planted her fingers in the turning pages, flicking back to where she thought she had seen the name, and couldn't find it.

I hadn't been mistaken, I saw it she told herself. She would recognise the shape of those letters anywhere, they were burned into her soul, and she had written them out herself enough times. Russian script was notoriously difficult for her to read, especially handwritten, but she was sure of the name.

Maybe this is his diary she thought, hardly daring to hope. *Maybe I have lost his letter to gain his diary.* She picked up the small lock of hair, holding it up to the lamplight. It certainly looked exactly the way she remembered Olaf's hair shining in the lamplight. She stroked it with a finger. *And as soft, if not softer* she thought, her lip trembling.

She shut her eyes tightly, then pushed aside the urge to rush into her bedroom and read the diary cover to cover. *It is too hard to read right now, and I am tired from this evening. Besides, I won't be able to read it in one sitting, and even if I could what would be done with it? It must be kept secret and safe. I need to repair the flower.*

She made a move to place the book on her small writing table then changed her mind and deposited it back in the drawer. She pushed it shut then picked her way across the debris field again, opening the door to her parlour.

It was not Roman outside her door, but a guard she recognised as Spanov. He saluted, shooting her a sympathetic look.

'Bring me -' she started before realising her voice was thick, her cheeks wet with tears. She quickly brushed them away and cleared her throat. 'Bring me some strong glue' she instructed. 'And a brush and shovel' she added.

'I can send a maid to clean -' he started but she interrupted him.

'Please do only as I ask' she said and shut the door on his second salute.

She paced restlessly until the tap on the door, then rushed to answer it in fear that he might push open the door and see the fireplace, see the mess she had created. She took the items from him, acknowledging his salute briefly then closed the door again, wondering if she could lock the door, or place a chair in front of it. Instead she shook herself, took off her silk gloves, and repaired the fireplace carefully and firmly.

After pressing the petals in place for what felt like an eternity she removed her fingers and inspected the join. The crack was barely visible, and looked like a vein in the marble. *You would only know it was there if you knew to look for it* she assured herself, then carefully pressed the button again. The drawer slid out easily.

She smiled then bent down to carefully sweep up the broken shards, dropping them all into the footbath. She righted the now empty decanter, and left the window open to blow the strong smell of liquor out of the room. She picked up the stems of flowers, scattered in the pieces of the vase, and took them to her dressing room, sitting them in the ewer of water, then took them out again to pour a little of the water into the porcelain basin to wash her face.

She sighed, patting her face carefully dry and sitting down to tug out the jewels in her hair. But it was a long task, and a laborious one, and more than one jewel got hopelessly stuck in her tresses. The frustration of trying to remove them caused the tears to come back and she gave up, crying herself to sleep leaning over her vanity.

41

'Your Majesty!' Anna gasped, arriving in the dressing room.

Laura woke blearily, her back and neck aching, groaning as she sat up.

'You poor dear' Anna soothed as she came to support her mistress. 'I heard all about Maksim's ball from Anya, who works for him.'

'Tell me everything' Laura said dully.

'I'll run you a bath, Your Majesty' Anna said, quickly stepping out to send a guard to the kitchens to heat a dozen water pots over the roaring fires. 'Nikolai arrived early yesterday morning in a horseless carriage. He woke up Maksim's household, but no one knew who he was then. -'

'So that's who I heard at three that morning' Laura mused out loud as Anna began to detangle the stubborn jewels from her hair. 'I thought it was Uvarov.'

'Well, the household was in an uproar all of yesterday trying to get ready for the ball. No one really knew who he was, but he talked a lot with Tatiana and Anya heard some of the conversation when she was outside the room, dusting the paintings.'

She freed the last of the gems then brushed Laura's hair out gently, directing the army of kitchen girls who came in with pails of steaming water to the clawfoot bathtub. They poured in the water then slipped out with their empty pails, closing the door behind them. Laura stood and Anna helped her out of the rumpled dress, steadying her as she stepped into the bath.

As Anna washed her back and massaged the tight feeling out of her shoulders and neck, the story; garnered through over-heard conversations and second-hand accounts; was dutifully retold to Laura.

Nikolai, it seemed, had grown up in St Petersburg with two younger sisters. He had served in the Imperial Army as a colonel, and had a rather remarkable education. His father, who had died four years ago, had lived embittered with the knowledge that he would have been Tsar of Dalnerechensk, were it not for the slight inconvenience of Peter's recovery and subsequent lineage. He had given his son the education worthy of a great monarch, and had charged him, under oath on his deathbed, to seek the throne that had so desperately eluded him.

He had, by all accounts, respected his father's wishes, but had found himself too content to find urgency in fulfilling them, as he was newly married, and very much in love. It wasn't until Maksim sent him a letter, many months ago, inquiring after the descendants of Viktor, that Nikolai finally decided the time was right to fulfil his father's wishes.

The gossips were clear last night, no wife Laura reminded herself. *That's who he grieves for, his dead wife.* Laura could not help but feel sorry for him. *To lose his father and wife in so short a time. His father could not have been more than five and forty, no doubt Nikolai will die young too. All Vakhtangov men die young. Perhaps it is their due for being so handsome…*

She stretched carefully, feeling how wonderfully relaxed her muscles were.

'Anna you are a godsend' she smiled, though in truth she didn't really feel so jovial. 'Help me dress for Parliament.'

She stood and Anna brought her towel, folding her into it. Something suddenly caught Laura's eye, looming into the sky through her window.

'Good God, what is that?' Anna cried, frightened.

Laura was surprised to see it here, but she knew what it was.

'An airship' she said, then corrected herself when she saw the basket hanging below it. 'No, an air balloon.'

She could see two small figures in the basket, and knew without a doubt they were Nikolai and Tatiana, though they were too far away to see their features clearly. *Oh yes, that would be Maksim's plan alright. Bring in a man to be Tsar, with a pure bloodline all the way back to Vsevolod, and marry his daughter to him. Then, when he undoubtedly dies young, Maksim will step in as Lord Protector, crafting a grandson to rule in his image. He would have at least until the child grew to maturity to rule, maybe longer if he died young too. Maksim was definitely not a Vakhtangov man.*

And it looked like Varvara had other plans for the new Tsar, parading Anna before him all night. Poor Anna, she looked so deeply unhappy. I wonder if she is in love with Kurt.

'Close the curtains and help me dress' she said, turning away from the window.

She waited patiently for Anna to tug her into her clothes and pin her hair up again, then slipped down to the Parliament Chambers, formulating excuses for her tardiness. She need not have bothered. All the ministers were standing in the courtyard, mouths agape as they looked up at the air balloon, which was now descending to the fields south of Tcherepnin. She saw the sunlight wink at them from the glass of an eyepiece, and realised Nikolai was surveying the Principality.

'Good morning, Your Majesty' Fedor said loudly, and she watched the ministers start in surprise and turn quickly, bowing to her.

She bowed her head to them and slipped into the west wing, leading the way to the Parliament Chambers, listening to them shuffle in behind her. Laura took her seat on the dais, pleased to see that it was Vsevolod's throne, back in its rightful place, and motioned for the other ministers to sit too. A part of her had wanted to arrest Maksim for theft, but she knew what his cunning arguments would be: The throne was not her personal property, but a symbol of state government, of which he was now part, and if it belonged to the Vakhtangov family there were plenty there who would have consented to Nikolai's sitting on it. As much as his brazen actions galled her there was to be no consequence for his taking of the throne and she decided to let the matter rest.

Two other things she noticed had not surprised her in the least. *Knjaz* Uvarov sat in Parliament, albeit in one of the more distant seats, and Ilich and Luka did not. Maksim made some speech requesting the position of foreign attaché in Yekaterinburg for his cousin which his party wholeheartedly approved of, and the Revolutionists, defeated doubly by the loss of the election and their leaders, made no objection. *Knjaz* Uvarov made some small words of thanks, then the report of the work detail to exhume the graves of the Heroes was called for.

The Heir of The Nine Week King was not mentioned. Laura could see them all very carefully *not mentioning* him. It would have been amusing, were it not so serious. *They could have a tsar again, and a bloodline back to the beginning.* She could see how it would appeal to the population at large, who by now, no doubt, were gossiping violently about the ball last night and the appearance of Nikolai. The revolution had never really been popular with Dalnerechensk, despite the large number of men who had gone to hear Ilich rail on the bar top. They had been angry, yes, and bitter, and blamed Aleksei for their sufferings, but they had not wanted to be without their ruling family. They had wanted a son of Aleksei's to come to the throne. Or the return of Alexander Andrei. Or possibly even a son of the Mad Prince. They had wanted a new tsar.

And now they could have him she mused. *Yet their loyalties do lie with me. I wonder how long it will be before someone suggests —*

'You could marry him, Your Majesty' Ivan said, interrupting Maksim's rather verbose discourse on the state of the mining industry.

Laura eyed Maksim as the arguments broke out. It was not an unexpected proposition, no doubt he and his cousin had spent many days carefully constructing a case against her suitability.

'A widowed commoner? She is beneath him, as she was beneath Aleksei' Lev sneered, reckless now that the Vakhtangovs' hand had been revealed.

'However she is not without her own merits' Yuri countered, and the shouting match continued, quite unmindful of Laura's presence.

It was no wonder Aleksei had grown weary of his council, especially when they argued like this for hours and hours Laura thought, sighing inwardly. *Though I doubt they were this rude about him in his presence.*

It was a perfect solution for Dalnerechensk she mused as the argument wore on. *They would get their tsar, and keep her. Happiness all round. Except my heart belongs elsewhere, and they know it.*

'Gentlemen' she interrupted them, stilling the cacophony. 'It is true a more perfect solution for the general could not be found, but let me assure you - in the most forcible terms possible - that I once was married for political satisfaction, and although there was affection at the beginning there could be no doubt that fondness did not last. I have no wish to be wed again in such a manner.'

She eyed them all severely, satisfied that almost all of them found it difficult to raise their eyes from the benches before them.

'Your Majesty, if I may -' Yuri started, then stopped himself, unsure or unwilling to proceed.

The silence dragged out, uncomfortable and thick, until Maksim banged his fist on the bench before him and called an end to Parliament for the day.

It could not have been, Laura mused as she watched them slip out of the room, *a resounding success for Maksim's first Parliament, but then what was he expecting?*

What was *he expecting?* she pondered, eyeing the empty room. *Surely he must have known that Dalnerechensk, even his own political party, would want to wed her to Vsevolod's descendant. In fact they would not tolerate any other match. Maksim would have to be masterful to* – she stopped. That was a word she had been using a lot lately, especially in light of his political manoeuvring.

So he had found another Vakhtangov for the throne, one with an impeccable lineage, if he was to be believed. Even now Fedor would be making discreet inquiries, trying to prove the validity of the claim. But Nikolai did not look sickly, nor did he seem weak and pliable. He seemed a strange choice for a puppet king. *But perhaps this was not about his own bid for power. Perhaps his hatred of her was so great he was prepared to give up anything to see her removed...*

She sighed and stood, slipping out of the rooms, meeting Fedor in the corridor outside. One look at his face was enough.

'It is true, isn't it' she said, resigned.

'Yes Your Majesty' he said, unfurling a document he had with him. 'But I am afraid there is something more. His marriage was fruitful Your Majesty. Nikolai has a son.'

Her eyes widened in shock.

'Forgive me for distressing you so' he apologised. 'But I wished you to know, that it not be used to humiliate you in another malicious act.'

She managed a smile for him. 'That is kind Fedor, I will not forget it.'

He bowed and she took her leave, heading up to her rooms, knowing miserably that her spies would already be there, waiting to gloat in that silent smug way of theirs. But to her surprise there was a sullen disharmony in her rooms when she entered. Two new women were in her chambers, and she could tell from the looks on their faces that there had been a passionate argument between them all.

Anna Vakhtangovna stood beside the newly wed Marie Borodina, wrapped tightly in a thick shawl, both of them holding skeins of silk thread. They all dropped curtseys, falling into a guarded silence. Laura crossed to her chaise lounge, welcoming the two young women into her apartments. For the first time in months there was silence as they worked, a sullen resentful silence that the balance was beginning to turn, that with the arrival of dissident members of the Vakhtangov family and the absence of Tatiana the conspirators were losing ground. Just as Laura wondered if she should call for musicians to play in her rooms they were interrupted with a knock on the door. Roman pushed it open and bowed.

'Nikolai Vakhtangov sent me to remind you of your appointment with him, Your Majesty' he said.

'*Naslednik* -' Polina snapped.

'Be silent' Marie commanded, and – to Laura's surprise – Polina did just that, biting her lip and shooting her an angry look.

'Very well' she said, setting aside the tapestry and beckoning for Anna to follow her into her dressing room.

For a brief moment she felt a pin prick of fear, wondering if they would search her rooms while she was absent, wondering if one of the women had found Olaf's letter and given it to Maksim, or Luka, or some other that she was not aware of. Perhaps they might even know of the hidden compartment in the fire surround already. *But then again, perhaps they will not* she reassured herself. The presence of Anna Vakhtangovna and Marie changed things. She wondered if they would start arguing again, it was clear they had been interrupted earlier and there were unresolved issues between them.

Carefully she dressed in a royal blue dress and her green overcoat, mindful of the cat and mouse game they were playing, and sat still while Anna pinned her hair back prettily. She debated wearing jewels, her crown or a hat, twisting back and forward in the mirror before finally settling on a gust of perfume and leaving the room unadorned.

Marie wished her well for her outing and Laura smiled, closing the door behind her. Roman made to follow but she stopped him, instructing him in a whisper to listen in to the argument that was to unfold in her rooms. He looked unhappy, but saluted and watched her slip down the stairs to the entrance hall.

To her surprise it was empty, but the door to the castle was open, and she could see him out in the courtyard, standing near a gleaming machine and surrounded by several soldiers and castle employees. Quietly she approached, keeping out of sight, watching him carefully. He lifted the hatch at the front of the automobile to show the men with him the engine, allowing them to come closer and inspect the gleaming compartment. Laura appreciated the way the soldiers craned to see but were still mindful of their duty, keeping a watchful eye on the gate to Vsevolod's Way.

Nikolai was dressed in crisp breeches and a thick leather jacket trimmed with fur. A pair of gloves were tucked casually into his pocket and his dark hair played in a slight breeze. His gestures were strong and confident, but casual and easy too, and he was courteous and pleasant to the servants who stared gog-eyed at the machine and the new prince alike. *Those with long memories will liken him to Alexander Andrei* Laura thought quietly. *How terrible it must have been for Aleksei!*

She stepped out into the courtyard and the soldiers saluted smartly, taking a step further back from the automobile. Nikolai turned and bowed to her, and she noticed there was a more relaxed movement to his limbs, it was a bow that was not so millimetrically precise in execution. She curtseyed to him, coming down the front steps, acknowledging the bows and curtseys of the servants.

'Good day, Your Majesty' Nikolai said, straightening. 'I trust you are well?'

'Indeed' she answered, stepping closer to the automobile, aware of the different way he was looking at her this morning.

Was that admiration in his eyes? she wondered. If it was, it was not a look that she had expected, given that he had just spent the morning with Tatiana, and was no doubt spreading her poisonous lies just as she had done with Fredrik.

'If I may be so bold, I have a gift for you' he said, reaching into the rear seats of the automobile and pulling out a thick ermine coat. 'The wind can make a drive very cold Your Majesty, I would hate for you to suffer' he went on, bowing as he presented it to her.

'How very kind and thoughtful' she murmured.

'Please allow me' he said, helping her into the coat.

'It is beautiful' she said. *And very hot* she added in the privacy of her head. 'Please tell me about this magnificent machine' she gestured to the automobile.

'It is a Spyker, model fourteen eighteen H. P. open tourer, made last year' he said proudly, and his eyes lit up as he spoke. 'A four cylinder bi-bloc of two thousand, five hundred and forty four cubic centimetre capacity. It has a top speed of about sixty kilometres -'

'Sixty!' Laura interrupted, astounded.

'Indeed, indeed!' he laughed. 'Spyker's were the first in the world to have six cylinders in their engines, and the thirty-six fifty was supposed to establish them with a racing pedigree, unfortunately they were never able to set a record because the top speed was not there. No, for that, you will need a Darracq, like *Knjaz* Uvarov's.'

Laura listened politely as he went on to extol the admirable accomplishment of Viktor Hemery, who had recently won the *Circuit des Ardennes* race in a Darracq, averaging an astonishing ninety eight kilometres per hour and beating the incomparable George Heath, who had won it the year before on a Panhard, and had certainly been the favourite to win again. 'It will be an exciting race when they meet again in America, for the

Vanderbilt Cup race in October' he went on excitedly. 'Heath won it last year, but I predict Hemery will win it this year. I only wish that I could be there to -' he stopped, mindful of who he was talking to.

'Do you race as well, Your Highness?' she asked sweetly.

'I entered in the Paris to Madrid race two years ago, but I broke the axle of my Mercedes and was forced to withdraw. But I was not alone, there were fifty participates who could not complete the race, and as there were such a high number of accidents the leg to Madrid was abandoned.'

'It sounds dangerous' she said, eyeing the gleaming bodywork and the strange, snake-headed tube that tapered to a thin point attached to a bulbous rubber balloon.

'I promise you will be in no danger with me' he assured her quietly.

He held out his hand, and after a small hesitation she placed her hand in his, aware that the heat of the sun and the ermine coat had made her so warm she was almost clammy. His hand, in contrast, was cool and strong, deftly leading her to the side of the phaeton seat that did not have a steering wheel in front of it. She fervently hoped the wind would indeed be cold, she could feel prickles of sweat forming on her scalp.

She climbed into the seat and sat while Nikolai raced to the other side, turning the crank to start the engine, explaining how combustion worked in it. He swung into the seat beside her, demonstrating how each of the levers worked, releasing the brake and turning in a slow circle inside the courtyard. He squeezed the bulbous horn twice and turned the automobile through the sharp s-bend at the top of Vsevolod's Way, guiding them down the busy street.

There were crowds lining the route, as they were all eager to see the horseless carriage, the new prince and the tsaritsa, and they called out and waved as they drove past. Laura waved, but she felt oddly pleased that Nikolai did not wave as well. Instead he honked the horn, garnering shouts and applause from the crowd each time he did so. When they reached the train station at the end of the road, in the shadow of the city walls, Nikolai turned down another street. It was less crowded, and Laura was able to begin a commentary of where they were, pointing out the hospital, school and cathedral as they drove.

She began to relax, Nikolai was skilful and experienced with the controls of the machine, and his absolute surety, even in an unfamiliar place, made it easier to trust him.

'What do you say Your Majesty?' he asked when they reached King's Gate at the end of Castle Street and passed out of the city of Dalnerechensk. 'Shall we see what she can do?'

Laura looked at him, at his eyes shining with excitement and pleasure, at the way the wind played with his hair, at his pretty smile, and suddenly felt reckless.

'*Da!*' she cried and was almost thrown back in her seat as he accelerated away, a cloud of smoke gusting out behind them.

The wind whipped at them but did nothing to cool Laura down, if anything it made her pulse race and flushed her cheeks with excitement. She stole a quick look at Nikolai, aware that he was stealing looks at her, and eyed the way his hair spilled boyishly across his forehead, how white his teeth were when he smiled, how handsome he looked darkly flushed with enjoyment.

They raced up Miner's Way, circling the town of Ladozhskoye before continuing to Macherna, laughing and enjoying each other's company. Her eyes were beginning to blur with wind-whipped tears and the softly suffused hardness of his jaw and his shining eyes, the rushing shapes that were hardly recognisable as houses and people zipping past them were exhilarating.

'God save the Tsar!' someone cried, and Laura turned away from Nikolai sharply, shutting her eyes tightly.

God save the Tsar. Someone had shouted it when her eyes had been filled with wind-whipped tears before, when she and Aleksei had gone sleigh riding together, when his cold hand had cupped her cheek and his lips had been hot when they had kissed for the first time, when their blood had rushed furiously in their veins - when he had loved her. *Nikolai might not be crowned, but he was Tsar in the minds of Dalnerechensk.*

She turned her face away, biting hard on her inner lip to stop the trembling, to force back the tears. She was dimly aware that they were slowing, that Nikolai was saying something, his voice filled with concern. They stopped with a jerk, the heat rushing back in the sudden stillness of the wind.

'Your Majesty?' Nikolai asked, worried, laying a hand on her arm.

They had stopped on the narrow road to the mine, and it was shift change. Grubby men were walking towards them, wearily swinging empty lunch pails, eyeing the automobile with interest.

'You're not supposed to touch the Monarchy' she said, turning to him.

'I *am* Monarchy' he said quietly.

Laura eyed him quietly, wiping away moisture from her eyes. *He's not shy about looking at me, the only one who really looks at me* she thought. *Though it is definitely not the same way he looked at me last night.* No doubt he had been gathering gossip and rumour about her, probing for weaknesses as she had looked for his. Yet he did not look at her with disdain or pity, rather, it was something resembling admiration, and perhaps respect. She wondered if she was anything like what he had been expecting.

A crowd was beginning to form around them and Laura looked away again, turning to talk to the miner nearest her. She did not miss the way he could hardly look at her, the hardness that lay underneath their curiosity. *So it begins again* she thought, and suddenly shivered.

'Do forgive me, Your Highness, but I must return' she said turning back to Nikolai, who broke off his conversation with the miner nearest him.

'Of course Your Majesty. Farewell!' he called to the crowd, who shouted back happily.

He started the motor again, and drove at a very sedate pace back to Dalnerechensk, eyeing her as they made their way through the city.

'Do you ride, Your Highness?' she asked as they arrived in the castle courtyard.

'I do' he smiled, leaping down and coming around to help her down, catching her around her waist to set her gently before him.

'Do call on me tomorrow afternoon, we shall ride through Hunter's Pass together' she said, aware of how he lingered.

He took her hand and kissed it, warmly accepting.

'I do hope you enjoyed your outing Your Majesty' he said.

She murmured something in reply and took her leave, heading up to her rooms where she found a bored looking Roman waiting in the corridor. He straightened up when he saw her approach and saluted.

'Do I have company Roman?' she asked.

'No Your Majesty, they left some time ago' he answered, opening her door for her.

'Good. Admit no one for an hour' she instructed. 'I wish for some peace today.'

'Yes Your Majesty' he said, saluting again.

Laura closed her door and locked it against him, then padded over to the fireplace and pushed the button for the secret drawer in the marble surround. The leather book was still inside and she pulled it out carefully, sitting down on her chaise lounge, then hid it under a pillow while she went back to close the drawer, sitting once more and retrieving the book.

She flicked past the dedication at the beginning and eyed the strong letters underlined at the top of the page. It was easy enough to figure out it was a date, 15 May 1868, and she noted the way the letters were formed so she would recognise them in other words, and find meaning in the script. Eighteen sixty-eight, that was too early for this to be Alexander Andrei's diary, in fact it was before he had even been born. *It must belong to Tsar Constantinovich* she realised.

She looked up and away from the page for a moment. She had loved and respected the man deeply, and reading this seemed to be a violation of his decency and privacy. *Do I really want to do this?* she asked herself. No, she did not. But he had been one of the few who had known why Alexander Andrei had abdicated, if he had truly gone mad or not. *Of all the things he had told me, shared with me, he had never told me that* her mind whispered. He hadn't seemed mad, but then, neither had Aleksei.

What would you call it? To give up your birth right and shovel horse shit for the next ten years? She sighed gently and realised she could not leave it now, no matter what she might read in those pages.

Despite the bold strong lines of the script it was difficult for her to make out some of the words because of the cursive form of the letters and when the hour had passed she had only been able to read two paragraphs. It seemed there had been some party, and a woman called Jagna had given the tsar this diary. Perhaps it had been for his birthday, but it was unclear from the little she had read.

She sighed and closed the book, checking the little mantle clock as she slid the book back into the secret drawer, twisting her neck to ease the tightness there. To her surprise she could see Nikolai's horseless carriage still in the courtyard, and the man himself, being spoken to earnestly by the stable boy. She drew the curtain back, wishing she could hear them, wishing she could read the words forming on their lips.

As if aware that he was being watched, even though his back was mostly towards her, he dismissed the groom who bobbed several bows and swung himself back into the seat of the automobile. He pulled on his gloves and honked the horn twice then headed through the gate at Vsevolod's Way. Laura sighed, letting the curtain fall again.

She sent Roman to find Anna, instructing her to arrive with something to eat and waited patiently until the girl arrived. Anna set the tray before her on a little table then hung up the ermine coat that Laura had left on the chair by the door as she had come in. When she was done eating she dressed in her riding habit and led Roman down to the stable.

He followed her silently as they mounted and trotted towards The Avenue of Heroes, stopping to inspect the work detail there. There were now twenty graves that had been moved; the grass cut and peeled back, the earth scooped out and the coffins removed. There was evidence of each pile that had been exhumed in the loose scattering of dirt beside slightly concave rectangles, the cut grass stamped back down on top but bearing unmistakable signs of disturbance.

A canvas tent stood around the latest grave to be exhumed. Inside was the sound of shovels shifting soil and the angry voice of a man. As Laura approached the flap was suddenly thrown open and a young, red-faced man stalked out. He caught sight of Laura and pointed an accusing finger at her. 'You should have left them in peace!' he shouted. 'He already died for you, and now you're digging him up again! When will you have done with him?!'
'Be mindful of who you speak to!' Roman snarled, riding up beside Laura.
The man glared at him. 'I am. Be mindful of who they shall dig up next' he said and stalked off angrily, refusing to bow or even look back at them.

Laura shut her eyes, clutching her hands tighter in the reins. The next grave was Basil Barand's, Roman's childhood friend. *Maybe I have made a mistake* she thought.

'Did Vsevolod do anything that ever made him unpopular?' she wondered, half to herself as she watched the man walk away. 'Where did they bury them? Those who fought for him?' she eyed Roman.

'In Macherna, I think' he answered, subdued.

'No special dedication?' she asked, surprised.

He shrugged. 'Things were different back then. The only one I know for sure where he is buried is Vsevolod. It didn't matter about making a special grave for them.'

'He did not honour them?'

'No. But he never dug them up again either.' He looked away.

She was quiet, then said softly 'I dug up my father too.'

'I know why you're doing it' he said. 'I just wish you didn't have to do it.'

'Me too' she sighed, then turned her stallion towards the forests north of Hunter's Pass.

Roman followed her silently until they reached the secret glen where she dismounted and motioned for him to dismount too, draping her reins over a low branch.

'They argued only for about ten minutes, Your Majesty' he said, dropping his reins over the branch too. 'I never heard the young princess say anything, but Marie Borodina gave that nasty Nineczka an earful' he grinned. 'You have a real supporter there Your Majesty.'

She smiled. 'What did she give her an earful about?'

'That they all needed to be mindful of their place.'

'She impressed me today' Laura grinned, remembering the way Polina's face had twisted.

'Why don't you do that?' Roman asked, turning to her. 'You don't have to put up with them Your Majesty. You can tell them to shut up and go away. I know you want to.'

'Yes, I want to' she said quietly.

'It's your home and you are the tsaritsa, Your Majesty' Roman pointed out. 'The way they waltz about the place, like they own it, it rankles me, and the things they say to you! They would never dare say that to any other, and you've let them!'

'They're spying on me too Roman' she snapped. 'I let them because they cannot fault me. They have not witnessed once any indiscretion or sin. I cannot be a whore if I am never given the opportunity!'

He was quiet, a muscle working in his jaw.

'And what about Lvov?' he asked finally, tightly. 'He will think me a liar if they say you are spotless and I say you are not.'

'Does he suspect?' she asked, a flutter of fear in her words.

'I do not think so' he shrugged. 'But I feel another game is afoot. He used to ask me time and again when the *Tsesarevna* was born, he has not asked me the last two times.'

'That information has been common knowledge since I sent my letter to Ilich, before I even came back' she said.

'I know. I don't know why he kept asking. Maybe he thought the date was false' he shrugged.

She sighed, shutting her eyes tightly and turning her face up to the sun.

'Tell them I will be wearing Bavarian Blue on my birthday' she said tiredly. 'Tell them I want – I want to marry Fredrik.'

'They already know that, Your Majesty' he said quietly.

'Then tell them – tell them -' she stopped, sitting down on the grass.

'What?'

'I don't know. I'm tired of playing these games. Nikolai has a son.' Her chin crinkled. 'What shall I do Roman? They will want me to marry him. Of course he is handsome and charming and I dare say he could make me happy but – but -' she took a shaky, wet breath, pressing her lips together but the sobs exploded out of her anyway.

Roman hesitated then sat awkwardly beside her, but he did not touch her. *If he did, what would happen?* the longing in him whispered. His hands itched, remembering the feel of her night dress, the heat of her body. *To feel that again, to feel her hot and supple in his arms…* he shut his eyes tightly, forcing the feeling away. *If he touched her he would kiss her, he would strip her here and have her, again and again if he could.* He sighed. *And then it would be resignation, and disgrace, and god knows how he would ever be able to look at her again.*

He shook away the thoughts. He knew why she sobbed so helplessly on the grass beside him. *Aleksei had sent his father to the New World to bring back a fortune, and if it came with a pretty face so much the better. And she had come, too young and vibrant for a man old enough to be her father, wanting romance and courtship and love. She hadn't realised she would be property, and left alone until Aleksei sent for her, a man too awkward and stuffy to seduce her correctly.*

It was hardly any surprise that she had sought company with the young Norwid family, with the scandalous Nikita Rurik, company that twisted Aleksei's jealousy and anger and impotence into a weapon of hate and violence. He had been there, that night in the dining hall. He had heard Nikita's bold taunt at the cuckolded man. *Send your wife to me* he had said, and he had seen the look in Aleksei's eye when he dismissed the court for the evening, dragging his struggling wife up to his bed chambers.

Everyone knew what he had done to her that night. Everyone knew of the torn sheets, the broken furniture, the blood they had to clean up. And everyone knew it was the last time they had been together. It was easy, so easy to assume she had been unfaithful, that she had found a gentler lover who had fathered her child.

But they were wrong he whispered to himself fiercely. *They hadn't seen what he had seen. They hadn't looked in her eyes as they had barred her from seeing Aleksei in his rooms, hadn't seen her heart break when she heard Tatiana laughing inside with him.*

Roman never doubted her fidelity after seeing that terrible look, that way she stepped away from her pain and commended Basil and himself for a difficult job. He had hated Aleksei in that moment.

And they had never seen him, the night of the revolution, when he had that same look in his eye…

His blood had been hot; violent and maddened, and the courtyard had rung with her screams each time the whip descended. Roman had been too shocked to do anything, not even when Mikhail, Aleksei's manservant, had tackled him. He hadn't dared lay a hand on the monarchy.

Beside him Laura lay down, curling into a little ball on her side, still crying. He reached out to touch her then drew his hand back, gripping his wrist tightly with his other hand, sighing again.

*

It was late when she woke and the glade was bathed in the silvery light of a young moon. She gasped, sitting up quickly and looking around for Roman. He was seated on a log a little way away from her, his arms wrapped around himself and hunched against the chill of the air.

'We must go' she said, getting unsteadily to her feet. 'Help me mount.'

He boosted her up onto the horse and swung himself onto his own, following her out of the glade. It was darker in the forest, and so still he could hear her breathing. It was quick, and shallow, and he wondered why she should be afraid of the dark, she had spent nearly two weeks in the dark forests of Russia after the revolution.

The moonlight was too weak to see where they were going, but the horses knew the way back to the castle and Roman was content to let them go as they wished. Even so he was conscious of Laura falling behind him, and as he turned to look a passing moonbeam showed that her eyes were shut tightly, her mouth a thin line of fear. He slowed his mount, letting her come up beside him.

'Your Majesty?' he asked softly.

Her hand shot out and grabbed his, surprising him.

'Tell me if the beacon is lit' she said urgently. 'The Tcherepnin Beacon. Tell me if it is lit.'

Her hand was trembling.

'I don't know, I can't -' he began, turning to peer through the trees. Just then an opportune gust moved a tree branch and he saw it. 'It is' he confirmed.

Her hand went still, then began to shake violently, a whimper escaping from her lips. There was a distant shout, and her fingers tightened harder on his. *Of course* he realised. *She wasn't afraid of the dark, she was afraid of that light. She had been in the forest with her servant when the riot had happened, perhaps crying herself to sleep in that very glade, and the beacon was lit when she had emerged. Dalnerechensk had been dark, shuttered and humming with fear and anger, and that brilliant light had glittered balefully above it all.*

'They would have to light it, to call troops for a search party' Roman soothed, squeezing her hand back. 'You've been gone hours' he explained.

They have never seen fit to light it before when I have been gone too long she thought. *And why should they panic now and send so many looking for me? And who had sent them? They were either hoping to find me dead or in the arms of a lover. Either way it gets rid of the problem of me.*

Roman suddenly slipped off his horse and fished around in his pocket, pulling out a small folded knife. He bent down in the dark and made a sharp thrusting motion, then a wrenching one. His horse screamed in pain. 'What did you do?' Laura cried, frightened.

He flung out his arm, and there was the dull thunk of a metal horse shoe hitting the trunk of a tree some yards behind them. He folded away the knife, stroking the horse's nose softly.

'I'm sorry' he whispered to her gently, then gathered the reins, handing them to Laura, taking her own off her.

A thrown shoe and a lame horse would give them some innocent pretext for staying out so long in the forest together she realised. There was another shout in the distance.

'Answer them Roman' she said quietly and he did so, cupping his hand around his mouth to amplify his shout.

Within ten minutes a group of searchers had reached them, and more were making their way over.

'Are you hurt, Your Majesty?' Gustav asked, holding his torch up to see her better.

'I am fine' she smiled, controlling her stallion as it shied at the open flame, and Roman marvelled at her composure. 'My Captain's horse threw a shoe, we had to walk back such a long way' she went on, slipping down from the saddle.

Gustav offered his elbow and she slipped her hand into it gratefully.

'Forgive me for the ill timing of this message, I did try for an audience with you earlier but regrettably I could not be seen. I would not raise it now, except it seems a matter of some urgency and I could not distress Gertrude further.'

'Gertrude?' she asked, shocked. 'Alexandra -'

'Is well and unharmed' he soothed. 'No, this matter concerns Gertrude herself. It seems she received a letter from her brother this morning with the distressing news that her mother is ill, and not expected to regain her health.'

'That is terrible news indeed' Laura murmured.

'She has begged me to intercede with you on her behalf, and regrets that she must leave her employment immediately. She is beside herself with anxiety, and wishes to leave tomorrow.'

'Tomorrow? It is a long journey for a woman alone, I could not arrange a chaperone at such short notice -'

'Have no fear, I have given my word to accompany her' he soothed.

Laura stopped, looking at him. 'You are leaving? Will you return?' she asked, surprised by the depth of the loss she felt.

'Of course' he smiled. 'Countess Ivanova has quite beguiled me with her plans for your birthday, I should not want to miss them!'

'That is good news' she smiled, relieved. 'Please see Fedor when we return and let him know the particulars of the travel arrangements. All Gertrude's costs will be met.'

'That is most generous' he smiled.

She smiled too, falling into a comfortable silence with him as they reached Castle Street. At the other end of the city the Tcherepnin Beacon suddenly went out, and the walls were dark once again.

42

Laura rocked Alexandra gently, eyeing her as her little hands held the bottle all on her own, tipping it up to drink from it. *It was only a few short weeks ago and she could not do this without help* she marvelled, and she let her fingers run through the fine wisps of blonde hair, picking up small clumps and inspecting the way the sun shone through them, looking carefully for any sign that her hair would turn dark.

'*Maam maam maam*' Alexandra burbled, flashing small white teeth when she smiled and Laura smiled too, sitting her upright and kissing the top of her head.

Gertrude, Gustav and Grigory had left that morning, and the departure of Ekaterina's husband had saddened her more than the other two. *Grigory will not return to Dalnerechensk* she told herself. *They had lost everything they had here in the revolution, and although he was not a proud man it had embarrassed him to have lived on her charity. His departure also meant that Ekaterina would leave her soon too, a prospect that grieved her terribly.*

She looked over at her friend, who was sitting at Laura's small writing table, jotting down plans for the birthday party and conversing with Fedor quietly, who held a small leather book, jotting notes too. Between them were several women, stitching industriously at the tapestry. Tatiana was again absent, and Marie Borodina sat with Anna Vakhtangovna, both of them quick and skilful embroiderers, who had taken it upon themselves to stitch the intricate border for the third tapestry.

The other women were straining to hear Ekaterina's plans, hoping that she would let slip details of her secret project for Laura's birthday, or – even more scandalous – the cost of these festivities, and how much was being paid for by the government. There were more of them than ever in her chambers, all eager to see how she behaved knowing that Nikolai was spending the morning in Tatiana's company again, including some faces she had never seen before.

'*Bab ba ba bab*' Alexandra burbled, waving her fists excitedly, kicking her feet against Laura's thighs and wiggling.

'My clever girl is learning the alphabet already' she laughed, kissing her cheek, and was rewarded with a delighted squeal from Alexandra, who planted a bity kiss on her cheek too.

There was a sudden commotion outside her door and it was thrust open in time for her to hear Roman shout:

'You cannot go in there!'

Varvara, frail though she was, managed a spritely sidestep past his outstretched arm, dismissing him rudely, and Elena and several of her daughters, including Polina, barged past him too, inviting themselves into her presence.

'I'm sorry, Your Majesty –' Roman started, his fists tightening on his rifle but she waved away his protest.

Varvara and the seven women with her made only the smallest motions of courtesy, eyeing Laura with all the affronted dignity and pride of the Vakhtangov bloodline in their bearing. Laura raised her eyebrow slightly.

'Good morning *madames* and *mademoiselles*, what pressing business seems fit to violate the sanctity of protocol and force yourself into my presence?' she asked archly.

Some of the younger women suddenly looked uneasy, but Varvara was unfazed, glaring at the squirming baby on her lap.

'This matter cannot be left to rest, it has gone on long enough' she snapped, putting her hands on her hips. 'It is an embarrassment!'

Laura forced herself to stop from looking around her, knowing all eyes were on her. *Here it comes, the accusation of infidelity* she told herself. She was surprised, she had expected to be arrested, a tsaritsa's infidelity was treason. But Peter Kamanin was not with them, and a small glimmer of hope surfaced.

It did not last. Frail and small though she was, Varvara's overbearing demeanour was frightening, and she was reminded, in no small way, of Lady Ramkinson. She fought the urge to look around her, to see if any of the women with her were carrying a riding crop, and the scars on her back and legs itched. *It was no wonder Marie's aunt had been so cowed she allowed her niece to be disgraced.*

At the thought of Marie Laura shifted her attention to her. There was a complicated emotion on her face, mirroring her inner turmoil. *Stand up to her* she seemed to plead, *you outrank her; she has to do what you say, even if she does not like it.* But tempering that fervent desire was disappointment, as she knew Laura had not stood up to lesser members of the Vakhtangov family, or even an unpleasant commoner. There was also resignation, she knew just how difficult it was to stand up to Varvara, but the hope was still there, hope that she would put that scheming woman in her place. Laura suddenly didn't want to disappoint her.

'That child' Varvara pointed, distaste dripping from every syllable, 'must have a nurse and a governess.'

Laura was momentarily surprised at the turn of the conversation and Varvara went on relentlessly.

'You insulted this family when you brought that woman with you and have shown an embarrassingly small knowledge of raising a child, I won't stand for it -'

'You won't stand for it?' Laura interrupted, forcing all the regal outrage she could muster into her tone. 'Gertrude is an excellent nurse -'

'Do not insult us!' Varvara hissed, malice glittering in her eyes. 'Vakhtangov children have always had Vakhtangov nurses and Elena is more than qualified to raise a child, as would be any of her daughters -'

'My daughter has a Vakhtangov nurse' Laura snapped. 'Marie Borodina was appointed this morning.'

Varvara blinked, stunned.

'Preposterous!' she boomed.

'Do not dare to presume to tell me who I appoint as nurse to my daughter' Laura said, raising from her seat and drawing herself up to her full height. 'I have suffered this outrage as long as I could bear it and *I* will not stand for it. You and these women will depart now from the castle or you will be arrested. You are henceforth no longer welcome here. I will not repeat myself.'

Varvara spluttered with outrage, the other women looking shocked too. Polina turned and fled from the room and two more wavered. The others in the room held their breaths in horrified fascination. Varvara had no choice but to comply, but she hesitated too long. Laura raised her hand and made a signal at Roman.

He lifted his whistle to his lips and blew three sharp bursts. The guards on duty rushed to her rooms, their rifles at the ready, blocking the doorway and fanning out behind the women, eyeing all the people in the room distrustfully.

'Spanov, you will go immediately to summon *Graf* Pavlodar. *Madame* Durova, *Madame* Petrova, *Madame* Koneva, and the *Mademoiselles* Petrovna are detained here until the arrival of Peter Kamanin, who alone can arrest members of the Vakhtangov family' Laura said, stressing each of the last names of the women. It was petty, but not pointless, she was making it very clear that although they could claim common ancestors within the Vakhtangov family tree they did not bear the name. They were property of their husbands, and, as such, they could not wield the power of the name like she could. It had taken her too long to realise it, but the truth of it made her forceful, and slightly giddy.

'Malenkov, Repnin, bring in a settee from the room next door for these ladies to wait in comfort' Laura went on. 'Anna, some tea. Marie, please take the *Tsesarevna* back to the nursery.'

They rushed to do her bidding, and when the settee was brought in Varvara alone sat on it, taking a cup of tea with bad grace from Anna. Elena and her daughters still stood, shooting each other alarmed and miserable looks. Laura sat on her own chaise lounge, sipping thoughtfully at her tea. She was aware of the uncomfortable silence, of how the women stared at her, and the concerned look on Ekaterina's face.

She knew her friend well enough to know what was on her mind. *It would be a mistake to arrest members of the Vakhtangov family, no matter how much they deserved it.* She set down her tea and picked up her section of the tapestry again, busying herself with stitching Vsevolod's face. She was surprised that her hands were so steady, her insides were twisting and jumping with a strange excitement. With each passing minute that she ignored them the tension in the room grew.

'Do you truly mean to arrest us?' one of the younger girls suddenly asked.

'Be quiet' Varvara said.

'Please Your Majesty, forgive us!' cried the other, clasping her sister's hand.

'Be *quiet!*' Varvara thundered, setting her tea cup down so hard she chipped it.

'Speak' Laura said.

The two looked at each other again then came forward, going down on their knees before her. Laura listened to their entreaties, her eyes on Varvara. There was no repentance in the old woman's features, it was incomprehensible to her that she was under arrest. *You wouldn't dare* her posture seemed to say. Laura held up her hand, cutting off the pleading of the two girls.

'I have heard enough' she said, waving them away.

The girls stood miserably, avoiding looking at Varvara as they scuttled back to their mother's side, who was looking a lot less defiant now. Laura picked up the tapestry again, stitching in the jacket of another figure. Those who were working on the tapestry would stitch a loop of silk every now and then, watching the power play with interest, and only Anna Vakhtangovna bent industriously over the material, ignoring everything else in the room. Laura wondered how she might be feeling right now.

Roman announced the arrival of *Graf* Pavlodar, saluting, and Peter Kamanin bowed low to the assembled room before acknowledging the salute. Laura, still maintaining an air of disinterest, instructed Roman to make his report to his commanding officer. Peter listened as he talked, then turned to Laura.

'What would you have me do Your Majesty?' he asked quietly.

'Only what the law instructs' she answered, snipping the thread loose.

He bowed, turned and arrested Varvara.

'You impudent wretch!' she exploded, leaping out of her seat, anger and affronted dignity lending her strength. 'The *Naslednik* will hear of this' she hissed. 'He will not allow this!'

'Perhaps he will wonder what will happen when the Vakhtangovs feel he has outlived his usefulness' Laura said. 'But you are in a better position to know his mind.'

There was a flicker of doubt on the old woman's face; fleeting, but clear, and Laura rejoiced, she knew what she was thinking. Nikolai had been horribly disturbed by the behaviour of his cousins and their supporters at Maksim's ball and he had no doubt heard many tales about her in the hours following; some bad, but many that were exalting. Dalnerechensk held her in high regard, it would be an unpopular move to replace her. *It was not clear who he would marry either, he could marry me, and he would not be pleased with his family's treatment of his wife. They have recklessly overplayed their hand and have lost. I will not be so openly challenged again.*

There was a sudden creaking of ligaments, and Varvara slowly, painfully, got to her knees. Behind her Elena and her daughters dropped to their knees too, but none of them spoke. Very slowly, wincing in pain, Varvara bent forward and touched her forehead to the carpet. Laura knew the gesture. It was called Peter's Bow, one that Tsar Vasilievich II had introduced into his court, one he had forced his brother Viktor and his entire family to perform, right before he banished them. It was one of the unpopular laws his son had reversed upon his ascension. *It must have been humiliating.*

'Very well' she said finally, quietly. 'Repnin, Malenkov, help her to her feet. *Graf* Pavlodar there will be no arrests today. But there will be punishment' she added. 'Escort these women from the castle then return to your posts' she instructed the rest of the guards, who saluted and did as they'd been told.

There was silence when the women and guards had left. Laura was momentarily surprised by the smile of satisfaction and approval on Nineczka's face, and looked quickly at Ekaterina, who still looked troubled. *Whatever the outcome of this confrontation, none of it could ever be good* she sighed, calling for Anna Vakhtangovna to show her the progress she had made on the border.

An hour later the tension was gone and Ekaterina had slipped away, excusing herself to set in motion her plans for Laura's birthday. Fedor had followed her, and some of the other women excused themselves and scuttled out too, rushing off to spread the latest gossip and rumour.

Roman had gone off duty and so it was Spanov who knocked on her door, announcing the arrival of Nikolai. Laura motioned for him to be brought in and was aware of how the other women fluttered. She had to force herself to stop from doing the same thing, carefully stitching another loop of gold thread into the tapestry.

'I hope I am not interrupting?' Nikolai queried, bowing and eyeing the hive of activity. 'Is this the famous tapestry project *Mademoiselle* Yegorovna spoke about, to replace the ones destroyed in the second battle for Dalnerechensk?'

'It is' Laura smiled, pleased with the way his enthusiasm made his eyes light up.

He held up the tapestry, admiring the skill of the stitches, the brightness of the colours and the intricacy of the design. Laura explained the tapestry they were working on was the second one, they had already completed the gigantic tapestry that depicted the siege of Novgorod by Ivan the Terrible and Vsevolod pointing the way to salvation in the Ural Mountains, to the three valleys that would become their home. She showed him Gustav's detailed drawing for the last tapestry, the chaotic defence of Dalnerechensk and he praised the drawing, surprised at how much they had stitched in such a short time. The ladies fluttered and wittered at his compliments, curtseying and blushing as he kissed each of their hands. Even sour Nineczka sweetened briefly for him.

'I dearly miss Tatiana's needle, she is extremely skilled' Laura said, hoping that Nikolai would take the hint and stop spending the mornings with her.

He placed the drawing back on her writing table, turning to her.

'I hear tell, Your Majesty, that you ride better than all the cavalry officers of the Polish army' he smiled. 'Almost as well as the Tsar of Russia!'

'Better than a tsar' she grinned. 'I let him win.'

'Now that is a large boast indeed, one I would like to see for myself!' he smiled.

'Do you propose a race?' she asked eagerly.

'I do. To the Eastern Border, for the sum of a hundred roubles. Is that acceptable?'

'It is' she accepted, beckoning for Anna to join her in her dressing room.

She quickly dressed in blue and green again, hurrying down to the stables where Nikolai was already mounted on a fine white charger. She mounted her stallion quickly and guided Nikolai to King's Gate, Roman following behind on a brown mare. People called out to the two of them, waving and bowing as they rode past, some even trotting along behind them, calling blessings and for others to come and see the two royals.

'You are very dear to the people of Dalnerechensk' Nikolai said as they rode. 'The common folk tell tales with awe in their voices and *Mademoiselle* Yegorovna speaks highly of you. She has taken great pains to assure me there is no truth to the terrible rumours.'

That's because she started most of them she thought nastily, and she wondered if Tatiana would first have to explain what those rumours were before pretending to defend her honour.

'I'm rumoured to be an excellent horsewoman and I believe that is true' she said, then kicked sharply at her horse's flanks, sending him leaping forward.

Nikolai called out loudly, spurring his horse after hers. They raced across the valley floor and thundered into Hunter's Pass, neck in neck. Laura leaned forward and rose in the stirrups, spurring the stallion faster. Beside her Nikolai rose too, urging his mount to keep up with hers, both of them aware that Roman was steadily falling behind them.

They broke out of the pass, flying down the road to Kalach, first one marginally in the lead, then the other, both urging their mounts faster and faster. Nikolai laughed, surprised at just how hard he was straining to best the pretty tsaritsa, and dug his heels in again, aware that she was beginning to pull away from him. The low stone wall of the border was rapidly approaching and he leaned further forward, urging the horse faster.

Laura had won her race against Aleksei's Polish nephew and his friends by leaping over the wall while Filip had turned his mount from it, but it seemed Nikolai had heard of that trick as he sailed over the wall too, moments behind her. He laughed again, calling out and naming her winner, reining his sweating mount in.

'Magnificent!' he shouted, watching her wheel the stallion and leap back over the wall again. 'There is no shame in being bested in one so skilful and daring as you Your Majesty' he grinned, turning his mount a little way so he could leap back over the wall too. 'I confess I thought your boast fanciful, yet you have proved you are a woman of your word' he said, bowing to her. 'Well met!'

'Thank you, Your Highness' she smiled, breathing hard too, leaning forward to pat her stallion's neck.

In the distance Nikolai saw Roman break out of the pass, urging his horse on.

'Forgive me, I have grieved you terribly' Nikolai suddenly said, quiet and sincere. She looked up, surprised. 'My father always believed Peter's descendants were as corrupt, fickle, fanciful and vengeful as Peter had been, and I was raised on tales of the wickedness of a brother's betrayal. He bade me promise him, on his deathbed, that I would seek the throne of Dalnerechensk. It was a promise I made, but did not think I could keep it. It was one I didn't want to keep.' He looked away briefly.

'When Maksim's letter arrived, it spoke of hate, and a despotic regime, and many other terrible things and it begged, on behalf of Dalnerechensk, to save them from this terrible affliction. I was swayed by it. I do not deny that I once coveted the throne, for myself, for my father's dying wish, for my son.

'But then I met you ...' he stopped and sighed.

Laura heard so many things unspoken in that sigh. She looked away, watching Roman approach.

'Who won?' he cried, halting before them.

'I did' she smiled.

'Bravo!' he shouted, bowing to her.

'Thank you Roman' she said, patting her stallion's neck again. 'Your Highness, please do accept my warm invitation to my birthday celebrations'

'With pleasure' Nikolai smiled.

'Let me show you the beauty of the forests' Laura said, turning her horse back towards Hunter's Pass. Nikolai and Roman fell into step behind her, their horses still snorting with exertion.

43

15 May 1868

A splendid party. Jagna came with presents for all, this journal for me. I am remiss in keeping any kind of personal record, action calls me more than a pen does, but as she so earnestly pressed me I shall persevere. S and I danced with many of the cousins and their retinue, much wine was consumed. Many plans to go hunting have been made. N and S have wager on largest prize.

Jagna dances well. Cousins and retinue planned to stay two months. Many balls to be had? S promises at least one more with court. Mama promises many feasts and gifts in return. S looks happy with mama's choice, she is very pretty and rich. Relieved and pleased so strenuous choice does not need to be made for me.

My head and hand hurt. I waver already in a promise. I shall quit now while I still have some fondness for it.

Laura rubbed her eyes, tired, and pulled the oil lamp closer to her. She fluffed her pillow and curled up tighter on her side, snuggling into the covers. The next date was 20 April, and she smiled to think so little fondness had been kept that it had been over a month before he had penned another entry, as blunt and short as the first. She yawned, shutting her eyes in a long blink, and debated trying to translate the entry. It was late and her eyelids were drooping. She feared falling asleep with the book so visible, in case Anna saw it. It would mean nothing to her, but she would see it nonetheless.

She rubbed her eyes and sat up, trying to reduce the chance that she might fall asleep and began to read again.

20 April 1868

Guilty. Jagna asked if I had been writing in the journal, I could not lie to her, but her look of disappointment was wrenching. Vowed to write more frequently. Abominable she did not give me a band of musicians and press me to dance every day with her, I would do nothing else. Finding myself attached to her. She loves dancing, music and literature, she is a woman with strong understanding. S is very taken with her. Cousins have nearly drunk Dal. dry but have had splendid time.

Many days we have been at the gorge, we dare each other for more wild displays of courage and foolhardiness. I have the record for holding on the longest to the branch, N was incensed I beat his time. Jagna very impressed. S, N, V and I have been riding every day. Most of the court has accompanied us at one point or another.

Cousins pressed to extend their stay. Only slight resistance, most very willing to enjoy hospitality for longer. S very happy they are staying. Another party planned tomorrow night. Jagna has promised to stay. I am very happy.

Addendum: *N won the wager, mighty buck he found, antlers like a tree. Proudly mounted in his drawing room.*

Laura shut the book and yawned, forcing herself out of bed to return it to the secret drawer, her fingers finding the button easily, even in the darkness. *"N" might be Nicholas Riminov* she mused as she headed back to her bed, and wondered briefly who "S" and "V" could be. She suspected that Tsar Constantinovich liked this woman Jagna more than he let on, it was the only name he wrote in full.

She blew out the oil lamp and pulled the covers up to her nose, shutting her eyes tightly. *I know Jagna is not the woman he married* she told herself. She found it difficult to think of Tsar Constantinovich having a mistress. *He was clearly devoted to his wife, he was devastated by her death, so much so he lost all heart and abdicated, thrusting an unready and awkward Aleksei onto the throne.* She yawned again, curling up. *Perhaps I am wrong, perhaps he is merely admiring. Perhaps it was nothing more than a fleeting fancy.*

She sighed quietly, slipping into sleep, dreaming of dancing.

44

Laura and Ekaterina breakfasted alone in her dining room, shrouded in silence. The days were inching closer to when she would leave, and Laura couldn't find the words to ask her to stay. She knew she couldn't speak them anyway. She wondered if she would ever find genuine friends in this small Principality.

When they had finished they headed back to Laura's apartments, steeling themselves for another morning of guarded interaction. But they were both surprised to find no one at all in her rooms, not even the wives of junior ministers.

'What is this?' Laura asked, puzzled.

Ekaterina looked unhappy. 'The Vakhtangovs have decided to snub you for your treatment of Varvara -'

'But -'

'And no doubt the others would have been ordered not to come. They want to punish you Laura, they know why you left *that* tapestry till last. They want you to sit alone with the memories of that terrible battle, and to think about the sons you are digging up.'

'Marie Borodina?' she queried desperately.

'In the nursery with Alexandra, and Anna has taken to her sick bed again.'

Laura eyed her empty rooms despondently. She knew of one other reason why they were not here. She had boasted to Nikolai that it would be finished by her birthday, and now she would look like a fool.

'Roman' she called and he stepped in, saluting. 'It's a nice day, we shall stitch in the sun by the village green. Find someone who can carry all the things we will need, and I will take Alexandra with me.'

He saluted and rushed off to accost a servant or two to carry the silk threads and the giant tapestry itself, rounding up a few guards that could be spared from the castle to accompany them.

Ekaterina made her apologies and left to organise more secret activities for her birthday. Laura hid her disappointment, heading to the nursery to collect her daughter. Marie smiled and tied a sweet bonnet on Alexandra's head before bringing her to Laura, falling into step behind her as they left the castle.

Roman had thought to bring her a blanket to sit on and the servants spread it out for her. Laura thanked them and sent them back to the jobs they had interrupted and sat on the blanket with Marie, taking a corner of the tapestry and pulling it onto their laps. Alexandra giggled and wiggled on Laura's lap, her little fingers pulling at the material of the tapestry. Roman and three other guards fanned out, taking up strategically unobtrusive positions close to her.

Several of the townsfolk had seen them and stopped to look, watching the two women with surprise. Laura greeted those who came close, bobbing curious curtseys and inquiring after the tapestry, cooing and waving handkerchiefs at Alexandra. Soon a crowd had gathered around them.

'Do you sew?' she suddenly asked the woman nearest her.

'Me?' she gasped, flustered. '*Da*, of course. Your Majesty' she said, flushing.

'Would you be so kind to stitch that little piece of sky there?' she pointed, handing her a needle threaded with blue silk.

She blushed and accepted, bobbing a hundred small bows as she came to sit beside her, thanks and praises tripping over themselves on her tongue. Another announced that she could sew too, and Laura beckoned her forward, asking her to stitch a small figure.

Within an hour fifty women were seated around the spread out tapestry, gossiping and laughing, shooting the tsaritsa and the baby surreptitious looks, whispering behind held-up sections of the tapestry to each other. Laura knew what they were saying. *She was one of them, a common girl who made it good, one for whom the fairytale had come true. She had ruled wisely and well, there was peace and prosperity in the kingdom, and she did not lock herself away in her ivory tower, forgetting what it was like to walk in their shoes. She had knocked the upstart nobles back a peg or two as well.*

She also knew how it looked, sitting here stitching the defence of Dalnerechensk with the wives, daughters and mothers of the sons who had defended it again. Her decision to move the graves had not been popular, but she had ensured it had been done with great solemnity and respect, and she knew the grave diggers had heard her soft words to Roman. *I dug up my father too.* Those words had been told to wives, to neighbours, to passing acquaintances until Dalnerechensk realised she hadn't made the decision lightly, until they knew she knew what it was to watch this too.

The crowd watching them was jovial, and respectful, some staying over an hour to watch, others hurrying on to finish their errands, still others clutching their own sewing needles and waiting for a place to open up so they could help too. Towards the back of the crowd there was a sudden shout and a commotion, and some shuffling to and fro.

The crowd parted like the swishing back of theatre curtains and an aisle formed to reveal Nikolai, and, holding his hand and marching solemnly beside him, his two year old son Ilya. The crowd curtseyed and called greetings, and those who were sitting around the tapestry scrambled to their feet, curtseying too, leaving Laura seated alone. She smiled as she watched them approach, but her heart was doing horrible things inside her chest.

Ilya was blonde, and dressed in a military jacket, decorated with braids and cloth medals, his white breeches tucked into sweet little riding boots. He carried a rolled up material bundle with him and it was tied with blue and green ribbons. Nikolai stopped, and with a quiet word to Ilya they bowed to her. Nikolai shook his hand gently, and he took a deep, theatrical breath.

'High Miss, I have a pres'nt for you!' he said loudly.

Some of the crowd laughed and more cooed, and Laura let herself smile deeper.

'You do? How wonderful!' she said. 'Please come forward and give it to me.'

Ilya marched around the women, who turned to follow him, and saluted before Laura. She handed her daughter to Marie and got to her feet, curtseying low before him, trying to hold back a laugh at his serious little expression. He handed her the bundle, which she took with another curtsey, untying the ribbons and unrolling the material.

It was a pretty, golden sewing kit, with matching thimbles, scissors, needles and all manner of instruments necessary for a seamstress, albeit a very rich one. She smiled and thanked him, sitting down so she was the same height as him.

'What a lovely present!' she exclaimed, giving his cheek a kiss. 'Shall I use it now?'

Ilya nodded, beaming, then turned to look at the material spread out before him.

'What are you doing?' he asked, leaning against her shoulder to look at the tapestry.

She let him climb onto her lap and put her arms around him, showing him the tapestry and explaining what they were doing.

'Who is Vis'lod?' he asked.

There was a quiet, shocked gasp from the women and several turned to look at Nikolai questioningly, who had either not heard or was tactfully ignoring the comment, engrossed in conversation with several people in the crowd.

'Well, once upon a time there lived a kind man in the city of Novgorod' Laura began. 'It was a beautiful city, and a rich one, and the people were happy. But nearby in a neighbouring kingdom was a jealous, evil man -'

'Peter Vas'livich!' Ilya shouted excitedly. 'And all his des'dents!'

There was another careful pause and all eyes turned to Nikolai, who looked very embarrassed.

'My father told him many stories' he said quietly. 'Stories that had more to do with his resentment than with truth.'

'No, not Peter my dear, it was many many years before him. Right back to the beginning of this Principality' Laura said, then went on to explain the story that all little children knew about Dalnerechensk.

'And they live here now?' Ilya inquired.

'Yes, ever since Vsevolod led us here' Laura said, snipping the thread with the golden scissors. 'But the new Tsar of Russia, Ivan's son Feodor, wanted to take back the valleys from Vsevolod, didn't want them to have a home away from Russia. So he came here, with cannons, and men, and a terrible battle happened. And then, many many years later, another Russian came, with cannon and men, and wanted to take back the valleys again. The beautiful tapestries, the ones that Vsevolod's wife had sewn, were torn up in that fight, torn up to protect us. So we sew them again, and hope. We hope they will not be torn up again, but if they are, we hope it will be because they protected us, like the first ones did, like Vsevolod did.'

'Like you did' said the woman sitting on Laura's left, while others said 'Amen', and it was echoed around the circle of seated women sewing the tapestry.

'Tell me about Peter' Ilya demanded. 'He 'trayed his brother, and sent him away, never to see his home again. And all his des'dants never let them come home. They were bad men!'

There was a quiet hiss of indrawn breath from some of the older women, who had lived through Tsar Constantinovich's reign and remembered their ruler with fondness and reverence, from those who hated the words from a little boy's mouth. But there were sidelong looks at Laura, because there was one bad man they remembered well.

'Peter had a son, called Igor' Laura said quietly. 'He was young, very young, when he became Tsar of Dalnerechensk, and he did not want to be like his father, he wanted to be a good man. And he was. I think the one thing he regretted was not letting his uncle come home.'

'But why?' Ilya asked. 'I don't un'stand!'

'Well, that is something we can never really know' she said, snipping another thread. 'Perhaps he wanted people to forget about his uncle, it is hard to be a good tsar if everyone remembers someone who was better.' She bit her lip at that, forcing away the thought of Alexander Andrei. 'And perhaps he distrusted his uncle, perhaps his father had told him about a brother who stole his throne while he was sick. There are many reasons why people do the things they do, and not all of them we understand.'

Nikolai approached, calling to his son, who scrambled off Laura's lap and went to hold his hand. It was at this particular moment that Alexandra exercised another of her alphabetic burbling.

'Papa!' she cried. 'Papa papa!'

There was a horrible, crowded moment, and everyone looked at Nikolai. Laura hadn't been ready for this and the shock of it ripped her already fracturing heart into little bits. She knew she would one day have to tell her about her father, she just never knew her daughter would remind her of that so soon, and so publicly. *And everyone looked at Nikolai* she thought, her eyes stinging. That's what she would remember, afterwards. *Everyone had looked at Nikolai. That poor man.*

She lifted her daughter onto her lap and cuddled her, one tear splashing onto the top of her head which she wiped away gently, stroking back her blonde hair. Alexandra hugged her, mouthing kisses against her cheek and Laura smiled despite the tears, kissing her cheek too. Alexandra giggled, laying her head on Laura's shoulder, her crown tucked into the curve of her neck. She buffed at her tears with a dainty knuckle, sniffing.

'Why're you crying?' Ilya asked. 'Doesn't she have a papa?'

'No my dear, she does not' Laura managed.

'I don't have a mama' Ilya announced. 'She died birthing me.'

Unable to help herself her eyes flicked to Nikolai, and she saw in his face the grief and pain he still felt, how he struggled to hide it in this public place. His eyes met hers, briefly, then looked away again, picking up his son who was still babbling away, quite unconcerned, about the mother he had never known.

He bowed and excused himself, stating he wished to show his son the markets, and Laura told him about the exquisite carved wooden toys one seller made, guaranteed to delight a small boy. Father and son bowed to her, then said their goodbyes to the crowd, making their way slowly towards Vsevolod's Way. Laura watched them until the crowd surged back behind them, all eyeing her.

Quietly but deliberately she began to put away her sewing things, folding up the golden set and tying the ribbons again before smiling at them all.

'My dear friends, I thank you all for your skilful help. I shall bring the tapestry to the green again tomorrow, will you help me again?'

'Da!' they cried, and bowed as she stood, folding her arms around Alexandra.

She gave instructions for two of the guards to fold up the tapestry and the blankets and carry them as they made their way back to the castle, Roman falling into step behind her silently. At the gate she turned and waved to the people again, blowing kisses which Alexander copied clumsily, and bid them farewell, trying not to run away from the tears that were building up in her.

45

30 April, 1868

Week of both glad and miserable tidings. Funeral for V. His death quite sobered us. Can't forget his face as he fell, the sound he made hitting the rocks at the bottom, his moans as death took hold of him. E and N beside themselves with grief. Aunt M has taken to her bed since. None can console them. Mother is furious. Even if she had not banned us from the gorge we would no longer go.

Laura stopped reading and pushed back the covers, sighing deeply. She put the book back into the secret drawer and pulled on her silk dressing robe, fastening it tightly around her. Roman looked round in surprise when she opened the door.

'Are you alright, Your Majesty?' he asked softly.

'I cannot sleep' she said, collecting the oil lamp from the hallway table beside him. 'I thought to find something in the library to read.'

Roman saluted and followed her soundlessly as she padded along the corridor, the lamp casting long, flickering shadows on the walls that danced after them, twisting and flapping like demonic birds. Laura was tempted to blow out the light, the shadows were unnerving. But they stopped when she opened the door and set it down on the table, warming the cold room with a yellow glow.

Her fingers ran along the stiff leather spines of the tsar's collection, dancing past titles in French, Greek, Latin and English, looking for the books Fedor had found for her when Maksim had tried to thrust poor Piotr Vakhtangov at the throne. She found one book and pulled it off the shelf, flicking it open. *Let's see, Aunt M…*

She found the entry she wanted quickly. Tsar Constantinovich had an Aunt Maria, who had three children: Elena, Natasha, and her oldest, a son called Vasili. *Aunt M, V, N and E* she realised. She also realised that the inconsolable 'N' and the winner of the hunting bet 'N' could not have been the same person. She sighed quietly, Tsar Constantinovich wrote so cryptically sometimes she would never quite be sure what he was referring to.

Roman peered at her choice of book, confused.

'Do you think this will make me fall asleep Roman?' she smiled.

'Yes Your Majesty' he grinned.

She closed it and tucked it into the crook of her arm, lifting the oil lamp again. Roman followed her back to her room and bid her good night when she closed the door, retrieving the book on the way back to bed. She pulled the covers up to her nose, placing the reference book beside her, ready to consult should she need it.

She opened the diary and found the entry she had half read, squinting in the lamplight at the script.

Jagna confessed she is relieved we will no longer dare ourselves at the gorge. Confessed she feared she might have watched me fall. Or S. There is an unusual stir in my breast that she thought of me before S. I have tried since then to press her for meaning but she evades my questioning masterfully. Her elusiveness is both frustrating and alluring. Does she consent to my attentions so flatteringly because she is vowed to my family or through genuine affection for me?

Laura rubbed her eyes, tired. *Vowed to my family?* she wondered. *Did he mean engaged? Was Jagna his brother's fiancée?* Radomyr had never married, but had he never loved? Perhaps he did not marry her because she was his brother's mistress. *Was there a law against that?* she wondered. Probably. There were many laws about sex in Dalnerechensk.

Fedor had told her that Nikolai had requested books on the laws of Dalnerechensk, in particular those on marriage and succession. She knew what he would read there. She was, technically, his cousin's wife, it was a questionably legal act to marry her. Though the legality might be glossed over in the clamour to have a man on the throne again. The crown could only pass to men. Her daughter would never sit on the throne, not unless she fought...

She sighed, tired, and forced herself out of bed to put the journal back in the secret drawer, forgetting to blow out the lamp before sleep took her, cocooning her deep in dreams of a blonde haired man.

46

There were six days before her birthday, and a nervous excitement had taken hold of her, one that made her fingers flutter and tremble, despite how many times she forced herself to be still. She was well aware of the scrutiny she was under now. She folded her hands in her lap, clutched one firmly with the other, and tried to stop her mind sliding away from Maksim's discourse on the healthy state of the economy.

But it was no good. *Fredrik promised he would be back in time for my birthday* she mused, and again she felt the strange, almost guilty shiver at the thought. It had been so long since she had seen him last, and so much had happened since then. She wondered what he would make of Nikolai. She wondered if he knew.

She shook herself mentally, letting her eyes glide over the ministers seated before her. Some political musical chairs had taken place again, Uvarov was now seated quite close to the front, and – to her surprise – so was Luka. It had taken a long time for Ilich to rejoin his political party in the Parliament, and a power shift seemed to have taken place. Luka sat near the front, and Ilich lurked in the back, surly and deflated.

She sighed inwardly. She did not blame the revolutionaries from seeking a new leader in the fallout of the elections, but Luka was a dangerous choice. There was fury in his eyes when he looked at her, a rage that scared her despite her cool dismissal of him. She was very glad Roman had followed her to the nursery that night and she wondered, frightened, what would happen if he ever caught her alone again.

She looked away, shifting uncomfortably on her chair. Maksim droned on, strutting occasionally, posturing mostly, and she had to resist the urge to lean her cheek on her fist, shutting her eyes against the complete boredom she felt.

Again her mind drifted away, this time to her small triumph against Nineczka yesterday afternoon. As she had promised on Monday she had returned to the village green with the tapestry, to waiting crowds of a thousand women, all clutching needles and skeins of thread. Peter Kamanin had wisely sent a delegation of soldiers to bolster the numbers of the Vsevolod Guards accompanying her. But the crowds had been respectful and well behaved, waiting patiently for their turn at the tapestry.

She had not been surprised to see Tatiana, and other members of the Vakhtangov family, join her on the green, silently stitching in the midst of a gossiping gaggle of women. Only Tatiana tried to engage with the commoners, but the conversation was awkward and forced, and it soon petered out. That evening a message had been sent to the castle, begging Laura to once again stitch in her rooms, as the "emanations had distressed the Vakhtangovs and they wished to stitch in comfort."

She had agreed, but it wasn't long before she had finally grown tired of unpicking the mess Nineczka had made of the stitches and had sent her unceremoniously from her rooms. Nineczka had been furious but could do nothing about it, bobbing an insultingly low curtsey and storming out. She hadn't missed Roman's grin when he had reached in to close the door after her. A small smile touched her lips and she coughed quickly to cover it. No doubt Ilich had heard an earful last night, which might account for his temper today.

Maksim's discourse finally ended and he sat, cutting off Yuri's motion by calling end to the Parliament.

'I will be heard!' Yuri snapped.

'Not today' Maksim announced imperiously, then swept out of the room, the rest of his ministers following him to the dining room.

Yuri's mouth pressed into a tight line of anger and he clenched his hands, swearing under his breath. He turned to look at Ilich, who had already gone, and shook off Luka's hand when he grabbed his arm. He looked at Laura fleetingly, opened his mouth to say something to her, then changed his mind, blushing, and followed the rest of Parliament out of the room.

Laura sighed, wondering what games they were playing now, and rubbed her eyes, tired. Maksim had spoken for nearly three hours, all the time allotted for Parliament's session, on a pointless and painstakingly thorough account of the Principality, to the exclusion of all other motions. It was the second time in as many days he had done so, and Laura wondered what he was preventing her from hearing. *Another plot, another coup de 'tat…*

She stood, letting herself out of the chambers, greeting Roman quietly as he fell into step behind her. Instead of going all the way up to the third floor she turned off the stairs on the first floor, heading down the corridor where the old offices of Aleksei and Grigory had been.

Neither had been damaged by the cannons of Nikita's army, unlike the Advisory Council room between them. The office right at the end, the one that had belonged to Aleksei, was now the office of the Prime Minister. Laura had not set foot in it in all the time she had been back. But the one closest to the stairs, that used to belong to the Treasurer of Dalnerechensk, was now the office for the head of her household.

Roman knocked and announced her arrival to Fedor, who stood and bowed, inviting her to a seat by the small fireplace. After a small inquiry into her wellbeing that morning Fedor selected a folder of figures from his desk and presented it to her with a quick bow. Laura flicked through it, pleased to see her recent investments had been successful as well, she had nearly ten times the fortune she had less than four months ago.

Fedor handed her another portfolio, this one with several new investments detailed in it, their risks and returns, and she read them carefully, making quick notations before signing her agreement on the last page. She handed it back and accepted another, this one with figures and notations for her birthday celebrations. Laura baulked at the number under the double ruled line, biting her lip. She knew Parliament was paying for some of the celebrations, and a large sum was coming from the Ivanovs themselves, but the number on that page seemed astronomical.

'So much?' she gasped, begging Fedor to tell her he'd made a mistake.

'Yes Your Majesty' he said.

She worried at her lip again, wondering how much more she would need to pay for. She was spending her money just fast as she was earning it, faster even, and her hand shook slightly as she signed her name beside it.

'There will be rich gifts, and presents to offset the cost now' Fedor assured her. 'Such as it always is.'

She managed a small smile though she did not feel comforted, and handed back the folder. She stood, Fedor standing too, and sighed, stretching out her hands to the small fire.

'Tell me Fedor, have you ever heard the name Jagna?'

'Jagna? Where did you hear that Your Majesty?' he blinked.

'In some old papers of Tsar Constantinovich's' she said. 'I don't believe I have ever heard of that person.'

'It is not commonly known' he said, shrugging. 'It was a pet name for Agnieszka, but she did not like it, and begged people not to use it.'

'Ah, I see' she smiled. 'Thank you' she nodded and left, heading back to her rooms.

So it was his wife after all she smiled to herself. She hesitated only briefly at the door to her rooms, schooling her features carefully, then stepped in. The hubbub of voices cut off abruptly and the women in her rooms turned as one to look at her.

'What is it?' she asked, eyeing them, noticing they all held something in their hands.

They drew apart, stretching out the material for her to see.

The tapestry was finished. Laura's eyes roamed over it, searching for any blank space or hanging thread, but found none. A heady flush of pleasure and satisfaction welled up in her and she clasped her hands together, pressing her index fingers to her lips as she admired it.

'Congratulations Your Majesty' Ekaterina said.

'Thank you, thank you all' she murmured, unable to take her eyes off the material.

Natasha's tapestries were complete, recreated faithfully to the last stitch, except for this last one. It had been her little secret, her twist of history. Unlike the other two tapestries Vsevolod was harder to find in the battle for Dalnerechensk. He was harder still in this copy, as another figure had been added which partially obscured him. A woman, dressed in white, knelt at his feet. With one hand she held a white handkerchief to her face, in her other hand she held a sword resting across her lap. No one who looked at this tapestry could doubt who that woman was.

'We must make an announcement!' she said excitedly. 'Anna would you be so kind as to send for Fedor?'

'Yes Your Majesty' Anna smiled, bobbing a curtsey on her way out.

'And send in the court musicians too' Laura called after her, then stepped closer, running her fingers gently over the stitches of the castle.

She let them set it down, and chatted with them graciously until Fedor arrived two minutes later, followed by the musicians. She sent them up to the castle wall overlooking the village green, instructing them to play the national anthem and all the folk tunes about Vsevolod they could remember, while Fedor set up speakers and a microphone for her, as well as a secure way to fasten the three completed tapestries to the wall.

Laura penned a quick speech then dressed in royal colours, heading to the nursery to collect Marie and Alexandra. Maksim was roused from his lunch in the state dining room, and Lev followed them up to the wall, munching on a chicken leg, tossing the bone over his shoulder to land somewhere in the flowering garden. Laura had half a mind to make him dig it out again, but she gritted her teeth and ignored it as best she could.

She was pleased to see the three tapestries rolled into spools and placed end to end along the parapet of the wall. The microphone had been set up behind the middle tapestry, and the musicians were crowded together at the far end of the little space. They had done their job and the commons were teeming with people. Fedor, with great presence of mind, had sent an urgent telegram to Tcherepnin for soldiers to be stationed at the foot of the wall, keeping the crowd back. They cheered when Laura appeared at the top of the wall, and she waved to them, blowing kisses.

It took a while for the noise to die down enough for her to be heard, even with the microphone, and she wondered how on earth they had heard her before, and all the tsars that stood here before her. At the end of her short speech two livery men pushed the rolled up material for the tapestries, letting them unfurl down the wall, one after the other.

The crowd cheered and surged forward, pressing as close to the armed soldiers as they dared, craning their necks to see the finished pictures, shouting at each other and pointing at the figures. Laura took Alexandra from Marie, sitting her on her hip and waving to the crowds below. Alexandra copied her, staring fascinated at the sea of noise and colour below them.

'Leave them up for three days' she told Fedor, her gaze flickering at the clear blue sky. 'Guard it day and night. And pray it doesn't rain' she added, before taking her daughter to play in the rose garden.

47

Laura flipped idly through the diary, using one nail to select a few pages and flick them over. She could see the entries grew longer and more detailed as they had progressed, filling page after page with the blossoming feelings for the woman that would become his wife. She had lost that sense of anticipation the diary had first woken in her, instead she was filled with a disquiet wistfulness, a fervent wish that it would just tell her what she wanted to know.

She was sure that he had not told Jagna how he felt, pouring his sentiments into this dairy instead, and she saw so clearly the resemblance between father and son. Perhaps Tsar Constantinovich had been just as awkward and uncomfortable with expressing his feelings as Aleksei had been. He did not seem so in his old age. Perhaps Aleksei would have grown more comfortable as the years and children had wound their lives intricately together. She would never know now.

I will be eighteen tomorrow, and Fredrik still has not arrived.

She shut her eyes, flicked over a few more pages, then rubbed her eyes tiredly. She shut the book, her fingers drumming on the leather cover, then opened it again, found the last entry she had read, and flicked on a few pages until she found an entry over a page long. She lay back and rested the book on her knees, propping her feet up to read it more comfortably.

28 June 1868

My hand trembles as I write this. I fear a sickness might have taken hold of me, but I cannot determine whether it be attributed to the cold I endured or the result of the conversation between Jagna and myself. My other symptoms are a tightness in my chest, a quickness of breath, and a maddening quivering of my stomach.

'Sounds like love to me' she told her empty room.

S and court decided to ride through forest today. Jagna and I rode together, and fell so deep in conversation that we did not notice how we had become separated from everyone else, nor how the sky had grown overcast. We were caught in a violent summer storm out in the open with no shelter save for the cave behind the waterfall in the glen.

Laura was surprised by that information, and vowed to go looking for it that afternoon. She shifted position and kept reading.

It was a bitter shelter, we were soaked from the rain and spray from the waterfall would occasionally douse us with heavy droplets. Jagna was indeed suffering with the cold and graciously accepted my own jacket with which to fortify herself. We laughed about our lack of attention, of how we had come to be so involved in our words that we should now find ourselves hiding behind one deluge to protect us from another.

By and by our conversation turned to Dal, to the place which would be her home, and she confessed how eager she was now, to know us as well as she does, how dear she now holds me. She knows how precious the alliance between our families is, but she worried she would be so unhappy here. She said that having met me, and my brother, all her fears had been put to rest. Then she looked directly at me, and claimed she would not feel so at home, were it not for me, and the affection she has for me.

I wish now I had said all the witty things I can think of afterwards, wish now I could have told her how my affections for her had grown so strong I could not bear to think of her leaving Dal, could not bear to think of what would happen when she married. I dared not confess that, too unsure of her feelings for me, too unwilling to cause a rift that would tear our families apart. But oh how I wished to kiss her, to fold her in my arms and dry us both with the heat of passion.

Instead we just stood there, listening to the waterfall, until she finally turned away, and I knew I had missed a chance to change our lives. I am filled with regret that I could not speak when I knew I should, yet I hear her words still, and see her eyes when she spoke them, and part of me knows that we will get the chance to speak again, that we will both contrive to have that chance, that we will fill it with words we shouldn't say, but will anyway.

Laura closed the book, feeling that desire twist in her to read Olaf's letter, and the words he couldn't say to her. She knew them by heart, but it was not the same as holding the last thing he had touched, letting her eyes follow the sweep and loop of his handwriting, smelling the scent of him in the fibres of the paper.

She shut her eyes, folding the book to her chest and sighed quietly. *Why am I reading this?* she asked herself. *What am I hoping to find in these pages? Does it really matter, now, why he abdicated?*

She shook herself, avoiding answering her own question, and blew out the lamp, slipping out of bed in the dark to return the diary to its hiding place. She slipped between the covers and shut her eyes but sleep would not come. She tossed and turned for three hours restlessly, trying to get comfortable, trying to turn her thoughts off. But it was no good.

At dawn she rose and washed with the ewer of water in her dressing room, dressing in a pretty blue dress and wondering if it was too early to go riding through the forest. Instead she forced herself down corridors to the nursery, slipping over to the crib. Marie had not risen from her bed yet, and Laura had these precious moments with her sleeping daughter alone.

She smiled and stroked her cheek with the back of a finger, tracing down her arm to circle around her palm, feeling those little fingers curl around her. Alexandra woke and smiled at her, rubbing at her eyes as she stretched.

'Good morning my precious one' she said, lifting her out of the crib, moving to the nursing chair to sit with her on her lap, planting kisses on her cheeks while Alexandra giggled.

There was the sound of running feet and a breathless moment of flurried adjustment before Roman pushed open the door, amused, and announced a flushed Marie, apologising profusely for sleeping in. Alexandra squealed in delight at seeing her and reached out, jiggling earnestly on Laura's lap. *I don't think she has ever greeted me like that* Laura thought, surprised. *Does my own daughter not know who I am?*

'I'm sorry, she's hungry, and knows I bring her food in the mornings' Marie said apologetically, who knew what she was thinking.

'We shall eat today with the court' Laura said, scooping her daughter up. 'Perhaps I do not spend enough time with her' she kissed her cheek again, and led Marie down to the long dining hall.

Alexandra, unused to this change in her routine, fussed and grizzled until hunger and Laura's patient ministrations made her more compliant. The court was surprised to see Laura feeding her own daughter at the table, just as she was surprised to see Nikolai seated there too, near the centre, but not under the royal canopy. *I have missed much while secreted away in my private dining room* she thought, and made a vow to eat more frequently with the court.

When she had eaten her fill and Marie had taken Alexandra back to the nursery Laura summoned her ministers to Parliament. She half expected to listen to Maksim talk non-stop for three hours over the state of the castle silverware, or some other inconsequential matter, but was somewhat surprised to find the minds of Parliament turned to the pageantry of her birthday.

With some disappointment she realised she was to be somewhat of a spectator at her own birthday celebrations, much the same way as she was in her own wedding. There was the riding through the streets of Dalnerechensk so the population could wish her a happy birthday, and the formal receiving of gifts to take place in the ballroom, for which three hours of her day had been set aside. There was the formal reception of dignitaries, and a royal banquet of thirteen courses, the opening of the theatre house, and only after that would there be music and dancing, if anyone was still awake to enjoy it.

It sounded so tedious and dull. She had expected her birthday party to be full of excitement and feasting, music and dancing, presents and Fredrik; not this stuffy ritual. In fact she quite longed for it. Last year, pregnant and recoiling from the shock of all that had happened, it had taken her some time to become aware of how much time had passed, and to her horror she realised her seventeenth birthday had passed without her even knowing.

I can't imagine Ekaterina, vivacious and fun loving – even tempered with the careful way she behaved now – would plan something so dull as this!

'Gentlemen' she said, interrupting them. 'What of Countess Ivanova's plans? Are these what she has devised for my birthday?' There were confused looks from the ministers. 'Has Parliament conversed with her at all?'

'We have not' Maksim said, and there was a barely contained sneer in his voice.

'Ivan, would you be so kind as to summon Countess Ivanova to Parliament?' she smiled sweetly. He bowed and left but was back quickly, having sent a guard to make the necessary summons. 'It would grieve my closest and dearest friend, who had so earnestly made plans for my birthday, were I, at the bequest of my Parliament, to discard all her efforts *and before you protest* I understand that there are formalities to observe.

'Unless my dear friend Countess Ivanova has planned activities that are more suited to share this happy occasion with my people, more gracious to the bestowers of those wonderful gifts and above all *more entertaining*, it is my will that the formal reception of gifts will take no more than two hours, the banquet will begin one hour earlier, and the theatre performance must not take longer than two hours.'

'But Your Majesty!' Lev protested. 'You cannot do that! What will you do for the rest of the evening?'

'Dance' she smiled. 'Have you forgotten what it was like to be young?'

'I dare say he has' Ekaterina said, curtseying low in the doorway. 'Good morning Your Majesty, Ministers' she curtseyed to them too.

'Good morning Countess, I would not think to summon you so, but it occurred to me that two factions had made plans for my birthday, quite unaware of the other. It would insult both of you too greatly should I favour one over the other, so I humbly beg that you work together to make my birthday a wonderful occasion.'

'Of course, Your Majesty' Ekaterina curtseyed again. 'Might I be so bold as to humbly suggest that you leave? I could not ruin the surprises by discussing them so vulgarly in your presence.'

'Very well' she smiled. She rose and the room bowed before her.

She excused herself from Parliament, and headed up to her rooms to change into her riding habit. Anna pinned her hair up quickly, seeing how restless Laura was to get to the stables, and she rushed down the stairs, fidgeting impatiently while the stable boy saddled the stallion and the mare. She debated leaving Roman behind but forced herself to wait just a little longer.

The stallion fretted at her restlessness, pawing at the ground and she reined it in tightly, calming herself and finding a suitable smile to wear while riding through her people. Roman swung up into the saddle and trotted after her, adjusting the rifle strap around his shoulder, his eyes probing the crowd warily. Laura smiled and waved, greeting those who called out to her, heading down Castle Street.

She could see the slightly concave depressions, neat and regular, along The Avenue of Heroes, the excavation tent gone. Fedor had told her they had laid the last body to rest in Macherna yesterday, and the road now had an empty, wistful feeling to it. She turned away, urging the horse towards Hunter's Pass.

She was surprised to find Nikolai's automobile on the road, canted slightly to one side, its wheels sinking in deep mud. Nikolai was stripped to his shirtsleeves, his back soaked with sweat, and he was digging at the ground around the front wheel with a thick tree branch.

'Might we be of assistance Your Highness?' she called, reining in her horse.

He turned and bowed to her, wiping the sweat from his face with the upper part of his arm. Laura noticed the way his shirt clung interestingly to his chest as well.

'Alas, it is stuck fast' he said, resting the branch against the wheel. 'It will need a team of men and horses to get it out.'

'Perhaps you would like to accompany me on a ride through the forest instead?' she asked, trying to hide her disappointment when he reached into the back of the phaeton and pulled out his jacket, slipping into it and fastening it closed. 'Roman will gladly give you his horse and see that your automobile is returned to *Monsieur* Yegorov's house.'

Roman hesitated.

'Your Majesty' he began to protest, swinging down from the saddle, but left the rest unsaid.

'I understand, *Sotnik*' she said gently. 'Roman once saved me from poachers in the forest, he fears greatly he may not be there to save me again. But he worries too much, the Hunting Forest is for royals and ministers alone, no poacher will ever mistake me for a deer again' she told Nikolai.

It's not poachers but assassins I fear Roman wanted to say, but bit his lip and said nothing.

'*Whoso list to hunt*' Nikolai grinned, leaping up into the saddle of the mare. 'Your *Sotnik's* dedication is a credit to you, Your Majesty' he said, aware of the effect Thomas Wyatt's opening line had had on her. 'But rest assured I will let no harm come to you' he promised.

She turned her stallion into the forest, leaving Roman alone in the road. Nikolai followed, and they lapsed into a coy conversation, one where Nikolai chased her through history and literature, art and technology, poetry and philosophy. Laura ducked under a branch and they stepped out into the sun-drenched clearing, blinking in the brightness.

'What a delightful place!' Nikolai exclaimed, his eyes drawn to the waterfall.

'It is my favourite in all the forests' Laura said, swinging down from her horse and looping the reins over a tree branch.

Nikolai dismounted too, his eyes drinking in the pleasant pool, the lush meadow, the dotted white mountain daisies, which glowed against the green in the kiss of the sun. Laura left him ambling through the flowers, skirting around the pool beneath the waterfall, looking for the entrance to the cave.

There was no obvious entrance, just a small gap between the rock face and the water, one that did not look as if it turned into a cave. It was thin, she realised she would have to press close to the rock face and hold her skirts gathered tightly around her to avoid saturating them. *A Gibson Girl mermaid dress would be appropriate about now* she thought wryly, shuffling behind the water.

Stray drips splashed at her back, and a rushing wind pulled at her, threatening to topple her backwards into the thundering waterfall, threatening to pull her down in its wet grip, pressing her to the floor to pin her in a watery grave. She shuddered as the terror washed over her. She had nearly drowned once. It had been the strong arms of Olaf that had saved her, arms she wished to feel steadying her now.

The rock face suddenly opened in front of her and she nearly pitched forward onto her face. It was only the hand she held against the rock that saved her from a painful embarrassment, as the floor was littered with stones. It was gloomy beyond the water, and she blinked several times while her eyes adjusted, before stepping into the cave proper.

It was quite small, only a couple of feet across and extending no further into the rock than twenty paces. The walls were green with lichen and moss, and wet with dew. Carved into them were initials, some in hearts but mostly not. Some were old, mostly obscured with moss, others sharp and defined against the green. A+T, B+Λ, C+A...

Some of the initials had small crowns carved over them, though many did not. *The royals must have been coming here for years and carving theirs and their sweetheart's initials into the rock* she realised, touching an obscure Δ+И. *Or possibly it was H.* She wondered, briefly, painfully, if Aleksei had come here, and carved their initials into the rock. *Unlikely* she told herself, and did not look around to prove herself wrong. *In all the time they had been married Aleksei had barely left the castle, and if he were to carve their names he might have done it that day they had ridden to the glen together. But we found other ways to declare our love...*

Nikolai suddenly called out, alarmed.

'Your Majesty?!'

'I'm here! Behind the waterfall!' she answered, moving closer to the entrance so he could hear her.

Following her instructions he clambered behind the water but stumbled, tripping on a rock as he stepped into the cave, accidentally grabbing at Laura for support. Off-balance, she stepped back, rolling awkwardly on a rock herself, and the two of them engaged in a tripping dance to keep upright, crashing against the rock wall on the other side of the waterfall.

Nikolai grunted as he fell against her, heavy and smelling of sweat from his earlier endeavours. Thick and violent longing rose in Laura and she struggled to push it down, struggled not to want the feel of a man again. Nikolai hesitated and she wondered if desire was stirring in him too, though she couldn't see it in his eyes. She wondered if he was going to kiss her.

'*Noli me tangere*' she smiled, slipping away, peering at the rocks he had overturned.

There were three of them, and each of them, neatly preserved where they had been pressed into the mud of the cave floor, had P+Я engraved on them. Using her toe she overturned two more stones. Each had P+Я carved on them too.

'Look!' she said, pointing them out to Nikolai. 'Why would someone do this?'

'Perhaps they were secret lovers' he said. 'Or it was unrequited and not meant to be discovered.'

Laura looked away, then edged out of the cave, blinking as she emerged back in the daylight. Nikolai followed her, shielding his eyes from the hot sun while his vision adjusted. He bent down and picked up the bouquet of flowers he had gathered and set aside near the entrance, offering them to Laura. She was surprised, and blushed, sniffing them as she accepted the posy.

'I expect you know this is the national flower of Dalnerechensk' she said. 'I wore them in my hair when I married Aleksei.'

'May I?' he suddenly asked, plucking some from the posy and threading them into her bun, then stood back to thoughtfully eye her.

She blushed deeper under his scrutiny, reaching up to tug out the flowers, adding them back into the posy. By pure chance she missed one, and Nikolai didn't tell her, following her back to their horses, watching as she tucked the flowers under a strap of the bridle before swinging up into the saddle.

'It has been such a long time since I have entertained, do come to dinner and dancing tonight' she said, turning to face him.

He bowed. 'It would be an honour' he smiled, swinging himself up into the mare's saddle.

48

Laura regretted lacing her corsets so tight, and regretted the last glass of wine she had drunk. She was out of breath, and giddy, and knew that sitting out the next few dances would be a good idea. But she couldn't bring herself to say that. The music was lively, Nikolai was an incredibly good dancer, and she had not had this much fun in over a year. Even the sour and reserved ministers had joined in the fun.

Luka and Ilich had excused themselves early after dinner and, once the wine had been flowing for an hour, shrived of the watching eye of their leaders, the other ministers had thrown reserve to the wind and joined in the dancing too. She could almost imagine that the revolution hadn't happened, that this royal prince had always been here, that Tsar Constantinovich had retired early for the night, that she had momentarily lost sight of her husband but no doubt he was around somewhere. It was a dangerous road of thought to be following.

The music finished and she bowed to Nikolai, who kissed the hand she offered him.

'You are enjoying yourself Your Highness?' she asked him, puffing.

'I am, I trust you are too?' he smiled, a high colour on his cheeks.

'Immensely' she grinned, fanning herself. She was aware that she hadn't let go of his hand, but didn't want to. 'It has been too long since I last had so much enjoyment.'

'For me too' he admitted, dropping his eyes briefly. 'Your Majesty, it would please me very greatly if you would -'

The rest of his words were cut off with her sudden cry of delight.

'Fredrik!'

The ballroom fell silent. Even the musicians paused, and Laura could feel the weight of their eyes as they swung between her, Fredrik and Nikolai. She let go of Nikolai's hand and gathered her skirts, coming forward while schooling her features. But she was unable to stop the pleasure shining through.

'My dear friend, how delightful it is to see you again!' she cried, offering him her hand.

His touch was electric, even through her glove, and her skin burned where his lips touched her.

'Your Majesty' he smiled, straightening up. 'It pleases me to see you again. I have thought of nothing but your birthday since we have been apart' he said, and to Laura's surprise, and pleasure, he spoke in Russian, his words repeated in whispers behind fluttering fans, rippling out across the ballroom.

He turned, and her heart wrenched as he let go of her hand, extending it to a beautiful woman who stood behind him, leading her forward. Her hair was dark and sensuous, her dress the colour of rubies and cut in the new mermaid style, her curves so daringly accentuated that Laura found herself staring at her shapely legs.

'Your Majesty, may I present Lilia Bellagio, esteemed soprano of the Athens Opera company' he said switching to French, and Lilia took Laura's extended hand, touching her forehead to it, curtseying low and gracefully. 'And this is Aris Paskalis, famed tenor of the same' Fredrik went on, introducing the swarthy Greek. He clicked his heels, thrust up an arm before flinging it across his waist and bowing theatrically low, his magnificent moustache bristling against her silk glove as he kissed her hand.

Aris spoke bad English, but Lilia could only speak Italian, her words lilting and musical, and Fredrik would translate for her, attentive and kind.

'It is a great pleasure to meet you' Laura said. 'I have heard so much about you. How very kind to bring such splendid singers to Dalnerechensk! We must have you sing sometime in the theatre.'

'It pleases me to say that they will, Your Majesty' Fredrik smiled. 'The Athens Opera Company, in their entirety, is here for the inaugural performance for your birthday.'

'Delightful! Splendid!' she cried, and couldn't help but notice how close Lilia stood to him when he translated her words to her.

She could feel all their eyes very deliberately not turning to focus on Nikolai. She should have introduced him before now, but she was strangely reluctant to do so. The sensible part of her was clamouring to do so, insisting that Nikolai would be appalled at this snub. Her words tripped out in a rush.

'Allow me to introduce His Royal Highness Nikolai Viktor Antonevich Vakhtangov, a distant relative of Aleksei's, who has been here these past two months' she burbled.

Fredrik bowed low.

'It is an honour to meet you at last, Your Highness' he said. 'I have heard so much about you.'

'And I you' Nikolai answered. 'Your cousin, Countess Ivanova, speaks highly and with deep regard for you.'

They know of each other Laura realised. *Of* course *they know of each other!*

'My dearest cousin speaks so highly of those she holds most dear in her heart that no one else could feel any differently' Fredrik went on and Nikolai smiled at the truth in the words.

'Tell me, Baron von Schmidt, do you fish?'

'Occasionally Your Highness.'

'Do join me one day. I believe I shall enjoy your company.'

'I accept gladly' he smiled too, bowing deeper as Nikolai took his leave, nodding to Fredrik before turning and bowing deeply to Laura, who was still flustered and out of breath.

There was curiosity in Fredrik's eyes but he was discreet enough not to mention it. He took her hand when she reached out to him again, and led her to where Gustav and Kurt were standing, watching what had happened with wide eyes. Laura greeted them, with more decorum this time, trying to force her heart rate to slow, to stop her blood from rushing around her ears so she could hear what they were saying.

'Gustav, it is good to see you again. I trust Gertrude returned safely home? How is her mother?'

'And you too, Your Majesty' he said. 'I am sad to report Gertrude's mother passed away, but with her daughter at her side. She will be cheered that you remembered her.'

'That is terrible news' Laura murmured, turning her attention to Kurt, who was straining to see everyone at the party, and knew who he was looking for. 'Kurt, how good of you to return for the opening of the theatre' she smiled.

He murmured something, distracted, and Laura took pity on him, directing Fredrik to take her for a dance. She was slightly put out that he turned to Lilia and spoke to her briefly, bowing, before leading her away, but loved the way Italian sounded on his lips.

'Tell them to play a waltz' Laura hissed in Ekaterina's ear as she slipped past her friend, knowing that a vigorous dance now would be the death of her.

The musicians complied, and Laura gratefully fell into the slow steps, surreptitiously looking around for Nikolai.

'I have missed you Fredrik' she said quietly. 'You don't know how much I looked forward to your letters.'

'I am pleased to hear that' he answered, his cheeks heating. 'I am sorry I did not write more.'

'You are here now, that is what matters' she whispered, dropping her eyes.

But his decorum stopped her from saying more. He could be nothing less than kind and attentive, but she could feel the wall of protection he had built for himself, could see the way he kept himself restrained. *And he turned up with* her…

Innocent, like a kitten Ekaterina had said. *Well she looked like a vixen now, and she was surrounded by a crowd of admirers already.* She pushed away the nastiness unhappily.

'Tell me, *Euer Hochwohlgeboren*, can you dance the *ländler?*'

He blinked, surprised. 'You know the *ländler?*'

'Ekaterina was kind enough to teach me' she smiled, stepping closer to him, waving to the musicians. 'Play *Dance Two* of Mozart's *Teutsche K. 605*' she called to them, impressing Fredrik with her knowledge of music.

He took her hand, sliding one arm around her, and Laura wished she wasn't wearing gloves so she could feel his skin against hers. *I want to dance naked with him* she thought giddily, and let him whirl her through the steps.

But it had been a mistake. The hopping, stamping liveliness of the German folk dance made her head swim crazily, and it felt like she was drowning in her ballroom. She could not catch her breath and could feel herself growing sluggish, knocking ungracefully against Fredrik.

'Your Majesty, are you alright?' he asked, concerned.

The dance finished and she bowed clumsily to him, stumbling slightly.

'Excuse me, I – I must retire – briefly' she managed to get out then turned and pushed out of the ballroom, stumbling for the stairs.

Somehow she made it up them, pressing one hand to the wall for support, swaying and gasping, her other hand tugging uselessly at her too-tight bodice.

'Your Majesty!' Roman cried, shocked when he saw her.

She pushed past him into her rooms.

'Anna!' she cried, feeling hysterical, her voice strangled and weak. 'Can't breathe! Can't -' and she fainted, crashing onto the rug.

Anna screamed, running over and dropping to her knees, shaking her.

'Roman!' she shouted.

In two great strides he was beside her, shaking Laura too.

'She's not breathing' Anna said, beginning to undo the thousands of seed pearl buttons holding her dress closed. 'I shouldn't have laced her so tight!'

Roman pushed her hands away and seized the dress, tearing it open in one great tug, sending pearls tinging and pinging off furniture in the room. Anna tugged at the knotted mess of her corset strings, picking at the tangles.

'You shouldn't see her like this' she babbled.

In an instant Roman's knife was out and he slit the silken strings of her corset, rolling her over.

'Smelling salts' he demanded, patting Laura's face gently.

Anna rushed to her dressing room, running back with a small bottle she uncorked and held under Laura's nose. He head jerked and suddenly she was coughing, sobbing in great sucking breaths, struggling feebly. Roman helped her sit up, aware that Anna had slipped a rug around her shoulders, hiding her dishevelled state from him.

'Olaf?' Laura said, dizzy. 'But, you're dead...' she trailed off, shaking her head to clear it of the muzzy cotton wool feeling.

'It's Roman, Your Majesty' he said quietly, lifting her off the floor and seating her on her chaise lounge.

'Yes of course' she said quietly, pulling the rug around her tighter, her breathing beginning to return to normal. 'Thank you. Please return to your post outside my door.'

He saluted. 'Are you sure Your Majesty?' he asked.

'Yes. Please go' she said quietly, accepting the small brandy from Anna.

Roman saluted again and slipped out of the room, closing the door behind him. Laura swallowed the liquor and leaned back against the chaise, shutting her eyes and breathing deeply.

'Did I faint in the ballroom?' she asked quietly.

'No, in your rooms Your Majesty' Anna said, taking her glass. 'Although God alone knows how you made it here. I will not lace you so tightly again, please do not ask me!'

'Alright' she soothed her friend. 'It was stupid of me to ask anyway. I don't know what I was thinking.'

She sighed, massaging the pounding headache with the hand that wasn't holding closed the rug.

What had *I been thinking?* she interrogated herself. *I'm losing control!*

She sighed again, getting carefully to her feet. The dizziness was gone, and her breathing was now slow and easy.

'Help me fasten my dress again Anna, I will return to the ball.'

'Forgive me, the dress is ruined' Anna said. 'You stopped breathing, Roman and I were desperate to revive you. He didn't see' she rushed on, assuring her.

'But what can I do? I need to go back there. Will they comment if I change dresses?'

'They will comment more if you go back in a ruined dress. Or worse, naked' she giggled. 'You should know by now Your Majesty they will comment no matter what you do.'

Laura paused then shrugged off the rug and pulled the remnants of her dress and corset off her, heading to the dressing room in her chemise. Anna followed, pulling open the large wardrobe for her. Almost unconsciously Laura reached out and fingered the Bavarian Blue dress she had been longing to wear. *I want him to see me in it* she thought, but pushed that emotion away hard.

He was so strange now, so distant. Did I imagine that moment together in the ballroom? Did I misinterpret the want in his voice? Her hand fell away from the dress. *I need to be sure...*

'Anna, wake up a seamstress, and give her this dress' she said suddenly, pulling Fredrik's dress out of the wardrobe. 'Give her a picture of that Gibson Girl in the mermaid dress, the one whose husband just shot a man, what is her name... Evelyn Nesbit. If you can't find a picture ask any one of the soldiers, I don't doubt they would have one. This is to be re-cut in that new style, ready as soon as possible' she said. 'And get me one of those swan-bill corsets to wear with it.'

'Yes Your Majesty' Anna giggled, folding a new corset around her, tugging it into shape.

With Anna's help she struggled into a new dress, refreshed her make-up, fixed her hair, and dabbled on perfume. She looked at herself carefully in the mirror, turning this way and that in the green dress, fanning herself with the black lace fan. Sober now, and more comported, she headed back to the stairs where she found Fredrik and Nikolai waiting worriedly for her.

'Are you in good health?' Nikolai asked in French for the benefit of Fredrik, bowing low as she appeared.

'Yes yes, just a moment of sickness. I'm afraid the wine is quite strong tonight' she flushed prettily, sliding her hand into the crook of his elbow.

'That is a relief' Fredrik said. 'You looked so pale, I thought -' he broke off, not finishing his sentence.

Laura turned and allowed Nikolai to lead her back to the ballroom, Fredrik following two paces behind. She had been gone less than an hour, but rumour and malice had done its work. She smiled charmingly, and tried to ignore the fluttering fans, the stares and the twisted smiles.

49

Laura woke to the sounds of Anna running water into a bath for her. Excitedly she pushed back the covers and rushed into the bathroom, greeting her warmly.

'Happy birthday, Your Majesty' she smiled, coming forward to help her disrobe.

Laura sank into the hot water, sighing in bliss. She had precious few moments to herself this day, but she couldn't stop the excited butterflies with the thought of the day's festivities. She washed and dressed quickly, skipping down to the nursery to greet Alexandra.

She was standing in her crib, holding on to the rails and wailing in hunger when she arrived. Laura lifted her out, kissing her head quickly, and took her down to the dining room, seating her in the carved high chair that now sat beside hers under the royal canopy.

It was early, but the table was crowded with Ministers and Vakhtangovs alike, who rose and bowed, with varying degrees of respect – but all at the correct height, she noted – when she arrived. She waved them back to their food, thanking those who wished her happy birthday, and sat, accepting a small side of cut meat from a servant.

Alexandra wiggled impatiently, and Laura fed her while she ate herself, letting her eyes glide over those seated around the table. Nikolai and Fredrik were seated together, quite near to the centre, and Ekaterina was with her younger cousins, seated further along. Maksim and Luka were sitting closely too, across the table from each other, and Ilich lurked in a chair near the door, drinking heavily.

When Alexandra was full Laura gave her to Marie, instructing her to dress her daughter in royal colours. Laura quickly ate a few more bites herself, then rushed upstairs to dress in full regalia. Anna worked fast, pinning her hair into a fantastic creation, perching the feminine crown on top. She wore Jagna's black diamonds, the only jewellery she had that had belonged to the royals before her, and a royal blue sash across her body. Anna helped her into the thick ermine robe of state, securing it to her shoulders, brushing away any loose strands of fur.

Laura headed down the stairs carefully, Anna and Roman trailing after her, both trying to carry the heavy mantle for her. She could hear the noise of the early morning crowd already, loud and festive even before the guards in the entrance hall opened the doors to the courtyard.

A gleaming open coach sat at the bottom of the stairs, the team of six horses sporting royal plumes from their bridles. Peter Kamanin, resplendent in the uniform for the commander of the army opened the door to the carriage and Roman lifted her gently inside, helping Anna to arrange the mantle around her, pooling it on the floor.

Maksim swung himself into the carriage and sat opposite her. It was a role neither of them relished, but he was the Prime Minister. To not be with her, to send some other junior minister, would be an insult. So they traded impersonal and flippant pleasantries, watching as the honour guard took up positions around them. Marie handed Alexandra, dressed in a sweet blue coat, to Laura, who kissed her cheek to soothe her, as she was looking wide-eyed around her, starting at the noise from the crowds.

Roman had insisted on riding behind the carriage, a position that should have been given to a junior guard, while he had taken his rightful place beside his commanding officer at the head of the honour guard. *There still are pockets of resentment* he had explained. *If any attack comes I want to see it coming, and I want to be close, to do something about it.* Peter Kamanin had agreed reluctantly, and headed the column of riders alone.

The trumpets atop the gate to Vsevolod's Way blew, and the crowd roared in delight. Drummers struck up a beat and marched out into the road. Laura couldn't remember if the old Palace Guard had had a military band, but the new army seemed full of musicians, and quite competent ones at that. Peter Kamanin followed them, the column of soldiers following him.

Alexandra gave a little, worried mewl when the carriage jerked, but Laura soothed her, kissing her cheeks and holding her up, letting her stand on her thighs so she could see the crowds. She was pleased to see she wasn't crying, even though it must have been quite frightening for her. *She will take to royal duties like a duck to water* she smiled.

Vsevolod's Way was jammed with people, so many that some were in danger of being caught by the carriage wheels and crushed underneath. It was stupefying, not even on her wedding day had so many people lined the streets to see her. She was sure that the hamlets and villages of Dalnerechensk were completely empty; they were all standing on the streets of the capital.

And they were all calling Happy Birthday *in English* she realised, the words sounding strange from tongues not used to speaking them. She blew kisses to them all, waving at the children, one hand firmly around Alexandra's middle to stop her tumbling off her lap.

They made good progress in spite of the press of the crowd forcing them to drive at no more than a walking pace. The procession was smaller than her wedding one had been, and it managed to weave through the streets of Dalnerechensk in less than two hours. Still, the drive had been too long for Alexandra, who was red-faced and wailing with discomfort, and nothing Laura could do would soothe her.

Marie took her quickly and sympathetically, whisking her up to the nursery for peace and quiet and a bottle of milk. Laura stood and waited for Roman to dismount, coming forward to help her down from the carriage. She could feel tension in him, his eyes quartering the courtyard, and he didn't help pick up her train, leaving Anna to struggle with it alone.

Fear pushed deep into her stomach but she ignored it, smiling, and led the way into the castle, heading to Parliament Chambers. Ministers who had not been part of the official procession followed her in, taking their usual places in the benches. Behind them came a crowd of foreign attachés, secretaries and adjutants, and a whole army of servants carrying boxes, scrolls and even one with some kind of strange contraption.

Laura sat herself gingerly on Vsevolod's throne, knowing – from painful experience – that the weight of the state robes could topple the rather light chair and send the unbalanced occupant sprawling. It gave her no comfort to know it had done the same for virtually every other occupant that had sat here before her. Anna quickly pooled the material at her feet and walked backwards down the steps of the dais on which she sat.

In the three hours that followed Fedor announced hundreds of dignitaries who presented many fantastic presents on behalf of the ruling families of Europe, or indeed around the world. His Majesty The Emperor of Japan had sent her a chest full of blue and green silk, and one bolt of yellow, almost hidden at the bottom of the chest. Laura noticed it was Romanov yellow, and wondered if this was a nod to the small Principality's defeat of Russia, from one victorious nation to another.

Armand Fallières, President of France, had sent her a whole cellar full of rare vintages from Bordeaux and Champagne; Wilhelm II of Germany had sent her the luxurious pelts of eighteen various animals, including a bear and a wolf. King Edward of England had sent her a complete silver dinner set for a table of two hundred and even President Theodore Roosevelt had sent her an automobile: a Model F from the Ford Motor Company. Tsar Nicholas II had sent her one of Fabergé's beautiful jewel encrusted eggs and she was delighted, upon opening it, to discover an enamelled duck sitting on a lake of aquamarine. It was mechanical, and dibbed its head in quite a realistic way, waggling its tail in pleasure. It had all the technical mastery and beauty of the famous swan egg that Nicholas had presented to his wife the previous Easter. Laura loved it.

Her presents from the Principality were by no means any less dazzling. There was a tin model of Dalnerechensk, painted and delightfully detailed, and dazzling in its accuracy. The streets bustled with people at the Harvest Moon Festival, and there was even a tiny child clinging to the topmost branches of the trees on the Western flank. Maksim presented her with a delicately engraved vase of Austrian crystal, snidely remarking that he hoped it lasted longer than the last two vases she had been displeased with.

She was given more jewels than she could count, and fine boxes made of rare and precious woods to keep them in; dresses and furniture; even a gramophone with a collection of vinyl platters. Gustav had presented her, blushingly, the bound book he had made of the study of Dalnerechensk's flora, and Laura praised the beauty of his drawings and the meticulous French explanations. Finally Jurek Titov stepped forward and presented Laura with a large, bulky object which he called a Kinetograph.

'It is, Your Majesty, the machine that produced the first ever moving pictures in Dalnerechensk' he announced proudly. 'I wish I could present to you the Kinetoscope, but alas it is being used in the new theatre to screen that first film.'

'We are all impatient to see it' Laura smiled. 'Would you demonstrate it for us this evening?'

'Of course Your Majesty' he bowed.

Laura smiled then turned to address the assembled guests.

'Thank you all so much for the wonderful presents. Please do all join me in the dining hall for luncheon.'

She rose and the room bowed, waiting until she had left the room before straightening. As she passed Nikolai she stopped and extended her hand to him, letting him lead her, with a quick kiss to her hand, to the dining hall, seating her under the royal canopy.

Ekaterina had ensured the modest six-course luncheon would not detract from the gastronomic thirteen course seating that had been planned for that evening. Small though it may have been it still took over two hours to finish, and Laura was impatient to get on with the rest of her birthday celebrations. When the last dish had been cleared a fanfare played and Ekaterina appeared, curtseying deeply before her.

'Your Majesty, please do allow me to present to you the first of many surprises for your birthday' she announced, then ushered in a gaggle of village children, who were star-struck in the presence of the assembled dignitaries.

Ekaterina and the music teacher managed to get them singing for her, though it started badly. But by the end the children had slipped into their well-rehearsed routine, and it was a pleasant end to the lunch. Laura spoke to all eighteen of them individually, and they left, giggling to each other and bobbing a hundred small curtseys on the way.

There was a shout, scattering the girls, and an armoured knight rode into the hall, brandishing a sword. His horse reared impressively, forelegs pawing at the air, and crashed down on the flagstones. Peter Kamanin raised his visor, announced he was Ilya Muromets and challenged men to joust for honour and the favour of their tsaritsa, reaching down to pull her up onto the saddle behind him.

She laughed as they cantered out into the courtyard, rounding the back of the castle. Here, before the blooming gardens, a medieval tilt yard had been erected, complete with a viewing gallery with two viewing towers, one each end of the yard. In the middle was a carved throne, draped in cushions and furs to make it comfortable for her to sit and watch the activities. Near the walls of the castle bright tents had been erected, most of them sporting several horses, breastplates, helmets and jousting sticks with their ends padded.

Laura slipped to the ground, Peter's firm arm letting her down gently, and perched quickly on the throne, the dignitaries and Parliament filling the seats in the gallery. Although there were very few men who were young and athletic enough to participate in jousting, there were, nevertheless, many who indulged in their boyhood fantasies and rode again and again against each other.

Guards had laid down thick sawdust layers over the gravel of the yard and the padded ends of the lances greatly reduced the injuries. They rode with no stirrups, and only those most skilful in the saddle managed to retain their seats. Not surprisingly it was the young and most reckless who were the most successful, but even they did not escape without bruises and pains. Laura was sorely tempted to ride herself, it looked like so much fun.

After the jousting there was just enough time to refresh in her rooms, changing her dress for one more suited to the banquet, donning a number of jewels. Anna unpinned her hair and refastened it in a new creation, threading yet more jewels into her locks. Laura wore the enamel medal for the Order of Vsevolod and the blue sash across her body, knowing that this was mostly an official engagement as well as a personal one.

She heard laughter inside the dining room when she reached it and paused to listen. Nikolai and Fredrik were comparing battle wounds, laughing as they recounted how each had been received. Laura pushed open the door and they stopped, bowing to her. She smiled, and offered her hand to Nikolai, who took it gently, leading her down to her seat. Laura would have dearly loved to have given her hand to Fredrik, but Nikolai outranked him, and she could not snub this man.

Perhaps it is best she told herself, trying to remember how cold and distant he seemed now. But she pushed that unhappy thought away too.

She managed a smile and Nikolai sat her under the royal canopy, Fredrik taking his leave to sit with Kurt, who looked unhappy, and Ekaterina, who was as smiling and charming as Laura remembered her. *Maybe she has forgotten herself so much she has remembered her old self* she thought, smiling at the idea.

Despite their early start the extravagant courses took five hours to complete and the hands were lagging towards eleven when they finished. Laura had only seen such finery and complexity in the confectionary on her wedding day, and wondered if Ekaterina had employed a new chef for the occasion, as they had when she had married.

She excused herself from her company, heading upstairs to change yet again for her outing to the new theatre, marvelling at how ridiculous this seemed. She saw to her toilette and then tiptoed into the nursery to kiss her sleeping daughter, stroking her soft skin with the backs of her fingers. Alexandra nuzzled her unconsciously and Laura smiled, kissing her again before heading down to the courtyard, hugging her stole around her shoulders.

Roman and Nikolai were waiting patiently for her to join them. Most of the other ministers and dignitaries had left already, and only the drunk and sleepy stragglers were left. Laura couldn't stop herself glancing around for Fredrik, but was able to stop herself from looking disappointed when she realised he wasn't there.

'The night is chill Your Majesty, would you care to drive rather than take a carriage?' Nikolai asked, taking the hand she offered him.

She agreed, and Roman shifted uneasily. Protocol dictated he could not ride in the carriage with them and the horses were skittish with the new machines, especially the brown mare. It would be horribly undignified to run alongside the carriage, getting breathless and hot, and unable to see the other side of the street, where any assassin could be hiding.

'You must teach me how to operate the Model F' Laura said when Nikolai opened the door for her, helping her up into the phaeton.

'It would be my pleasure' he smiled, eyeing Roman in surprise when he leapt onto the running board, gripping his rifle tightly.

The carriage rocked slightly as Spanov took up station on the other side of the carriage and Nikolai said nothing, cranking the engine over before climbing into the front seat and releasing the brake.

The short ride to the refurbished grain warehouses was in silence, but Laura could hear the excited buzz of people outside the theatre. They alighted, meeting a nervous Jurek Titov at the doors, who bowed deeply before them. A thin red ribbon had been stretched across the double doors of the theatre and the expectant crowd turned to face the newly arrived royals.

Laura was a little shocked to discover Kurt was not standing on the steps, beaming and proud of his investment. She caught Gustav's eye, who shook his head almost imperceptively, making an apologetic face. She couldn't see Fredrik either, and turned away, taking the scissors that Petrovich Kamanin gladly handed to her. She made a short speech, mindful of everyone's impatient desire to see the theatre, being careful to stress Kurt's modesty as the patron of the theatre.

She cut the ribbon to wild applause and followed Petrovich Kamanin into the elegant entrance hall, aware that the crowd of dignitaries and the upper echelons of Dalnerechensk society were jostling each other in their rush to see the refurbishment.

The entrance hall was narrow but long, running the entire length of the building. On one side was a small ticket booth where a proud attendant stood beaming in his blue and gold uniform. Rich green carpet stretched between the ticket booth and a wide set of stairs at the other end, which led to the balconies and the boxes. Directly opposite the entrance doors were three sets of double doors, decorated with gold rococo acanthus leaves. Above each door was a small plaque with Stalls A, B and C written in bold black letters. Two uniformed attendants stood each side of the doors and they all bowed respectfully before the two standing at the middle doors reached forward to pull them open for their guests.

The theatre itself was no less opulent, with red velvet seats and gold painted details, the heavy red velvet curtains of the stage closed. Jurek Titov and Petrovich Kamanin led the royals and their guards, Ekaterina and Gustav, Maksim and Tatiana through the auditorium to the stage, ushering them through the backstage area and along the narrow gantries, pointing out the mechanism for raising and lowering sets, including the newly finished canvas screen for moving pictures. Far below them Laura could hear the rustling of murmured excitement as the seats filled with people.

Laura praised the theatre, marvelling at the beautiful design and the impressive mechanics, making Petrovich Kamanin grin till the top of his head threatened to fall off. They made their way back down to the stage where Jurek Titov bowed nervously in front of Laura.

'It pleases me greatly to show you the projection room Your Majesty, Your Highness, but I regret that the room is rather small and cramped' he said apologetically, leading them to a narrow set of stairs in the main foyer.

Laura dismissed both her guards despite Roman's protest, giving them leave to watch the screening in the auditorium. She and Nikolai climbed the narrow stairs, and greeted Jurek's assistant, who stood to attention in the small, dark room, sweating with nervousness. He bowed over and over until Jurek kindly brushed him aside, bringing a film reel over for the royals to admire.

'Celluloid is a wonderful invention' Nikolai said, pulling a length of the film from the reel and holding it up to the light so Laura could see the little frames of pictures.

She was disappointed to see that all the pictures were still, as she had somehow expected to see them move, almost as if by magic.

'It doesn't move?' she said, confused.

'Allow me' Nikolai said, handing the reel to Jurek, who surreptitiously tried to check the celluloid for any damage before wrestling it back onto the bulky object that took up a large portion of the room. A lamp at the front of the contraption was aimed out a small, square hole cut into the wall, and there was a second hole cut close to the first, allowing the projectionist to easily see if the image was projecting correctly.

From his pocket Nikolai pulled out a disk with leather straps attached each side. A painted red cardinal with outstretched wings adorned the front of the disk; a golden cage the back.

'It is an optical illusion' Nikolai explained, spinning the disk. 'You are shown the images so fast it appears as if they move.'

'Well, not exactly' Jurek hastened to correct him.

Laura, fearing another technical lecture was about to begin, hastily said: 'We would be most grateful if you would show us this moving picture.'

Jurek blinked, caught off-guard, then he and his assistant tripped over each other to comply. Jurek signalled wildly out the small window and after a small pause there was an excited flutter of noise from the crowd. Nikolai guided her to the small hole beside the large machine.

'Look out through here' he said quietly, and she stepped closer to him, hardly aware of the lamp of the kinetoscope spluttering to life.

The curtains of the stage had been drawn back revealing a white screen. Below them, in the darkened auditorium Laura caught sight of Fredrik and Kurt. Fredrik's hand was on the boy's shoulder and he had leaned close to speak quietly to him. *Whatever he is saying it was not congratulations* Laura realised. Kurt looked upset, even in the dark, and she could tell he wasn't really listening to his older brother. Fredrik's face was stern, and while she knew his words could never be harsh, it was unsettling to see him so grim.

A flicker on the screen caused an excited tremor of response in the audience and an attendant quickly announced, from the little stage to the left of the screen that also held the latest Bechstein upright piano, that they were going to watch the first motion film made in Dalnerechensk. Another ripple went through the crowd, and they gasped as an image of the castle appeared on the screen.

It was autumn, as far as Laura could tell from the black and white images, and before the revolution, the Vakhtangov flag above the castle was snapping back and forward in the breeze. *It* was *magical* Laura thought. *Even with the machine clicking and whirring beside me as he turns the handle, even knowing how it was done, it's magical.*

The screen suddenly went black and the words "A magnificent occasion" appeared. Several excited patrons shouted them out, and even Laura felt her own lips move to form the words. A picture appeared again and she cried out in shock, grabbing Nikolai's hand. There was an equally loud gasp from the auditorium as Aleksei and Laura appeared, standing in their wedding clothes at the top of the cathedral's steps.

'Forgive me!' Jurek said. 'Stop turning!' he hissed frantically at his assistant.

'No. Keep going' Laura instructed quietly.

There was a hesitation, then the clicking and whirring of the crank started again. Aleksei unfroze on the screen, turning to look at her as they waved at the ecstatic crowd. Tears welled up in Laura's eyes in the dark room. *I never knew he had looked at me with such love in his eyes then* she sniffed. *I had forgotten what that glance looked like.*

On the screen she and Aleksei, slightly too fast to be natural, walked down the stairs and after some awkward manoeuvring because of the way their hands were tied together from the hand fastening ceremony, they were seated in the waiting carriage. She threw the bouquet of flowers she had with her, and blew kisses to the crowd before the procession moved off, riding out of the frame. The mounted guard of soldiers followed them, and the crowd surged into the vacant places, waving their handkerchiefs and hats after the carriage.

Laura moved to mop her face with her sleeve, forgetting she was still holding tightly onto Nikolai's hand. Quickly she let him go, mumbling an apology, and wiped away her tears, sniffing loudly. Wordlessly Nikolai handed her his handkerchief and she took it, wiping her eyes again.

The rest of the reel was very short, showing her arrival by train back in Dalnerechensk with her daughter and the von Schmidt family, and Laura's heart did another little flutter when she saw Fredrik step down from the train, so handsome and refined in his movements. She wondered how he felt seeing himself on the screen.

The picture disappeared and thunderous applause broke out in the auditorium, breaking her out of her reverie.

'Are you alright?' Nikolai asked quietly.

'It was such a shock to see him again' she said, lowering her eyes and dabbing at more tears.

She suddenly noticed that they were alone in the room, and eyed Nikolai, surprised.

'I sent them away' he shrugged by way of explanation.

'Did you operate this?' she asked, surprised.

'Yes, it is quite easy' he said. 'When I travelled to Paris I often spent time in Georges Méliès' theatre, and he was kind enough to allow me to frequently visit his studio in Montreuil.'

From below them in the auditorium a voice rose above the hubbub.

'Again!' it cried. 'Again! Again!'

People around them took up the cry. Without saying a word Nikolai pulled the reel from the machine and swapped its place with the empty reel, threading it through the machine carefully. Rather than watch the screen again Laura stepped closer, studying the whirring, clicking sections as it pulled the perforated strip of celluloid past the lamp, winding it onto the reel again. Nikolai stepped aside and she turned the crank, stopping when the tail flap of celluloid came free and slapped against the machine.

There was a timid knock on the door.

'If it pleases Your Majesty, Your Highness, I have another moving picture to show you' Jurek said, carefully pushing open the door.

Laura smiled when she saw him eye the Kinetoscope carefully, inspecting it not so subtly for any damage.

'We shall watch in the auditorium' she said, extending her hand to Nikolai, who took it, leading her towards the royal box.

He held her chair for her as she sat, then sat beside her, pulling the chair closer to hers. He then surprised her by taking her hand in the darkness, stroking the back of her gloved fingers comfortingly. She wondered if she should pull her hand away, but it was nice to sit here and feel the touch of another human being.

The Bechstein piano rattled into life, tinkling through the accompaniment of *Jack and the Beanstalk*. The crowd watched, enrapt, and

Laura gaped at the fairy who appeared and disappeared as if by magic. She let Nikolai's hand go for her applause at the end.

'Did you enjoy the Kinetoscope?' Petrovich Kamanin asked worriedly, appearing behind them in the entrance to her box.

'It is the most magical piece of technology I have seen' Laura said, surprised she felt so composed now. 'When does the theatre open for the public?'

'Tomorrow. We have three exciting moving pictures to show them -'

'Please make the screenings free of charge for the next three days' Laura said, holding out her hand to Nikolai again. 'I would encourage everyone to see the pictures. They really are astounding.'

'As you command, Your Majesty' he bowed, and Laura let the Vakhtangov prince lead her down to where her guards and the automobile were waiting.

50

It's so quiet Laura thought, gazing out over the valleys of the Principality. The air was still, and the balloon barely drifted on the end of its tether. *I am standing on air...*

She had been terrified, and shook noticeably when Nikolai had helped her up the steps to climb into the wicker basket beneath the helium-filled balloon. But she had smiled and talked pleasantly with the servants who were untying the mooring ropes, who were passing in hampers and baskets to take into the air with them. She had held on, her knuckles white, as she saw the faces of those on the ground drift further away from her.

But the fear had gradually subsided as the wonder of what she was seeing stole over her. To look down on mountains, to see all of her Principality, laid out like some living model, was marvellous to behold. She could see Russia, and far away on the horizons she could see the smoky smudges of towns and villages. *Russia had always seemed so far away* she mused. *Even just over our borders it had been so far away. Not like it seems now...*

Nikolai came to stand beside her, breaking into her thoughts. She smiled at him before turning back to the view, gazing down at the castle far below her. The tiltyard that had adorned the gardens yesterday had been dismantled that morning and some busy activity was happening in the ballroom. Laura was pleased, the newly re-cut dress of Bavarian Blue had arrived that morning, she would wear it for Fredrik tonight as they danced.

Ekaterina's festivities had centred around the theme of water for the second day of her birthday celebrations. They had bobbed for apples in the

262

palace fountains, raced toy boats down the river and ate a large banquet of seafood for lunch – rare delicacies that Laura had never sampled before, even living in the port city of Boston. Nikolai had then taken her into his air balloon, showing her all her empire as the sun sank towards the horizon.

He took another step closer to her, laying his hand on hers on the edge of the wicker side of the basket.

'You're not so frightened now' he said quietly, a statement rather than a question.

'No' she confirmed, letting his fingers twine around hers.

She looked away briefly, at the small, folding table where they had shared a meal and champagne, at the stools where they had sat while the day had waned around them. They had brought no servants with them, and had spent the afternoon in candid and unguarded conversation. It had been rather special, these few hours together, but Laura couldn't help but feel a small pang of jealousy. Nikolai had taken Tatiana ballooning on his first day in the Principality; he hadn't needed a special occasion to take her.

But she pushed that thought away as he moved closer, tilting his lips towards her. Laura turned her face up to him, wondering how many people had eye glasses trained on them, wondering briefly if Fredrik was one of them. The thought was given a jolt with the gentle pressure of Nikolai's lips on hers, his hand taking hold of her arm gently.

Laura couldn't help analysing the kiss. It was the right moment for it, with the sunset colouring the landscape beneath them in dusky lavenders and roses. It was romantic, but it wasn't spontaneous or passionate. There was an element of – of what? Calculation? Possibly. It was what was right and should happen at this moment.

He would do what was right in our marriage, and be dutiful too. She could tell that from his kiss. There was attraction there, no doubt. His kiss was soft and almost tender; he would be caring, gentle and attentive – even fond and loving, in a way – in their lives together. *He would try to make me happy.*

But there was no passion a small part of her whispered. There had been more passion, more *want* in the way Fredrik had whispered her name that night in the ballroom, than in Nikolai's kiss. She wondered what making love to him would be like, then flushed at the thought, breaking away from him. Her eye caught by the bright flash of sunlight reflecting off glass below her. *Who had watched them kiss? Was Fredrik watching her? What would he make of it?*

She shut her eyes at that. *If he still loves me, that kiss would have broken him in two.*

'Do you sail Laura?' Nikolai suddenly asked.

'What? Sail? No' she said, confused by the question.

'I do. I adore it. My grandfather loved to sail, he would always take me with him. I learned my love of the sea from him. Do you know why ships must be careful when they pass close by?'

She blinked, having difficulty following the flow of his thoughts. 'No I do not.'

He touched the gravy boat and the mustard boat on the table, pushing them into roughly parallel lines.

'When they are close, the water between them becomes calm, and the water on the outside of the boats has more of an effect on them. If captains do not make clear and conscious decisions, the outside forces slowly push them together' he slid the serving boats past each other, gradually pushing them closer until they grazed each other with a metallic scratching sound.

He's not stupid Laura told herself. He knows the political pressure I am under to marry him. It would fix so many things; he would get the throne, Dalnerechensk could keep her, and they would have the male heir they craved. Any more children Laura would have would be of the blood too, heirs and spares to safeguard the throne.

'Dearest Nikolai, you are kind and thoughtful and – and attractive' she faulted briefly 'I most certainly am fond of you. But let's not be pushed into this. We will make the conscious decisions, not have them forced on us. Should we wed it would be our choice; should we not, that is ours too.'

He smiled and kissed her again, and Laura couldn't help thinking there was more passion in his relief than there had been before. She broke away again.

'But it is not so simple Nikolai' she sighed unhappily. 'We are sailing in the tempests of duty and public opinion -'

'I know' he sighed. 'But there is a solution that may be agreeable to us both. I have a son, and you have a daughter…' he trailed off. 'If there must be a marriage, why not them?'

Laura blinked at him, reeling in shock. *You don't want to marry me?!* she wanted to ask him. She was both relieved and affronted. *He should want to marry me, and if our children are betrothed we can never marry. But we can marry others.* She stopped. *Could I really arrange my daughter's life to suit mine? Promise her to a man she barely knows so that I can have what I want? What if she doesn't like Ilya? I don't want her to be a pawn in the games of politics…*

Laura pushed aside her hot indignation and looked at Nikolai carefully; at a man still in love with the wife he had lost, at a man who had no wish to be pushed into something he was not ready for, despite the charms of a new bride. *Despite my charms* she smiled softly, feeling a deep understanding open between them, something that would be unfathomable to others.

'There is yet another solution' she said gently. 'A political union that does not need a marriage.'

'You speak of co-regency' Nikolai said.

'Yes. I shall share the throne with you, completely and equally. I shall make the announcement when Parliament meets again.'

'You honour me' he said, taking her hand and kissing it.

'Indeed, you shall have new honours too' she smiled impishly. 'Dalnerechensk finds herself in need of an Admiral for her Navy.'

Nikolai blinked, caught off guard, then the valleys rang with his laughter.

51

They had stared. She had stared too, turning back and forwards in front of the mirror, shocked that she was daring to wear something so scandalously tight. She felt naked, and restricted, and somehow wonderously free at the same time. The swan's corset she wore made her stand with her breasts pushed forward and her hips jutting backwards, her backside pert and noticeably more round. Fredrik's dress hugged at her, accentuating every curve she had, and she wore no gloves, jewels dripping from her throat and wrists.

Anna had twisted long strands of pearls into her hair, weaving and plaiting a fantastic coif that had taken nearly an hour to complete. Delicate branches of fiery coral were also pinned in her locks, and she carried a fan of the same colour, every inch a beautiful mermaid come to life.

Fredrik had stared, though he had tried hard not to. He had called her Undine and Lorelei while they had danced, and in the silences where his eyes said so much her heart sung and stung at the tender gentleness, the unbearable sadness in his manner.

Ekaterina had outdone the decoration of the ballroom – it was draped with shimmery blue, green and silver material, long thin strips that waved in the hot air, making everything look like it took place at the bottom of the sea. There were fishing nets and hunks of coral, shallow troughs in which candles and lily leaves floated, and seats designed like giant clam shells lined the walls.

Many of her guests had come in nautical fancy dress: there were pirates and fishermen, sailors and smugglers, mermaids and sirens and a whole array of other fantastic creatures of the deep. Laura was surprised how many wives and daughters of the court had the new Gibson Girl inspired dresses, then realised that they had been in fashion for several years now, but they had had to wait until Laura wore hers before they could do the same.

Most of all she danced with Nikolai, and noted the relaxed change between them almost immediately. She had teasingly called him Admiral and he had smilingly called her cousin, while fans and tongues wagged around them.

The eastern rise of Liberty Valley was picked out against the soft pink of coming dawn when they retired from the dancing. Laura awkwardly made her way up the stairs, still unused to the restriction of the new style of dress and pushed open the door to her empty room.

Anna was gone, and Laura was desperately in need of a bath, and someone to help her unfasten her hair. She dithered a bit before opening her door again, instructing Roman to send maids with pails of boiling water to her room. She waited until the bathtub had been filled then opened the door again, calling Roman's name.

'Anna is not here, I cannot do this myself' she whispered, closing the door behind them.

His hands twisted on the rifle, and he swallowed hard, eyeing her. She looked away, stepping over to her vanity where she sat down, eyeing Roman in her mirror, who had not moved. She turned her head and raised her arms, trying to find the hundreds of pins that secured her hair, aware of the effect the shape of her body was having on him.

Haltingly he crossed to her, his face dark, his hands twisting the rifle hard. He set it down, leaning it against her dressing table, ready to grab again should he need to, and his hands shook as he reached for her dark tresses. She half expected him to be rough, but there was tenderness in the gentle way he found the pins and unwound the strings of pearls. She shut her eyes, massaging her temples as the release of tension from the tight coif made her light headed.

My hair must feel terrible she thought. *It's soaked with sweat, yuck!* But Roman didn't seem to mind, gently laying down all the jewels and bits of coral before her on the vanity, his thumb surreptitiously stroking a lock still captured in her hairstyle. His breath was hard but carefully measured, his mouth working as he fought with himself, swallowing hard against the words stuck in his throat. Laura knew what he wanted to ask, to do, but knew asking him to unbutton her dress would be dangerous. Still, she had no idea how she was going to get it off without help.

Roman laid the last of her jewels on her vanity, his hands working as he forced them down to his sides, still unable to say anything.

'Take this, it is one of a set, everyone saw me wearing them tonight' she said, selecting a large sapphire she placed in his hand. His fingers closed over hers, his touch hot and urgent, but at the same time he tried to push her hand away. 'Let someone see you with it, brag about it even' she went on.

'I can't do this anymore' he said, interrupting her.

'You must' she said simply.

'I can't -'

'You will.'

She managed to extract her fingers and turned away from him, dismissing him. For an instant she wondered if he was going to disobey, if he was going to lose control of himself completely, but he took the rifle, his fist tight around the jewel, and he slipped back out into the corridor, shutting her door behind him.

She sighed with relief and crossed to her dressing room, managing to undo the buttons of her dress after some undignified contortions. She tugged undone the strings of her corset and groaned out loud as she straightened up, massaging her lower back as she stepped into the hot water, removing her chemise and sinking down gratefully.

It had been a long time since she had washed her own hair, and she delighted in massaging more of the tension out of her head, tipping ewer after ewer of water over her head to wash out the suds.

'Laura?' Ekaterina suddenly called from inside her sitting room.

She gasped in surprise, pulling her knees up and folding her arms across her chest, feeling fluttery and embarrassed.

'I am bathing!' she called back, hoping her dear friend would not push open the door and see her naked, see her scars.

'Well done Laura, you looked stunning last night. Roman is standing guard with an erection he can sling his rifle from' she grinned, and Laura heard her moving something about.

She jumped out of the bathtub and didn't bother drying herself, wrapping her robe around her body and fastening it tightly. Ekaterina was sitting on her chaise lounge when she stepped out cautiously, her feet propped up on a chest she had with her. *It didn't seem to have much effect on your cousin* she wanted to say, but held her tongue.

'What is in the chest?' she asked instead.

'Your costume for tonight' Ekaterina grinned.

Laura grinned too, and knelt, pushing aside Ekaterina's feet. But the chest was locked fast.

'Where is the key?'

'That you will find in the course of the day' she laughed. 'Come come, dress in your riding habit, Odin is going hunting today.' She patted her hand and stood, heading for the door.

Odin Laura thought. *King of the gods of the Vikings and the Teutonic tribes, from whom the Russians and the Germans claim as their distant ancestors. Clever Ekaterina has something stunning planned for this evening* she mused, smoothing back her wet hair. *I must get dressed!*

Anna arrived, surprised to see Laura up and wet from a bath, but quickly helped her dress, pinning her hair back simply. Laura avoided looking at Roman as she headed up to the nursery, greeting Alexandra who stood in her crib, bouncing with excitement when she saw her.

'Hello precious one!' Laura smiled, lifting her out of the crib, planting kisses on her plump cheeks as she carried her down to the dining room.

Alexandra burbled away in her own language, talking to people only she saw in her imagination, hugging at Laura's neck. She seated her daughter in the high chair and greeted those who were already at the table. Most of them were already dressed in various hunting attire as well, all eager for the day's festivities. *I should spend astronomical amounts on frivolous entertainments more often* she thought wryly. *I have never been so popular with the snobbish Vakhtangov family and the rest of the court...*

Gustav, Fredrik and Ekaterina joined her, calling good morning, all looking fresh and smart in riding attire, despite the little sleep they had all had. Again Laura wondered briefly where Kurt was, who seemed particularly mopey since returning to the Principality, but she pushed away the thought and greeted Nikolai when he joined her with Ilya. The small boy gave Alexandra a soft toy, and Laura couldn't help but feel this was a childish courtship gesture.

She pushed away the discomfort that gave her, and chatted pleasantly with the court, finally returning her daughter to the nursery when she had eaten her fill. Nikolai followed her, depositing his son into the welcoming embrace of Marie Borodina, kissing him warmly and wishing him a good day before following Laura back down to the stables.

A sharp hunting horn blast startled them and Peter Kamanin, dressed in fur robes and crowned with magnificent stag antlers, rode into the courtyard, brandishing a silver horn.

'Who dares ride with The Wild Hunt?' he cried, his voice bellowing easily above the hubbub in the courtyard. 'Who rides with Wodan and his army? The Valkyries? The Fair Folk? Heroes? Lost Souls and the Damned? Who dares for wealth unimaginable? Who defies me shall catch me, and be richly rewarded!' he shouted, and spurred his horse out of the castle gates.

Laura leapt into the saddle of her stallion, spurring it after him, the rest of the host falling thunderously into the chase behind her. Peter was already far ahead of her, and she knew he would not play some coy game designed to be caught easily; he so rarely got to test his skills that catching him would indeed be a worthy prize. She rose in the stirrups, ducking under a branch as they swerved into the Hunting Forest, the cries and shouts of the others ringing around them.

Fredrik, Gustav, Luka and Nikolai managed to keep up with her, and some deft manoeuvring saw Nikolai's charger slip into the lead of the pursuers, spurring his horse faster, trying to get in front of Peter Kamanin. Laura turned her stallion to the west, surprising those near her, who shouted for her to join the hunt again. But Peter, to avoid Nikolai, had also turned his stallion to the west, and Laura intercepted him, daringly grabbing his reins and yanking sharply, bringing them both to a stop.

Peter laughed, forgetting himself, then saluted her, grinning, the disappointment of the others ringing in their ears.

'It has been a long time since there was a Commander in Chief worthy of that title' Peter said, slipping off his headdress and tying it to her saddle. 'It is an honour to serve one now. I will follow you anywhere you lead' He saluted her again.

'Thank you Peter, that is kind of you to say' she said, while the others of the hunt applauded her success.

'That was very daring of you' Nikolai remarked, impressed. 'Countess Ivanova has instructed that I take you to the gorge. I do not know where that is, but she assured me you would.'

Laura answered that she did, surprised that Ekaterina would instruct Nikolai to take her there.

'Allow me, Your Majesty' Gustav offered. 'I have become quite familiar with these woods in the course of my studies.'

'Lead on' Nikolai gestured, turning his mount to follow.

Laura walked her stallion slowly to allow it time to cool down from its exertions, eyeing Fredrik's back as he rode alongside Nikolai. Their French words drifted back to her, jovial and warm. It was clear Fredrik greatly admired Nikolai and the prince deeply respected him too, once telling Laura *I should hate him were he not so likeable.*

So Nikolai counted Fredrik as a rival, at least on some level Laura mused, and wondered if Fredrik saw Nikolai as a rival too. He hid his heart too well, she couldn't read him. He looked at her with such sad kindness sometimes, and at other times with miserable want. Once she thought he was on the verge of proposing to her, she could feel the question struggling on his tongue, but he refused to speak them.

Yes she wanted to shout out loud. Surely he knew she would say yes if he asked her. She didn't think she had imagined his desire for her. She didn't imagine the way her heart skipped a beat when he looked at her, smiled at her. Nor did she imagine the way her skin still tingled with the heat of him, long after his touch had disappeared.

I am in love with Fredrik, and I have never loved anyone like this.

She sighed gently, letting the truth of that thought settle through her. In the quiet moments of the night she had sometimes doubted if what she felt for Aleksei had ever been love. There was affection, yes, and the giddy rush of fervour, of finding herself in a real life fairy tale, of the handsome prince falling for the cruelly treated heroine, of - if she was honest in those dark moments - the smug satisfaction that she would outrank all the snobbish cows in Lady Ramkinson's boarding school so that they would be twisted up in jealousy for her.

She had liked Aleksei, that she couldn't deny. Maybe it was a kind of love. But it was different to the love she felt for Fredrik, and for the love she had felt for Olaf, which had seemed old and comfortable, even when it was new. There had been no swooning infatuation, no courtship, no caught breaths and bitten lips. Just two people who had drawn together. He had been her guardian, then later her companion and friend, sometimes her only friend in the Principality.

And he had loved me more than I had loved him.

She found it difficult to face that fact, turning her head away, to look through the trees into the forests he had loved so much. She hadn't wanted to untangle the strong mess of emotions that had surged through her in the last few weeks of his life. But as time had passed, as she had returned to the familiar places they had gone together, as she began to think less often of him, they had begun to unravel from the hurt knot inside her, letting her begin to recognise what they truly were.

She had looked to him for happiness and refuge, but that was not love. He had spoken to her honestly and treated her with respect when no one else did, but that wasn't love either. He had saved her life several times, and a sense of obligation could masquerade as a kind of love, but none of this had mattered. What she had felt, *really* felt, was fear and guilt.

The fear of her near drowning, of the torture and rape Nikita might have put her through, the gnawing fright of Russia's imminent attack had sent her into his arms, for the comfort he always gave her. She had allowed him to strip her, kiss her, make love to her, and his body had done things to hers that had never happened before. She had enjoyed the sex, and because he had loved her a good man had died.

She shut her eyes against the tears that threatened. She had railed against the injustice of his death, against the tragedy of circumstances that had seen him fall from the throne to the hangman's noose. The guilt that had gnawed at her in the months that followed had coloured her memories of him, the depths of her anguish making her believe that her love had been equally as deep.

I'm sorry I didn't love you more, but you are gone, and there's nothing I can do about that she thought. *We have a beautiful daughter, and I love her with all my heart. Goodbye, Alexander Andrei.*

A bird whistled, off to her left, seemingly in answer, and she smiled sadly, urging her horse to catch up to the others.

Nikolai dismounted when they reached the chasm, which was only a few feet wide, but at least ten feet to the jagged, sharp rocks at the bottom. He peered over the edge, eyeing the tree that grew from the side of the gorge, overhanging the drop.

'I am told that many men have hung on to this branch to prove their worth to a pretty maiden. Or their friends.'

Fredrik dismounted too, peering down at the tree beside Nikolai.

'How foolhardy and dangerous' he said.

'Shall we?' Nikolai grinned.

'Of course' he smiled too, following Nikolai in swinging down to the branch that stretched into the void.

'Oh please don't!' Laura cried, dismounting too. 'Gustav, stop them!'

'That's an ash tree' he said, dismounting too, coming over to peer down into the canyon.

'What? So?' Laura demanded.

'So, if my memory serves me correctly,' he said, lying down on his stomach to inspect the bark better, 'the ash tree was Yggdrasil, where Odin hung himself for nine days to gain knowledge.'

'*Nine days?!*' Laura cried.

'That would be a challenge' Nikolai grinned, adjusting his grip.

'Please climb back up' Laura begged. 'Fredrik, please! Too many people have died here, falling onto those rocks. Please climb up!'

Fredrik hesitated then did as she asked, soothing her gently as he brushed away the dirt on his clothes.

'There's a key' Gustav suddenly said, pointing at a branch near Nikolai.

'No doubt Countess Ivanova wanted me to collect this key' he said, managing to grab it and pushing it between his lips for safekeeping as he climbed back up, accepting Fredrik's hand to step up to the edge where they stood. 'I wonder what it unlocks.'

'I suspect it is for the chest the Countess gave me this morning' Laura said, calmer now that they were both safe.

She held her hand out for it, and Nikolai kissed it before laying it in her palm. She smiled, tucking it into a pocket then mounted back up on her stallion.

'Come, dear friends, come with me to my favourite place in all the forest' she said, and waited for them to mount too before leading them deeper into the trees.

52

Laura stole another look at Fredrik, trying to read his face in the darkness of her theatre box. She wanted to reach out and take his hand, to stroke back a wisp of hair from his brow, to turn his attention from the stage and Lilia, dressed as a Valkyrie, and lying so sensuously curled on a bed surrounded by flickering flames that even Laura was finding it difficult not to stare at her. She could only imagine how uncomfortable he was sharing the royal box with her and Nikolai.

Aris, dressed as Siegfried, began to strip Lilia of her armour in a way that managed to reveal a good deal of her legs as well; a scripted piece that would not be out of place in a burlesque show, making Laura flush and steal another look at Fredrik. *There was no way she could have been mistaken for a man, even before her armour had come off* she thought, flushing. She desperately wanted to fully understand what they were saying to each other, wanted to ask Fredrik to translate for her, but couldn't bring herself to speak. From the small smattering of German words she could understand, and their passionate gesticulations, she gathered it was some prolonged and protracted courtship; a thought that was confirmed when Aris took Lilia in his arms and climbed above her on her bed as the curtain fell to thunderous applause.

Laura stirred, the spell broken, and applauded as the curtain rose again for the cast to bathe in the appreciation of the Principality.

'Wonderful performance' Nikolai said. 'Richard Wagner's epic *Ring Cycle* is a momentous piece of work, though I gathered *Die Walküre* was more popular than *Siegfried*. The acoustics of your new theatre are just right for a ringing rendition of *The Ride of the Valkyries*.'

'It was my intention that *Die Walküre* be performed tonight' Fredrik interjected, sounding embarrassed. 'However, *Signorina* Bellagio insisted on performing *Siegfried*. She was so enthusiastic I could not refuse.'

I know why she insisted Laura thought. *Ekaterina told me one of your given names is Siegfried. Lilia Bellagio is in love with you too.* The pang of jealousy twisted painfully in her heart.

Kurt climbed onto the stage and handed Lilia an enormous bouquet of red roses, kissing her hand gallantly. She clasped the flowers to her and kissed his cheeks, applauding the theatre's patron loudly, encouraging the audience to do the same. Kurt scuttled down to his seat again, red faced.

The cast had not yet finished their curtain calls, but Laura could already see patrons making a hasty exit, rushing off to don their fancy dress for the third night of dancing for her birthday. It promised to be the most lavish yet, and an extraordinary amount of money had been spent on this night. Laura wanted to run off too, it would be nearly ten o'clock by the time she dressed and returned to the ballroom.

But she could not, Ekaterina had given her strict instructions to see Lilia before she returned to the castle. After the third curtain call she lost patience and gave her hand to Nikolai.

'Please take me to the stage, I will congratulate the cast personally' she said. '*Euer Hochwohlgeboren*, please translate for me.'

Both men bowed and Fredrik pushed aside the curtain to the royal box and nodded to Roman, who was standing guard outside, bowing as Nikolai and Laura passed him. He followed them down to the auditorium and through a small side door that led to the back stage area. When Lilia saw them she rushed over excitedly, curtseying deeply before them, Italian words pouring out of her mouth.

'*Signorina* Bellagio wishes to thank Your Majesty for the privilege of performing for your birthday and hopes that you have enjoyed the evening' Fredrik translated.

'Delightful' Laura assured her, and waited for Fredrik to translate her next words.

'She is so very pleased to hear you enjoyed it, and wishes Your Majesty many happy returns for her birthday. She says that she has a present for – *Cheido scusa?*' he broke off, surprised.

Lilia, clearly in an excited, flustered rush had begun talking again, even before Fredrik had finished translating for her. But Laura understood what she had called her. *Brünnhilde*, and she had taken off the helmet she had worn herself for the role of that Valkyrie, and was presenting it to Laura with another deep curtsey. Fredrik blinked, caught off guard, then finished:

'My dear cousin has named you as Brünnhilde, favourite of Odin, for the festivities tonight, and *Signorina* Bellagio presents a helm for that most worthy head.'

'It is no *Tarnhelm*, to be sure, but I gladly accept it' Laura said, taking the proffered helmet and Fredrik smiled at the reference.

Quickly she spoke to Aris, congratulating him on his performance, and the debonair Greek planted many kisses on her hand, repeating several times in bad English:

'I thanks that you like!'

She spoke to each of the main cast members individually but briefly, as well as to the conductor and to the stage manager who had designed and built the Fafnir dragon; a spectacular creature that had spouted smoke and fire and beat its wings as it fought with Siegfried. Finally satisfied that she had been gracious enough she bid them a good night and let Nikolai escort her back to the castle.

Anna was waiting impatiently in her rooms for her, and Laura quickly disrobed with her help, washing her face and limbs carefully before collecting the key to the chest that was still in the pocket of the dress she had worn earlier, throwing open the lid.

Inside, under a layer of straw, was an intricately carved cuirass, clearly designed for a woman. Laura gasped, holding it up and eyeing the detail of the swirling, twining serpents that adorned the stomach.

'Many of the court have raided the armoury in Tcherepnin' Anna revealed excitedly. 'And I have seen what they did to the ballroom, you will be amazed, you really will!'

'I am sure I will' she grinned as Anna helped her into the white flowing shift she was to wear under the armour.

Together they then strapped her into the cuirass, fastening the numerous buckles. It held her firmer than a corset could, and was rigid, restricting her movements.

'How am I going to dance in this?' she wondered, shifting uncomfortably, trying vainly to tug it into a more forgiving mould against her.

'I'm not sure, Your Majesty, but you have to ride a horse as well' Anna grinned, selecting her hairbrush from the vanity.

'Leave my hair loose' Laura suddenly said, shaking it out and retrieving the helmet from where she had dropped it onto her chaise lounge, placing it on her head.

A copper armband, twisted and bent into Celtic coils, and a pair of leather vambraces completed her look and she quickly pulled open her door, tossing thanks over her shoulder and running swiftly down the stairs to the entrance hall.

She stopped in surprise, because her stallion, cloaked in furs and a round shield fastened to his saddle, was standing in the middle of the wide entrance hall, his reins held by Spanov. She laughed in surprise and then ran forward, boosting herself up into the saddle. Roman, who had followed her down from her rooms, handed her the spear he was carrying then stood back to eye the full effect of her majesty. Laura was surprised by the weight of the spear, but knew it would look impressive if she held it without help as she rode into the ballroom.

She took the reins from Spanov and urged the horse forward, feeling strange to be riding through the castle. *I wonder if anyone has ever done this before* she mused, but the thought was interrupted when the guards at the ballroom saluted and pulled open the doors to admit her. She stared, her mouth falling open in shock.

Thin strands of gold, red and orange material hung from the walls, waving in the heat of the candles, so that the court danced in a ring of encircling fire. At one end of the ballroom a fantastic fountain filled with amber liquid flowed and tinkled, surrounded by tables groaning under the weight of honey cakes and other sweet treats. Simple wooden benches, covered in furs lined the walls of the room, and above them hung round shields and an assortment of swords, maces, halberds and poleaxes. Far above them, hanging from the ceiling, was an enormous piñata in the shape of a dragon.

At the far end of the ballroom there was a tree - *a live tree!* - she gasped, and beyond it, a painted backdrop of Valhalla. Between the two hung a rainbow bridge of light. *There must be a prism somewhere* she gaped, but it could not detract from the wonder of the spectacle.

Her guests were dressed in a mixture of armour and fur; as warriors painted with blue woad, as gods, as dwarves, as elves, Rhine Maidens and Valkyries. They bowed and curtseyed as she urged her stallion forward, slipping out of the saddle when she spotted Malenkov, waiting to take her horse back to the stables. She gave her spear and reins to the guard and greeted her guests, bidding them rise from their courtesy.

The musicians struck up, and Nikolai bought her a goblet of mead, dipped straight from the fountain. He was wearing full upper body armour, without a helmet or gloves and Laura was not surprised to see it was Vsevolod's armour. She had recognised it from the portrait that hung in the library and from the tapestries she had spent months stitching. She wondered if Ekaterina had given him the armour, or if he had selected it himself.

Her thoughts stopped when she saw Fredrik. He was stripped to his waist, wearing a pair of breeches and knee high moccasins that were strapped to his legs with strips of leather. His arms were decorated with woad swirls and he wore buckled to his chest a moulded plate of steel that wouldn't protect much of him in a real battle. He wore a short fur cape and his blonde hair was loose, spilling out from under a horned helmet. She swallowed hard, simultaneously dry mouthed and salivating, blushing hotly.

She drained her goblet of mead and quickly went to fill it again, tearing her eyes away from him.

'Allow me Your Majesty' Ekaterina said, appearing beside her and taking her goblet from her, dipping it into the fountain.

Is he your handiwork too? she wanted to ask, but saw from the impish look on her face that it was, and she was quite aware of Laura's reaction to it as well. Her blush deepened but she hugged her friend, thanking her for her attention to detail. But they didn't have long to talk, as Nikolai interrupted them with a bow, asking Laura for a dance.

He whirled her through the evening, through many cups of mead and wine. They all drank far too much, growing raucous and loud in their merriment. Sometime in the evening the clay dragon was lowered, and Nikolai managed to shatter it with a wooden sword, showering the crowds with roubles, sweets and memorial tokens Ekaterina had especially commissioned for the party.

Somehow she found herself as Fredrik's dance partner. She didn't remember asking him, or him asking her, only suddenly became aware of the electric sensation of his hand on hers, and his other around her waist, his fingers clutching at the ends of her hair. There was a thin sheen of sweat on his body, and his cheeks were dark with wine. She couldn't resist, and slid her hand under his cloak, pressing her palm against his back.

His skin was hot, and dewy, and she felt his breath catch at her touch. She stepped the wrong way in the waltz, and her body collided with his, metal on metal ringing startlingly loud in the room. She felt the hot flush start again under the weight of their stares.

'Forgive me' she said. 'Too much wine has made me ungainly.'

Fredrik bowed and took her hand.

'Allow me to escort you to a seat, I would not want for you to hurt yourself.'

She hesitated, looking around the room, realising it was half empty, and nearing dawn.

'No, I shall retire now. Thank you, dear friends, for this wonderful celebration. Good night and sleep well!' she said, then realised she had to let go of Fredrik's hand, and didn't want to. 'Escort me to my rooms, in case I hurt myself' she said.

Fredrik flushed deeper, but bowed, leading her out of the ballroom and up the stairs to her room. He bid her goodnight and kissed her hand, managing to extract his fingers from hers. She wanted to pull him into her room with her, but he bowed and stepped back, saying goodnight to Roman before taking his leave of her.

Laura stepped into her room and closed the door, pressing the back of her hand, where he had kissed it, to her lips. The taste of him was too faint, she shut her eyes tightly, wanting to throw open the door and run back to him. The yearning grew as she undid the buckles of her cuirass, as the firm metal fell away from her body. She took off the helmet she still wore, wishing it really was *Tarnhelm*, the magical helmet that could make her invisible, disguise her, or transport her great distances instantly.

'Transport me into his arms, right now' she whispered, wishing desperately that there was a secret passage in her room, so she could go to Fredrik without anyone knowing.

Roman will know where I am going, and for what she thought, embarrassment rising in her, but it couldn't hold her in check. She pulled open the door and rushed out.

'Stay there!' she told Roman, and rushed along the corridor to Fredrik's rooms, letting herself in and leaning against the door when she closed it behind her.

Fredrik emerged from his dressing room, shorn of his cape and breastplate, his skin wet where he had washed away the woad paint. He was surprised to see her, and embarrassed by his state of undress, one arm coming up to protectively cross his chest.

'You have lost your armour Brünnhilde' he said quietly.

'Are you afraid?' she asked.

He did not answer, but the arm that covered him dropped to his side, aware of the way she looked at him. But he did not approach her.

'Even now' she said quietly. 'Even now, with me here, you are still so reserved, so thoughtful of others. Be reckless, for once! Tell me you want me!'

'Laura please...' he whispered.

'*Mein*...' she started hesitantly, hoping she had the German words right.

'*Meine Haut brennt noch, wo du mich berührt.*'
  My skin still burns where you touched me.

Fredrik seized her arms, pulling her against his mouth, his arms sliding around her back to press her hard against him. She wrapped her arms around his neck, clasping his blonde hair, responding earnestly to his fevered kisses. A hand cupped her breast, slid down to grip her thigh, caressing and stroking her body. She stroked his arms, ran her hands across the fine hairs on his chest, slid one hand down to stroke the front of his breeches.

'*Gott!*' he groaned as her hand slid inside. '*Noch nicht!*'

'Now!' she begged, pulling him out, feeling him thickening in her grip.

He thrust her up against the door in a hard, passionate move, pressing her there with his body. Laura mewled deep in her throat, a need that was visceral, full of anguished want.

'I'm sorry, I'm sorry' he said, breaking away, turning his back on her, fighting with himself.

Laura gawped at him, stunned and confused, her breath harsh in her throat, every inch of her aching to feel him again. The seconds passed, stretching away between them, and Laura could see Fredrik's will was winning, a supreme effort to control himself.

'Fredrik -'

'I can't' he said quietly, tucking himself away. 'I won't – hurt you.'

And shame branded her in the silence that followed. *He knew what Aleksei had done.*

'It was not pain' she said quietly but he cut her off, pleading her name. 'Or fright -'

'Please go' he whispered.

She shut her eyes, misery stirring.

'Tell me you love me, at least give me that' she whispered.

Fredrik relented.

'I love you' he said quietly. 'You pierced my soul, and every atom of me filled with you. I cannot *be* without you. I love you more dear than I could ever love myself.'

Laura sniffed, her chin crinkling, her tears hot on her cheeks. She pressed one soft kiss on his shoulder blade, then slipped out of his room, closing the door gently behind her.

53

Laura sat in Fedor's office and sipped tea, watching him sign several documents for Parliament. He tucked them into a manila folder and set it aside, screwing the cap onto his pen before setting that aside too.

'Your celebrations were a great success' he smiled. 'The attendant reader in the theatre is hoarse, but every single person has been to see the moving pictures, many of them several times. And the telegrams that left Dalnerechensk for various embassies have been complimentary in their reports.'

'You must invite them all to stay longer on my behalf' she said, setting down the cup. 'Nikolai Vakhtangov will be crowned Tsar of Dalnerechensk and co-regent with myself.'

Fedor blinked rapidly. 'When?' he asked, pulling a piece of paper towards him, unscrewing his pen cap again.

'Not so far away that to host such an extensive and extravagant multitude will be too much a drain on my already taxed finances, and not so soon that other guests will not have time to arrive. I suggest a month from now.'

'Other guests?'

'I gather Nikolai's family, the banished branch of the Vakhtangovs, might like to come home. And if not, his sisters and mother should be here when he is crowned.'

Fedor made some quick notes, then paused, his pen hovering over the parchment.

'Parliament has agreed to co-regency?'

'Not yet' she admitted. 'I intend to raise it with them today.'

He hesitated again, then delicately tried to broach the subject of her rooms, trying to suggest – without doing anything so crass as suggesting – that she should take up residence in Tsar Constantinovich's old rooms, the rooms all ruling tsars had occupied.

Everything within her rebelled, she could not bring herself to move into the rooms of a man who was now gone, to touch the objects he had touched, to sleep where he had slept, to lie where he had fathered her husband. She wondered if other wives had felt this way, if other tsars had had any qualms about sleeping in the bed where his parents had made love and probably conceived him...

And yet she knew what others whispered, that she refused to move into them because she secretly knew those rooms were waiting for the *true* ruler...

Laura heard Fredrik's voice wander past the floor, heading down the stone stairs, deep in conversation with someone in German. It was a welcome distraction. She caught the words *Ich fürchte für unseren Bruder*, and he sounded worried. *I something for our brother* Laura translated in her head, and knew he was talking to Gustav about Kurt.

'- unlucky rooms' Fedor finished, breaking into her thoughts.

'My rooms are unlucky?' she asked, surprised.

They had been unaired for many years before I took them over she remembered. *But Ilich assured me there was no reason to keep them so. Maybe he was not superstitious, or maybe he did not care.* She found it so difficult to read him nowadays.

'You do not know' Fedor said, realisation dawning. 'Forgive me.'

'Why are they unlucky?' she pressed.

'The last three occupants to inhabit those rooms met unhappy ends' he said quietly. 'The *Tsesarevich* held them, as did his uncle Radomyr, and his mother, before she married. They had not been opened for more than ten years before you returned.'

Laura dropped her eyes then sighed and collected the folder of signed documents, standing. Fedor stood too, bowing to her as she dismissed his concerns and took her leave, heading to Parliament Chambers.

As she rounded the corner she saw Ilich drinking furtively from something he slipped back into his jacket pocket. He had just enough self respect left to look embarrassed and avoid her eyes, apologising.

'Ilich -' she started, then stopped, unsure what to say to him, unsure what she *could* say.

'I know' he said quietly. 'It won't happen again.'

He bowed as she passed him, stepping into the chamber that was already full of ministers. They rose and bowed as she made her way to the throne, sitting again when she gave them permission. Ivan bowed and took the folder of paperwork from her, opening it and reading it through quickly while Maksim called Parliament to order.

'Gentlemen, I have news. Nikolai and I have reached an agreement' Laura announced, then watched Maksim carefully when she told them of her decision to rule jointly.

That was not what he had been expecting she thought, noticing the tightness in his jaw, the coldness that settled into his eyes.

'What about marriage?' he snapped, sharper than he had intended.

'*I will not be forced*' she answered. 'But we have not discounted it. I am of the impression that Parliament - indeed, Dalnerechensk - is in want of an expeditious union, political or other. You can have what you want.'

'But you could marry another!' Lev shouted, aghast.

'And so could he' Laura pointed out.

Lev opened his mouth to protest again, but shut it when *Knjaz* Uvarov placed a restraining hand on his arm. A disgruntled silence fell over the Parliament, and Laura wondered at Maksim's reaction to her announcement. *He can't have* wanted *me to marry Nikolai…* she stopped. *Of course he did, because then I would be his property, and lose all claim and authority to the crown. If Tatiana became his mistress she would have more power than I. She and Maksim could get him to sign all sorts of little decrees, like barring Alexandra from the throne.*

She inwardly sighed. How much more of this could she take? What would stop him, once and for all, in his malicious attacks on her?

Parliament droned on, and Laura fought the boredom she felt, letting her mind drift back to that brief moment in Fredrik's room. *He loves me.* There was a hot glow in her, one that had never dissipated, and grew hotter every time she thought about his words, his touch, his desperate want for her. She had been deeply humiliated to learn that he knew what Aleksei had done, but later, as she had lain awake while the sun came over the Eastern Range, she realised she shouldn't have been surprised.

Unconsciously she reached up and patted the fresh daisy in her hair. It had been lying on her plate when she came down to breakfast this morning, and she knew without a doubt that Fredrik had placed it there for her. It was a small courtship gesture, and all the more intimate that it was a flower and not some expensive diamond jewellery.

Part of her knew that her courtship with Fredrik would be as unconventional as Aleksei's and hers had been, where attraction and union were not just matters of the heart but of state policy and governance as well. She didn't want her new marriage to be as romantic as tax laws. *How did Royals go courting?* she wondered. *Maybe they gave each other empires...*

She giggled then coughed to cover it, realising with some horror that she had been day dreaming, and several ministers had noticed.

'You find this discussion of pensions funny?' Maksim snapped, pouncing on her indiscretion.

'Forgive me, I was distracted' she blushed.

'What could possibly be more important, to occupy your attention so fully, than the governance of the Principality?' he sneered.

'Succession' she answered.

'That a laughing matter too is it?' Lev said snippily.

'It is if you are thinking about how to create it' someone said bawdily, and Parliament laughed.

Maksim lost his temper and dismissed them, sending them scuttling out. Laura was surprised to see Ilich had not complied with his instruction, and was still sitting in his seat with a manner of quiet, insolent defiance.

'Did you hear me?!' Maksim thundered.

Ilich gave him a long look. 'I heard' he said quietly. 'I have a matter to discuss with Her Majesty. In private' he added.

Maksim glared at him, then at Laura, his fists tightening. Then without a word he left, slamming the doors behind him.

The silence fell between them. Ilich didn't move, or even look at her, and she wondered if she should say something first. No doubt he was embarrassed with being caught drinking so early in the morning, and she could see some kind of deep internal struggle was taking place in him. Quietly she rose from the throne, coming down to stand near him, wondering how she was going to deal with this. *I could have monarchs eating out of my hand but I don't know how to deal with a man apologising to a little girl for being a drunk...*

'Marry for love' he told her. 'Nothing else.'

He stood, brushing away a fleck of dirt from his pants, bowing briefly. 'Nothing else' he repeated, and took his leave.

Laura was left staring open mouthed after him.

54

Roman knocked on her doors then pushed it open to admit Nikolai, who bowed before her.

'Admiral' Laura smiled, setting aside her embroidery and offering him her hand, which he kissed.

'Sweet cousin' he smiled in return. 'I trust you are well this morning? What is it you are stitching?'

'Very well' she answered, then showed him the blue sash, one small section secured with an embroidery hoop. 'I am stitching a new coat of arms onto this sash' she said, lifting the dangling thread out of the way so he could see her progress. 'I would be honoured if you wore it to your coronation.'

'The honour would be mine' he said, his smile deepening, then presented her with a small box. 'A present for you, Your Hind-ness' he quipped.

She grinned and opened the fine box, inspecting the glittering diamond necklace inside. Thomas Wyatt's poem, *Whoso List to Hunt*, had that famous hind wearing a diamond collar with the words "*Noli me tangere* for Caesar's I am" engraved on it. She wondered whether this necklace made Nikolai Thomas Wyatt or Henry VIII.

'It is clear where your heart truly lies' he said. 'I wish you all the happiness in the world.'

'Fredrik is not a king' she said quietly.

'No. But any man who secures *your* heart would be a Caesar indeed' he smiled.

She smiled too, and handed the necklace to Anna, instructing her to put it away with her other recently acquired jewels. She curtseyed and did as she was told.

'Would you care for some tea?' Laura asked.

'Alas no, I have only called to, regrettably, tell you of my impending departure.'

'Leaving so soon?' she said, surprised.

'I must return to St Petersburg and see to the packing up of my household, and I need to appoint someone to manage my estates while I am not there. It is something I personally see to, I like to see the measure of a man before I employ him.'

'I see. And are you a good judge of character, Your Highness?'

'I am famed for it' he replied.

'When will you return?' she asked, wondering if she should ask his opinion on several of her ministers.

'My mother is frail, and needs my assistance to travel. I hope to be no more than three weeks. Do not worry, I shall not miss my own coronation' he grinned.

'Please do keep me informed of your progress' she smiled, giving her hand to be kissed. 'God speed and good luck on your travels. When do you plan to leave?'

'I hope to reach Chelyabinsk by nightfall, there is a train leaving for St Petersburg in the morning.'

'You will not drive?' she asked, surprised.

'Good heavens no, it is too far, especially for Ilya. No, I will be storing my automobile here in Dalnerechensk and taking the train.'

'Sadly Dalnerechensk no longer has a royal carriage, else we might have used it for your journey. Perhaps we shall look at purchasing another' she mused. 'No matter. Farewell Your Highness, I shall wait anxiously for your safe return.'

He kissed her hand again and then bowed, taking his leave of her. At the doorway she called out to him, unable to resist asking him.

'Your Highness?' Nikolai stopped and looked back. 'How would you judge the character of my Prime Minister?'

There. There was a flicker on Nikolai's face, but she had read in it all she wanted to.

'I believe you are a good judge of character yourself, Your Majesty' Nikolai said. 'I believe you have the make of him already. Good day.'

Roman shut the door behind him and Laura collected her embroidery again, her quick fingers making fast progress in the design. But her attention to her work could not dispel a growing sense of unease, and she could not identify its cause.

She forced herself to finish the coat of arms then gave it to Anna to be pressed properly, heading to Ekaterina's rooms. She let herself in, only to discover an army of servants packing clothes into travelling cases. Ekaterina was sitting on her chaise longue, sipping tea thoughtfully.

'I thought I might have a visit from you today' she said quietly, setting aside her tea cup. 'Anya, be so good as to pour Her Majesty some tea, then all of you please give us some privacy.'

They bobbed curtseys and Anya poured Laura a cup, bobbed another curtsey and scuttled out, closing the door behind the retreated servants.

'Leaving so soon?' Laura asked, despairing.

'I promised to wait until Fredrik came' she said quietly. 'He is here now.'

Laura shut her eyes, trying to push away her misery.

'He does love me, doesn't he?' she asked plaintively.

'How could you doubt that?' Ekaterina asked, surprised.

'Why won't he ask me to marry him?' she wailed.

'He won't ever ask you' Ekaterina said. 'You are an Empress. You outrank him. *You* have to ask *him*.'

Laura began to laugh at how stupid she felt, then came to sit beside her friend, hugging her tightly then collecting the tea and sipping it carefully. Ekaterina sighed sadly, setting aside her empty cup.

'I know you want me to stay. I hear you thinking so loudly sometimes' she smiled. 'But I have no friends here now, except you, and I miss my husband. I am irrevocably changed by all that has happened and – something miraculous has happened. I hardly dare believe it, to speak of it out loud might make it false, or make it real, I hardly know which!'

'What do you mean?' Laura asked, confused.

'I think I'm pregnant' she whispered, then looked defiant, as if she expected Laura to disagree. 'I don't know if I am, but I had to say something, or go insane! I don't want to wait in case I can't travel. I want to be with Grigory.'

'Does he know?' Laura asked.

'No. Not yet, I wanted to be sure, before …' she trailed off.

Laura couldn't blame her. She could only imagine how disappointed Grigory might be if such a miraculous event turned out to be a false pregnancy. She set aside her tea cup and took her friend's hands.

'Then you must go to him' she said, tears welling up in her eyes. 'And I shall miss you all my days.'

They hugged tightly, and kissed each other's cheeks.

'I shall miss you too. But rely on Fredrik, he is your most ardent defender. I shall, of course, come back for your wedding.'

Laura grinned, the tightness squeezing all of her insides in the giddy rush of love.

55

Laura hardly slept a wink, tossing and turning fitfully. She would grow too hot and throw the covers off, then shiver and be forced to don them again. She tried to read some more of the diary but her heart was not in it and she put it back almost as soon as she had collected it from the secret drawer. *Just how on earth could she propose to Fredrik? What would she say to him?* She had stopped herself from running directly to his apartments and demanding he marry her after she had left Ekaterina to her packing, but now she was tying herself into knots trying to think of the most perfect proposal she could utter.

Nothing was working. Words that had never failed her before now refused to come, or sluggishly moved across her tongue like thick porridge, forced and awkward. She finally sighed, sitting up when the Eastern Range was picked out against the light of a new dawn. She dressed quickly, and went to the nursery, sitting in a chair by Alexandra's crib to watch her sleep.

She heard Roman shifting uncomfortably outside the door and wondered if she should ask him what she should say, if she should use a line from great literature in her speech. *You must allow me to tell you how ardently I admire and love you…*

'Why is this so difficult?' she wondered out loud, and her voice woke Alexandra. 'I'm sorry my love' she said, reaching in to scoop her into her arms.

'Mama' Alexandra smiled, and Laura's heart melted, kissing her head.

'That's right my love, I'm your mama' she smiled. 'Are you hungry? Let's go downstairs for breakfast.'

She rose from the seat and closed the nursey door behind her, her gaze sweeping across the window as she did. In the cool greys of the morning light she saw Fredrik moving across the courtyard below the window, and in his hand was something red, probably one of summer's late blooms. She was filled with a delirious happiness and quickly ran down to the dining room, catching him placing the wild rose on her plate.

Alexandra burbled, catching his attention, and a charming blush coloured his cheeks. Laura crossed the empty room, picking up the flower and sniffing it carefully, closing her eyes. Alexandra tried to take a bite and Laura laughed, giving it to Fredrik.

'It's not food my love' she smiled, then turned her attention back to Fredrik. 'I love the flowers you give me' she said quietly.

'I love seeing you wear them in your hair' he said quietly, his cheeks darkening more.

'Would you do me the honours?' she asked, stepping closer and tilting her face up to him.

His hands came around her, sliding the stem of the rose into her hair, his fingers brushing against her shining locks. He brushed a wisp of hair back from her face, his fingertips tracing their way down from her temple to her jaw, then sliding back to cup her face, watching the way she nuzzled into his palm. She moved closer, parting her lips, watching the way his adam's apple bobbed when he swallowed.

Outside in the corridor Roman greeted Luka loudly and they reluctantly parted, Fredrik placing the kiss he had meant for her lips on the back of her hand.

'I would be greatly pleased if you would -' she started in a rush, but Luka stepped into the room, scowling, and she felt too frightened to continue with the words she wanted to say, changing them quickly to: 'accompany me riding this afternoon.'

'Of course Your Majesty' he accepted, then retrieved the carved royal chair for Alexandra.

They sat near each other, discussing Alberto Santos-Dumont's successful powered flights in Europe, comparing his wheeled machine to the Wright Brothers' mono-rail contraption, their eyes saying what their mouths could not. Maksim called for Parliament to enter session, and Laura gave Alexandra to Marie, reluctantly parting from Fredrik.

'Till this afternoon then' she said, giving him her hand.

'I shall count the minutes' he murmured, planting a lingering kiss on her fingers.

'So will I' she whispered as she left him, letting her fingers brush against him as they parted.

Maksim looked less than happy to see her when she made her way inside chambers, but she smiled sweetly at him, sitting on Vsevolod's throne and motioning for others to sit, looking around for Ilich.

He looked ragged, but he had shaved, and was wearing a clean shirt. He was also sitting closer to the front benches than he had been previously. Laura wondered if that meant he was taking an interest in politics again, or that he was gaining back the favour he had lost when he had lost the elections. Unable to help herself her eyes sort out Luka, deep in furtive conversation with Lev, both of them with their eyes on her. It gave her unease another twist and she tore her eyes away quickly, acknowledging Ivan's bow and taking the presented folder from him.

It took an extreme amount of prudence to keep her mind on the matters before Parliament, and time passed so slowly the hands on the clock seemed not to move at all. But at last Maksim dismissed them, and Laura ran up to her rooms, yanking on her riding habit. She sent Anna to send word to Fredrik that she was ready to go riding and hesitated before plucking the rose from her hair so as not to crush it under her hat.

Fredrik joined her at the stables, managing to hide his disappointment when he saw Roman mounting up to ride with them. He boosted her up onto her stallion and mounted a grey mare himself, riding beside her down Castle Street. They hardly spoke, too mindful of Roman's company, too shy to voice the things they wanted to say to each other.

They dismounted in the glen and Fredrik unpacked a hamper of food, laying out a blanket for them to sit on near the water's edge. Laura's stomach growled and she blushed, praising Fredrik for his thoughtfulness. He grinned and they sat in silence again, eating the assortment of sweetmeats he had packed for them, shooting each other blushing looks, both aware of how awkward Roman's presence made courtship.

Roman diplomatically wandered off to give them some privacy, sitting on a log across the clearing from them, turned slightly away from them, but still facing them to keep an eye out for trouble.

'Please read me this' Fredrik suddenly said, handing her a small book.

It was a collection of Heinrich Heine's poems, and he had marked a specific poem. Laura cleared her throat, the blush coming up in her cheeks as she read the German aloud. *I know this poem* she flushed. *It was talking about how the poet had had a woman, and couldn't forget what it was like, still desiring her body, and claiming we must make our bodies and souls one.* She was surprised that Fredrik had wanted to hear such eroticism from her lips.

'Are you playing an erotic trick on me?' she asked, embarrassed.

'I like to hear you speak German' he answered, shifting closer to her, his voice dropping. 'I hope to hear you say the things I feel...'

He clasped her hand, and her breath caught in her throat.

'*Ich*' she started hesitatingly, '*ich lieb' dich.*'

He kissed the inside of her wrist. 'Tell me again' he murmured. She did, and he kissed her forearm. 'Tell me again.'

'*Je t'aime*' she whispered, and he kissed the inside of her elbow. '*Ti amo*' she said in Italian, but he hesitated. '*Ya lyublyu tebya*' she tried in Russian, but still no kiss was forthcoming. 'I love you' she switched to English.

'I cannot kiss you again' he said in English. 'I will never stop.'

'I don't want you to stop' she interrupted.

He blushed, eyeing Roman miserably. She suddenly stood and walked nonchalantly along the edge of the lake, shooting Fredrik a beckoning look. He stood too and followed her, right up to the cliff face beside the waterfall. She waited until Roman looked away and then darted behind the waterfall, pulling Fredrik in behind her.

They shuffled along the ledge, pressing close to the rock face, and stepped into the cave, hesitating while their eyes adjusted to the gloom. Fredrik eyed the romantic graffiti on the walls then quickly dug out his pocket knife, carving their initials into the soft green moss as well.

'Fredrik,' she started, hardly knowing what to say next, but knew it was now or never.

'Yes' he said. There wasn't a question or inquiry in his tone, it was an answer to the question that was coming.

'Yes?' she blinked, surprised.

'How could it be any other answer?' he asked, dropping the pocket knife and stepping closer to her, taking hold of her arm.

She stepped into his embrace, her lips parting as his pressed to hers, his arms circling around her.

'*Ya lyublyu tebya*' he whispered as her arms slid around his neck, her body arching against his.

She sighed happily, tangling her fingers into the long locks tied at the nape of his neck, liking the way his arms pulled her tightly against him, till every breath he took felt like it happened in her own chest, every tremble of his stomach was her own too.

'Don't stop' she pleaded, pulling open his jacket and sliding her hand inside his silk shirt.

He groaned, trying to slide his own hand inside her dress, but she was laced too tightly and he had to settle for cupping her breast through the material. Her gasp that made her swell into his touch inflamed him and his other hand slid harder around her waist, then lower, cupping her buttock firmly. *Touch me like you touched me before* he wanted to beg. He wanted to lift her up against the wet walls of the cave, to lie her in the sweet grass of the glen, to stop imagining what it would be like to make their souls one.

'Your Majesty?' Roman called, alarmed.

Laura cursed, hesitating, torn between answering him and pressing more kisses into Fredrik's chest.

'We must stop' he whispered, pushing her away gently, though she could feel the reluctance in his touch.

'Come to the library tonight' she said urgently. 'Midnight.' She kissed him again. 'Wait there for me.'

'Your Majesty, where are you?' Roman called, closer than he had been before.

She cursed again and pulled away, wiping her lips to stop the tingling feel of his kisses. Fredrik turned away, retrieving the pocket knife he had dropped, folding it closed and sliding it back into his breeches, righting his clothing.

'You better answer him' he sighed unhappily. There was no answer. 'Laura?'

He turned. He was alone, she had already left the cave. He sighed again, wiping his mouth to dampen the taste of her, then shuffled out into the sunlight and the knowing grin of Roman.

56

'Wait outside, I may be some time' Laura whispered to Roman, before slipping into the library, closing the door behind her.

A fire had been lit earlier that evening, and it was now dying down, casting red shadows across the rug. Fredrik was sitting in a chair, still dressed, a book open on his lap. His eyes were closed, his hands gently folded across his lap, his head resting back on the warm leather of the chair.

She tip-toed over to him, stroking his loose hair back from his face, tracing lines on his soft skin. Her fingers slid across his lips, so supple and warm, delighting in the way he spoke, the shape of her name on them. He kissed her fingers, opening his eyes.

'I was afraid you would not come' he said quietly. 'But it is warmer than waiting for you under the willow tree in the grounds of Varennikov Castle.'

She kissed him, cutting off his words, and after a second of surprise Fredrik melted into the sweet embrace. Eager to feel his body pressed along hers again she hesitated only briefly before climbing onto his lap, sliding her arms around his neck. He shifted uncomfortably, hesitant in his touches.

'What's wrong?'

'Not like this, upright, like some common strumpet' he groaned.

'You sleep with many common strumpets do you?' she teased.

'You will be my first' he admitted.

'Your first strumpet?'

There was a fleeting look of annoyance on his face. She apologised, moving against him. He groaned.

'Laura, please' he begged.

'Fine, come to my rooms, you can fuck me in my bed.'

'Laura!' he gasped, pained and shocked and wanting...

She arched against him again and could feel him wavering. She kissed him again, her hands falling to his shirt, undoing his buttons.

'I am not common, or a strumpet' she whispered, opening his shirt, planting a kiss in the centre of his chest. '*Wir müssen ganz Leib und Seele sein*' she said, quoting the last line of the poem he had made her read that afternoon. *We must be one soul and body...*

Then she gave another line a dirty twist.

'Blow half your soul into me.'

'*Berühre mich*' he begged, folding his arms around her, opening against her lips.

She arched harder against him, into the hands he placed on her breasts, delighting in the way they moulded to the heat of him. Quickly he pulled undone her robe and tugged at the string for her chemise, opening the neck of her night gown. She flushed at the way he looked at her naked breasts, gasping at the heat of his hand against her bare nipple.

He kissed her breasts, took a nipple into his mouth, and she shuddered at the sensations, clasping his head tightly to her, aching and hot with desire. He pulled aside her robe, dropping it onto the floor, divesting himself of his shirt as well. He moaned when he pulled her against him, liking the unfamiliar chafe of her skin against his. He moaned again when she stroked the front of his breeches, gently undoing them.

He trembled in anticipation but was still unprepared for the electric sensation of her hand on his manhood, thick and bulbous with want for her. He could feel the heat of her sex though her thin chemise, wet with want, and the rough sensations as she moved against him were almost too much to bear. Her hands tangled in his hair, her body moving rhythmically against his, her lips fierce and passionate as she kissed and licked at his chest, his throat.

His hands fell to her thighs, pulling up her chemise, the soft cotton sinful in his fingers. He cupped her thighs and felt her gasp, then cry out as his long fingers found the soft wetness between her legs. He cupped her buttocks, his hips rising to meet hers, stroking the skin – she stiffened, pulling away.

He stopped.

'Laura, what ...?' he trailed off and she hid her face from him. 'Laura...'

She got off him, leaving him with an ache that went deeper than skin. He held onto her chemise and it slid off her, leaving her naked before him. 'What...' he started, and she turned her back on him.

Laura heard him gasp, heard him leap to his feet. She could feel his anger and hurt, could feel his eyes roaming over her scars.

'I was nine when my mother sent me to Lady Ramkinson's School for Decorum' she said dully. 'Whenever I was naughty or disobedient or did something wrong she would beat me with a riding crop. It was the first lesson I learned, *to fear the riding crop*. I was beaten for climbing trees, for making mistakes in French, for forgetting to lower my eyes when speaking to her...' she trailed off, and Fredrik took hold of her shoulders, gently kissing the nape of her neck.

'I am so sorry my love' he whispered, his lips tracing patterns across her shoulders.

'If you no longer wish to marry me -'

'I do' he interrupted. He turned her around, gazed down at her. 'I do' he repeated, gently.

He's already fastened his trousers again she noticed. *And his erection is gone.* She probably could stir it again with some gentle ministrations – he did respond so well to them – but the moment was gone now. She sighed and bent down for her chemise, pulling it back on and fastening it closed with the ties at her throat. Wordlessly Fredrik passed her robe to her, collecting his shirt and shrugging into it too.

'Please don't tell anyone' she said quietly.

'Your secret is safe with me' he soothed. He caught her hand as she turned away. 'Don't go, not yet' he begged, pulling her into his embrace. 'I don't want to be without you yet.'

She complied, sliding her arms around him and leaning her head against his chest. He sighed gently, kissing the top of her head, stiffening when he heard the floorboard creak outside the door.

'It is Roman' Laura said quietly.

'Did he hear us?' he flushed.

'I'm not sure, but he's a fool if he doesn't know who I was with.'

'Will we ever…?' he broke off, embarrassed.

'When we marry there will be no Putting to Bed Ceremony' she vowed. 'On my wedding night, when Aleksei dismissed the court they all followed us into his bedroom. I had to change into my nightclothes behind a screen, Anna saw me naked before my husband did. Then I had to get into his bed and I was mortified, I thought they would all stand there and watch while he – deflowered me. My *father* was there…' she trailed off, embarrassed again. 'There will be no such ceremony for us' she vowed again. 'But it will not matter. I will make you moan so loud Russia will hear you.'

He snorted, amused.

She sighed gently, content, and shut her eyes, nuzzling her cheek against him. But dawn was coming and the castle was beginning to stir, fleet footed servants bustled past on their way to light fires in the kitchen and prepare the Parliament Chambers for another day of arguing.

'When can we meet again?' he asked, his hand stroking her back gently.

'After Parliament. We will lunch in my private dining room, and admit no one, so we can consume all that we desire.' She flashed him a look that set his pulse racing again.

He leaned down to kiss her but she stopped him, pressing fingers to his lips.

'You burn me with your lips' she said. 'You'll set me aflame and I cannot leave, not till consumed, but like a phoenix I will rise for another little death.' She gave him an arch look.

He groaned at the thought of her *la petite mort*.

'I already smoulder' he said, kissing her fingers.

'You tempt me' she sighed. 'I cannot bear to be apart from you. Every second will seem an eternity until I am in your arms again.'

'Stay' he begged, trying to kiss her again, but she gently pushed him away.

'I need to go. And you need to *be*-flower me' she teased.

He groaned again, his fingers reluctantly letting her go. She pulled her robe around her tighter, grabbed a random book from a shelf and slipped out, not looking back.

Roman had gone off duty, so it was Malenkov who followed her back to her rooms, then followed her, now dressed, to the nursery.

'Mama!' Alexandra shouted happily when she saw her and Laura scooped her up, kissing her cheeks.

'Your mama's in love' she told her. 'And I'm going to marry him!'

She spun around the crib, waltzing with her daughter on her hip, who laughed excitedly.

'Yes I am!' she said, nuzzling her. 'I'm sure you will love him too my darling. He is so kind and gentle, he will be a good father to you. I'm sorry you will never know your real father. He was a good man too. Fredrik will love you like his own, and treat you no differently.'

She sighed, hugging her, smiling when Alexandra kissed her cheek, bouncing and wiggling in her arms.

'Are you hungry my love?' she asked, leaning back to look at her. 'Hungry?'

'*Da!*' Alexandra answered, surprising her.

The door opened and Marie stepped in, calling good morning to her.

'She can talk now?' Laura asked, surprised.

'Just a few words: *Da, Nyet,* -'

'*Net!*' Alexandra chimed in, shaking her head, laughing.

'- Mama and Marie.'

'Wee!' Alexandra shouted, reaching for Marie.

'Though she does call me *wee* rather than Marie' her embarrassed nanny finished.

'Does she understand me?'

'I don't think so, maybe a few basic words. Hello Your Highness' she said, taking Alexandra from Laura. 'Hungry?'

'*Da!*' Alexandra said again.

Laura led the way down to the dining room, meeting Fredrik in the entrance foyer.

'I'll take the *Tsesarevna* to the table' Marie said diplomatically, leaving the two of them alone.

Fredrik handed a deep-throated blue crocus flower to her, his fingers brushing hers. She smiled, tucking it into the simple bun in her hair, enjoying the way he watched her. He offered her his elbow and she took it, squeezing his arm as he led her into the dining room. As they approached they became aware of a conversation taking place just inside the room by the open door.

'- they'll be at clicket again this afternoon' Lev said.

'Well, Her Majesty *is* particularly fond of green gowns' Luka chortled.

They laughter stopped when Laura and Fredrik stepped into the room.

'That is good to know,' Fredrik said. 'I shall be sure to give Her Majesty a green gown.'

Laura's eyes widened in shock. The ministers bowed to them as Fredrik led her to the table.

'Do you know what you said? To give a girl a green gown?' she gasped in an aside.

'I am aware of the euphemism' he answered.

She stopped short, goggling.

'You just made a dirty joke!'

'I am not incapable' he answered. 'Ekaterina *is* my cousin, you know.'

He held her chair for her. She hesitated then sat, still eyeing him. She had thought Fredrik was so reserved to be almost innocent, and that he would be shocked at the carnal actions of the marriage bed. *But he wasn't shy about touching me* she reminded herself, *and not shy with his want for her. Maybe it had been there all along, and it was only his gentleness and decorum that had prevented him from displaying it.*

He did try to begin an affair with you all those months ago at Varennikov Castle she reminded herself. *You have misjudged him. I think you will enjoy finding out how wrong you were...* Her thoughts turned to the sight of him, glimpsed briefly in the firelight last night. *He'll make me enjoy that very much...*

Fredrik excused himself, quickly moving to accost Gustav, who had just stepped into the dining room. Laura wondered what was going on, why the two of them looked so grim. But she didn't have long to wonder. She had hardly begun to eat when Maksim called Parliament to session. She quickly kissed Alexandra's head, instructed Marie to continue feeding her, shoved some more food into her mouth and chewed industriously as she made her way to chambers.

Maksim looked even less pleased to see her today, and was visibly annoyed by the ingratiatingly sweet smile she shot him.

'My lords, I have happy news' she said, her voice trembling with excitement when Maksim had called Parliament to order. 'Baron von Schmidt has consented to be my husband.'

There was a loud gasp.

'*You ignorant bloody fool!*' Maksim thundered, slamming his fist down on the bench before him.

Parliament erupted, shouting and gesticulating wildly at each other. Some effort was made to quieten the floor, but no sooner did one minister raise objection or approval and it was interrupted by an opponent until they descended into chaos again.

Laura watched them with a sinking heart. Some ministers looked at her with open hostility, vitriol and vehemence in their words. Others looked exasperated or confused, but most were red faced with anger and aplomb, nose to nose with an adversary and shouting over each-others' words. Only Ilich was quiet, and watching the spectacle before him, occasionally shifting his glance to look at Laura.

He's no defender of mine she thought unhappily. *For all the "advice" he gave me.*

I wish they would all just shut up and let me live the way I want!

It was after midnight when Maksim finally, grudgingly, let them leave. Laura was red-eyed from crying, bitter and ashamed that he had reduced her to tears at least twice and frustrated doubly from the stagnated arguments and being kept from Fredrik's arms. She rushed up the stairs to her dining room, throwing open the door, apologies on her lips.

The room was empty, the table bare and gleaming with polish. But there was a lingering aroma of the waxy, phosphorous smell of extinguished candles. She shut her eyes against the hurt, too tired to cry again, definitely too tired to throw herself in his arms and make love passionately all night.

She turned away wearily, making her way laboriously up the stairs to her rooms. In her parlour she stripped off her dress and chemise, leaving a trail of clothes all the way to her bedroom where she slid between the cold covers and shut her eyes, her ears still ringing with the curses that had made her cry.

57

Laura woke late and quickly dressed, running down the stairs to the dining room. Fredrik was not there, but a wild pansy sat on her plate. She stared at it, a blush coming up in her cheeks. It had many common names, including Heart's Ease, Heart's Delight, Come-and-cuddle-me and Love-in-idleness. She wondered if he was angry with her, for teasing him into a frenzy then leaving him idle in his love, wanting her to come and cuddle – and more – and ease his poor aching heart.

She never got the chance to find out. Or even to eat or see her daughter, Maksim spitefully called Parliament to session while ministers were still arriving at the castle. She followed him to chambers, dreading the day of bullying that was to follow, wondering if starving her was a tactic to get her to break down and comply. *Lady Ramkinson tried that many times, it didn't work* she thought defiantly, sitting in Vsevolod's hard chair and watching disgruntled ministers file into the room.

Ilich's demeanour interested her as soon as he walked into the room. It was markedly different from yesterday's, his stride was measured and purposeful and – and *angry*. She could see in him a spark; a faint, frail ember of the fire she had seen in him once before; in a bar, standing on the tables, revolution on his lips. It felt like so many life-times ago. Something had changed in him, something fundamental. Laura was curious to see what would happen next.

If she had expected to see him rally to her cause and shout down the opposition with witty rhetoric she was sadly disappointed. She had watched him carefully in the endless hours of arguing, but again he said nothing, only watched and listened.

Under pressure from the ministers, some of whom were now in open rebellion, even in his own party, Maksim called an end to the Parliament at ten in the evening. Scuffles broke out between warring ministers and the guards were forced to separate them, pushing them out of the castle grounds. Laura was too exhausted to be alarmed at the depth of feeling in her ministers, barely managing to make it up three flights of stairs, her knees wobbling with the effort.

'God bless you Anna' she said aloud when she arrived in her rooms and noticed the tray of food waiting on her small writing table.

Her stomach gurgled painfully and she fell on the plate of cut meat, stuffing it into her mouth with her fingers. Then, still dressed, she collapsed onto her bed, the blackness stealing her away in a heartbeat. But her slumber was not restful and she woke in the grey light of dawn, stiff and cramped, her head ringing with arguments her dreams had had with her.

Disgruntled she sat up, wincing with the pain as sore muscles contracted and stretched, as her corset jabbed her uncomfortably. She was sorely tempted to not go to Parliament today, unsure how much more of this she could take. *I know they berated Aleksei mercilessly when he wanted to marry me* she told herself. *He must have either been incredibly stubborn or deeply in love then, to have insisted. Maybe both.*

She stood and washed, dressing in a deep navy blue, surprised by the dark circles she saw under her eyes in her mirror. She twisted her hair into a simple bun and pinned it in place with seed pearl clips, wondering what flower he would leave on her plate today.

Whatever else happens I'm going to see my daughter and have breakfast she thought, heading up to the nursery. Alexandra was sitting up in her cot, sleepily rubbing her eyes when she stepped in. She smiled when she saw Laura.

'Hung-ngy!' she announced, pulling herself to her feet on the rails of her crib.

Laura laughed in surprise and shock, pulling her out of the crib and kissing her cheeks.

'Clever girl!' she said, carrying her down to the dining room and sitting her in the high chair.

The table was empty of all others and for that she was grateful when she saw the particular flower Fredrik had left for her, flushing hotly. The deep purple flower was commonly called Touch-me-not, and sometimes Impatiens. This particular flower stored its nectar at the end of a long, thin tube, where only a creature with a long and skilful tongue would enjoy its delights. She picked it up and stared at it, the hot ache starting between her legs again.

Long fingers plucked it from her grasp and Fredrik threaded it into her hair.

'Be-flowered' he muttered, his voice thick with want. 'When can I deflower you?'

She kissed him, hard, pulling away when she heard footsteps approaching the dining room.

'Will you meet me for luncheon?' he asked.

'It is more likely to be dinner' she sighed ruefully.

'I am *impatient* for you' Fredrik whispered, his breath hard in his chest.

'I know' she plucked the flower from her hair. 'But this is also called *Patience*, my love' she said, tucking it through his button hole. 'I must eat, I suspect Maksim is trying to starve me to break down my resolve.'

Fredrik looked shocked.

'Eat, I will see to the *Tsesarevna*' he insisted, quickly placing morsels on a plate and setting it in front of her.

'No need' Laura smiled when Marie stepped into the room.

Marie bobbed a curtsey then greeted Alexandra, kissing her cheek before getting her a plate of soft food. Fredrik sat beside Laura and pulled out a small book of poetry to read to her, avoiding conversation least it detract from the time she could spend eating.

The dining room filled up quickly with ministers, all with one aim in mind: to eat as much as they could before Maksim called Parliament to session. The table was quiet, a few were surreptitiously stuffing bread rolls filled with cold cuts into their pockets. Despite their speed many still had not eaten when Maksim flung open the door, calling for Parliament.

All eyes swung to Laura. Quite deliberately she picked up her knife and sliced the top off a boiled egg, dipping a silver spoon into the shell. Ministers, who knew they could not leave the table till she was finished, settled back with happy smiles on their faces. She debated helping herself to another cut just to spite Maksim, but the door slammed open again.

'*Parliament now, damn you!*' Maksim thundered, and again all eyes turned to Laura.

She deliberately, and slowly, finished her tea, but her insides were jumping. Only Fredrik noticed the shake in her hand when she gave it to him to kiss. He squeezed her fingers comfortingly, then let her go, marvelling at the way she held herself. Laura stood, causing a reluctant rising in the ministers, and slowly made her way to chambers, dreading the day of haranguing that was to follow.

*

'…you must retract your offer of marriage!' Lev snapped.

'I will not' she answered.

Maksim slammed the legal tome he was holding down on the bench before him.

'You are not allowed to be a stubborn, stupid little girl!' he shouted. 'You cannot marry a man less than a tsar and you cannot open your legs for any pretty cock that comes along!'

Ilich, who had been silent again all day, now spoke one word.

'Enough.'

There were harmonics in his tone, notes of warning and authority and iron will. It was a cadence Laura had not heard for a very long time, and she was not the only one shocked at its emergence.

'What?' Maksim blinked.

Ilich's eyes bored into them. He spoke again, his voice no louder than it had been before, but all the more hardened. It was a voice that brooked no disobedience.

'Enough.'

Maksim opened his mouth. But it was late, he was angry and he knew if he tried to argue with Ilich now he would lose. He shut his mouth, then dismissed Parliament. If he could have spat he would have.

Laura wondered if she should say something to Ilich, but he left with the press of ministers before she got the chance. She sighed and got to her feet, making her way to the dining room on the first floor. Again the room was empty but for the smell of extinguished candles and she shut her eyes miserably, heading up to her rooms.

Roman saluted, eyeing her worriedly when she appeared.

'Good evening Roman' she said, tired.

The little clock on the hall stand began to tinkle ten o'clock. Roman was just in the process of telling her Fredrik was in her rooms when she pushed open the door and saw him sitting on her chaise lounge, a book lying abandoned beside him. He stood, hope rising in him, but it was dampened when he saw how tired she was. Laura closed her door and crossed to the decanter on her side table, pouring a small glass.

'I have missed you these past days' he said quietly. 'What have you been discussing in Parliament so long?'

'It is nothing really' she said dismissively, placing the crystal stopper back into the decanter.

A subtle change behind her made her turn and look at him, at the frustration she saw in his eyes. *Had he spent the day with his desire winding him tighter and tighter with thoughts of deflowering her at diner only to be denied again?* she wondered. But it was deeper than that, a frustration she well remembered when Aleksei brushed off her inquiries, that he was locked away with his Advisory Council and could not conduct a proper courtship with her. *He's slighted, but holding his tongue.*

'I am sorry' she said, coming back to him and seating herself, exhausted, on her chaise longue. 'I know how frustrating this is for you, I was once in your place. It will sound utterly stupid, *stupid* and ridiculous when I tell you. We have been arguing what your title shall be.' She drained her glass.

'*Three days* over what my *title* will be?' he cried, astounded.

He took her empty glass and put it back on the table, then sat gently beside her. She shut her eyes, leaning her head back, her body feeling sluggish and heavy.

'Among other arguments' she said despondently. 'It sounds so simple, but it really isn't. It's the blood you see, that's all that matters.' She sighed deeply.

'Ekaterina would have told you how Dalnerechenskers revere Vsevolod. And even if she didn't you would know it in all the subtle clues in the Principality. Vsevolod: the first tsar, defeater of Russia, saviour of Dalnerechensk. Each ruler is not just a son, a descendant; but a legacy, as if each new tsar is a pure continuation of him, as if he is reincarnated each generation. Each tsar takes his father's name, and his father's bed, in his official title: "Son of Vsevolod", "Son of Constantine", "Son of Stephan" – one unbroken line stretching all the way back to the first.'

She stopped, rubbing her forehead tiredly. Deep in her subconscious something stirred but she was too exhausted to pay it much heed.

'It's broken now' she said quietly. 'Dalnerechensk has *never* had a female ruler, not even of Vsevolod's blood. Not even as guardian while a son came of age, uncles always stepped in for that.' She looked at him. 'Four hundred years of men. It was unconscionable that there would ever *not* be a man on the throne.' She closed her eyes again, tired. 'I may not be his blood, but they can't deny I married it, and Aleksei's heir is of his blood too. But she's a woman.

'The trauma of all this is compounded by Dalnerechensk's marriage laws. Put simply, when I marry you, I will belong to you, not just metaphorically but literally too. You will *own* me. I will be property, and all my belongings, wealth and titles will pass to you. *You will be the Tsar of Dalnerechensk.*

'But you will not, because you are not his blood, and not even Russian, and that galls most of the ministers. I thought co-regency might pacify them, but I was wrong. One man, one tsar!' she said bitterly. 'Alexandra is his blood, but anyone she marries will become tsar as well. We are something that affronts the very souls of these people so stuck in history and legend and – and *medieval* mind sets.' She sighed again, rubbing her temples.

'They have forbidden me from marrying you. Insisted I recant my offer and marry Nikolai. They even went so far -' she paused, embarrassed. *Even went so far as to suggest they might change the law, so it would not be treason if I took you as a lover. They were thinking up* – rosters – *to try to differentiate between legitimate children and our bastards!* She was too embarrassed to tell him that.

'They are insisting I betroth Alexandra to Ilya. Others insist they change the law, to make me an honorary man, others insist I am not entitled to be Tsaritsa and that the crown – in its entirety – be passed immediately to Nikolai. But that is all knotted and complicated too.

'Russian society sets great store by the titles and standing of their nobility. They must give you a title that is royal, and above the members of the Vakhtangov household, but also one that does not supersede mine or my daughter's, one that does not allow any sons we might have come to the throne before Alexandra and any son she might have, but still allow them to inherit should Alexandra have only girls. Though some have argued that no children of ours be allowed on the throne.

'I know they argued when I married Aleksei, but never like this. My official title was *Velikaja Knjaginja*, the title for a wife of a royal prince but not the Heir Apparent. Tsar Constantinovich would affectionately call me *Tsarevna* – daughter of the Tsar. Those who knew which side their political bread was buttered on would call me that too. It meant, unofficially, that I was to enjoy all the privileges of the Royal Family, including inheritance. Afterwards a few began to call me *Tsesarevna* – wife of the heir. But Aleksei was never called *Naslednik*, not even unofficially. No one could bear the thought he was all they had' she stopped, her chin wobbling.

'Lev Dostoevski insists that I was only a prince's wife, and have no right to be tsaritsa, but it all got so messy after the deaths of Tsar Constantinovich and Aleksei and the revolution. They want the problem of me to go away, to neatly tie the two branches of Vsevolod's family tree back together in a little bow, placing Nikolai or Ilya squarely and completely on the throne. But at the same time they respect me here, their new Vsevolod, who saved them from Nikita and the second Russian invasion. That means a lot to my people.

'And the world is turning; changing. Some are enthusiastic, some are terrified, and all of it makes them argue and argue and *argue* and my poor head ache...' she trailed off.

'They cannot just let me love you.'

Fredrik was silent for a long time.

'I will truly be the Tsar of Dalnerechensk?' he asked. He sounded appalled.

She nodded wearily.

'If they do not change the law, yes. You will own me, and can take as many mistresses as you like, putting me aside when you feel like it. You can even have me flogged for embarrassing you.'

He winced at that, moving closer to her and taking her arms, turning her to face him.

'You could come home to Bavaria with me' he said urgently. 'You could marry me there, live with me there. You could give the throne to Nikolai -'

'No.'

'In God's name why not?' he cried.

'I fought for this place, and lost everything for it! -'

'And you are haunted by it' he interrupted. 'I saw you on the train journey here, saw the fear in your face. You hide it well but it is still there, isn't it' he demanded. 'Laura, my love, I am offering you everything again, please! -'

He was interrupted by an urgent knocking on her door. Roman pushed it open and revealed an agitated Gustav, a piece of paper clutched in his hands.

'Forgive me' he bowed to Laura. 'Fredrik!'

'*Was ist?*' he asked, crossing to the door.

Wordlessly Gustav handed him the paper. Fredrik took it and read it quickly.

'*Kleine Narr!*' he exclaimed, horror etching his voice.

He called someone a little fool Laura thought. *Something terrible has happened.*

'Fredrik?' she whispered, frightened.

He turned, and she saw the agony struggling on his face. It took him a moment to marshal his thoughts, and when he next spoke it was in English. 'Kurt has eloped with Anna. I must go after him.'

'I will go with you, they have been gone hours' Gustav added.

'Take my stallion, and the roan gelding, they are the fastest horses I own' Laura said.

'Forgive me' Fredrik said, turning to leave.

Then he turned back and pressed a firm kiss to her lips, his arms crushing her tightly against him. Then he was gone, running down the stairs after Gustav.

'Is everything alright, Your Majesty?' Roman asked, worried.

'No Roman, it is not' she answered, then quietly closed the door, wondering if she had any tears left with which to cry herself to sleep.

58

There was no flower on her plate this morning, and Laura sat alone at the table with her daughter. As much as she missed the flowers she was slightly relieved there would be no overtly sexual names forth coming. She was sure he was working up to give her flowers called Ladies Delight and Nymph's Thighs, maybe even the Cockhold Herb. She wondered briefly whether there was a flower called Fuck-me-lots, and if she would find it one day on her plate.

Or maybe I would find visually sexual flowers, like a deep-throated orchid, snapdragons or the peony daisy, with its proud and fleshy stamen. She wondered, briefly, whether she might come downstairs one morning to find *him* naked and erect, sitting on her plate, though she would have considerable trouble tucking *that* behind her ear.

She snorted out loud and quickly shook her head to dislodge her thoughts, turning her attention to Alexandra, who was managing to get at least some egg into her mouth. Laura laughed and cleaned her face and hands, wiping away the mess, then kissed her cheek. Alexandra grinned happily, grabbed another fistful of egg and mashed that to her face, slobbering on her hand in great gastronomic delight.

Laura was not surprised to see so few attend breakfast this morning, what with Maksim's marathon Parliament sessions and the wildfire gossip of Anna Vakhtangovna's elopement; very few wanted to be in the line of fire today.

'Did you know about this?' Lev demanded, storming into the dining room.

'Lower your voice, you are upsetting my daughter' Laura said archly. 'And no, I did not.'

'Can you not see how unsuitable a family you desire to ally yourself with? They are not the *Uradel*, not even *Hochadel!* They are nothing more than Paper Princes! Lettered Lords! This callous and ruinous action is a deliberate slander on the good name of the Vakhtangovs -'

'He is only a boy' Laura interrupted. 'And no doubt no one knows the full story.'

'You must -'

'I must do nothing' she cut him off. 'I understand there are many search parties looking for them and when they are found and returned they will answer to me. You grow too presumptuous' she warned him.

Lev scowled but bowed and left.

Laura sighed, and picked up her daughter, taking her back to the nursery. Marie was inside, upset and unwilling to go down to the dining room.

'Your Majesty!' she cried when she saw her. 'Such terrible a thing is happening!'

'You were close to Anna, weren't you' Laura said, placing Alexandra on the floor and giving her a woolly snake to play with. 'I did notice Kurt seemed to have feelings for her, but I thought it was just a harmless infatuation. Did you know of her feelings?'

'Yes Your Majesty' she admitted. 'She had feelings for him too, but I also thought it was something innocent. I never thought she would agree to – he hasn't forced -' she started to ask, but stopped herself.

'I don't believe so, I wouldn't think him capable' Laura said.

'Only I heard Varvara was angry with him because he kept asking to see her. She was going to make a complaint!'

Laura started to feel a little sick. She knew the old woman would seek revenge for her arrest and wondered if this was it; barring a young lover from seeing the object of his affection and then making a formal complaint that would have far reaching consequences. It was hardly a move that would topple her place in the monarchy, but would keep the malicious gossips entertained for months.

'The longer it takes to find them the worse this will seem' Laura said sadly.

She kissed her daughter farewell, then made her way down to Parliament, wishing she could avoid the hours of abuse that were to follow. To her surprise Maksim had effected an emergency closure of Parliament for the day, and the chambers were empty. Instead she went to Fedor's office, letting herself in and sitting down opposite him, waving him back into his seat.

'You are going to have to make an announcement regarding the young *Herr* von Schmidt and Anna Vakhtangovna' he told her. 'It is a scandal that will hurt your public personality, and Baron von Schmidt's too. No mention of the word *elopement* can be made.'

Laura was quiet, thinking.

'Anna has been confined to her sick bed of late' she mused out loud. 'Perhaps, so concerned for his friend's health he rushed her to one of the best physicians in Germany, youthful impetuousness not thinking through the perception nor the consequences of such an action. Our thoughts and prayers are with them for their safe return, and an improvement of young Anna's health.'

Fedor nodded in approval, jotting down her words.

'Perhaps not mention Germany, perhaps "world renowned physician", just in case they are found in Siberia, or Greece -'

'Would they really travel so far?' Laura gasped, shocked.

'Anna is in very poor health' he said quietly. 'I doubt they will get far, and I pray she is still alive when they find them.'

Laura sighed unhappily and selected the latest figures of her finances that Fedor had jotted down for her, finding some small comfort in the recovery of some of the expenses she had paid for her birthday.

Fedor handed her another sheet, this with investment recommendations jotted down, and Laura forced her wandering mind to focus on the task at hand. She approved of his choices and signed her agreement, then left him to organise a public proclamation for her at midday, returning to her rooms to write the short speech. *I better add in that I don't condone their actions, though I can forgive their youthful recklessness* she told herself, and wondered how Fredrik was feeling right now.

Somehow she managed to keep herself occupied until she had delivered the speech to the waiting commons below the wall, then tired of being cooped up in the castle she made her way to the stables, Roman following behind her as she mounted and rode out into the Hunting Forest.

When they reached the Northern Wall they stopped and dismounted again.

'Roman, you're a man with your ear to the ground, what are the people saying about Kurt and Anna?'

'Lots' he shrugged. 'There are plenty of rumours.'

Laura sighed, rubbing her temples, wondering what good her speech had done.

'Are they all really bad?' she wanted to know.

'Depends on your perspective' he shrugged again. 'Everyone is talking about how shocking it is they ran away together, but they also kind of… approve too. Everyone knows Varvara is a domineering hag and that poor girl is being used in a political game of musical beds -'

'What?!' Laura interrupted, shocked.

Roman blushed. 'I – I mean, there was talk that they were trying to arrange a marriage between her and the *Naslednik*, but there was also a rumour that Maksim was seeking a marriage with her too.'

'He's old enough to be her *grandfather*' Laura said with a shudder. 'I can't imagine Tatiana calling her mother!'

'Most everybody feels the same way you do, it ain't right' Roman agreed. 'So everyone kind of *approves* the kid got her out of it, even if he did it the wrong way.'

Laura sighed again, tipping her face up into the dappled sunlight, shutting her eyes against the warmth of it on her cheeks.

'And what says Lvov?'

'I will be going this afternoon, when my duty ends' he shrugged.

She smiled at that. 'Dear Roman, your duty never really ends does it. You are always my defender and my champion.'

'Yes Your Majesty' he said quietly.

'What will you tell him?'

'By now he should know I got the sapphire valued at Grünbaum's jeweller. The look he shot me was despicable.' He rubbed his arms, suddenly agitated. 'I don't like this Your Majesty' he protested. 'They all think I am your lover!' he stopped, agony twisting his face.

'I know' she sighed. 'Don't confirm it. There is no better way of getting people to believe a falsehood than to deny it. But tell them you took that jewel from my hair yourself.'

'I can't do this!' he cried. 'You don't know what you ask of me!'

'I know exactly what I ask of you' she said, rounding on him. 'I know exactly how twisted and terrible this is.'

Roman clenched his fists.

'Did your other servant ever deny you?' he wanted to know.

'No. But he was Aleksei's spy long before he ever was mine.'

She sat down on the northern wall, briefly putting her face in her hands. 'Roman' she pleaded. 'I know how this hurts you. I would not ask if I did not feel it necessary. You serve me in the slander and the lies and the misdirection. And if it makes you feel any better I believe they will make their move soon, probably before Nikolai returns. I am alone, my most ardent supporters are gone. This will soon all be over.'

'Not all your ardent supporters' he said thickly.

She took his hand and kissed the back of his fingers. He dropped to one knee before her, clutching in sudden fright at her hands, pressing them to his forehead.

'What will they do to you?' he asked.

He felt her hands tremble and he squeezed them tighter, looking up at her. She turned her face away.

'Maksim rules by pieces of paper. Most likely he will gather the signatures of all the ministers claiming I have no right to the throne and transfer all titles immediately to Nikolai. They might allow me to continue to call myself *Vdova*, but not Tsaritsa. He will argue and twist the law until it does what he wants it to. And he will stop the co-regency.'

'What will you do?' he wanted to know.

'Take my voice to the people. And Nikolai will be back in sixteen or so days. I can hold out.'

'I hope that you're right, Your Majesty' he said, kissing her hands again.

She gently took her hands away, and smoothed down his hair.

'Come, no more talk of these unpleasant things' she said, standing up. 'It is a pleasant day and you are pleasant company. Let's ride to Davostok and back, they should have finished the work on repairing the road by now.'

Roman bowed and swung himself back into the saddle, following her as she moved off through the trees.

59

Two more days of arguments and propositions had passed, though neither of the sessions in Parliament had lasted more than eight hours. She had received only one terse telegram from Fredrik, they had had no luck locating Kurt and Anna Vakhtangovna so far. It had made her heart sink to read it.

Uneasy and unable to sleep she had paced around her room until the clock in the hallway had tinkled past one o'clock. She forced herself to stop, and collected the diary from the drawer in the fireplace, taking it back to her bed. She had made her way through half of the entries, and she had not seen the name Alexander Andrei again, the name that had forced her to pry into the private thoughts of Tsar Constantinovich.

Idly she flicked through the remaining entries, back and forward disinterestedly. But she couldn't leave well alone. *I need to know why he abdicated* she told herself, then selected a random entry, beginning to read.

3 September 1868

S signed a trade agreement today. He is so young, yet his negotiations with Russia means the price of tin will not fall for another 5 years. N is very impressed with him, as is mother, and I know Father would have been proud of him too. He was not a man to show affection often, but there is no doubt in my mind how affectionate he would have been on hearing that news.

S is nearly delirious with happiness. The announcement was made, and Dal celebrated, how could they not? I am so conflicted. I wish him all his happiness, yet wish so fervently, so angrily against him too. But I could not bring myself to quarrel and hurt him, when he has only ever been kind and just and loving to me.

Oh Jagna, I am so desperately unhappy!

Laura shut the book and pushed back the covers, stealing across her quiet room and deposited the diary back in the secret drawer. *A trade agreement for that date shouldn't be too hard to find.* She pulled on her robe and opened her door, stepping out into the dimly lit corridor. Roman didn't look surprised to see her, and followed her wordlessly, somewhat preoccupied, to the library again. She lit one of the oil lamps and turned the flame up, heading to the furthest shelves, where the legal documents were held.

'Something on your mind Roman?' she asked quietly, pulling a tome off the shelf.

'Hmm?' he asked, then seemed to come to his senses, a little alarmed. He cocked his head, his eyes probing the dark corners of the room, before looking at her again, worried.

'It's not like you to forget to do that first' she said, eyeing him. 'It seems we are both preoccupied and restless tonight.'

'Forgive me' he said, searching the corners again. Then he stepped closer, his voice falling. 'He was not there, Your Majesty' he whispered. 'He always makes me wait, but he always meets me. I don't know how he knows, maybe someone sends a runner to him, but he is always waiting when I leave the tavern. He wasn't this time.'

Laura felt cold.

'You have either been discovered, or they have all the information they could want on me.'

'I don't know how you do it Your Majesty, this world of intrigue and assignation. It would drive me crazy!'

'How many times have we gone to the library because I have been unable to sleep?' she smiled. 'How many times did you listen to me cry?' She stopped and sighed. 'It is difficult. You suspect everyone and trust no one. It makes you so very lonely.'

She looked away and his arm brushed hers as he shifted beside her. She doubted very much that it was accidental, and her fingers played with the book nervously, carefully checking the dark corners of the room again.

A small piece of cardboard fluttered out from between the pages and she stooped to pick it up, aware that Roman had moved too, so close to her that she could feel the heat of him. She glanced at the piece of paper and gasped in shock, moving away to the lamp to squint closer at it in the light of the flame. Behind her Roman fell silent.

The world was crystalising around her, cold and sharp and brittle. Her hand shook, and she used both hands to steady the piece of cardboard, staring at the familiar script. It was Tsar Constantinovich's handwriting, and it was *not* the script in the diary.

'Ess!' she said out loud, shocked.

S and the court… S signed a trade agreement… Of course he would, because Stephan Constantinovich was Tsar, and the tsar made those decisions, but a brother would still call him by his own name she realised. It had been nagging at the back of her mind for some time now, and it was all beginning to make sense. Her rooms had been Jagna's rooms, and Radomyr had moved into them after she had married. The diary belonged to Radomyr, and he was in love with his brother's wife.

And she was in love with him too she realised. *Did they have an affair? Was Alexander Andrei their child? Is that what he had discovered?* Her soul was growing colder by the second. *Fedor had said the* Tsesarevich *had had those rooms, and he hadn't meant Aleksei. Alexander Andrei had had her rooms, and he had found the diary, and read what was written there.*

The piece of cardboard fluttered from nerveless fingers. She pressed her hands to her mouth, sinking down to her knees in misery. Roman came forward, taking hold of her arms.

'Go stand guard in the corridor' she snapped at him, recoiling from his touch.

He was hurt by her rejection; she could see it in his face. He couldn't answer, but bowed stiffly, slamming the door harder than he needed to behind him. Laura stared at the piece of card without seeing it. *Was that what had driven him mad? Was he illegitimate?* She rose and abandoned the book carelessly, making her way back to her rooms.

'Admit no one, not even Anna' she instructed Roman, then closed the door, pulling out the diary from the secret drawer.

She took it to her bed and found the last entry she had read in proper chronological order. She turned up the flame on the oil lamp and pulled it closer to her, beginning to read.

Evening was approaching when she had finished. The last entry had been difficult to read because the hand that had been writing had been shaking. The ink had run and smeared in places, as if someone had wept over the words. She wasn't surprised. It was Radomyr's last confession, and was dated the same day of his death.

They had been lovers. But they had only been together one night, one *passion filled night, before her engagement to Stephan*. Neither Laura nor Radomyr could understand why Jagna continued with the marriage, especially knowing how she felt about him. *Maybe it was because Stephan was so kind and gentle she couldn't bear to hurt him, or maybe she had panicked when she realised she was pregnant and had slept out of wedlock with Stephan too. When she had revealed that she was pregnant, Stephan would have married her to preserve her honour, in the belief that the child was his.*

Agnieszka had given Radomyr a lock of her golden hair, the lock that lay beside Laura on her pillow now, and allowed him to call her Jagna, the only one who could. Radomyr had carved their secret initials under every rock in the cave, and poured his grief and joy at the birth of his son into his diary, a child he could never call son, tormented to watch him grow into a fine man, never knowing how deeply Radomyr loved him.

He called my son Alexander Andrei…

She had also found in the pages of the diary a mention that Radomyr had been the one to give the Countess her lucky black diamonds, a present for Alexander Andrei's birth. No wonder they had become Jagna's favourite jewels. And she had been lucky, it seemed Tsar Constantinovich had not suspected. Laura doubted he had ever known his *Naslednik* was not his.

The diary entries had grown infrequent again, but Laura could tell his feelings for her had never abated. They had loved long and passionately, but had never been together again, not even a kiss or a clandestine touch. The diary entries grew so infrequent there was a period of five years between the penultimate entry and the last, and Laura could read in it the heart-breaking change.

Between the entries it seemed Radomyr had moved out of these rooms, and Alexander Andrei had moved into them. The diary must have been left behind in the fireplace, where it had lain undiscovered until the death of the Countess.

Her end had been cruel and painful and short; sudden and devastating for all. The terrible shock of her passing had sent Alexander Andrei into a rage, he who had been so close and fond of his mother, and the impotent fury had seen him destroy his room, where a lucky blow with a thrown object had revealed the drawer and the diary.

Radomyr's shaky confession had detailed what had happened next. Maddened by grief and hate and disgust he had confronted his uncle, who admitted, with a hand shaking with remorse and agony, that the confrontation had come to blows. Laura never knew whether that meant he had hit his son, or whether Alexander Andrei had hit him, but the emotional agony of Alexander's breakdown was raw and visceral to read.

Tsar Constantinovich's disbelief and hurt at his abdication was palpable in Radomyr's words. He had begged him to reconsider, pleading with him to no avail. There was a hint, only a mere suggestion, that Alexander Andrei might have tried to hurt himself, which put an end to the attempts to dissuade him. Laura's heart ached at his actions, a man so distraught to find his world turned upside down, and he could not bring himself to tell his father that he could not take the throne because his wife, who had not even been buried yet, had had an affair.

Radomyr had finished his entry with a direct appeal to his son, begging him to forgive him and his mother for what they had done. Laura wondered if the tears that had blurred the words been his or Alexander Andrei's, weeping for everything he had lost.

Aleksei had been the true Heir all along, but he had grown his whole life believing he was not. She wondered if he ever knew his older brother was illegitimate. She doubted it.

An illegitimate child had fathered her illegitimate child...

She sighed and shut her eyes, sore from all the weeping she had done. Her fingers stroked the soft edge of the silk bedsheet, tracing patterns on it. *These were his rooms. He had slept here, dreamed here...*

Once that might have stirred a painful longing in her heart, and a desperate, miserable want to feel him again, to read the words he had written and sob brokenly into her pillows. Now she only felt a deep sadness, an empathy for the agonies of his life. She finally understood why he had turned his back on his birthright: Because he *had* no right. It was a gesture that had been both gallant and terrible.

Laura rolled over, folding her arms around the book and pulling her knees up, shutting her eyes. She was desperately tired, she had not slept at all, but did not think sleep would come. *I have not eaten either* she thought, and pushed back the covers, padding through her silent parlour. She put the diary back in the secret draw, pushing it closed with a click that sounded so final; that seemed to signal it knew she would never open it again.

'Roman,' she started, pulling open her door, then stopped in surprise.

There was a young guard outside her door, one of her personal bodyguards, but one so young he was rarely used outside her doors. He saluted nervously.

'Your Majesty, the *Sotnik* is not here, Your Majesty' he said.

She blinked, shocked.

'What?' she gasped. 'He has abandoned his post?!'

He saluted again. 'Your Majesty, I don't know, Your Majesty. He was supposed to come back on duty half an hour ago, Your Majesty. He's late, and they made me stand here to protect you, Your Majesty.'

He saluted again, in case protocol would save him from the stammering mess he found himself in.

Laura opened and closed her mouth a few times, the memory of the look on his face when she had rejected him last night opening a chasm of dread in the pit of her stomach. *What have you done Roman...*

'I am hungry, have something sent in' she said instead, closing the door on his nervous salute.

She heard him leave, but then stop and come back, unsure how to fulfil her instruction when his duty said he could not leave his post. She heard him step away again, then heard him say:

'You're late! Where have you been? I was supposed to have gone off duty half an hour ago!'

'None of your business' Roman answered gruffly.

'You're drunk!' the younger guard cried. 'You stink of alcohol! You can't do your duty like this!'

'Don't tell me what I can or can't do. I'm your damn captain, not you' he answered viciously.

'You're a disgrace!'

There was the sound of a blow, and the younger guard yelped.

'The Commander will hear of this!' he yelled.

'Stop that noise and be off' Roman snapped and there was another thump, possibly a boot to a backside.

The younger guard's voice retreated, still reproachful and indignant. There as a creak as Roman settled into position outside her door, and she wondered whether to open the door and berate him for his behaviour. *Something has gone terribly wrong* she realised. *And I doubt I'm going to get some food.*

She sighed, tired, and went back to bed, winding the covers tightly around her and wishing, quite fervently, that she was not alone.

60

It was the scuffle outside her apartments that woke her just before dawn. Roman was struggling with someone, grunting with effort.

'You are under arrest, dammit, be under arrest will you?' someone snapped.

Laura suddenly felt cold. She sat up in a rush, then tumbled out of bed, pulling on her robe as she ran for the door.

'You cannot leave her unguarded!' Roman protested. 'Malenkov, you will -'

There was a sound of a slap and Roman broke off.

Laura yanked open the door, eyeing the tableau before her. *They were Parliament soldiers, not her Vsevolod Guards who were arresting Roman* she realised. Malenkov and Spanov were hovering nearby, their rifles gripped in their hands, unsure what to do. Roman's gun was lying on the floor, and his hands were already fastened in iron handcuffs behind his back, his cheeks dark with rage.

'Stay in there and barricade yourself in' he snapped when he saw her, his words cut off when the butt of a rifle was driven into his side, making him double over, wheezing.

'You dare abuse a prisoner in your custody?' Laura snapped, folding her arms, sounding more authoritative than she felt.

The guard shot her a look of hatred, but it was mingled with unease, and he grabbed Roman's arm, beginning to hustle him down the stairs. The three remaining Parliament soldiers grabbed hold of Roman too, and all but lifted and carried him out of the castle. *Barricade myself in* he had instructed. Fear and confusion were knotting tightly around her stomach and backbone. *From what?*

'Malenkov, take up station in your *Sotnik's* place' Laura instructed. 'Spanov, take his gun and report to Peter Kamanin, Roman was drunk on duty and has been arrested, therefore someone needs to replace him in his duties today.'

Both of them saluted and Laura closed her door again, squeezing her hands tightly together to stop the fluttery nerves in them. A deep sense of foreboding was stirring within her. *Get dressed* she told herself. *And wear white. You will not be in your nightshirt when they spring their trap.*

I will not be hungry either she thought, fastening her dress and pinning her hair into a simple bun. She hesitated, torn between collecting Alexandra and leaving her in the nursery. No doubt Maksim would be smug and unpleasant as he tore power away from her. She knew if she cried it would upset her daughter, who wouldn't understand what was happening.

She decided to eat on her own and pulled open her door. To her shock the corridor was empty, Malenkov was not at his post. She blinked and looked left and right, but she was alone. The unease wound so tight it nearly strangled her, and she knew she could not eat now, the little she would be able to force down would be so upset by the fluttering butterflies in her stomach that it probably wouldn't stay there.

Anna appeared at the top of the stairs, alarmed and apprehensive to see Laura standing in her corridor, and without a guard. Laura quickly beckoned her in, closing the door behind her.

'Roman has been arrested' she whispered to her.

Anna's mouth fell open in shock and she stared, stupefied, at Laura. Before she could go on there was a knock at the door and Tatiana pushed it open.

'If it pleases Your Majesty, we have come to embroider today' she said, curtseying affectedly, Polina copying her.

Laura tried not to look pained. *Of all days!* she thought irritably, only half aware that Tatiana had sailed into her apartments without waiting to be given permission.

'I have no wish to embroider today' she said, and watched the two of them shoot each other sly looks.

'But Your Majesty!' Tatiana protested. 'We cannot leave you unprotected in your rooms now that your Captain has been arrested! It is terrible! Shocking!-'

'Scandalous!' Polina added helpfully.

'How frightful it must be to have been so close to one arrested for treason!'

Treason.

The word chilled her blood. And suddenly she understood what was happening, that these harpies were here at the kill. She heard the marching feet in the corridor seconds before her door was pushed open again. Peter Kamanin and four Parliamentary soldiers, armed with poleaxes, stamped noisily into her room, their gazes distant and carefully blank.

'*Vdova* Laura Aleksa Stephanovna Vakhtangova, you are under arrest' Peter Kamanin said, his voice curiously flat, as if he were somehow detached from what was happening, as if he couldn't hear the words coming out of his own mouth.

Laura ignored the gasps and exclamations of Tatiana and Polina. They were forced and fake, the sneer and the smirks were obvious. Anna screamed in anguish and threw herself at Laura's feet, hugging her skirts, protesting her innocence.

Barricade myself in she told herself bitterly. Roman knew what was coming. Is that why he had been drunk? Unable to protect her, to stop what was coming? *He could have taken me away, or warned me. I wish I had thought to take his dropped rifle myself...*

Gently she reached down and took Anna's hands, stilling her.

'My faithful friend' she said quietly, gently, stroking back her hair and lifting her chin to smile at her. 'Rise and see to my guests who were so thoughtful of me in my time of need. This matter shall pass soon enough. *Graf*

Pavlodar, must I be handcuffed?' she held out her wrists, aware of the hateful look Anna had sent Tatiana and Polina.

'No Your Majesty' he assured her.

'To where will you take me to be imprisoned?' she wanted to know.

'The tower in the West Wall, Your Majesty' he answered. 'Please follow me.'

'Very well' she said calmly, folding her hands gently in front of her.

The four soldiers took up positions around her, and Peter Kamanin marched, stiff-backed, out of the castle and across to the tower in the castle's curtain wall.

'What is the charge?' Laura asked when Peter knocked on the narrow wooden door.

He looked pained. *He knows, but the soldiers do not, and he's not going to say it in front of them* she realised. Laura was grateful, and did not press the matter further.

The door was opened by the castle's jailer, a fat and slovenly fellow with piggy, squinting eyes and legs so skinny they had bowed under the weight of his enormous stomach. He looked like a particularly vile egg that was hatching upside down. He eyed Laura lecherously and eyed the soldiers distrustfully.

'Need all of yers for one little girl do yers?' he said.

'I will escort Her Majesty, you are not needed' Peter Kamanin said, dismissing the guards. They saluted and left.

Peter hesitated, and Laura wondered if he was giving her an opportunity to escape. They were near the stables; one quick dart and a lack-lustre pursuit could see her bare-backed on a horse, successfully avoiding incarceration. *The innocent don't run* she told herself, and the moment passed.

The jailer led her up a winding, circular staircase, passing many heavy iron doors in the process. She wondered, briefly, whether Roman was in one of these cells too. She pushed that thought away roughly. At the top of the staircase a short corridor led the way to a single iron door, black with age and soot. The jailer unlocked it, and Laura was escorted in.

It was a small room, with a single, hard bench as the only furniture. There was no glass in the tiny, arrow-slot window, and Laura was glad it was not winter as the room would have been unbearably cold. As it was the fresh breeze made the room almost pleasant, if a cell could ever be called pleasant. There were fresh rushes on the floor and a chamber pot tucked under the bench.

'What happens now?' Laura asked, only a tiny amount of the fear she actually felt obvious in her voice.

'Now yers my pretty bird' the jailer cackled. 'And I keeps yer till yers sings!'

He slammed the door shut, and Laura heard him turning the key in the massive lock. *He will be watching* she knew, so she crossed to the bench and sat down, folding her hands in her lap, schooling her face carefully to hide her fear. It was nearly twenty minutes later before she heard him grunt and move away, his footsteps disappearing down the steps. Only then did she let herself cry, pressing her hands to her mouth to stifle the sound of her fright.

61

She woke when she heard the key twist in the lock. She was still sitting upright on the bench, and her cell was dark, only a faint glimmer of moonlight illuminated a bar of the floor. The door was pushed open, the sullen orange glow of an oil lamp spilled in from the corridor. Peter Kamanin, looking tired, stepped in, followed by the jailer, who was holding the light.

'Up yer gets pretty bird, time to sing!' he crowed.

There was a fleeting look of disgust on Peter's face. The jailer held up a pair of iron cuffs.

'I am to be handcuffed?' Laura asked, surprised.

'He has insisted' Peter said.

Laura didn't envy him, he hated doing what he had to do. She held out her hands, and the cuffs were fastened uncomfortably tight around her wrists. Peter took hold of her arm gently, guiding her down the steps and out into the night.

There was no sound. Dalnerechensk slept, the deep slumber of a city who did not know of the recent events. The guards in the castle were all Parliamentary soldiers, and Laura wondered what had happened to her Vsevolod Guard. *Perhaps Maksim had worried that her loyal, well armed and well trained body guard would have staged a rescue and summarily incarcerated all of them too.*

The jailer had not left his kingdom in the tower, so Peter alone walked her to the ball room, where a table had been erected at the far end. Behind it sat Luka, his hands folded together on the table top, watching her dispassionately. A smaller writing desk had been set up against the wall, nearly hidden in shadows, and a second man sat behind it, scribbling industriously on several sheets of paper.

There was no one else in the room. Laura blinked, surprised that Maksim, or even his cousin was not there. In fact she was surprised the entire Parliament and Vakhtangov family was not here to sit in judgement of her. The clandestine nature of this meeting gave her some hope. *But who was that second man? I feel I should know him…*

He looked up briefly, leaning forward to place a finished piece of paper onto the pile set aside at the top of the desk, the moonlight momentarily falling across his features. *I know him, Seryeshka Shcherbakov, Nineczka's brother.* The realisation gave her no comfort. Maksim was conspicuous by his absence, and Laura wondered if she had read the political landscape wrong. Maksim's coup would have been bloodless, she didn't know where she stood with these two. *Nowhere good…*

Luka finally moved, reaching for an ewer of water, pouring a glass for himself. He placed the jug carefully on the table and took the glass, sipping it slowly, watching her over the rim. But Laura was not cowed by his tactics to intimidate her.

'Well?' she demanded. 'You did not drag me from my cell to watch you drink water.'

Luka looked annoyed and placed the glass with a thunk back onto the table. He stretched his hand back towards Seryeshka, who handed him the stack of paper he had been adding to. *Reports of some kind* Laura guessed. She suspected he was Lvov's contact. *Roman had gone to meet Lvov when she had rejected him, and told him something in a fit of anger.* Within hours they had both been arrested. *The ink would have still been damp on her warrant when Peter had been given his orders.*

Maksim knew she suddenly realised. *Tatiana and Polina had* certainly *known. Maksim knew, but he was letting Luka do this. This was going to be dirty…*

Luka put the papers in front of him and made a big show of reading them, delicately turning over each piece and aligning it squarely with the one below it.

'Laura Vakhtangova -'

'*Vdova* Laura Aleksa Stephanovna Vakhtangova' she interrupted.

Annoyance flickered over his features again.

'You are accused -'

'Who accuses me?'

He blinked, caught off guard.

'You are accused -'

'*Who accuses me?*' she demanded.

'- of adultery and treason' Luka finished, speaking over her. 'Do you understand these crimes?'

Laura scanned the sentence for hidden meaning but could see none.

'Yes' she answered.

'I sentence you -'

'I demand a trial' she interrupted.

Luka glared at her.

'I sentence you -'

'*I demand a trial!*' she shouted.

'You have *confessed!*' he shouted, slamming down his pen, incredulous and frustrated.

'To what?' she asked, surprised.

'Adultery and treason!' he shouted, agitated, looking at her as if she were stupid.

'Admitting I am in full possession of my cognitive ability to understand what crimes of treason and adultery *are* is *not* a confession' she snapped. 'What right do you have to act in the interest of the law? I demand a lawyer, a trial and an unbiased judge.'

Luka slammed his fist down on the table.

'No.'

'Every citizen of Dalnerechensk is given the right to face their accuser in court. Who accuses me and where is the court?'

Luka slammed his hands repeatedly into the table.

'You will never have a trial and a judge!' he shouted.

'Then they will hang you.'

Luka froze, his voice dropping to a whisper.

'You dare *threaten* me?'

'You of all people know what happens when men are enraged by injustice and contempt for their rights' she said calmly, though she was beginning to shake.

The air suddenly felt dangerous.

'Get her out of my sight' Luka snarled at Peter.

He saluted then took Laura's arm gently, guiding her away.

'Well done' he whispered when they were out of ear shot.

'I need a lawyer, quickly, but I don't know any' she said.

'I do' he answered.

'Would you be so kind as to ask him to help me?'

'Yes Your Majesty.'

'Where is Roman being held? In here too?' she asked when he knocked on the tower door.

'No Your Majesty. I don't know where he's being held. He's not in the barrack's prison, nor the civilian one. He's not in the castle or the towers, I've been looking for him.'

She felt cold at that. *Had he played me for a fool all this time?* she wondered.

The door opened and the jailer leered out, grumbling about the late hour.

'Ain't sung yet 'as yer?' he grinned as he shut the door behind them. 'Ne'ermind, we's gat all manner of things to makes pretty birds sing!'

Laura gasped, grabbing Peter's arm with shaking hands. The jailer rocked back under his punch, screaming and clutching at his nose. Peter hauled him up by his collar and held him, feet dangling, against the wall. He stepped close and began to whisper, and Laura watched the jailer's face grow paler then greener at his words. Finally he set him down.

The jailer managed a small bow. 'It pleases Yer Majesty to come this way' he mumbled, looking askance at Peter, then headed quickly up the stairs to her cell.

'You are to unlock her handcuffs then give us a moment alone' Peter said. 'And you are to send up some food.'

'Yer 'onnor' he said, touching his forelock and unlocking her quickly before disappearing down the stairs.

'He will be unpleasant, but he won't hurt you now' Peter promised. 'Is there anything I can get for you?'

'Is Alexandra alright?' she asked, worried. 'She must think I have abandoned her. Please tell me if she is alright. And a lawyer is all I need now. Thank you Peter, for your kindness. I will not forget it' she swore.

He kissed her hand and reluctantly left her, closing the door behind him. Laura sat down to wait for whichever came first: the lawyer, news or the food.

It was the food, arriving two hours later, cold, and with a glistening glob of phlegm floating in it. She sighed and placed the bowl under her bench, sitting back and hoping the lawyer and news of Alexandra weren't too far behind.

62

Night had fallen again when she heard her cell door unlock. She had waited all day but Peter had not returned with news of Alexandra, or a lawyer, and she was irritated at the lack of progress. She had drifted off some time in the afternoon, dozing in the heat of the late summer day, but the key jangling in the lock startled her awake. She wondered just how late it was.

The door was pushed open and Luka stepped in. The jailer gave Laura a lecherous look and retreated down the stairs, leaving them alone.

'Where is Alexandra?' he asked.

She blinked.

'What do you mean where is Alexandra?' she cried, jumping to her feet. 'She should be in the nursery, with Marie Borodina!' She stopped talking, realising that this might be just a trick to break her.

'Where is Alexandra?' he asked again, taking a step towards her.

'She is in the nursery with Marie Borodina' she answered, forcing herself to be calm.

Luka asked her the same question three more times, growing more irritated at each repetitive answer. He stopped asking, his fists opening and closing, then he folded his hands in front of himself; a small, knowing smile touching his lips.

'Surely you must realise the evidence we have against you is compelling' he said. 'You cannot hope to win a trial. -'

'Then why so frightened of giving me one?'

His face hardened. 'I am not frightened' he snapped. 'We will be kinder if you confess.'

'I will not' she said quietly.

'Confess!' he shouted.

'If your case is so compelling take me to trial. You are wasting your time trying to intimidate me into a false confession.'

'You fucking whore' he spat, lashing out.

The blow caught her across the cheek and she stumbled, twisting away from him. He grabbed her, his lips crushing against hers, and she could taste the fetid stench of stale alcohol. The weight of him pulled her down and they crashed onto the floor, his bulk pinning her to the ground. She drove her knee hard into his groin, her questing hand finding the chamber pot under the bench. She whacked that with all her strength across his head, breaking it.

His fist struck her temple and she screamed, and again as another blow landed. Luka was screaming, blowing reeking breath into her face. Suddenly his collar was grabbed and he was yanked off her, swearing, and pushed out of the room. Laura scrabbled to her feet, sick and swaying dizzily, pressing one hand to the wall for support.

Ilich her groggy thoughts supplied. *It's Ilich.*

'What in God's name do you think you are doing?' he shouted.

Luka said nothing, spat and left. Ilich's ire fell to the jailer, lurking behind the door.

'You dare – *dare* – stand idly by while a woman in custody is violently mistreated?!' Ilich thundered. 'You will arrange forthwith, and *with alacrity*, to have her detention commuted to house arrest -'

''Ere, I can't do that!' he protested.

'Last year there were *five* cases that were commuted just so, and you signed every one of them' Ilich went on, then began to quote chapter and verse of each of the cases and the arrests.

The pain in Laura's head was making it difficult to follow the conversation. The rancid taste of alcohol on her lips made her violently sick and she threw up against the wall that was supporting her.

'- and you will do so at once' Ilich finished, moving closer to Laura.

'But -'

'*At once!*' he roared, and the jailer scuttled off, cowed. He took a deep breath then turned to Laura, taking hold of her arm in case she fell over. 'Are you hurt?' he asked quietly, kindly. 'Do you need to see your physician?'

'Where is my daughter?' she asked, grabbing his arm to steady her.

'I do not know.'

'Is she missing? Tell me, is she missing?!'

'I don't know. I will find out' he promised. 'Are you injured at all?'

Her voice suddenly became small.

'Please don't leave me alone here.'

'I won't' he said quietly.

The jailer returned and handed Ilich a piece of paper. He took it and read it carefully. The jailer hadn't expected him to do that, and suddenly looked very nervous. Ilich thrust it back at him.

'The *correct* papers, please' he said coolly. 'We shall accompany you, to ensure such a silly mistake is not made again.'

The jailer grumbled, but headed back down the stairs, Ilich and Laura following him. Ilich placed one firm arm around her waist, aware of her dazed and sluggish reactions. He could feel her trembling, like the last leaf of autumn in a gale. The correct papers were handed over with bad grace, and Ilich gently guided Laura out into the chill of the midnight air.

'House arrest' she said, aware that he was leading her away from the castle, towards the stables. 'Where will I go?'

'Home with me' he said gently.

She wanted to refuse, she had no wish to suffer Nineczka's sneering contempt, but nothing could have persuaded her to go back into that jail now.

Four Parliament soldiers met Ilich at his small carriage, announcing that they were there to guard the prisoner. Two got into the carriage with them, and two climbed onto the footplate at the back of the coach, instructing the driver to go no faster than a walking pace.

Laura was not surprised to see a unit of soldiers waiting outside the modest home where Ilich lived. They climbed down from the coach, and the ones that had accompanied them from the castle followed them up the stairs as Ilich produced a large key from his pocket, unlocking the front door.

But on the threshold Ilich turned and spoke to them.

'I understand you are ordered to stand guard over Her Majesty but unless you have the proper documents, and I know for a fact that you do not, then you are not permitted to set one foot inside my home without my express permission, and that, gentlemen, you do not have' he said. 'The law will be upheld, you have my word' he finished, then shut the door, leaving the soldiers outside.

'Your wife…?' Laura asked.

Ilich suddenly looked strained.

'She is not here' he said. 'Come into the parlour, put your feet up. I would feel better if you would at least allow me to fix you a cold compress.'

She sat on the small settee and leaned back, gently feeling the side of her head where Luka's blows landed. Ilich bustled about making her comfortable, then presented her with a cold compress which he laid gently on her temple. She winced and held it in place, looking at him carefully.

'Why did you come to the jail?' she suddenly asked.

'Peter Kamanin said you were in need of a lawyer.'

She eyed him, shocked. 'You're a lawyer?'

'I was, before I was a politician' he answered.

And you had debated with yourself, hadn't you she thought. *All day; wanting to reject being my counsel. You don't want to defend the monarchy you once so passionately denounced.*

'Can you send word to Fredrik, or – or Nikolai?' she asked.

'I am afraid not, they have seized control of the post office, and the wireless office too. There will be no rescue or help for you.'

She shut her eyes at that.

'How does Luka know Lvov?' she wanted to know.

He seemed surprised that she knew that name.

'Since childhood, I believe they might even be distant relatives. He has never been very clear on that.'

'How long have your brother-in-law and Lvov been his spies?'

He blinked rapidly, caught off guard.

'Probably since University' he admitted. 'We all met in lectures on law. And in a tavern…' he trailed off. 'Luka is my oldest friend, but he and Seryeshka have always been closer political allies. Do you understand the position I am in? I have always stood with them.'

'Why did you agree to represent me then?' she wanted to know.

He shut his eyes, sighing, and she saw the inner turmoil he was in again.

'They pervert the law for their own ends' he said quietly. 'This is an injustice. Whether you are guilty or not they cannot circumvent the law.'

'It is more than that, isn't it' she said out loud, realising he was holding back.

He sighed. 'I tell you this now because as your lawyer you will need to disclose your secrets to me too. Nineczka has always loved Luka. She married me because I was the better lawyer.'

Richer Laura's cynical side provided. *And that's why you told me to marry for love.*

'I am sorry, Ilich' she said quietly.

He smiled sadly.

'No matter now' he said quietly. 'Allow me to show you to your room, you can refresh and sleep, it is very late. We shall prepare your case in the morning.'

She stood, feeling better and more stable, following him to the guest room on the ground floor. Ilich apologised that he had no nightshirt for her to wear, folding down the slightly dusty covers of the bed.

'It doesn't matter, I am too tired to care' she assured him.

'Sleep well Your Majesty and sweet dreams, for what they are worth' he said, and closed the door behind him.

63

Laura woke with the soft tap on her door. Anna pushed it open, carrying in several dresses and a small jewel case. She hung the dresses in the wardrobe and rushed to Laura, taking hold of her hands.

'They questioned me today' she told her. 'And my husband. All about our time in Russia after the revolution.'

'Who was the judge?' Laura wanted to know, pushing back the covers and getting to her feet.

'There were five. Maksim, Lev, *Knjaz* Uvarov, and two others I don't know.'

'*Sud'ya* Gorbunov and Iosif Osin' Ilich said, appearing in her doorway. 'Court Justices and neither a friend to you. Get dressed Your Majesty, things are progressing quickly and unfavourably.'

'Their signatures are already dry on my sentence, aren't they' she said, with no hint of surprise.

'Get dressed and join me for breakfast. We must make some haste.'

He closed the door and Anna stripped Laura out of the dress she had been wearing for two days, helping her wash quickly then don clean clothes. She had done well, selecting a dress of light grey silk, sombre enough for the gravity of the situation but not the colour of guilt. From the small jewel case Anna drew out the Countess' lucky black diamonds. *How fitting* Laura thought. Anna pinned Laura's hair up then promised to wait here until she returned from the court.

Laura found Ilich's breakfast room and sat beside him at the small, round table, suddenly ravenously hungry. *I can't even remember when it was that I last ate properly* she mused as she helped herself to some cold cuts of meat. Ilich drained his tea and set down the cup carefully.

'Your Majesty' he started quietly. 'Roman has signed a confession. I have read it. It is detailed, precise, and obscene.'

'And false' Laura added. 'Roman is my spy, not my lover.'

'He was Seryeshka's spy, there is evidence of his pay -'

'And mine' Laura said. 'Roman accepted his pay at my insistence. He was a double agent, and loyal to me. They will use his confession against me, won't they. Call him as a witness, that confession was signed under duress. I suspect that he is infatuated with me, but he was never my lover. He will tell you that much himself, and he most certainly can't be the father of Alexandra -' she broke off. 'My daughter! Where is she Ilich?'

'I don't know. No one seems to know.'

'She is missing?' she whispered, horror twisting hard inside her. 'How? *How?! What happened to the guards that were supposed to be protecting her?!*'

'There was confusion in the castle. Some of them even deserted.'

'*What?!?*' she cried. 'I don't believe that! They were all *especially* chosen for their loyalty to me -'

'Roman was not the only guard they bribed, and one of them was seen riding for his home in Macherna shortly after Roman's arrest.'

Malenkov had not been at his post she reminded herself. The betrayal was a blow and she sagged, shutting her eyes miserably. Alexandra had been taken. Perhaps some doctor was examining her, measuring her face and eye colour and size and comparing them to known facts about Aleksei, to prove she could not be his...

'If they harm her, *I will kill them*,' she said vehemently. 'And put Roman on the stand. That confession was signed under duress. If he has lied he can look me in the eye and lie again.'

Ilich was quiet for a very long time.

'I have lost a wife, a friend and an election' he finally said, quietly, 'but never a case. I don't want this to be my first.'

'It will not. I am not Roman's lover.'

'He named others. Six others.'

'*Seven* lovers?' she asked, drily. 'How on earth did I find the time to rule and stitch the tapestries?'

'Don't jest, they are all credible. He has named Fredrik von Schmidt, Gustav von Schmidt, Nikolai Viktor Antonevich Vakhtangov, Fedor Smolin, Olaf Yazov and *Knjaz* Nikita Rurik.'

'Not one of those men, save Fedor, is here to answer for their alleged crimes. But that is what they hope for, yes? They have to rely solely on Roman's confession, Fedor will certainly refute his false claims.'

A knock on his front door interrupted them and Ilich excused himself to answer it. Laura popped a few more cuts of meat into her mouth, acutely aware that she had to make the most of this opportunity to eat, as she did not know when she would next get a meal. Ilich came back with a sheet of paper.

'We have been summoned' he announced. 'We must leave at once.'

Laura stood and followed him nervously to the front door where he collected his hat and coat. A handsome cab was waiting in the street outside his house and Ilich quickly helped her into it, instructing the driver to head to the castle.

'They will tell you what the charges are, in blunt detail, and then ask you to enter your plea. Roman's confession will probably be read out loud, then you will be given time to address and refute the charges. Luka will also be allowed to cross examine your testimony -'

'Which I will only allow if you can cross examine Roman's' she answered.

'You cannot prevent him, he has the right to examine your testimony.'

'Then I have the right to examine Roman's, or else his testimony cannot be used.'

Ilich agreed then sat back, shutting his eyes, his lips moving occasionally as he marshalled his thoughts and arguments. At the castle doors he spoke briefly to a Parliamentary guard, instructing him to bring forth Roman for testimony at once. The guard saluted and left. Ilich took Laura's arm and led her quietly to the ballroom.

'One more thing. Bow to them' he instructed her.

'Bow to *them*?!'

'They are the law. No man is above the law, and it will be respected.'

'Even if it is perverted?' she demanded.

'Even so' he answered quietly.

He knocked loudly on the ballroom doors and they swung open. *They have made changes* Laura thought drily. The five judges sat at Vsevolod's table in the centre of the ballroom. Two tables had been quickly erected, parallel with each other, separated by five feet of space and facing the judges. Luka sat at one, his back to her, and did not look around when they entered. The other table was empty. Directly between the counsel tables and the judges sat a small wooden chair, as hard and as unforgiving as the judges looked.

Laura and Ilich came before the judges and bowed low. After a long pause Maksim graciously allowed her to sit, sending Ilich to his own counsel table. Lev stood and unrolled a scroll of parchment, clearing his throat noisily. *Roman accuses me* she thought as he read the charges to her. *That was a nasty touch. And Ilich was right, the details were obscene: dates, times, paramours, acts... I don't even know what some of them are...*

'Do you understand these charges?'

'No. What is sodomy?' she asked.

There was an embarrassed, squirming silence.

'If she is innocent of what that is she is innocent of the act' Ilich said.

'Objection! Just because she doesn't know what it is called doesn't mean she hasn't done it' Luka snapped, then added in an aside to Ilich that the judges did not hear but Laura did: 'You will have to try better than *that*.'

After a small hesitation, Lev, red-faced, explained what it was.

'That is possible?' she asked, shocked. 'And if you please, what is *cunnilingus?* And *fellatio?* And fornication?'

Actually I know what that one is, but you're going to say it out loud she thought, and tried not to admit that some small part of her was enjoying this. Lev looked like he wished he hadn't agreed to this, stammering through the explanations as diplomatically as he could. She was quiet when he finished. 'Ye-es' she said finally, slowly. 'I understand the charges.'

'Confess and sign this' Maksim said, holding out a piece of paper. 'We will be merciful.'

Laura stood, but Ilich was faster, snatching it out of her hands. 'Do not sign that' he snapped, then rounded on the five that sat before him. 'This is not justice!' he cried. 'She has not even entered her plea!'

'The evidence is overwhelming' said the elderly Gorbunov, glaring at Ilich. 'There can be no other plea but guilty.'

'No!' he shouted. 'The law must be untaintable! No one above it, no one below. If you pervert it now, for the Tsaritsa, how could you ever hold the authority of justice sacrosanct again?'

'We only wish to spare her the pain and embarrassment of a trial -' *Knjaz* Uvarov began, but Ilich interrupted him.

'Her Majesty has insisted. I must insist' Ilich said, and his tone brooked no argument.

'Very well, let us begin this farce' Maksim grumbled. 'How do you plead to the charges before you?'

'I plead innocence' Laura said.

'Not guilty, Your Honours' Ilich translated.

'Luka Nevsky, you may begin' Iosif Osin said, eager to have some say in the proceedings. 'Return to your table, counsel. Take her with you' he told Ilich.

Luka moved the chair she had occupied to his side of Vsevolod's table, turning it to face sideways with the judges on his left.

'Your Honours, Her Majesty is irrefutably guilty of all charges. Not only do we have a signed confession from one of her lovers we have the testimony of another. Call in the *Archimandrite.*'

Laura blinked. *A priest? Granted, one in charge of a large monastery, or several monasteries, but who on earth —*

Her thoughts stopped. Stepping through the doors, wearing the rich, sable-black garb of an *Archimandrite*, was Nikita Rurik. *Disgrace has been kind to him* she thought. *When he left Dalnerechensk he had been stripped of his titles and wealth. How quickly he had recovered.* She forced herself not to react, knowing that the eyes of the judges were on her, scrutinising her.

'Whatever he says will be a lie' she whispered to Ilich.

'No talking!' Lev snapped.

Nikita stopped at her table, and made the sign of the cross over her and Ilich.

'Bless this poor, misguided child' he said before turning to the judges and bowing so low his chin touched his knees.

That was a cruel little gesture Laura thought, fuming, though she didn't let her face twist in a way that would convey that to the judges. Maksim welcomed him, then pointed to the chair, asking him to sit and swear to tell the truth. Nikita did, clasping his hands around the ostentatious gold cross he wore around his neck.

His tale was lurid, and took three hours to tell. He spoke of her infatuation for him when he had been an ambassador from the Russian Court, and told tales of sex in his army tent as he made his way back to Dalnerechensk, of bathing her in perfume and her insatiable appetite for him.

Laura stayed silent, her hands clenched tightly in her lap. Ilich made an occasional note on a sheet of paper he had with him, his face betraying nothing. But when Nikita talked of her dancing naked around his tent for him she took the pen from his hand and wrote one word on his paper, underlining it twice. He blinked, then looked at her carefully; reading her unspoken shame and determination in her eyes.

'She had not slept with Aleksei since the night he took her forcefully. The child is mine' he finished, then crossed himself.

'Thank you, High Reverend, you may leave' Maksim smiled.

'I have right of cross-examination' Ilich reminded him archly.

Maksim sighed and waved his hand irritably to begin. Ilich stood and bowed, but Laura noticed it was a lot less respectful than it had been before.

'High Reverend, you claim Her Majesty's daughter, Alexandra, is your child; conceived sometime in your tent en route to Dalnerechensk, is that correct?'

'May God forgive me, yes' he said, sighing with pain and crossing himself.

'Are you sure? -'

'I was in her to the hilt when I came' he said crassly. '*Every* time.'

'How many times were you "to the hilt" with her?' he asked, the quotations dropping neatly around the words.

'I cannot exactly recall' he said. 'It is something God calls me to reject and not dwell on.'

'For the sake of truth, High Reverend' Ilich pressed.

'Perhaps twenty. Twenty times "to the hilt", on her back, on her knees, bouncing above me when I could take no more. I did say she was insatiable' he added slyly. 'For all manner of things.'

'What do you mean?'

'*Fellatio. Cunnilingus. Sodomy.* She liked it in her ass. She would beg for another soldier to pleasure her at the same time I was. She sucked my stick, I tickled her tits, nibbled her nipples, licked her lips, kissed her clit, bit her bean, delved her *derriere*, fondled her flower, poked her pussy, fucked her fanny and came in her cunt! May God have mercy on my soul' he added, crossing himself again.

'And in all of this … activity' Ilich coughed, 'you were able to see her body?'

'Intimately. From every angle' Nikita smiled, and there were fangs in his look.

'Tell the court about her disfigurements.'

Nikita smiled, enjoying himself.

'She is not disfigured. It was a vile rumour spread by Aleksei's spurned lover Tatiana. The poor girl was only a virgin, and shy about taking her clothes off in front of others. But it wasn't long before she'd made a whore of herself.'

'She is completely unblemished?'

Nikita grinned like a cat with a mouse.

'There are three long scars across her back. Aleksei gave them to her, he whipped her the night of the revolution.'

'They were still not completely healed when she returned. It must have been quite painful for her, to lie on her back.'

'She cried some' Nikita admitted. 'But I was gentle, and she begged me for more.'

Ilich paused, eyeing the effect Nikita's testimony had on the judges, on Luka.

'No further questions for this witness' he said quietly, looking down.

'*Archimandrite*, you may leave' Maksim said, and he was crowing with spiteful pleasure.

Ilich sat next to Laura, cutting off her protest.

'Say nothing' he instructed quietly.

Laura dearly wanted to argue, but the harmonics in his tone prevented her from disobeying. *He has never lost a case* she reminded herself, but she found it very hard to trust him. *He still thinks he is going to lose this one.*

She turned her face away when Nikita paused at her table. He opened his mouth to say something, but then closed it, made the sign of the cross, and left the room.

'I have the testimony of -' Luka started, but Ilich interrupted him, his voice low and dangerously quiet.

'You dare bring that man back here.'

'I -'

'You *dare*' Ilich interrupted. '*That* man, to *this* place!' He stood again, seeming so much taller than his physical height. *You!* he rounded on Lev and Maksim, pointing an accusing finger at them. 'You who sat in the old Advisory Council, who knew of this man's insidious political behaviour, *you*' he looked at Luka, 'who fought against him, as did I, *you dare bring him here?!*

'He came to steal the mines, first with a bit of paper, then with cannons, and he stole the lives of a hundred and thirty men. Sons of Dalnerechensk! You dare bring him here, knowing what he was, to trot out these vile lies? -'
'Whatever else he was, he was her lover too' Luka snapped. 'Why would he need to lie?'
'I don't know, what did you offer him?'
There were audible gasps from all those present.
'I will hold you in contempt of court if you utter another accusation like that!' Gorbunov shouted, outraged.
'Good! It could not be more contemptable than this perversion of justice!'
'This is your last warning! And it will go most severely for your client should I charge you with contempt!'
'Three scars, he said' Ilich reminded them quietly. 'Three. No more, no less. And able to inspect every inch of her.' He turned to Laura. 'Your Majesty?' he prompted.
'I – I need help' she whispered as she stood, turning her back to the judges.
Gently Ilich began to undo the buttons of her dress. Laura shut her eyes, bowing her head in burning embarrassment. Ilich said nothing to her, but she could feel his gentle apology radiating out of him as he undid the strings of her corset, folding it open, and then her thin chemise. There were shocked gasps when he stepped back.
'Three scars, he said' Ilich repeated quietly. 'Danced naked around his tent, he said. Close enough to have seen every inch from every angle, he said.'
'It might have been dark -' Luka started.
'*He would have felt those*' Ilich said, his voice whipping out like a snake. 'That lothesome man was never her lover. *He has lied.* He might have said he had forced her, even clothed; but he did not claim that. You didn't want him to say that, because you could forgive a victim. You needed her to be his whore.
'But he was not her lover, or her rapist, because we know she knows how to deal with those.' His gaze bore into Luka, then he turned away, fastening her clothing again for her.
Laura turned around and sat down, uncomfortable, as Ilich was not used to lacing corsets properly. She didn't dare raise her head to look at their faces, her cheeks still dark with shame.
'You'll have to do better than *that*' Ilich murmured to Luka, who went red faced.
'Your Honours I submit the signed confession of Roman Prokofiev as proof of her crimes.'
'Your Honours I ask this document not be admitted' Ilich interrupted. 'Her Majesty has the same right as all citizens, to face her accuser in court.'
'His word accuses her, it will be admitted' Maksim snapped.
'You cannot cross-examine a written statement!' Ilich pointed out, annoyed.

'No cross examination is needed' Lev said. 'It will be admitted!'

'This is not a trial, it is a conspiracy!'

'Another word, I *beg* of you' Gorbunov snapped. '*One* more, to damn you and your client!'

Ilich gritted his teeth.

'Proceed' he told Luka curtly.

With a flourish he opened the folder that was sitting on his desk, pulling out many sheets of paper. It took him two hours to read out all the reports. They were the tidbits of information he had given to Lvov over the course of several months, most Laura knew about but some she did not, including the confession that had gotten them both arrested: Roman had carnal and frequent knowledge of her. The last page had been a statement that the reports were accurate and factual, and gave more details to the nature of their sexual couplings.

She fought down the blush that was threatening to brand the shape of her body into the chair she sat on. *I had no idea he fantasised about me like that* she burned.

'These claims are as false as Nikita Rurik's were' Ilich said, crossing to the wooden chair and carrying it to his side of the courtroom, setting it down sideways so the judges were on his right. 'Call in the guard.'

Luka was too slow to realise who he meant.

'You can't call in him!' he cried, but it was too late, the judges had seen Roman.

Laura saw their looks of horror and turn quickly, leaping to her feet and pressing her hands to her mouth, her eyes filling with horrified tears. *They tortured him* she realised. They tortured him!

'Bastards' Ilich swore violently.

He could only walk supported by two soldiers, who both held him under the arms. The white shirt he wore was stained with blood as were the bandages wrapped around both his hands. Clumps of his hair and beard had been torn out, his nose was broken, his face swollen and black and blue. One arm was in a sling and he limped with every step, his teeth, such as were left, gritted in pain. There were livid garrotte marks around his neck and Laura suspected most of his ribs were broken from the way his breath laboured painfully. He was broken and crippled.

It took a long time for him to reach the chair, and he couldn't bring himself to look at Laura, his head drooping with the effort just to walk half the length of the ballroom. The guards helped him sit as gently as they could, but he still grunted in pain, stiff and exhausted.

'Roman' Ilich started gently. 'Did you sign this confession of your own free will?'

One glance at Laura was all it took. He broke down weeping.

'Please Ilich, he needs a doctor' Laura sobbed.

Through his tears Roman began to talk, detailing his spying operations, what he had told Lvov, what he had told Laura. He told them how he knew she had never been unfaithful to Aleksei, told them of the look in his eye the night of the revolution. *I know he forced her that night, then whipped her, still so frustrated…*

He recanted all his confession, pausing often to catch the breath that pained him.

'Forgive me' he sobbed. 'He cut me, he *cut* me. I failed you, but not Alexandra. *Protect my daughter Roman.* You told me that, and I did. She's safe, they won't find her. He didn't ask me those questions.'

'This is your proof?' Ilich asked, and his voice was as cold as a midwinter grave. 'An insidious snake and a poor boy you tortured, who told you anything to make it stop? That is not a confession' he pointed at Luka's paper. 'It is a plea for help, the fabrications of a victim who knew the only way to make his pain stop was to tell you the lies you wanted to hear. *And there was so much pain…*' he trailed off, his fists tightening.

'Two men have falsely accused her, and one more will certainly deny the claims. The others cannot answer the accusations as they are not here. Should they be, what do you think they would say? Dismiss these charges, and cease this persecution of Her Majesty.'

Maksim and his cousin put their heads together and whispered until they reached a nodding agreement. They then turned and whispered to the other judges, who nodded as well.

'Court is adjourned' Maksim said. 'We will reconvene at nine tomorrow.'

Luka and Ilich rose as the judges stood and made their way out of the ballroom. Without a word Luka followed them, leaving Roman, Ilich, Laura and a smattering of shaken guards alone in the room.

'Am I free?' Roman asked, not daring to hope. 'Don't send me back to the house they held me in.'

Ilich sent one of the soldiers who had helped Roman in to collect a wheelchair from the hospital, and to ask Doctor Pushkin, at the direct request of Her Majesty, to examine Roman and provide what relief and treatment he could.

'Your name?' he asked the other guard.

'Zimin' he saluted.

'Protect this man' he said. 'He knows where the *Tsesarevna* is, and it is clear they will do anything to know that information.'

'Yes sir' he said resolutely, saluting again.

'Sit' Ilich said gently to Laura, guiding her to the chair.

She did as she was told, too horrified and guilt-stricken to do anything else, weeping until no more tears would come.

'Who did this to you?' Ilich asked gently, finally.

'Lvov' he sighed, shutting his eyes.

Twilight had pressed against the window panes when the guard returned with the wheelchair. Together the two soldiers carefully manoeuvred Roman out of the hard chair and into it, gently placing his feet on the wooden footpad.

Ilich pushed the chair while the guards took up stations before and behind them, escorting them out into the castle courtyard. There were several Parliamentary soldiers standing around, and all of them had seen what had been done to Roman. There was anger in their faces.

Instead of using Ilich's handsome cab they hitched the largest carriage in the castle to a team of four horses, lifting the wheelchair in completely to avoid causing Roman any more pain. Laura and Ilich also climbed inside, and the other soldiers piled onto the carriage, clinging to any available handhold. Laura wondered if they were guarding them or protecting them.

The ride to Ilich's home was in silence. Roman's head sunk exhaustedly onto his chest, he could not bring himself to weep or acknowledge his surroundings anymore. The carriage stopped and the guards jumped off, pulling open the door and gently lifting Roman out, carrying the wheelchair up the front steps of Ilich's home. Laura and Ilich climbed out, following the soldiers.

Whispered conversations were happening with the guards stationed beside the front door, volumes said in the looks and the stiff backs of those that had ridden with them from the castle. Laura could feel their shock and bewilderment and anger.

Ilich unlocked the front door and a carriage pulled up behind theirs in the street, Doctor Pushkin stepping down and clasping his medical bag to him, a little surprised to see so many soldiers standing on the street.
'Good evening doctor' Ilich said. 'Please come in, your services are urgently required. Gentlemen, please remain, as ever, outside' he said to the soldiers.
'Will he be alright?' one asked, worried.
'I hope the good doctor could tell us that' Ilich said, then wheeled Roman inside, Laura and Pushkin following him.

Laura insisted Roman be given the guest rooms she had occupied the night before and Ilich and Pushkin gently manoeuvred him out of the chair and onto the bed, while Laura shut her eyes against his grunts of pain.
'Your Majesty, what has happened?' Anna asked, joining her in the narrow hallway. She gasped when she saw the state of Roman, her hands flying to her mouth.

Ilich diplomatically shut the door to give the doctor and his patient privacy, ushering the two women away from the room.
'Something smells wonderful' he suddenly said, aware of the rich smell of roast meat.
'I thought you would be hungry when you returned, I have made an evening meal' Anna managed, then wondered if anyone could actually

stomach it.

'Thank you Anna, that was most thoughtful' Ilich said quietly, then guided Laura to his small dining room.

Laura wondered how she could eat, but her body seemed to take over, pushing small morsels into her mouth in response to a hunger she was no longer aware of. But she fought against her need, desperately wanting to know the extent of Roman's injuries, quite sure that that knowledge would sicken her. She sent Anna to prepare a broth for Roman, unsure when he last ate, unsure if he could eat at all.

Doctor Pushkin finally emerged, subdued, and joined them in the dining room. Anna quickly set a plate for him, and he helped himself to a few morsels while Laura and Ilich sipped wine, waiting for him to speak. It was an agony of twenty minutes before he swallowed his last bite and patted his mouth on a napkin.

'How fares he, doctor?' Laura finally begged.

'Poorly. He is at great risk of turning septic. You must get ahold of some mouldy bread and warm soil dressings and change them frequently to avoid this.'

'What are his injuries?' Ilich asked quietly.

'They are acute' he dropped his eyes briefly. 'Please steel yourself Your Majesty for what you will hear. He has been beaten severely. His organs are bruised and he has multiple fractures to his ribs. His jaw is fractured, as are both orbital bones and the nasal bone. Most of his teeth were traumatically extracted, as were his fingernails. There are numerous burns to his body, most on the souls of his feet, some made by open flames, others by heated metal objects. The most trauma is to his hands and feet. All his phalanges have been smashed, and many of his metacarpals and metatarsals. And there was -' he stopped briefly, aware that he was talking to a woman. 'Genital mutilation' he finished.

He cut *me...*

Laura swallowed against the thick lump in her throat.

'Will he recover?' she wanted to know.

'He will need surgery to address most of the damage to his hands. Amputation may be the only option for some of his fingers and toes. He will eventually heal, but please understand he has been through great trauma. He may never fully recover.'

Laura shut her eyes. There were no more tears, but the ache in her chest was biting. Anna returned with a bowl of broth she placed on a small tray. Laura rose and took it from her, padding down to the guest bedroom where Roman lay. Anna opened the door for her but stepped back when Laura dismissed her quietly.

He was weeping again, silently and motionlessly, the hitching of his breaths causing him pain. Laura set the tray down on a small table, pulling it closer to the bed.

'Forgive me Roman' she said quietly. 'It's my fault they did this to you. If I hadn't have -' she stopped, biting her lip hard. 'I am so sorry.'

'I am crippled' he answered dully. 'I can't ever guard you again.'

She sniffed loudly, pushing away her grief.

'Doctor Pushkin says you will heal, given time. You will grow well and strong again, and you will always be my *Sotnik*. Unless Commander becomes available' she mused out loud. 'Whatever happens Roman, your loyalty to me will be recognised, and you will be rewarded for it.' She managed a gentle smile for him. 'In the meantime, you have my leave to grow fat and lazy while you heal. I have brought you some broth, I know you can't manage on your own, please allow me.'

'You don't have to do this' he said huskily.

'It is the least I could do' she answered, dropping her eyes.

Roman hesitated, worried she might accidentally hurt him as she fed him, but she was gentle and so precise with the spoon she never touched anything but his lips.

'You are very good at this' he said, managing a smile that was more smile than grimace of pain.

'I have had much practise with my – where is she Roman?' she stopped, every inch of her yearning for the answer.

'Malenkov took her' he answered. 'I don't know where exactly, it was better for me not to know, they wouldn't be able to get that information from me. All that intense scrutiny about her, I knew when they made their move against you they would take her too. She is safe and cared for. Malenkov knows I will send all the demons in hell after him if he did not keep her safe.'

Laura leaned forward and kissed Roman's forehead gently.

'Thank you' she said quietly. 'You can't know what that means to me. When will he bring her back?'

'Send this message to Lady Grey: *My flowers are lovely this time of year.* But please Your Majesty, I know you chafe to see her. Do not send that message yet. He will bring her back as soon as he gets that message; make sure it is safe to bring her back first.'

She smiled gently and stroked back a little of his hair.

'Get some rest Roman' she said quietly. 'Thank you for everything you have done for me.'

She put the empty bowl back on the tray and left, closing the door behind her.

64

The cold grey of dawn was rising in the east when Laura woke, stretching uncomfortably in Ilich's bed. He had insisted she slept there after giving up the guest bedroom for Roman, and Anna had been given a small cot in the attic. Laura didn't know where Ilich had slept; perhaps he hadn't slept at all. She stirred and slipped out of bed, trying to twist the stiffness out of her back and hips.

She dressed quietly, sending Anna when she arrived to help Roman, knowing his injuries made him almost helpless. Ilich was dressed and in his kitchen, preparing breakfast for them when she stepped into the small room. He greeted her quietly, somewhat apologetically.

'My house keeper only comes once a week. With all the commotion the last few days I forgot to procure her services for groceries. I am afraid I only have boiled eggs and bread.'

'Which will be fine' she answered, finding crockery and cutlery to take to the breakfast table.

Ilich followed her to the dining room, setting down his tray and watching her set out plates and spoons.

'I never thought I would have a tsaritsa set my table for me' he smiled.

'I thought that would be exactly what I would do, if I survived the revolution' she replied, sitting down. 'It must have crossed your mind. It certainly crossed Luka's.'

Ilich winced, sitting opposite her. They ate in silence, till Ilich finally sighed and put down his empty tea cup.

'I spoke to Roman last night, at great length. He told me more details of his espionage for you, and he swore to me there is no truth to any of the accusations against you. I believe him, I think he knows you better than most.'

'Maksim wants me out of power. Revolution did not work, The Nine Week King did not work, now he lies and it will not work. He will have assassins after me next.' She dropped her eyes, pushing away the fears.

Ilich opened his mouth to speak and was interrupted with a knock on his door. He excused himself, annoyed, and was back, quickly pulling on his coat.

'We are summoned again' he announced.

'It is only seven, they could not want us now!' Laura protested.

'*Now*, Your Majesty' Ilich said, buttoning his jacket closed.

Laura sighed and stood, catching sight of a nervous Anna as she did so.

'Will everything be alright?' she asked, and Laura knew it wasn't the trial she was asking after.

'I think this house is the safest in Dalnerechensk' Laura assured her. 'The soldiers will protect Roman, and you, with their lives.'

Anna looked mollified and bid Laura good luck. *Luck* Laura thought as she headed out the doors. *I'm not wearing the lucky black diamonds.* She dithered about heading back for them, but changed her mind when Ilich shot her a withering look, scrambling into the carriage.

The drive to the castle was in silence, and Laura marvelled at how quickly she had come to feel like a guest rather than the occupant. There seemed to be more soldiers in the courtyard than before, and they saluted smartly when the carriage came into view. Laura stepped down and greeted them quietly, aware of the thoughts that hovered over each head.

'*Sotnik* Prokofiev is recovering slowly, and will be grateful for your kind thoughts and prayers in his time of healing. He thanks you, as do I, for the loyalty you have shown him' she said quietly.

Ilich stepped down from the carriage and guided Laura inside. They had just turned into the West Wing of the castle when Luka stepped into their path.

'Might I have a word?' he asked Ilich, beckoning him privately further along the corridor.

Ilich looked strained but excused himself from Laura's side.

'This will not be a moment' he promised, following Luka to the far end of the corridor.

Laura sighed but then her heart leapt into her mouth as she was grabbed from behind and swung bodily out of sight. One hard hand pressed across her mouth, the other gripped her arm so tightly she could feel the blood strangulating in her veins. An unpleasant gust of garlic sausage breath blew against her neck, sticky and repugnant.

'Do you know what happens when a red hot knife is pushed into an eye?' Lvov whispered, his lips almost caressing her ear. '*If you resist me, you will find out.*'

The icy flood of fear was drowning her mind as Lvov dragged her away from the West Wing and the safety of Ilich, up the stone steps of the castle to the top floor, twisting and turning through some little used corridors. Through her terror Laura realised there were so many guards standing in the courtyard when they had arrived because not one of them patrolled the castle interior. They were utterly alone.

I don't want to be tortured! she wanted to scream, but was too terrified that any noise, any action except total compliance would begin the pain she wanted to avoid. Lvov opened a door and pushed her in backwards, then – surprising her – he shut the door again. *It's not locked* she realised, but other senses were calling to her now, senses that told her it would be imperative to turn around.

A small table stood in the room. Behind it sat Maksim, *Knjaz* Uvarov and *Sud'ya* Gorbunov. There was no chair for her to sit on, and she had to stand before them like a naughty child.

'I see' she said quietly.

'Speak only when you are spoken to' Maksim snapped. 'And only then you will answer yes or no.'

'I will speak to plead my case and only answer with the truth' she said, to Maksim's considerable annoyance.

He slammed his fist down on the table, opening his mouth to scream at her. His cousin's hand gripped his arm, and he subsided, swallowing back his rage and hate. Gorbunov cleared his throat, lifting a sheet of paper so he could read it clearer.

'You are accused of carnal knowledge of Nikolai Viktor Antonevich Vakhtangov. You are guilty of that crime.'

Laura laughed, but she did not feel it; terror still had her in its fearsome grip.

'You will have to do better than that' she snorted. 'You spent three days telling me I *had* to marry him. Some of your ministers would have dearly loved to have dragged me to his bed. I am innocent of that knowledge of him, but if I was not, how could it be treason? Aleksei is dead. -'

'He is not' Maksim said quietly. 'You have given me no proof he is dead.'

'You give me no proof he is alive. But if he was alive – as you seem to believe – what sin did you commit urging me most fervently to wed Nikolai? If he is alive, *why has he not come back here?* Your agents could find the Heir of the Nine Week King; you could have easily found Aleksei.'

Being confronted by Lady Ramkinson's riding crop in a snorting rage was not as frightening as Maksim's cold fury she realised. Gorbunov held up a piece of paper and demanded:

'Who wrote this?'

'Who is the father of Alexandra?' *Knjaz* Uvarov demanded at the same time.

'I don't know what that is' Laura said, and hoped that the lie was not audible in her voice, not readable on her face.

It was Olaf's letter.

Gorbunov cleared his throat and perched his half rim glasses on his nose, glaring hard at the paper.

'*My Diamond of Dalnerechensk*' he started, reading aloud the French words of the letter. '*I was lost the moment I first laid eyes on you. You came into my life and disordered it, some bright and gentle comet that moved the cosmos of my soul. You made the dawn rise in the West, the rain fall from the ground; the sun with all its burning warmth reside in my chest. I love you with the depth of space and the earnestness of the growing vine. You are my Northern star, my east, south and west; my song and my silence.*

'I am a better man for loving you.

'This is not Aleksei's hand' he finished. '*Who wrote it?*

Laura knew what answer she had to give. She didn't hesitate.
'Olaf Yazov.'

There was a sharp intake of breath, and the men exchanged glances with each other. *They didn't expect that* Laura thought. *They expected me to deny, and now they don't quite know how to proceed.*

'You admit to an affair with Olaf Yazov?' *Knjaz* Uvarov asked, recovering the fastest, and unable to keep the glee out of his voice.

'That is not what you asked' Laura said reproachfully. 'You asked me whose script that is, it is Olaf's.'

'That boy was an idiot, he didn't speak French!' Maksim blurted out.

If only you knew Laura wanted to snap. But she kept her composure cool and calm, folding her hands together so they wouldn't shake.

'No, he did not. Olaf gave him the words, Aleksei translated them into French and told Olaf to write them down. It was not the first time Aleksei had turned to Olaf, both as scribe and composer. -'

'Why would Aleksei turn to a common labourer when he had so many belletrists at his beck and call in his Council?' Maksim asked, astounded.

'Maybe because they were arrogant enough to call themselves belletrists?' Laura arched an eyebrow. 'You sat in the old Advisory Council Maksim, you know Olaf spied for Aleksei. You know they had a strange and somewhat intimate relationship. Aleksei trusted Olaf with confidential details; courtship with me was no different. I could show you several examples of letters they wrote together, though they are all in Aleksei's hand. -'

'Then that is no proof' Maksim snapped. 'How could we ever know the words were someone else's?'

'Because you know him' Laura said simply. 'Stuffy, awkward, indecisive and – occasionally – pompous. Or should you need further proof perhaps we can ask your daughter. Did he ever call her his diamond of Dalnerechensk?'

Maksim leapt to his feet in white hot rage, slamming his hands onto the table. Both Gorbunov and his cousin placed restraining hands on him and he fought them off, stalking back and forth, his fists clenching and unclenching.

Gorbunov held up the letter again.

'This was kept, secretly hidden, in a drawer beside your bed' he snarled. 'Why would you keep that there if this was from Aleksei? *He hated you.*'

His words hit her like fists. She shut her eyes, fighting against the tears.

'Not at first' she whispered. 'He damned Dalnerechensk for me, you know that. He would not have done so if he had not loved me. And I him' she added quietly. 'And if your spy had searched my belongings more carefully they would have found a little lump of tin. It was once a statue of me, in my wedding dress, dancing for him on the happiest day of my life. And he was tender, and gentle and kind and I kept it to grieve for the man he was; not the man an ulcer and stress and envy and fear made him. And I kept that letter -' she broke off, pressing her lips together and shutting her eyes again. 'We know when Alexandra was conceived' *Knjaz* Uvarov said quietly. 'We have the testimony of all those who were in Russia with you. Not once were you left alone with Aleksei in all that time. But you were with Nikita and Olaf.'

'Not *all* the testimony of those who were with me, you don't have Olaf's' she said, wiping her face on her sleeve. 'But that is correct.'

'When you jumped into the river, Olaf and Aleksei jumped in after you, is that correct?'

'Yes.'

'When did Aleksei die?' Gorbunov interrupted.

Laura blinked, aware of the looks they had shot each other. *They're not sure* she realised. *If he came out of the river alive...*

'He drowned in the river' Maksim snapped. 'She was alone in Russia with Olaf for three nights. Nikita's men saw him drown -'

'Who told you that? Nikita? Are you sure he told you the truth that time?' Laura interrupted.

'Your daughter is a bastard!' Maksim hissed.

'She is of the blood of Vsevolod!' Laura snapped, angry now.

'That is no great claim, most of Dalnerechensk has his blood in their veins. Olaf is the father of Alexandra. Confess!'

'I will not' Laura whispered.

'*Confess!*' he screamed.

'It would not matter what I say, your signatures gather dust on my sentence!' she cried. 'I am innocent of all malicious rumours and gossip! You rely on the lies of Nikita and pervert the law for your own desire for power! You will not hear me lie.'

Maksim's fist lashed out, catching her lip. The meaty thump of the impact was echoed by the crashing open of the door.

'This illegal court will cease right now!' Ilich roared. '*Right now!*'

He was incandescent with fury. He grabbed the edge of the table and overturned it, scattering papers and ink onto the floor. A stopper fell out of a bottle and a black tide began to flow across Olaf's letter, obliterating the words. Laura had thought she would always feel an unbearable wrenching grief if she ever lost the letter, those last tender words. She felt nothing.

But she didn't have time to be surprised at her reaction; more people were pouring into the room. There were soldiers; Peter Kamanin and men dressed in both uniforms of her Vsevolod Guard and the Parliamentary Army rushed in, and one more face she didn't expect to see.

'Nikolai!' she gasped, flinging her arms around his neck, sagging with relief.

'Arrest these men' he said, his voice low and dangerous.

Laura was dimly aware of scuffles breaking out, and shouting that seemed to come from far away, as if in underwater caves; a curious hollow, echoy muffled sound. Her swoon deepened and she let it wash over her, thinking to herself as unconsciousness claimed her: *Lucky.*

Lucky, lucky, lucky...

65

The sun was high in the sky when Laura drifted out of sleep. She resisted opening her eyes, unsure of where she was, and what she would see when she did. But her bed was comfortable and she lay between silk sheets, something she had not had at Ilich's house. *I'm in my own rooms in the castle* she realised. Opening her eyes confirmed it.

She gasped, because her bedroom door was open and she could see into her parlour. Fredrik lay on her chaise longue, rumpled and exhausted. She pushed back the covers and fled into his arms, burying her face in the curve of his neck. He woke, and fastened his arms around her, kissing her hair.

'Thank God, I was so worried' he said, kissing her temple. Laura winced and he apologised, smoothing away the hurt from the bruise Luka had left.

'Did you find them?' she asked, and her heart sank at the way he went still. 'She died, didn't she.'

'I'm sorry' he whispered.

Laura climbed onto the chaise longue beside him, leaning against him when he sat up, and cried as he held her tenderly, stroking her hair and her arm. And when her tears stopped she stayed leaning against him, too frightened to let him go in case she never saw him again.

'Yes' she finally said. 'I'll go with you to Bavaria. I'll marry you there.'

He sighed gently, squeezing her arm tenderly.

'But I will not leave the throne to Nikolai. I will be co-regent, but he can rule here without me.'

He was quiet, then placed a soft kiss on her head.

'His Highness has been asking after you. I shall tell him you have finally woken.'

'Finally?' she quizzed him. 'How long have I been asleep?'

'Thirty-eight hours' he answered. 'You have missed much. Please dress, then come down to your private dining room, I will have a meal ready for us, and invite His Highness to join us.'

Her stomach snarled at the mention of food and she blushed, kissing his shoulder then pushing him out of her embrace. He left her and she crossed to her dressing table, catching sight of her reflection. It shocked her; the first time she had seen it for several days.

There was a dark bruise at her temple from Luka's fist, and her lip had split from Maksim's. She was pale, and rather gaunt looking now, with dull hair and dark circles under her eyes. She sat down and ran her hands over her face, feeling how tired her skin seemed. *I will need to heal too* she mused. *This was more traumatic than I realised.*

She briefly wondered where Anna was, but then realised she was probably still helping Roman, and picked up her hair brush, gently running it through her locks. She pinned her hair back and then dressed, tugging her corset on and choosing a pale pink dress to wear.

She was relieved to see Spanov stationed outside her door and realised her Vsevolod Guards were patrolling the castle again. Her curiosity had to be sated and she quickly ran up to the nursery, holding her breath and shutting her eyes as she pushed open the door.

'Mama!' Alexandra cried.

Laura's world melted and she rushed in, scooping her up and pressing hundreds of kisses to her cheeks and head, despite how much it hurt her lip. From quick checks of her she did not seem worse for wear for her ordeal; she looked healthy and happy. Laura hugged her tightly to her and carried her down to the dining room, letting herself in.

Fredrik and Nikolai stood when they saw her, both bowing low to her. Two serving girls stood in the room and Laura sent one to collect the high chair. She sat with Alexandra on her lap, motioning for the others to sit too. The servant came forward and removed the cover from Laura's plate. She tried to eat, but Alexandra kept grabbing at her spoon, spilling her soup.

'Allow me, Your Majesty' Fredrik said, taking Alexandra off her lap and sitting her on his own.

She thanked him, finally able to eat in peace. The servant arrived with the high chair and Fredrik placed Alexandra in it, pulling her closer to him and giving her small amounts of egg to eat. She burbled happily, waving her fists. While Laura ate, Fredrik and Nikolai told her of the events she had missed while she had slept.

Luka's insistence that he speak to Ilich when they had been summoned the second day was an agreed upon diversion to separate her from her lawyer. Lev Dostoevski and Iosif Osin were unaware of the earlier, secretive court Laura had been dragged to, not invited because they had been too shocked by Roman's injuries and too sympathetic towards Laura. It was hoped that their last, desperate gamble would result in a confession, legal or not, that would remove her from the throne. It was the arrival of Nikolai that alerted Ilich to her disappearance and started the search for her.

Malenkov had been given special instructions two days before Laura's and Roman's arrests: to take Alexandra out of the Principality should anything happen to Laura. He had heard the soldiers arriving to arrest Laura, their voices floating up the stairs and he had abandoned his post to collect the child, smuggling her out of the castle in the confusion that followed. He had ridden straight across the border in the North, stopping in the first town he came to and sending two telegrams; one to Fredrik, the other to Nikolai, alerting them of the treachery taking place in Dalnerechensk.

Nikolai had been travelling with his mother, sisters and their young families when he had received the telegram. He had abandoned them all to continue the journey without him, borrowing a horse and racing back, hoping he wouldn't be too late. Fredrik had been in Samara when he received the telegram, having caught up with Kurt, inconsolable with grief, clutching at the body of Anna Vakhtangovna in a shabby hotel room. He too had left Gustav to settle Kurt's debts, and to make arrangements to return the princess to her family for burial.

The train from Samara had been delayed, and he had arrived too late to make a difference: The three judges, Luka and Lvov had already been arrested, Ilich had been temporarily reinstated as emergency Prime Minister, Malenkov had been recalled from his Russian safe house and Laura had been tenderly placed back in her own rooms. Fredrik had nothing to do but sit and wait for her to wake up.

'A trial has been set for the judges, Ilich has insisted. It is likely they will be found guilty' Nikolai explained.

'Will I have to testify?' Laura wanted to know.

'Yes Your Majesty' Fredrik said. 'If you are strong enough.'

'And what will be their punishments?' she wanted to know.

'It will depend on the decision of the judges, the punishment for treason, as you know, is death. It is also most likely that there will be fines, *Sud'ya* Gorbunov will be forced to resign his position, *Knjaz* Uvarov will be deported and he will not be able to enter Dalnerechensk ever again. But this will not be enough Your Majesty' Nikolai said. 'You have much to learn about exercising your royal prerogative. Titles and wealth are granted at the pleasure of the Monarchy and you cannot be pleased with these recent events.

'I must urge you, with great resolve, to strip their titles from them, and a good deal more of their wealth. What the courts impose will not be enough. Should this not be done by the time of the coronation, I assure you it will be the first thing I do as tsar.'

Laura set aside her plate and sighed.

'I know; you are right' she said quietly. 'It will be better if I do it, they wronged me. But you must tell Dalnerechensk you give me your full support. They voted overwhelmingly for Maksim as Prime Minister, they will not wish to have been made to look like fools.'

Nikolai took her hand and kissed it. 'You have my support' he smiled.

She smiled gently then let his hand go, reaching across to take Fredrik's hand, to stroke Alexandra's cheek with a crooked finger.

'It is my intention after the coronation to leave Dalnerechensk' she suddenly said. 'Fredrik and I will marry in Bavaria, and I intend to stay away from politics for at least six months. Perhaps more. I want to be kept informed of decisions, but I trust your judgement. I am weary of this now.'

Nikolai smiled gently. 'We will of course discuss all the necessary terms later. Tonight you still need your rest, and I can see that I am intruding.'

He stood, forcing Fredrik to stand too, and bow to him.

'Sleep well, Your Majesty' he said, bowing. 'I am glad that you are safe.'

'Thank you, Nikolai' she said, bowing to him too.

He left and Laura quietly dismissed the two servants, letting Fredrik fold her in his arms when the door closed behind them. Gently he stroked back her hair, his fingers tracing around the bruise at her temple, then his thumb stroked her lip.

'What did they do?' he whispered.

'No, no talk of that now' she said, shutting her eyes. 'We both have hurts to say. But not now.'

'As you wish' he acquiesced gently.

Laura picked up her daughter, folding her tightly in her arms.

'I was so frightened, and alone. My daughter was missing, and I feared the worst. I have no wish to be without either of you tonight.'

'Let us retire to your parlour, and send a maid to collect Alexandra's crib' Fredrik suggested, and Laura agreed, sitting Alexandra on her hip to carry her comfortably to her rooms.

Malenkov was standing on guard duty outside her rooms when she reached the corridor to the third floor. He saluted when he saw her and Alexandra, trying hard to repress his smile.

'Yu!' Alexandra said, excited. 'Yu! Yu-yu!'

'That's right, Yulian!' Malenkov said.

'Yu-an!' she repeated, wiggling in Laura's grasp and reaching out to clasp at his shining buttons.

'Yulian Malenkov' Laura smiled. 'I cannot begin to express the debt I owe you in the service you recently performed for me. Please accept this small, personal token of my fervent gratitude and thanks.'

She stood on her tip-toes and kissed his cheek, trying not to wince when she hurt her lip. Malenkov knelt and kissed the hem of her skirt.

'I would do it again in a heartbeat' he swore, standing again. 'Ask of me anything and it will be done.'

'Thank you Malenkov' she smiled.

Gently she stopped Alexandra from tugging at the gold buttons of his jacket and stepped back, opening her door and stepping inside. Fredrik followed her, nodding in acknowledgement at Malenkov.

A servant was inside her parlour, lighting the fire against the growing chill of the deepening autumn nights and Laura sent him to collect the crib from the nursery. They sat on the chaise longue and Laura cradled Alexandra in her arms until the crib was brought back to her rooms. Then she placed her daughter inside, giving her a soft rabbit to play with.

She sat back on the chaise close to Fredrik, her thigh pressed against the length of his. She leaned back against his chest, turning her face into his neck to breathe in the scent of him. From his inside jacket pocket he pulled out a slim volume of poetry and began to read them to her, and she smiled at the sound of English on his lips.

His gentle voice lulled Alexandra to sleep and Laura stood again, unfolding the blankets and tucking her between them, planting a soft kiss on her head, avoiding pressing the cut on her lip.

'Fredrik...'

She straightened, and he heard the want in her whisper. He abandoned the book and stood, coming forward to take her urgently into his arms. She winced, turning her mouth away from his kisses, but pressed him to her throat and knotted her fingers tightly in his hair. She tugged out the black ribbon and ran her fingers through his golden locks, leaning back to look at how pretty he was.

Gently he turned her around, his fingers falling to the hundreds of buttons that held closed her dress, kissing her shoulders and neck as he undid them, gently unfolding the material from her. His hands came around her, stroking her corset, his fingers cupping her breasts and finding her skin, burning her. She squirmed into his touch, back against the kisses he pressed onto her shoulders.

Her wiggling aroused him, and he groaned, urgency in his movements as he tugged undone her corset strings, pulling it off her.

'Me, undress me' he begged, turning her around, pressing her hands to him.

Quickly she undid his jacket and shirt, pulling them off him, pressing gentle kisses against his chest. He groaned as she stroked him, and Alexandra stirred. They drew apart briefly, kicking off their shoes as they crept into her bedroom, closing the door behind them.

Laura stepped back, letting him watch as she undid her petticoats, letting them slip down her legs. She pulled off her chemise and her silk stockings, liking the way his breath quickened at the sight of her.

'Your breeches' she giggled, and he struggled out of them, trying to clasp her and remove them at the same time.

Laura folded back the covers of her bed and Fredrik lifted her into it, climbing above her. They were slick with desire, wet with want, and he moaned as she took hold of him, guiding him to her. He stiffened at the sensation of his penetration, at the damp, tight heat of her.

'Don't stop' she begged, and his lips fell to her throat, kissing away the perspiration there.

Laura tried to press kisses against him, to respond to his lips, but quickly stopped at the pain. Instead she began whispering instructions; how to kiss her, touch her, how to arch and thrust in a quick, firm rhythm until she cried out in pleasure, squeezing the breath from him. His grip tightened and his whole frame stiffened, thick ecstasy spurting into her.

He shuddered and moaned her name, breathing hard into the crook of her neck. She pressed sweet kisses against his brow, stroking his sweat drenched hair. They were quiet while their breathing calmed, while their hearts slowed and the perspiration dried on their skin.

'I didn't know it was like this' he whispered, tilting his head back to gaze at her. 'Can we do that again?'

She giggled.

66

Fredrik jolted awake, stiff with embarrassment. Anna was in Laura's room, well aware of what they had done last night, and trying hard to cover her smile.

'Good morning Your Majesty' she greeted Laura, dipping a curtsey to them.

'You are here? How is Roman?' Laura asked, sitting up, and Fredrik pulled the covers up, trying to hide himself and her from Anna's gaze.

'His Highness instructed that Roman was to be brought back to the castle, he has been given several staff to attend to his needs, including a personal nurse, a maid and a manservant. His Highness said you were more in need of me.'

'I am' she smiled. 'Please draw some hot water for a bath, but I won't need your assistance' she grinned.

Anna giggled and curtseyed, running out to do as she asked. Laura slipped out of bed despite Fredrik's attempt to hold onto her and turned to eye him, aware of how he was reacting to the sight of her; hot and longing and embarrassed that Anna might see him aroused.

'I should not have done what I did last night' he said, embarrassed. 'I did not mean to dishonour you.'

'Are you not going to marry me?'

'Of course I will!'

'Then there is no dishonour' she smiled.

She stretched, arching her back, aware of the helpless way he watched her.

'Anna will be back, she'll see you' he tried.

'Anna has seen me naked many times, she even helps me bathe.'

'Please dress' he begged.

Laura curtseyed, holding the skirts of an imaginary dress, then stalked across to her dressing room. Fredrik heard muffled sounds of dressing, and heard Anna return with several others, pouring steaming water into her bath. He heard them leave, then there was silence.

'Laura?' he whispered.

Quickly he slipped out of bed and found his breeches, pulling them on. He peeked out into her parlour but no one was in it. He called her name again, eyeing the almost closed door of her dressing room. He pushed it open then stopped, his knees going weak.

She was standing in the middle of the room, a shawl of Bavarian blue tied around her hips, thick strands of jewels dripping from her neck and covering her breasts. There were jewels in her loose hair, on her wrists, on her fingers. She stood in a sultry pose; one hip jutted out, her arms above her head, her breasts lifted and pert beneath the weight of the pearls. Her white skin was wet and glowed in the light of the dawn.

'I promised myself I would dance naked for you' she said quietly. 'Have you ever been to the Moulin Rouge?'

Fredrik's legs folded under him and he sat down on a stool near the door, running a shaking hand through his hair.

'I haven't, but Ekaterina has. She was most instructive' Laura went on, beginning to sway her hips.

That didn't take him long she thought, amused, and she turned her back on him, holding the hem of her shawl out and making circular motions with her rump. There was the soft sound of clothing being divested and then his hands were on her, pulling up the shawl, the hardness of him sliding into her again.

Their lovemaking was quick and carnal and Fredrik cried out at his shuddering climax. He held her tightly, his breath hitching his chest, and she nuzzled tenderly against him, feeling his heartbeat pound against her shoulder. He retreated from her, and Laura was amused to see his thick manhood slick with their passion, glistening in the morning sun.

She stepped into the clawfoot bathtub and lay back in the warm water, sighing gently. Fredrik stepped in too and took up the soft cloth, gently washing her with it. Tenderly he removed her jewels and washed her hair, pouring an ewer over her dark locks to wash away the suds.

'I do not wish to leave this bath' she said quietly. 'When I do, I must face them, and all the terrible things that have happened.'

Fredrik took her hands and kissed them gently.

'You do not have to face them alone' he promised. 'I will stand with you always.'

She kissed the top of his head gently then washed his hair for him, goose bumps appearing on her skin from the tepid water. Quickly she got out and wrapped a towel around herself, passing one to Fredrik.

They dried and dressed, Fredrik forced to wear the rumpled clothes he had worn the day before. He promised to meet her in the dining room, insisting he change into fresh clothes first. Laura smiled at the blush that was fighting across his cheeks again. He was embarrassed that everyone knew what he had done with her, and embarrassed that such intimacy would be the subject of scrutiny and gossip in her court. She suddenly was glad she had chosen to leave Dalnerechensk. Fredrik didn't deserve that life.

And neither did Alexandra she realised, crossing to the crib and lifting her out, kissing her cheeks.

'Hungry mama!' she announced. 'Hungry papa!'

She stopped in shock.

'Did she just call me...' Fredrik started softly.

'Papa!' Alexandra giggled again.

Tears welled up in his eyes, and he smiled, his heart expanding with joy. Gently he kissed Alexandra's head, taking her little hands and kissing them too. She giggled at the gesture. Fredrik excused himself and squared his shoulders before her door, stepping out and trying to ignore the eyes of her guards. Laura greeted them quietly, heading down to the dining room to sit with the court, to take stock of the political tides that had turned.

There were no Vakhtangovs at the table. Some ministers sat at one end, but there were scant few of them too. Ilich was not among them. They all stood as she entered the room and bowed, and she acknowledged the foreign dignitaries who greeted her.

She crossed to the royal canopy, placing Alexandra in the high chair that had been returned from her private dining room. She stopped in surprise when she realised there was a flower sitting on her plate. She picked up the small, trumpet shaped bloom, brushing the white petals gently, her cheeks darkening with pleasure. *It's still fresh* she realised, and sniffed it deeply, smiling as Fredrik stepped into the dining room.

It was a stephanotis flower, and a traditional wedding bloom, symbolic of marital happiness. She kissed the white petals then threaded it into Fredrik's buttonhole as he came to kiss her hand.

'I still love the flowers you leave me' she smiled.

'I did not leave you this one' he said.

'I did' said Nikolai, joining them.

Laura and Fredrik bowed low to him, noticing the small crowd of people he was with.

'Your Majesty, Your High Well Born, please allow me to present to you my family. This is my mother, *Princhessa* Wilhelmina of Bohemia' he said, taking the hand of a woman who did not appear to be very old, but nevertheless seemed as delicate and frail as a snowflake caught in a spider's web. The woman curtseyed, and Laura didn't miss how Nikolai slid a protective hand under her arm, helping her to rise at the end.

It must have cost him a great deal to have left this frail woman on the road, to come to her rescue she realised. Nikolai went on to introduce his younger sisters Sophia and Uliana, their husbands Semyon Novikov and Eduard Troshev, and his seven nieces and nephews, all of whom Laura greeted and let kiss her hand.

'I am so pleased to meet you all' she said. 'Do make yourselves at home, Castle Dalnerechensk is at your disposal. Please join me for breakfast.'

They bowed and curtseyed, and seated themselves at the table, small conversations shyly breaking out between them and the ministers.

'Forgive my impertinence' Nikolai said eventually, turning to Laura. 'There were some things that could not wait while you were in your deep swoon.'

'Such as?' she asked, concerned.

'The death of Anna Vakhtangovna' he explained. 'To avoid a scandal I made an announcement that Kurt had taken her, in the zeal of youth, to a doctor he believed to be one of the best in Germany, but the ill-advised journey was a terrible cost to the princess and she passed away before she could even reach the country. It seemed the message was well received, despite its dreadful news.

'I have also spoken to Fedor, and arranged her funeral, it will take place tomorrow in the cathedral. It will not be a state occasion, there will be no procession to Macherna such as there was for Tsar Constantinovich. Fedor has also arranged the coronation for one week from tomorrow. I trust this will be to your satisfaction?'

Laura thought about it. She wanted to be indignant; Nikolai was not even officially recognised yet, and here he was, throwing around proclamations and matters of state. But another part of her, normally so quiet and reserved, took control of her tongue.

'That is most satisfactory' she said, somewhat surprising herself.

'Very good' he sounded relieved. 'How is Kurt?'

'Heartbroken' Laura said sadly. 'Guilt stricken. Pining.'

Nikolai tutted sadly, but smiled when Marie Borodina arrived in the dining room with Ilya in tow. The boy's face lit up when he saw his father, running into his arms. Nikolai planted kisses on both his cheeks and sat him on his lap, hugging him.

'I missed you, papa' Ilya said, hugging him.

'I missed you too' he said, stroking down his blonde hair.

They ate in silence for a while, until Nikolai cleared his throat self-consciously.

'Since we are over-throwing four hundred years of rule, perhaps I might persuade you of another tradition to abandon?'

'What would that be?' she raised her eyebrow.

'Dissolve the court. No, I don't mean like that' he said hurriedly at her sharp intake of breath. 'Perhaps my word choice was ill-considered. I meant that you had instructed Ilich to consider the castle private property, the home of the Monarchy, did you not, and yet you still allowed many people who had no real concern to come and go as they please. You permitted them to plot treason against you in your very home. -'

'I permitted them no such thing!' she said hotly. 'And do you think that should I banish them all from the castle that the plotting will cease?'

'Now?' he queried. 'Yes. Most likely so. There may be disgruntled discussions in drawing rooms and sulky symposiums in saloons, but they have what they want. I am on the throne. And you will have what you want too. There will also be financial gains when you stop feasting the masses.'

He knows me well she realised. *And I him. We will make a strong monarchy together.*

'You speak sense' she said finally. 'We have much to discuss, you and I, in the coming days. But for now I must rest, I am still not recovered.'

'Of course' he soothed. 'I thought to show my family around Dalnerechensk today, would you wish to accompany us?'

'I would be delighted' she accepted.

67

It was ten days later. Laura sat in a chair beside the fire in the library, her head resting back on the warm leather. Nikolai sat opposite her, and they were both drowsy with the warmth and the late hour.

Anna Vakhtangovna's funeral had been small and understated. Kurt had only managed to be present because Fredrik and Gustav had broken down his door that morning and pulled him out of bed, washing and dressing him in sombre colours. Kurt had wept bitterly and loudly through the ceremony, and Laura had held him in her arms, feeling that great wracking misery shake her too. Anna had been interred in one of the smaller chapels in the cathedral and they were unable to tear Kurt away from a lonely vigil outside it that night. Nikolai had let him remain, posting a soldier to guard him as well.

Two days later Gustav had taken Kurt home, concerned with his unceasing watch at her grave. Laura had half expected him to fight; to scream and kick, clawing to stay at her tomb; but he left dull-eyed and placid, like some clockwork doll. Fredrik had made Gustav promise to send telegrams every week, sooner if he grew more concerned at Kurt's health, and the brothers had embraced before the two younger siblings had boarded the train, leaving Dalnerechensk, perhaps for good.

As Nikolai had suggested the custom of court and parliament dining in the castle had been stopped and a new system of admittance via invitation had been established. It had meant that something like the Secret Court could never happen again, and more Vsevolod Guards had had to be hired, as two of her guards had deserted or been fired in the wake of the arrests of the Secret Court. One of them had been the young guard Roman had assaulted the night before his arrest, and Laura was quietly pleased he had managed to land some blows on one who had betrayed her. Peter Kamanin had drawn up new rosters, and Malenkov was made *Sotnik* of the day shift, though he administered Roman's position while he recovered.

Laura had also discovered guards outside Tsar Constantinovich's doors, which could only mean one thing: Nikolai had taken up residence in the rooms of the ruling tsars. Laura hadn't known what to make of that when she had first seen the guards, but finally told herself it didn't matter. She had ruled Dalnerechensk from Radomyr's rooms, and Aleksei had ruled from rooms on the first floor. No one had suggested to him that he take over his father's rooms. *It seemed room occupancy was fairly transient anyway* she had consoled herself.

There were also guards stationed outside the door to the room where Roman recovered. Laura heard they were fighting for the honour of standing there, and Peter Kamanin had threatened swift punishment for those caught brawling or doing extra duties. Laura suspected that might not have been the first time he had to make that announcement, but she and Roman were both touched by their dedication to him. The soldiers often left the door open, and Roman would talk quietly with them, their murmuring gossip filling the corridors with reports from the streets of Dalnerechensk.

Laura, Nikolai and Ilich had once visited him all together, surprising him with their attendance, until Laura had informed him of their joint decision. He was to become *bez pomestnoye dvoryanstvo* – Estateless Nobility – for his services to the state and crown, and would receive the rank of *Graf*, entitled to be addressed as *Vashe Blagorodiye* – Your Well Born. His titles and privileges were effective immediately, though the ceremony to confer them would not be performed until he was well enough to participate. Roman had been overwhelmed with the news, and had managed a tearful salute and thank you.

The world was certainly turning for some Laura thought. The turmoil in

Parliament had been greater still. The Principle Party had collapsed without the leadership of Maksim and Lev, and Luka's arrest had dealt a blow to the revolutionaries. Ilich still presided over the Parliament, but he had no real support, and no real governing body. He had redistributed the portfolios to those most capable of the role, but every session now became an argument and three distinct parties were beginning to emerge: one monarchist, one socialist, and one of militant revolutionaries, of those who still wanted the monarchy abolished altogether.

Laura and Nikolai had sat in Parliament together, in two ornate, identical chairs hastily commissioned, Vsevolod's chair empty and behind them. Laura had liked the symbolism of it: the ruling monarch who currently occupied the castle would sit on Vsevolod's throne, with the two ornate chairs behind them, to show either they spoke for two - or as one, if the two of them sat together in session. The symbolism hadn't been lost on the Vakhtangov family either.

She had watched Ilich turn often to them for mediation in the arguments, and had watched Nikolai phrase commands as suggestions; plant his ideas skilfully into the minds of others until they suggested them as if they were their own. She had been very tempted to suggest the Monarchy be given the powers of veto, and sovereignty in extreme and emergency situations – it was clear that Parliament had disintegrated so badly no agreement could be reached while new alliances were drawn. Laura was glad there were no pressing social concerns waiting to be addressed.

She and Nikolai had begun to come often to the library together, and it was in these chairs, were she and Tsar Constantinovich had so often sat, that they had gently reached agreements for the future governance of Dalnerechensk. It was here that they negotiated the terms of the co-regency together, where Nikolai had insisted their own *entente cordiale* included clauses for their children to rule jointly; either as husband and wife, or as their parents had before them.

Laura had allowed herself to be persuaded into signing a contract for Ilya's and Alexandra's betrothal, but only after she had insisted that a clause giving Alexandra a right to dissolve the betrothal should she wish be included as well. Nikolai had agreed, and he had made his first public announcement from the walls of the castle to the ecstatic crowds waiting below in the commons. He spoke of the union of a divided family, of the joining again of Vsevolod's bloodline. Fedor had reported that approximately two thirds of the population were pleased with the announcement, and the same number would have preferred the betrothal to have been between Nikolai and herself.

Laura sighed quietly, shifting into a more comfortable position in the high backed chair, stretching her toes towards the banked embers of the fire. Nikolai smiled and shrugged his shoulders back against his chair, crossing one ankle over the other. The silence folded around them, comfortable and calming.

Their coronation had taken place yesterday. Laura had never been crowned, not even when she married Aleksei, so she had insisted she be crowned in the ceremony too. They had sat on their newly commissioned twin thrones, and Vsevolod's crown had been placed on Nikolai's head; the new, feminine crown placed on Laura's. They had decided between them that the resident monarch would wear Vsevolod's crown, but when the two of them were together, Nikolai would wear it, and in turn, Ilya after him.

Episcop Vasily had presided over the ceremony, and proclaimed them Tsar Antonevich and Tsaritsa Stephanovna. When the rites of conferring tsar-ship were completed they had been hand fastened together. Three different strips of silk were used; green, blue and white; the colours of the Principality, both royal and revolutionary. Nikolai and she had risen as one, making their way down the aisle to the doors that were thrown open for them.

They had stood on the top of the steps and waved to all the crowd gathered around the church, held back from the open carriage by the mounted honour guard. In the crowd, on his own little podium, Jurek Titov had stood, winding the handle of a Kinetograph. Laura had waved at him, then turned to the rest of the crowd, blowing kisses.

Malenkov and Spanov had carefully lifted her and Nikolai into the carriage, arranging their long ermine robes around them as they had sat next to each other. Nikolai had reached into the cushions between them, raising a small metal rod. It had a flat plate on one end, and a sturdy pole. At the other end it had a thin ribbon of metal, which – when they rested their arms on it – comfortably moulded to the shape of their arms, supporting them almost invisibly. It meant that they could ride through the Principality with their fastened hands held aloft for all to see in complete ease. She had wondered why Aleksei had not used this on their wedding day.

Malenkov and Spanov had then mounted and joined the procession as the carriage had meandered its way slowly through the main streets of all the villages and hamlets in Dalnerechensk. Laura had tried really hard to stop her thoughts returning to the memories of her wedding day. But it was difficult, with this handsome man beside her, and the same route that she and Aleksei had driven on that cold, sunny day. They had even rung the bells and fired the cannons as they had passed.

They had returned to the castle, to the dining room where twenty-seven courses had been served in honour of the great occasion. Everyone who was anyone in Dalnerechensk had been present in the room, and it had been crowded with conversation and heat. Then there had been hours of dancing afterwards, and the dining hall had been scrubbed from top to bottom and then abandoned, only to be used again on great state occasions, as Laura's smaller dining room was more than adequate to house the castle guests.

She smiled gently, sadly, to herself, feeling too sleepy to move. *Nikolai had called Fredrik* Velikij Knjaz *- Grand Duke - that afternoon and they had spent a pleasant evening together in front of the fire, discussing his titles and any legal claim he could have to the throne. Nikolai had been surprised that Laura insisted he had none, although she knew that was what Fredrik wanted. But she had reluctantly agreed to the conditions of Lord Protector for the throne, if anything ever happened to Nikolai and herself, if their children were still too young to rule on their own, and if Nikolai's chosen guardian for Ilya was not fit for the position. It was unlikely that he would ever be called upon in that role.*

All that was left now was for Ilich and Parliament to sign off on their decisions, and Laura wondered if he would; actually create another monarch. If he did, Fredrik's social elevation would be staggeringly dizzying. She knew he was distinctly uncomfortable at the thought. Perhaps that was why he insisted in returning to Bavaria, where he was comfortable with his land and his titles. Perhaps he thought he was undeserving of his rank; perhaps they both were.

Maksim certainly thought so. She shivered slightly, folding her arms around herself. His trial, and those of Gorbunov and *Knjaz* Uvarov, had begun yesterday, and Laura would have to give evidence tomorrow. She knew she would have to retire soon but was reluctant to do so. *Will they ask me the same questions in the pursuit of truth? Would she be as much on trial as them, if only to quell the rumours and gossip once and for all?*

She suddenly stood, stirring Nikolai. She bowed quickly to him, then headed out into the quiet castle, letting herself in Fredrik's room.

He woke when she let herself into his bed, and lay against him as he folded his arms around her, stilling her trembling.
'Everything will be alright' he soothed quietly, kissing her temple. 'It will be fair this time.'
'And if it is not?' she whispered.
'Ilich and Nikolai will not let that happen' he soothed. 'Nor will I. They have appointed *Monsieur* Louis Perret, the French Ambassador, as Justice for the proceedings. I have met him, and conversed with him over the weeks that he has been here. I believe he will be just.'

He yawned, settling himself, sleep pulling him gently back. Laura said nothing and let him go, listening as the sound of his breathing filled the room. Despite his and Nikolai's reassurances, she was still frightened of the things to happen. Maksim, *Knjaz* Uvarov and Gorbunov could all be executed for treason. *And she would have to sign the death warrant.* She was no stranger to death, but none had she ever ordered. *Could I even do it?* she wondered. The thought made her feel sick. *How could I ever look at Tatiana again, knowing I sent her father to his death?*

Her thoughts would not leave and sleep refused to come. Eventually she slipped out of Fredrik's bed and padded through the silent corridors of the castle to her rooms, letting herself in quietly. *I don't want to be responsible for the deaths of anyone. I doubt Ilich had this much reservation when he sentenced Olaf.* She sighed and put her face in her hands, shutting her eyes. The thought of signing their warrants frightened her even more than the thought that they might be found innocent of treason and dismissed.

She stayed motionless until the sound of her door opening stirred her and Anna stepped in.

'Your Majesty, Ilich waits outside. He says he must speak with you before court today.'

'Very well. Help me dress' she answered, and sat up so Anna could work her magic on her hair.

She dressed in pale blue, and wore the Tsaritsa's lucky black diamonds again. She sent Anna to let Ilich in and then to leave them alone.

'I would have invited you to breakfast with my household, but I suspect you are here to discuss the case privately' she said after he had bowed to her.

'That is correct Your Majesty' he answered. 'The procedure today will be very similar to the first hearing – the legal one' he clarified. 'Kapustin and I outlined the cases yesterday. He and I will examine your testimony today, and you should not be called again.'

'Will I have to answer to Maksim's charges again?' she wanted to know.

'No' he promised. 'You have already been tried for treason in the eyes of the law. Your case was dismissed and you cannot be tried for the same crime twice. Whether you are guilty or not is irrelevant now. Besides, Alexandra will not be the only monarch to have rumours of illegitimacy follow them. Tsar Petrovich was rumoured to be illegitimate too and no one could ever be certain. But it didn't matter. As far as tsars go, he was a good one, and so are you. If your daughter is anything like you she will be too. Of course she has no influence of her father, and Fredrik is a good man. No doubt she will become a good woman to help Ilya.'

'She will not "help," but rule in her own right' Laura said tetchily.

'Of course' Ilich said in a placatingly dismissive way. He went on: 'Kapustin will try to introduce the evidence they used at the secret court -'

'I thought that was destroyed?' she asked, alarmed.

'No doubt they would have made copies -'

'Dismiss it. Neither of them can answer for the letter, they are both dead. You can't cross-examine -'

'Olaf's dead?' he asked, surprised.

'You should know that' she snapped, turning from him. 'You had him hanged for treason.'

'I didn't execute him. I banished him.'

She stopped, one hand on the door she had just pulled open, the other reaching out to grab Malenkov to steady herself. Her knees went weak as she turned, only dimly aware that Malenkov and Repnin had reached out to support her swoon.

'You – he's -' she babbled, shaky. '*He's alive?!?* All this time I thought he was dead!'

'Bring her in and sit her on the chaise longue' Ilich instructed her guards, who obeyed.

'I thought he was dead, I thought you'd killed him!' she went on, tears of relief streaming down her face. 'I thought he was dead!'

'Alive and well, as far as I know' he said. 'I couldn't bring myself to sign his warrant.'

She gulped down a few shaky breaths, wiping her eyes clear.

Olaf was alive.

Ilich poured her a small measure of brandy from her decanter. She swallowed it and licked her lips against the burn, shutting her eyes, pushing down the deep turmoil of emotions.

'I have held you accountable, all this time, for the death of a loyal, good man' she said, her voice wobbling though she tried to stop it, hating herself for crying in front of him. 'It has guided my thinking and attitudes, and founded a deep mistrust of you. I was wrong. I am so sorry. He's *truly* alive?'

She broke off, laughing at her disbelief.

'It seems I have given you quite a shock. We could ask for an adjournment -'

'Thank you, but that will not be necessary' she said. 'I will do what I must.'

'As you wish, Your Majesty' he bowed.

'Please give me a moment, I shall join you in the entrance hall shortly. Thank you Malenkov, Repnin, please return to your posts.'

The guards saluted and did as they were told, Ilich following them out.

Laura put her face in her hands, feeling her emotions surge through her in a dizzying giddy rush. *He was alive!*

The guilt that had burdened her for so long was gone and she was light-headed with the freedom of it. *What had happened to him? Where had he gone?* Thousands of questions clamoured for attention. *Does he know he has a daughter? Has he a family of his own? What is he doing now?*

Does he still love me?

She stopped herself, gripping herself tightly.

He was alive. It was all that mattered.

She rose, placing the empty glass on her small table. Then she composed herself carefully and left the room, heading down the stairs to join Ilich waiting below.

68

Fedor coughed quietly, prompting her. She sighed, pulling the document closer to her and reading it again. She could hear him trying not to hold his breath.

'He could have done this to me' she murmured, half to herself. 'He ruled with bits of paper. Ilich never understood you don't need blood and guns for revolution. You need people and politics and pens. It might have been better that way too. It would have been what Fredrik wanted. He's uncomfortable with my titles. And I wouldn't have to do this' she stopped, sighing again.

Nikolai had already signed it. She eyed the blank space next to his where her signature was to go.

'This is right, but is this the right thing?' she pleaded with Fedor. 'You didn't see his eyes; he was so furious with me -'

'There is the clause' he reassured her quietly.

'Yes, the clause' she agreed, unconvinced. 'But his cousin has money, he could hire an assassin -'

'He did run a very expensive political campaign' Fedor soothed. 'I believe you overestimate his net worth now. This has broken them, Your Majesty. The point is to keep them that way.'

She sighed again. *Perret had found all seven guilty.* He had stopped just short of pronouncing death sentences for the Secret Court judges only because Laura had intervened. Instead, as Nikolai had predicted, *Knjaz* Uvarov had been deported and banned for life, and a sizeable hunk of his fortune had been confiscated for the trouble he had caused. Lev, Seryeshka and Iosif Osin had been sentenced to no less than thirty years each for the minor roles they had played. Luka, proud and arrogant to the last, had demanded banishment. *Nineczka would go with him if Perret agreed* Laura had realised. She had overheard the soldiers gossiping; Ilich had already filed for divorce. But Luka had been in for a shock: He had laid violent hands upon the Monarch; there was nothing but death for him.

Gorbunov's sentence had also been severe. He had been stripped of all his wealth, possessions and livelihood. He was sentenced to life in prison, mingling with those he himself had most severely, mercilessly, incarcerated in his long reign as Justice. His sentence was death, without the formality of a firing squad.

Which just leaves Maksim she thought, reading the sentence again.

Banished. All titles confiscated. All wealth and property confiscated. All privileges revoked. A clause that stated should he ever be associated with another plot or action to overthrow or harm the Monarchy then his generous and lenient sentence would be revoked and commuted instantly to death. *Would he risk it?* she wondered. *Would he dare?*

I am signing his death if he does...

You need this man and his poisonous daughter out of your life she told herself. *He would have no such moral struggle, should he be sat here. And he would show you no mercy.*

In a rush she picked up the pen and signed with a shaking hand, pushing the paper away from her when she was done.

'Thank you, Your Majesty' Fedor said quietly. 'I know it was difficult. It is for the best.'

It was done. Tatiana would have to leave Dalnerechensk too, she had no one to support her. Unless she weds Laura realised, and wondered if she would chance that desperate gamble. *Dear God please do not let her wed Nikolai.*

She can't she assured herself. *The daughter of a traitor? He couldn't. She couldn't keep her wealth and power.*

Mollified, but still uneasy she stood, letting herself out of Fedor's office. She knew he would send some junior clerk to the jail to read Maksim his sentence. It would be the final insult. Once she would have smirked at the discourtesy, now she took no pleasure in it.

I have won, and it does not feel like victory she thought as she headed up to her rooms. *It doesn't feel like victory at all...*

69

Roman's door was open again when she stopped by it at nine in the evening, but Laura could see he was already asleep. She acknowledged the salutes of the guards outside his doors, wondering if she should wake him up, then felt guilty for entertaining the thought.

His healing was painfully slow, and although Pushkin was pleased with his progress she knew Roman chafed abominably in his idleness. She had wanted to thank him personally for landing the blows on her young betrayer, but every time she had come to see him she had been reminded of the torture he had been through, torture her political games had caused, and she had no wish to remind him of that.

'Laura?' Fredrik asked, joining her quietly. 'What are you doing here?' he went on in English.

'I am debating offering him a job in Bavaria' she said quietly. 'I am debating offering Marie Borodina the position of Nanny there too, and taking Anna with me... But they all have families here...' she trailed off. 'Who will help me dress?'

'You are perfectly capable of dressing yourself' Fredrik pointed out. 'And should you require any extra help putting clothes on, or taking them off, I shall gladly assist.'

She giggled, and he offered her his elbow, which she took, beginning to lead her away from the door.

'No, my love, Roman's place is here' he went on gently. 'As is Anna's, with her husband. I know you are terribly fond of her, but I cannot separate her so far from her family, nor employ all and sundry so that I can.'

'But what about Marie? What will she do?'

'I would hazard a guess that she will stay and nurse Ilya, or return with her husband to Izhevsk, where she will need to hire her own nanny soon. -'

'She's pregnant?!' Laura blurted out. *I hadn't noticed...* 'I've really been selfishly absorbed haven't I' she said sadly.

Fredrik kissed her hand. 'A little' he smiled. 'But I do not blame you, what a terrible time you have been through recently.'

His next sentence was interrupted when Fedor appeared before them, bowing low.

'Your Majesty, Your Highness' he said, presenting Laura with a telegram. 'We have just received the news.'

Laura took it and read the short message quickly.

'Allow me to be the first to offer congratulations' Fedor went on.

'Most kind' she murmured, then turned to Fredrik. 'Lady Anne gave birth to Charles William Asanton at three o'clock yesterday, both mother and son are doing well, my father writes.'

'That is wonderful news' he smiled.

'I have a brother younger than my daughter' she said sadly, dismissing Fedor. 'I was so lonely as a child, I desperately wished for siblings. Alexandra will *not* be an only child' she swore.

He suddenly stopped, turning to her and laying his hand on her stomach.

'Could you be...?' he trailed off.

'No, not yet, though it has not been for lack of trying' she grinned, gently laying her hands on top of his.

'Perhaps we should wait' he blurted out, surprising her. 'At least until we are back in Bavaria, if not until our wedding -'

'So your child is not a bastard like Alexandra?'

There was agony in his pause.

'Her father was dead, that doesn't make her a bastard' he said quietly, his jaw working. 'I am tired of the slander against you. I don't want it to be true. I don't want to make it true.'

Laura pushed open the door of the unoccupied room they stood outside, backing into the room, her hands beginning to untie her dress.

'When we marry, I will want my family there. It will take them many months to arrive, and it will be many months before they can even possibly consider travelling' she said, pulling her dress off her. He stepped in and closed the door behind them. 'A *year* Fredrik, maybe more' she said, pulling her corset off her. 'You will deny us that long?'

'Don't need a maid after all' he muttered, but his voice was layered with desire, his breath hard with want.

They stripped and he lifted her up onto the sideboard that stood in the dark parlour, their lips eagerly finding the other. Any last resolve he had vanished when she curled her fingers around his throbbing shaft, stroking him.

'There are ways' she whispered through his kisses. 'A womb veil, rubbers -' she stopped talking under the press of his body, the earnestness of his lips, the parting of her flesh for his.

She wrapped her legs around him and he groaned, starting a masterly and forceful rhythm that quickly had them both nearing climax. She arched harder against him, shuddering in ecstasy and felt him retreat, felt the wet length of him rub firmly against her swollen pea of pleasure; thick, hot enjoyment squirting against her belly. The surprise of it, the feel of the ridged thickness of him rubbing back and forth against her made her climax again, the moan of pleasure starting so low in her it was in her chest.

He groaned quietly, folding his arms around her and gently kissing her, stroking back her hair.

'Or you could just do that' she giggled.

He laughed quietly and apologised, using his handkerchief to lovingly clean her. They dressed again and patted back their hair, smoothing down the heat in their complexions. Laura tucked her hand into his elbow and they stepped back out into the corridor, smiling gently at each other.

'Will you ride with me to the glen tomorrow?' she asked. 'I should like to see it one more time, before we leave.'

'Most certainly' he said. 'Do you know, I have always been surprised there is no swing there. It is such a beautiful place; the pleasures of a swing will just complete it.'

'You wish for *Les Hasards Heureux de L'escarpolette* do you?' she teased.

Fredrik blinked, reeling. Fragonard's sweetly erotic painting swam into his vision but it was ousted by the arousing thoughts of happily but accidentally impregnating Laura on a swing, her legs around his waist, her hands –

He groaned and pushed open the nearest door, dragging her giggling inside.

70

Laura stood at her window, watching several livery men load boxes and chests onto a milk cart to be ferried down to the train station. At least two of the portmanteaus belonged to her, but many belonged to Perret and several other guests who were also leaving today. As she watched the Model F swung around the corner into the courtyard, heading down Vsevolod's Way to the station too.

Nikolai had taught both her and Fredrik how to operate it, and how to check the levels of petrol and oil needed to keep the machine operational. The three of them had enjoyed their last trip around Dalnerechensk yesterday, stopping in Macherna to pay their respects at Vsevolod's tomb and say goodbye to Tsar Constantinovich one last time.

'There is a crypt on my estate in St Petersburg, where seven generations of Vakhtangovs are buried' Nikolai had said quietly. Perhaps I will show it to you one day. If ever you find yourself in St Petersburg, you would be most welcome in my home. I extend to you the courtesy you have in opening your home to me.'

They had thanked him, and together they travelled on to Davostok, admiring the new road and how smooth it was to drive on.

Laura shifted position at the window, trying to block out the sound of Anna's tears. She found herself almost unwilling to leave Dalnerechensk. *Had Anna cried a year ago?* she wondered. Quite possibly. But she had been in such a daze in the grip of her depression she hadn't noticed. She hadn't even noticed her courses had been late. *And now I leave again in sadness, but in great joy too* she thought, sighing quietly. A knock on the door interrupted her and Anna ushered in Ilich, who bowed.

'Your Majesty' he said, presenting her with a parchment scroll he had with him.

She took it and unrolled it, recognising the handwriting, and what it was, right away.

'I denied it to you, but it is your right' he said quietly. 'Consider it a dowry perhaps.'

Aleksei's will had left her two hundred thousand pounds sterling. She thanked him quietly and rolled up the scroll again, handing it to Anna to pack securely with her jewels.

Ilich bowed again, awkward and unsure what to do.
'I wish you safe travels Your Majesty' he said. 'And many happy returns for your marriage.'
'Thank you' she said, and Ilich was relieved when the knock on her door interrupted them.

It was Fredrik, Nikolai and Malenkov – who Nikolai had insisted travel with them until they reached Axel's house safely. They did not have to say anything for her to know that the hour had arrived.

Porters carried her remaining cases out of her room and she embraced Anna, thanking her for her good service and making her promise to serve His Majesty Tsar Antonevich just as loyally. Anna promised and she kissed her again before leaving, trying to outrun her tears as she headed to the nursery to collect Alexandra.

She hugged and kissed Marie Borodina, wishing her and her unborn child happiness and health, then gathered Alexandra up, looking around the barren nursery. All her furniture had been packed and sent to the train station, and Laura was on the verge of changing her mind, asking Marie to accompany them, at least to the border with Bavaria. But then she saw how Marie's hands fell unconsciously to her stomach, how her eyes looked when she turned inward in contemplation.

She kissed Alexandra's cheek and bid Marie farewell, following the army of livery men and porters down to the courtyard. Nikolai himself drove them to the train station, and Laura was surprised by the number of people who thronged the road, waving goodbye to her. It was not a formal occasion, just as it hadn't been the first time she had left, and she couldn't remember if people had lined the streets to see her leave then too.

Soldiers let the automobile onto the station platform, closing back behind them to stop the press of the crowds following them. Laura was not surprised to see Jurek Titov and his Kinetograph perched at one end of the platform, but was surprised to see a new train carriage at the other end.

It was a private carriage Fedor had managed to secure somehow to take them all the way to Munich. It wasn't the royal carriage that Ilich had sold a year ago, but it was similar in design. Fedor showed them the sitting room equipped with couches, a cards table, a small writing desk and a breakfast table for them to relax in during the long days. There was a small room for Malenkov containing a narrow cot, a washbasin and a chamber pot, and two larger, more comfortably appointed rooms for her and Fredrik. In one of the rooms was Alexandra's crib.

Fedor finished his tour and they stepped down to the platform again. Peter Kamanin shouted an order and all of her guards saluted in farewell. She acknowledged it, and kissed Peter's cheek, letting him kiss her hand.
'I will miss your fearlessness' he said. 'If I may be so bold' and Laura noticed his eyes glistened in the bright light of the day.

'And I your loyalty, *Graf* Pavlodar' she assured him.

He saluted her again and stood back. Nikolai came forward then, and kissed Alexandra's cheek before kissing both of Laura's, embracing her warmly.

'My dear friend' he smiled. 'Return as often as you wish, I will be glad of your company, both of yours' he added, clasping Fredrik's hand. 'It is a lonely vigil I return to, with few delights. How I envy you.'

He kissed her cheek again then stepped back to bow deeply. Fredrik and Laura bowed too, and promised they would return one day. He beckoned Ilya over, who had been waiting with his aunt and her family, a posy of mountain daisies in his fist. *They were probably the last blooms in Dalnerechensk* Laura mused as Nikolai lifted him up so he could present them to Alexandra.

She took them, waving them excitedly at her mother. Laura smiled and took the offered posy, tucking one bloom into Fredrik's buttonhole, and another into Nikolai's. Ilya placed one in Laura's hair, then bowed deeply when Nikolai set him on the ground. She curtseyed to him, tucking the remaining flowers into the front of Alexandra's coat.

'Farewell Your Majesty, Your Highness' Nikolai said, bowing again as he stepped back.

'*Auf Wiedersehen Ihr Magistät*' Fredrik said, bowing low then turned to climb aboard the train.

'Farewell Your Majesty' Laura said, her voice starting to wobble. 'May the days pass quickly until we meet again.'

'Amen' he agreed fervently, and she turned, passing Alexandra to Fredrik, taking Malenkov's hand to climb aboard the train.

The whistle blew, a joyous shout to the world, and the train bounded forward. Laura, Fredrik and Malenkov stood at the windows, waving goodbye to the crowds as they glided out of the city of Dalnerechensk. There was a great cry from Tcherepnin as the train passed under the gateway to the garrison.

Laura waved at the crowds, tears rolling down her cheeks, calling goodbye. The whistle gave another joyous shout and they picked up speed as they cleared the second gate at the far end of the village. She took Fredrik's hand as they flew past farms, past the southern border wall, and felt his arms come round her as they surged into the gold-tinted blue of the beckoning horizon.

~~******~~

ACKNOWLEDGEMENTS

Thank you to my family for their love and support.
Thank you Adam Schmidt for the revised map of the Principality of
Dalnerechensk, and Sarah Foster for the beautiful cover artwork.
Thank you to those who allowed me to use their names for characters, you
know who you are!
And finally, thank you for those who purchased my first novel, and offered
sincere encouragement. Thank you all.

www.ingramcontent.com/pod-product-compliance
Lightning Source LLC
Chambersburg PA
CBHW031425240626
47154CB00001B/200